Reviews for *Cleansed by Fire*, the *first* Father Frank Mystery

I0617702

By Nancy. RANK IT AMONG THE BEST!, October 9, 2014
The author does an excellent job teasing us with some interesting characters who aren't always who they seem and manages to intertwine everyday life of this church family into a suspenseful and heartwarming story.
Like so many of the great authors, Callan, weaves a bit of romance, suspense and mystery into his story and keeps you reading. I loved this book and rank it as one of my top ten.

By Roger Bruner
I really enjoy cozy mysteries when they're this good. And when a writer makes a crime-solving priest as interesting to a Southern Baptist reader as Jim Callan has done, he's really accomplished something.

By John Brantingham
Writing from a priest's point of view is difficult. Most people do so badly. So often, the writer descends into cliché. Priests in literature are often either so good that they are uninteresting or so bad that they are unbelievable. A few people have written priests well.
Graham Greene wrote priests well. Then again, he wrote everything well.
Gerald Locklin wrote priests well.
And James R. Callan writes priests well in his novel Cleansed by Fire.

By Gene
My first introduction to Father Frank happened in the pages of this captivating book. I picked up the paperback at an authors event, and didn't put it down until well after the midnight hour.

By Lorna Collins
James Callan knows how to write. He develops interesting characters and weaves compelling plots.

By Kindle Customer
very good book hard to put down.

By M. McGraw
Told with passion, realistic characters and a storyline that will keep you guessing, you'll want to read each new Father Frank book. I know I will.

By "the Marta"
Get hooked on Callan and start here.

By sunnyreader
There were a couple of real surprises that kept me fully involved in the story and several times I had to smile as I read. A really good book that I will not hesitate to recommend to anyone who likes a little mystery, a little murder and a wonderful main character
By Elaine Faber

A good Christian based mystery, with an unexpected end. We hope to see more Father Frank mysteries.

Mazama Maven
I look forward to reading more of Fr. Frank's adventures and will recommend this book to others

By AE from Texas
If you enjoy well written cozy mysteries, this is the book for you!!

By J.R. Lindermuth
In many respects, Father Frank reminded me of G. K. Chesterton's Father Brown, though Callan's creation is a more modern and athletic person, likeable and even human enough to be closely tempted to fisticuffs on a couple occasions.

By Jory Sherman
The writing will keep you on the edge of your seat until the very end. Well-written, with superbly drawn characters. This first of a series holds great promise for future novels by Mr. Callan.

By Carl Rogers
This book is captivating and will hold your attention. Exceptionally well written and although it is fictional there is a lot of realism.

By Linda Glaz
I was drawn in immediately. I'm anxious for the next Father Frank Mystery to come out. Mr. Callan, keep writing. America's gonna love this series!

By Jim Ainsworth
The author does such an excellent job of plot development and of weaving his characters into the twists and turns that we forget Callan's presence and just let the characters and action tell the story.

By Fred-Suz
Can't wait to see the next in the series.

By S. Sehon
I was very excited when I discovered it is the first of series, and can't wait to dig into the next Father Frank mystery.

By Maggie
I am looking forward to the next book in this series, and hope that it is not to long in coming!

Over My Dead Body

A Father Frank Mystery

James R. Callan

Pennant Publishing

Publishers Note:

This is a work of fiction. All names, characters, places, and events are the work of the author's imagination. Any resemblance to real persons, places, or events is coincidental.

Cover Art: Julie Medina

Copyright: © 2015 by James R. Callan

Manufactured in the United States of America

ISBN-13: 978-0-9646850-8-6
ISBN-10: 0-9646850-8-6

Pennant Publishing

Dedicated to Ethan, Chelsea, A.J., Ana, Evan, and James

Over My Dead Body

Chapter 1

Syd snorted and thrust his chin toward his adversary. "Over my dead body."

The man almost smiled. "If you insist," he said easily.

Seventy-two year old Syd Cranzler squinted against the bright Texas October sun and scrutinized the well-dressed man in front of him. Syd was probably six inches shorter than the man, but Syd's voice had more iron in it. "Was that a threat?"

"No sir, Mr. Cranzler," Duke Heinz said.

Syd didn't like this city slicker, wouldn't have even if he weren't trying to steal Syd's homestead. Even Duke's clothes irritated him. The conservative black pinstriped suit, power-red tie and black wing-tips polished to perfection made the man look like he was posing for a magazine picture in New York City. And what was this "Duke" bit? Did he think he was John Wayne? "Why don't you just mosey on down the road a mile?" He jerked his hand up and pointed. "Lots of land there."

They stood on pine needles under three towering trees. Forty feet behind them was Syd's small, frame house, looking like a giant, square tumbleweed.

Bud Wilcox, Pine Tree's City Manager pushed his straw hat back a little and took a step forward. "Syd, Pine Tree wants this shopping center *here*, inside the city limits. Think of all the tax revenue we'll get."

"So's you can waste even more'n you do now? It ain't your house and land, Pipsqueak"

Bud reddened at the nickname Syd often used on him, but kept his mouth shut.

A mud-caked '92 Camaro rattled to a stop half off the black-top road. A man got out and started across the yard to where Syd was shaking his finger at Bud.

Duke started to speak, but Syd cut him off. "And don't tell me again it's twice what it's worth. You don't know what it's worth to me. And what's this 'fee simple' bit?" He cocked his head to the side. "You think I'm simple? Take your money and go back to Jersey."

Bud waggled his balding head. "It's a lot of dollars."

"He don't need your money," said the man from the Camaro. "He stole enough from me."

"Stay out of it, W.C.," Syd snapped. But his focus never left Duke. "You keep your money; I'll keep my land."

Duke spread his hands. "Mr. Cranzler, the Supreme Court says eminent domain can be used to obtain land needed for a project in the public interest."

"I know all 'bout the Supreme Court, and how they trampled all over people's property rights. I'd like to see some private company try to take the land *they* live on. They'd change their tune right fast. But that case was decided for a Yankee town. This is Texas. We still believe in property rights down here. And this ain't in the public interest. It's in Lockey Corporation's interest."

Duke smiled as he pulled a folded paper from the inside pocket of his coat. "Here's the court order, and it's signed by a judge right here in Texas." He held the paper out to Syd.

Syd ignored it. "Judge McFatage, right? He'd sign anything for a price."

Bud Wilcox leaned in. "Now, Syd, you shouldn't talk about the Honorable McFatage that way."

"Honorable, my foot. He's for sale. Common knowledge. You know what they say: he's the best judge money can buy. And it looks like Lockey's the buyer."

"Look, Mr. Cranzler," Duke said. "We're going to start dirt work in three weeks. I'd like to have all the paperwork in order by then. You've lost this fight. You might as well recognize that. You can delay signing. But by fighting this, you may end up getting less money and paying a lot of it to lawyers. You can't stop it. This project *will* be built. And it starts in three weeks."

"Three weeks?" Syd pulled on his chin and a sly grin crept onto his leathery face. "I'm bettin' my lawyer'll have my appeal filed before then. And I'm thinkin' I can tie this up for years. You sure Lockey wants to wait that long?" His head bobbed up and down as he continued. "Be a lot faster to go somewheres else." Now he laughed. "Bet they're gonna cut you loose when this don't happen. Can your butt."

Duke's smile faded and his eyes turned hard. "Two months from now, this will all be asphalt."

"Like I said, over my dead body."

Duke put the paper back in his pocket. "Old man, you'll hardly make a bump in the pavement."

Chapter 2

"He did *not*." Georgia Peitz's emerald green eyes flashed fire.

Detective Mike Oakley looked up at the ceiling of the parish hall and let his breath out slowly. "Georgia, I'm telling Father Frank about one of his parishioners. I'm giving him the official police report on the cause of death. I wasn't really talking to you."

"I'm a member of this parish, too. And if you didn't want me to hear, you shouldn't have told Father in front of me. But, I want *you* to hear *me*; the official police report is wrong." She turned and looked at the priest. "Don't you agree?" Georgia was a petite, five feet three inch bundle of energy, with short auburn hair, a pug nose, and strong convictions she was not afraid to share.

Father Frank smiled. He knew the two were seeing each other and was amused at this clash of wills. He certainly didn't want to get between them. "Before I take sides, let's hear what the police have."

Mike shifted his focus to the priest. "This big company, uh, Lockey Corporation, got a court order to condemn Mr. Cranzler's land to make way for a new shopping center. He was very upset at losing his place. His brother..." He looked at his notebook. "Ah, Randall Cranzler, found Sydney Cranzler dead this morning in his house. The M.E. determined the deceased took an overdose of—." He glanced at his notebook again. "Digitoxin, a medication he used for his heart. In fact, the pill bottle was completely empty, and tests showed his body was loaded with it, probably twice as much as needed to kill him. Plus, the deceased left a suicide note in the printer output tray, saying he didn't want to live to see them bulldoze his house." Mike joined the Pine Tree Police Department eleven years ago. He'd been a detective for the last five.

Father Frank pursed his lips, nodded a few times, but said nothing.

Georgia laid a finger across her chin. "Let me guess. It wasn't signed, was it?"

The policeman looked down at the floor and ran his index finger under the neck of his shirt. "No, it wasn't." He looked up at Georgia. "But that doesn't prove anything."

"Thank you, Mr. Detective. Exactly my point. The note doesn't prove anything."

"What I meant—"

"Never mind," Georgia interrupted. "Whatever you meant is immaterial."

Mike looked from Georgia to the priest. "The eminent domain document had been torn and wadded up—totally destroyed. We found a letter from Lockey marked over with a black pen, cut to shreds and thrown in the trash. It was clear he was depressed over this eminent domain order. And losing his home."

The priest arched his eyebrows and looked at the detective. "Certainly sounds like he was angry. I don't know about depressed."

Georgia focused on Father Frank. "You knew Syd. I knew Syd. Does either of us really think he would get so depressed over losing his house, over anything, to commit suicide?" She answered for him. "No."

"He was pretty attached to his place," said the priest.

"And," Mike started, "he was very unhappy, make that angry, over the power of eminent domain being invoked for a private corporation."

Georgia jerked her hand up and stabbed a finger toward the detective. "Right. Angry. Not depressed. Not suicidal. Angry. He was planning to fight it." She tilted her head and gave Mike an angelic smile. "He did not commit suicide."

"Maybe he finally saw he couldn't win."

"I suppose some people might end it all if they couldn't win something that was important to them," Georgia said. The frown lines on Mike's forehead began to disappear. "But," she continued, "that was not Syd. Did you know him, Mike?"

"No."

"Then, you're not qualified to say what he would do in such a circumstance." Again, the angelic smile. "I am."

Mike sighed. "Actually, I'm not the one saying he did. The M.E. is. The facts are."

"Well, go recheck the facts." She turned to Father Frank. "Give me your honest opinion. Can you see Syd Cranzler taking his own life?"

For a moment, the priest said nothing, then slowly shook his head. "No. I can't." He turned to the detective. "Mike, I'm not saying the M.E. is wrong. But it is hard to reconcile Syd and suicide."

"Well, these are the facts. There was no forced entry. Nothing to suggest an intruder broke in. And with the overdose of the medicine he regularly took, plus the suicide note, it leaves little room for doubt." He inclined his head to one side. "Until we have some facts that say otherwise, that's how the police are treating it."

"Well, there's a self-fulfilling prophesy, if I ever heard one." Georgia folded her arms across her chest and glared at the detective. "You're not going to look for any facts to contradict your current opinion, so I don't guess you'll find any. Unless one comes up and bites you in the … the behind."

Georgia turned on one heel, sending her purse in a wide arc hitting the detective on the hip, and marched out of the room.

Mike turned to Father Frank.

The priest held up his hand. "Don't look at me. But if I were you, I'd start looking for more facts." He turned to leave. Over his shoulder he said, "That is, if you want any more romantic dinners with Georgia."

Father Frank left the parish hall and crossed the parking lot to the church. He was an inch over six feet tall, with black wavy hair, and dark serious eyes that looked ready to shift to playful at any moment. Except for the occasional pain in his left knee, he felt as good as he had in college. He still maintained the lean, muscular physique and easy gait of his college basketball years.

Inside the silent church, he knelt on the floor near the back and prayed for the soul of Syd Cranzler. He hadn't known Syd well. The man kept to himself, didn't join any of the church organizations, never came to any social events. But he never missed Sunday mass and often stopped to talk. The conversations were always interesting, generally short, and frequently centered on Syd's displeasure with the government intruding on people's private lives. Father Frank had heard Syd expound on the injustice of the "new interpretation", as he called it, of the constitution by the Supreme Court. Eminent domain supplied plenty of fodder. Even before the Lockey Corporation began to acquire land in Pine Tree, Syd found examples of eminent domain being used to further the aims of private corporations. He said private property rights were being trampled whenever a buck could be made. The priest found it difficult to refute Syd's arguments.

Dear Lord, whatever the manner of Syd's death, welcome him into your house. Grant him forgiveness for any sins he may have committed in his human weakness. He remains your son. Please extend your boundless mercy to him and let him dwell in the house of the Lord for all eternity.

#

Father Frank had finished dinner and was washing a few dishes when the telephone rang. "Prince of Peace Church. How may we help you?"

"I know he sounded gruff and unhappy a lot, but that was just his way. I don't think he was unhappy with life."

"Hello, Georgia. I assume you're talking about Syd." He dried his hands on his pants.

"Of course I am. You don't think I was talking about that blockhead policeman, do you?" The usual lilt in Georgia's voice had disappeared tonight.

"Wait a minute. I know for a fact that you and Mike have been getting along very well. I heard about those dinners and walks around the lake."

"You won't be hearing about any more for a while."

"Now Georgia, Mike is looking at things from a policeman's perspective. That's his job. He *is* a policeman. And you're being too hard on him."

Father Frank could hear Georgia take in a long breath and let it out slowly.

"You're right. And I *do* like Mike. Just not today. But, that's not why I called. Have you seen the local news tonight?"

"No."

"Well, KLTV had a brief story on a suicide in Pine Tree. A few words about Syd, career as a pharmaceutical salesman, investor in a number of oil wells in east Texas. Did you know Syd was in on Wood #34A?"

"No. What's Wood 34A?"

"An oil well. Biggest producer in the county. Anyway, the TV guy said the police speculated Syd was depressed because the Lockey Corporation was taking his land for a new shopping center. Dumb yokels. Still talking about suicide."

"Hmmm."

"Anyway, I've been thinking, and I can't come up with anybody who would want to kill Syd. You and he talked sometimes. Any clue who might have it in for him? Enough to kill?"

"The police still think it was suicide."

"And they're wrong. So, let's forget that and move on. Who would want him dead?" When Father Frank didn't say anything, Georgia continued. "See, that's my problem. He was such a nice guy. Who would want to kill him?"

"He was certainly trying to block that new shopping center. That could make a lot of people mad."

"Mad enough to kill?"

"Certainly possible." Father Frank took a sip of his Dr Pepper. "Some large corporations see people like Syd as merely a bump in the road that needs to be smoothed out."

"I'm wondering what kind of a company Lockey really is?"

"Georgia, let the police handle it. You can suggest things to Mike—over dinner—but in case you're right, and someone *did* murder Syd, you don't want to get in their sights. You're an important member of the parish. We don't want to lose you."

"Why, Father." The sound of innocence wafted through the phone. "I'm just a little old lady. No one would feel threatened by me." She giggled. "And don't you ever repeat that 'little old lady' bit."

Father Frank hung up the phone smiling. Georgia was petite. And she was a lady. But though she was a widow, she was hardly old at thirty-four.

Her comment resonated with him. Syd didn't seem like the kind of person who would commit suicide, nor whom anyone would murder. So, what was the story? If he didn't take his own life, who did? And why?

Did Syd have any money that might provide a motive? He gave a generous amount in the weekly offering, but hardly enough to draw attention. Of course, when Prince of Peace needed a new air conditioning system to battle the Texas heat, Syd wrote a check for the full amount, and included enough for the parish hall as well. Still, Father Frank had never heard anyone mention money and Syd in the same sentence. However, Georgia did say he owned an interest in a producing oil well.

#

Father Frank was working on the parish books, wondering why they didn't teach more accounting at the seminary. Papers, receipts, checks and sticky notes littered the old roll-top desk in his office. "Why, dear Lord, are we always short of money? There are so many good projects we could tackle if only we had more money." He sighed and resumed his search for a missing invoice.

Just as he found the bashful bill, the telephone rang, as if to give a cheer for the lost sheep now found. "Prince of Peace. How can we help you?"

"Father, this is Judith Kitchen, Syd Cranzler's sister. We met once at my brother Randall's house."

"Oh, hello, Ms. Kitchen. Yes, I remember. About a year ago, I believe. I'm so sorry for your loss. Please know that Syd is in my prayers. And if I can be of any help to you, please don't hesitate to ask."

"Thanks, Father. I live in Greenville, or I would have come to talk with you in person. What's going..." Her voice broke and it was a second before she could continue. "What's going to happen on Syd's funeral?"

"What do you mean?"

"I know the church's position on suicide. Sort of." A slight tremor invaded her voice. "But Randall says, and I guess I knew, that if a person commits suicide, he can't have a Catholic burial."

Father Frank was quiet for a moment. "The rules are not as chiseled in stone now as they once were." The priest thought back to his discussion with Georgia. "Besides, not everybody is convinced it was suicide. So, I see no problem with having a funeral mass for Syd at Prince of Peace."

"Oh, thank you, thank you, thank you, Father. I was so worried. Randall said he was sure we couldn't do that. He's already talked to the funeral home about a service there."

"Well," the priest started, but her sharp intake of breath stopped him.

"You said ... I mean, if he didn't commit suicide, ... are you saying it was murder?"

"No, no. No. What I'm saying is that as far as the church is concerned, we don't really know he committed suicide, so there is no problem with his having a Catholic burial."

"But." She paused. "He didn't die of natural causes. So, ..."

"Ms. Kitchen, that's the point. We don't know. Maybe it was an accident. He died of an overdose of digitoxin. Please, I didn't mean to upset you. As far as we know right now, it might have been an accidental overdose. Prince of Peace will hold the funeral mass for him. I'll call Randall in the morning and set everything up."

Father Frank hung up the phone feeling he didn't handled things very well. But the uncertainty of Syd's death made it difficult to know what to say. How had he died? Father Frank closed his eyes and tried to make sense of what he knew.

Three choices. Suicide. Accident. Murder.

If it was suicide and Syd wrote a note, why not sign it? Make it clear. Eliminate any doubt.

The note pretty much eliminates the accidental theory. Sorry I thought about that. But, I'm not ready to go with suicide yet.

Then there's murder. But who would want to kill Syd? That's the question. And until I know more about Syd, I can't begin to answer that. Or rule out murder.

Father Frank decided he needed to talk with Mike in the morning.

#

"Now Mike, I'm going to ask you a question and I want you to answer it, without giving me a lecture. Can you do that?"

Father Frank stood at Mike Oakley's gunmetal grey desk in the Pine Tree Police Department. The detective had the build and agility of a professional tennis player, and the confidence to go with it.

It was just after 9:30 in the morning and already three empty coffee cups surrounded his telephone. Stacks of paper covered every horizontal surface in Mike's tiny office. A marker board behind his desk was divided into four sections, each labeled with the name of an investigation-. The only one Father Frank recognized was Syd's death. The word "Suicide" was prominent. But what jumped out at the priest was the word in red: "Closed."

The detective's brown eyes studied the priest. "Depends on the question."

"Who was the last person to see Syd alive, and when was that?"

"Aw, Father. The case is closed. Finished. Terminado."

"I know you've closed it, but—"

"Not me. The M.E.."

"Okay. But, can you answer my question?"

Mike ran his hand over his broad forehead, then through his short, rich brown hair. He let out his breath. "As far as we know, Bud Wilcox, the City Manager; Duke Heinz, the man acquiring land for Lockey; and ..." Mike pulled out a small, brown leather notebook, flipped through a few pages, then put it back in his desk drawer. "W.C. Mayfield, apparently a friend of Cranzler. Now, don't go—"

"No sermon today. Thanks."

Before Mike could continue, Father Frank turned and walked out the door.

#

Father Frank knew Bud Wilcox, had met him on several occasions. He didn't go to Prince of Peace. Father Frank thought for a moment. *First Baptist, as I remember.* The priest crossed the blazing hot asphalt parking lot and entered City Hall, spoke to the secretary and was ushered into Bud's office.

Larger than Mike's, it was also much neater. The yellow pad of paper, telephone, and computer monitor and keyboard almost looked lonesome on the large oak desk. A matching credenza behind Bud's high-backed leather chair held a neat stack of paper and a few colored folders with bold labels on them: water plant, road works, city auditorium, and merchants' association. The largest folder was labeled "Grant Applications."

"What can I do for you, Father?" It sounded like a rote response with no commitment.

"I understand you were with Syd Cranzler shortly before he died."

Bud leaned back in his chair, relaxed. "I heard about his death. But I didn't hear when he died. So, I don't know about the timing. But yes, I did talk with him Monday afternoon. Duke Heinz and I were trying to convince him to settle with Lockey and not get into court over this."

"How did the meeting go?"

"Not well. Syd was being bullheaded, wouldn't really listen to what Duke had to say."

"Can you remember what Syd said? Exactly?"

Bud sat forward, muscles tense, attention sharpened. "Where are you going with this?"

"Frankly, Bud, I have a hard time seeing Syd commit suicide. I'm trying to get a picture of what happened shortly before his death." He paused only a moment. "What did Syd say, or do? How did he act?"

Bud looked down at his desk for several seconds, then refocused on Father Frank. "He said he had no intention of selling, would fight Lockey all the way." He picked up a pencil and toyed with it.

"Anything else?"

Bud looked straight into the priest's eyes. "He said Lockey would get the property over his dead body."

Father Frank's eyes opened wider. "Over his dead body? He said that?"

Bud nodded.

"And how did Mr. Heinz respond to that?"

Bud shook his head. "He said it would hardly make a bump in the parking lot, or something close to that."

For a moment, neither man said anything.

Bud gave a small laugh. "They were both getting mad. I doubt Duke meant anything by that. Just an angry comeback."

"I'd find it easier to agree with that if Syd weren't dead."

"But the M.E. said it was suicide. And the police agree."

"Only the three of you? You, Syd and Mr. Heinz?"

"Yeah."

Father Frank got up. "Thanks, Bud. I appreciate your help." He turned to leave.

"Oh, wait. There was another guy who came up while we were talking. Said Syd didn't need the money. Said, 'He stole enough from me,' or something like that."

The priest's interest flared. "Do you know who he was?"

"Naw. Never seen him before."

"What'd he look like?"

"Old. Maybe same age as Syd. Buzz cut, but I think his hair was grey. Maybe five feet seven. Thin, with a little pot belly."

"How'd Syd react?"

Bud shrugged. "Mostly ignored it. Told him to stay out of it. Didn't really seem to bother Syd."

"The guy say anything else?"

"Not while we were there. We were finished. Weren't accomplishing anything. Syd was as stubborn as ever. Duke lost his cool. We left. The guy was still there, jawing at Syd as he walked toward the house."

The conversation with Mike popped up in Father Frank's mind. "Did Syd call the man W.C.?"

"Oh, yeah. As a matter of fact he did. No last name or anything. Just W.C.."

#

Father Frank sat in his office, trying to work on his eulogy for Syd's funeral, but his mind kept straying. The more he thought about it, the less he believed Syd committed suicide. Mike and Bud both agreed that Syd was angry. That wasn't the same as depressed. He'd been planning to fight, not take his own life. He didn't sound intimidated by the court order or the man from Lockey.

The priest thought back on his interactions with Syd. He was strong. Not a weakling who would commit suicide rather than lose a battle. Of course, Father Frank didn't know Syd all that well. Perhaps there was more to it. Maybe he was terminally ill, and this was the last straw. *I wonder who his doctor was.*

And who was this W.C.? As City Manager, Bud knew a good portion of the Pine Tree population. But he said he'd never seen the man before.

The telephone rang, and Father Frank picked it up on the first ring.

"Hi, Father. This is Norm Winters. Got a minute?"

Norm and his family were members of Prince of Peace. Father Frank got to know Norm quite well last year when his son,

Sammie, got involved with the wrong person and almost got killed. Norm, a lawyer, actually helped defend the man who injured Sammie.

"Sure."

"Irene said I should call you. She was talking with Georgia today about Syd's untimely death. Georgia said the police ruled it suicide, but she wasn't convinced." There was a slight pause. "I'm not either."

Chapter 3

Father Frank sat up a bit straighter. "That makes three of us. Why aren't you?"

"I've done some legal work for Syd over the years. Not just his will. A week ago, he asked me to look into the possibility of getting a court order to stop the Lockey Corporation from beginning work on the new shopping center. I told him we would need to appeal the ruling, take it to the Court of Appeals in Texarkana. He said, 'Let's do it.' I got another call from him last Friday, checking on where that stood. He wanted to make sure I wasn't letting it slip, as the Lockey man said they hoped to start work in three weeks."

"Last Friday?"

"Correct. Then he called again Monday night."

"You're saying he called you only hours before he died?"

"I don't know the time of death, but I talked with him around 7 p.m. Monday night."

"And he still wanted you to file the appeal with the court for him?"

"That's right. He wanted it filed this week." The lawyer laughed slightly. "He got on my case, wanting to know why I hadn't filed it already. I told him I had it prepared, had discussed it with the judge, and had a couple of small changes I wanted to make. I said I would file it the next day." He paused a second. "Of course, he was dead the next day."

"What was his mood when you talked with him? Was he depressed? Disheartened?" The priest wanted to include angry, but decided not to lead Norm in that direction.

"Mad, I'd say. And organized. He even quoted some of the dissenting arguments on the Supreme Court's decision on eminent domain. I was amazed at his knowledge on the case. He'd obviously done some research." Norm paused a second. "If you're thinking he might have been glum or discouraged, enough to commit suicide, he didn't come across that way to me. He was actually looking forward to going to court, if you ask me."

"Have you filed the appeal, or whatever you do?"

"I've got the paper work ready to send to the appeals court. I told Syd that Monday. He seemed excited over the prospect. Of course, now, it will be up to … to those who inherit the house and land to decide if they want to continue the appeal or not."

"Thanks, Norm. And tell Irene I thank her also. Can I have Detective Mike Oakley call you? He still thinks it was suicide."

"Sure. Nothing says I can't tell him, or anybody, about Syd's request."

All thoughts about the eulogy ceased. Father Frank was now totally convinced one of his parishioners had been murdered. Who had a motive? Somebody connected with the Lockey Corporation? If Syd had won his appeal, it might have stopped the project altogether. Even if he was unsuccessful, it might have delayed the company's plans by months, maybe years. He remembered hearing about a highway planned in Connecticut that was held up for thirty years. Would that be enough motive to end a life? Could such a delay cost the man in charge, Mr. Heinz, his job? Neither of those reasons seemed strong enough to kill for. Not to Father Frank.

Perhaps enough for someone else.

#

"What are the principal reasons for murder?" Georgia caught Father Frank right after Thursday morning mass as he headed for the rectory.

"Keeping a man from his breakfast," answered the priest with a smirk.

"You can go eat breakfast as soon as you answer the question." Ten years of teaching had equipped Georgia to handle smart answers.

"Money, power, revenge, love. Not necessarily in that order."

"But you put money first." A sly smile crept across her face. "Syd was not poor."

Father Frank nodded. "Yes, I know. He paid for the air conditioning in the church, and then asked if we needed new AC in the parish hall. He wrote out a check for both, and never batted an eye."

"No. I guess not. I was talking with the mother of one of my students. She works at the bank. She had to help Syd out awhile back."

"Oh my." Deep lines formed between the priest's dark eyebrows. "I hope paying for the air conditioners didn't put him in a bind."

"Not quite. The help she had to provide was how he could adjust accounts so that his money would be fully protected by the F.D.I.C. She said he had to move some of it to other banks."

"But the F.D.I.C. insures each account up to $250,000." He tilted his head to the side and stared at Georgia. "Are you telling me …"

"Syd was not even close to poor. Best I can figure, without asking too many questions my friend shouldn't answer, Syd could be called rich."

Father Frank whistled softly. "Who would have guessed?"

"I think somebody didn't have to guess. Somebody knew. And you know what that means."

Father Frank nodded. "Motive."

#

Father Frank cooked breakfast on auto pilot, his mind mulling over this new bit of information. He had realized Syd would receive a nice sum for his land. He had not realized that Syd already had a considerable nest egg. And where did it come from? Before he retired, Syd had worked as a pharmaceutical salesman. He might have been more outgoing then. He could have been a top notch salesman. And he didn't have a wife or kids. Still, how much could he have put aside?

By the time he had finished breakfast, Father Frank knew he couldn't let it go.

"Pine Tree Police Department, This is Detective Oakley."

"Hi, Mike. This is Father Frank."

"Yes, I know."

"Of course. The police *would* have caller ID. I know you're busy, so I'll get right to the point. Were you aware that Syd has a considerable estate? I don't just mean the sale of his land to Lockey. He had hundreds of thousands of dollars in the bank."

Silence. Then, "What's your point?"

"Money makes a great motive for murder."

Mike sighed. "Father, the case is closed. Suicide. Confirmed by the medical examiner. Captain's happy. I'm happy. Everybody's happy."

"I guess the murderer is happy too. You close the case, the murderer gets off scot-free."

"It's a suicide."

"What can I do to get you to reconsider?"

"Not a thing. The case is closed. The chief has me on other things.

And you should be feeding the poor, or ministering to the sick. Let poor old Cranzler rest in peace. Case closed." Mike disconnected.

Father Frank placed the phone back in its cradle.

"Wrong, Mike. The case is not closed."

Chapter 4

The funeral mass started at 9 a.m. with a minimal crowd in attendance. Father Frank tried to lay the blame on the weather, which was dismal. A steady drizzle had started about 7:30 and was still falling an hour and a half later. To add misery to discomfort, the wind whipped around corners and carried the rain to every exposed surface. Even with a raincoat and an umbrella and only a short walk from the rectory to the church, Father Frank was drenched. His trousers were soaked from the bottom of his raincoat all the way down. His shoes sloshed with each step. Surely, a good many more people would have been here had it been dry.

Of course, Syd was somewhat of a recluse. He didn't socialize with others at Prince of Peace, probably hadn't spoken to fifteen people in the parish. Add to that his rather small family and it was understandable why the turnout was poor.

Father Frank had asked Syd's brother, Randall, and his sister, Judith, if they wanted to speak at the funeral. Judith declined through sobs. Randall simply snapped, "No."

But Randall's son asked if he could say a few words. Randall objected, but when Father Frank said he thought that was a great idea, Randall conceded.

When the appropriate time came, the priest nodded to the boy. Ben Cranzler was barely twelve, slender and clean cut. Father Frank could see the boy shaking. But he held his head high, stood straight, and made eye contact with those sitting before him.

"I just wanna say a few things, to make sure you all know the real Uncle Syd. I know he seemed grumpy a lot, and didn't smile a lot, at least in public. But I can tell you, he was fun and had a, you know, sense of humor." Ben had to stop for a moment to compose himself, then continued. "Uncle Syd used to take me out for ice cream, and stuff like that. And he taught me lots of things. I mean, not school things but, you know, important things. He taught me how to fish. He taught me *I* was important, and if friends didn't like me the way I was, they weren't my friends."

Father Frank could see tears forming in Ben's eyes, but he didn't brush them away. He just kept telling people how important Syd was to him.

While Ben spoke, Father Frank studied the people huddled in the pews. Of course, he knew Randall and his wife, Abby. He had met Syd's sister, Judith Kitchen, only a couple of times, both brief. Oddly enough, her husband had not come with her. Mike Oakley was there, probably because of Georgia who was seated next to him. Father Frank was surprised to see Bud Wilcox. Sitting next to Bud was a well dressed man. Father Frank finally decided he must be the Duke Heinz people had mentioned. At the very back of the church, a man sat hunched over, hands on the pew in front of him, eyes studying the floor, a grim look etched on his wrinkled face. Father Frank had never seen the man before. But he looked like the man Bud had described. W.C., no last name.

Could this be the man who said Syd was stealing from him?

The family had asked that there be no grave-side service after mass. Later, they would gather at the grave for a private good-bye. So, Father Frank followed the casket out, and waited at the door of the church. The rain had stopped, but the low-hanging clouds threatened more to come.

When the man sitting in the back came out, the priest grabbed his hand and started shaking it. "Thank you for coming. I don't think I know you."

The man tried to pull his hand back without speaking, but Father Frank held on. "Are you a relative?"

"A friend."

"I'm Father Frank, Syd's pastor. And you are?"

The man hesitated, but people were piling up behind him. "I'm Mayfield." With that, he slipped his hand out and left.

A few minutes later, when Bud came out, he introduced Duke Heinz.

"Mr. Heinz, could you wait just a few minutes while I speak to the family? I'd like to talk to you for a moment or two."

Duke nodded and stepped back out of the way.

#

When the last person had left, Father Frank walked over to where Duke and Bud were chatting. "Mr. Heinz, thank you for coming. Did you know Syd well?"

"No, not really. I'm with the Lockey Corporation and we're acquiring Syd's land. I had talked with him the afternoon before he died."

And it hadn't gone well. "Oh. Tell me a little about Lockey and this project."

"Well, it's all been in the newspaper. They're going to build a shopping mall on 160 acres, which as you know, includes Syd Cranzler's land. The hope was to start dirt work within a few weeks. But, that may be postponed now, due to this unfortunate circumstance." Duke assumed an appropriately concerned look.

"Why was it important that it be right at that particular spot? I mean, there's a lot of empty land just down the road."

Bud Wilcox took a half step forward. "Actually, the city is in favor of this location. Move down the road a mile, even half a mile, and the city wouldn't get much in tax revenue."

"But a couple of years ago in Mineola, didn't Lockey build just over the line?"asked Father Frank.

Duke's face broke into a benevolent smile. "We're trying to be good neighbors in Pine Tree. I think the corporate officers have learned it's better to pay the taxes and be community supporters."

Father Frank wondered what they had learned and how, but decided not to ask. "And the rush?"

"No rush. We've been working on this for over a year." Duke spread his hands wide. "Obviously, we didn't want the information out until we were certain it wouldn't fall through."

Father Frank looked at the smooth operator. Was Duke too smooth? Or was that just a requirement for a person in his job? He stuck out his hand. "Thank you for enlightening me. I'm just sorry it came under these circumstances."

"And so am I," Duke said as he pumped the priest's hand. "Though we were at odds with one another, I had to admire Mr. Cranzler's spunk. I'm sorry he died."

#

That afternoon, Father Frank sat in his study, lights out, Tuscany music playing very softly. His eyes were closed, but his brain was very much awake. Duke's words rang false to the priest. Except his last comments about Syd. *I think he might really have admired Syd's spunk, even if it held him up a bit. And Duke might have been sincere when he said he was sorry Syd was dead. Maybe. Maybe he thought it would go faster without the problem of a death of a land owner.* But how did all that fit together? And how was he going to get Mike to reopen the case?

Father Frank was sure Mike was just following the chief's orders. Mike was fair minded, liked to see justice, and wouldn't take the easy way if it weren't the right way. *I've got to give Mike enough so he can convince the chief to reopen the case.*

The priest opened his eyes, picked up his glass and took a small sip of Dr Pepper. His eyes closed again. Did he have anything, other than a gut feeling, indicating that Syd did not commit suicide? Syd had been planning to appeal the ruling. He was rich, whatever that meant. He felt Lockey was trying to steal his land. And Mayfield accused Syd of stealing money.

But, what did any of those mean? The appeal could delay Lockey, perhaps a lot. And that could cost the company lots of money. So, would that point toward Duke? Or someone else hired by Lockey? If Syd were rich, maybe someone in his family, who stood to inherit, might have a motive. His brother? Sister? Some other relative? And if Mayfield thought Syd had stolen from him, could that be enough of a motive? How much was Mayfield talking about? And how did Syd steal it? *If* Syd actually did steal from Mayfield.

Clearly, I don't have enough information to make any kind of a judgment. And until I do, I won't be able to get Mike to reopen the case.

The priest opened his eyes and sighed. Perhaps he should take his own advice. Stay out of it. That's what he told Georgia. He grinned. *Taking your own advice is like kissing your elbow.*

Father Frank got up and wandered into the kitchen. He picked up an apple from the bowl of fruit on the table and took a bite. His thoughts turned to the funeral—who was there, and who wasn't. Syd's brother, Randall, and his wife were there. Abby dabbed at her eyes with a lace handkerchief several times. But her husband sat stone-faced throughout the service. He'd looked more angry than sad.

Sid's sister had cried softly through the entire service. But where was her husband? Even if he and Syd weren't the best of friends, why hadn't Lance Kitchen been there for his wife? Father Frank had met Lance only once, briefly, and didn't have any feeling for who the man was.

The priest walked back to his study. He thought of Ben. What a touching, and brave, thing the boy did. Even now, as the priest remembered Ben's eulogy, his eyes misted over. *Whatever, I owe it to Ben to at least look into Syd's death a little. Find something that even the chief can't ignore. Get Mike back on the case.*

#

W.C. Mayfield answered the door barefooted, a can of Bud Light in his hand. "Hello, preacher, come on in. Can I get you something to drink?"

"No, thank you. I just finished dinner."

W.C. ushered Father Frank into the living room and motioned him to sit down. Magazines of all varieties cluttered the room—on the table, the top of the TV, the floor. Father Frank had to move two from the chair before he could sit. Mayfield plopped down in a worn recliner. He looked to be a few years younger than Syd. His grey hair was cut to a quarter inch long, and he had a short neck which gave the effect that he was constantly hunching his shoulders. His arms looked accustomed to heavy work.

"What can I do for you, Padre?"

Father Frank hadn't rehearsed what he was going to say and for several seconds his mind raced through the possibilities. "I'm going to cut right to the heart of the matter, W.C.. I'm not convinced Syd committed suicide."

W.C. stared at him for a moment and then took a long swig of his beer and for a few seconds said nothing. Then, "How come?"

"Nothing concrete. I just don't see Syd as the type to take his own life."

"You didn't know Syd as well as I did. He didn't like to lose." He held up one hand. "I'm not saying he did. But I read that the medical examiner had determined it was suicide."

Father Frank nodded several times. "That's true. It's just … it keeps nagging at me. I guess I have to ask enough questions to satisfy my inquisitive nature. Maybe I'll sleep better."

"Okay. So, what can I do for you?" It was delivered flat, without enthusiasm.

"Bud Wilcox told me you came up to Syd and accused him of

stealing from you. What was that about?"

W.C. leaned back and laughed. "I did say that. But Bud didn't know what I was talking about." W.C. tipped the can up, finished the beer and set the can on the table before continuing. "You see, Syd and I golf, and he's been cleaning my plow. I'm a better golfer. But whatever, Syd has took me to the cleaners the last few weeks. I told him he was stealing my money." He laughed. "'Course, we're talking penny-ante stuff. Ten, fifteen dollars."

Suddenly he turned serious. "Looking at it now, it was a stupid thing for me to say. But who would have guessed?" He raised his eyebrows and cocked his head to one side. "Besides, everyone knows I don't got any money to steal."

"Do you know anybody who might want to kill Syd?"

W.C. looked down, and considered the question for nearly a minute. "Not really. Lance Kitchen expects to inherit, well, expects his wife to inherit, a good chunk of Syd's stuff, whatever that might be. I know he had a loud argument with Syd about wasting money on lawyers when they both knew he was gonna lose. He wanted Syd to bargain with Lockey, get a sweeter deal, and take it and skip any legal fees." He raised his shoulders. "I don't know if that means nothing or not."

Father Frank nodded. "I don't either. But, at least it's something to consider. Anyone else?"

"Other than that land guy, or someone else from his company. Can't think of no one else."

The priest stood up. "I appreciate your help. Sorry to have bothered you. But I just can't believe it was suicide and since the police aren't looking further, I'm going to."

W.C. looked at the priest for a moment. "I'm really sorry to see Syd gone. We go back a long time. I lost a friend."

As Georgia said, maybe somebody else knew Syd was rich. Maybe Lance knew.

Chapter 5

Georgia stood on the porch of the rectory, eyes dancing, hands in motion, excitement in her voice—her usual state. "I've got the Saturday Morning Ladies' Guild meeting in five minutes, but I wanted to tell you what I've found out."

"About what?"

"Lockey. You said I should look into it, and I did."

Father Frank put up both hands, palms facing Georgia. "Whoa. I did not say you should look into anything. In fact, I remember telling you to stay out of it, let the police handle it."

"They're not as nice as their slogan says."

"The police?"

"No, silly. Lockey."

"What slogan?"

"Don't you read anything?" Georgia let out a fake sigh of exasperation. "It's been in the paper several times. 'Improving Communities, Graciously.' More like they grind communities ruthlessly. I talked with friends in two other towns where they built shopping centers. All of them were unhappy. Said Lockey broke promises, used unethical practices, tried to frighten people into doing what they wanted, all sorts of non-gracious things."

"Hmmm."

"And they're into oil as well. In one of the towns, Wilmet Mills, they drilled a bunch of wells with no regard for the environment. They're sitting in the parking lot."

'Strange combination: shopping centers and oil wells."

"Isn't it. At any rate, the people I talked to felt like Lockey was unscrupulous." She glanced toward the parish hall. "Oops. There's Marge; got to go. I'll get back to you when I get more information." She turned and headed toward the parish hall.

"Stay out of it, Georgia."

Without turning, she waved a hand.

#

Father Frank rang the doorbell at Randall Cranzler's house. He had grave misgivings about this, and knew he should not follow this path. He'd told himself as much for most of the drive over. Nonetheless, here he was, waiting for someone to answer the door. Something compelled him. Even now, one part of him wanted to turn and leave before the door opened. But his feet remained glued to the spot.

"Oh, hello Father," said Ben Cranzler. "Mom and Dad are gone."

"I wanted to talk with your father. Guess I should have called first." The priest didn't say he had been trying to talk himself out of coming. "By the way, that was a very moving eulogy you gave last week. You must have been very close to your uncle."

"I just wish I'd, you know, spent more time with him. He was really cool."

"Yes. Did he and your father get along well?" As soon as it was out of his mouth, Father Frank regretted it. What was he doing wheedling information out of a child?

"They used to. But, ever since this shopping center thing, they've been arguing."

"About what?"

"Oh, Dad wanted Uncle Syd to, you know, take the money and quit fighting. Said he'd waste his money on lawyers and still lose. He called Uncle Syd stupid." Ben's opinion of that was mapped on his face.

"I'm sorry. I hate to see brothers fight," said Father Frank.

"Just a few days before, ah, Uncle Syd died, he and Dad and Uncle Lance had a big fight. I couldn't hear all of it 'cause Dad made me stay outside. But all three of 'em were really mad and yelling. Uncle Lance said something about him not being fair to the family, or something. And Dad, ah you know, ah, was on Uncle Syd too."

Father Frank felt intrigued and embarrassed at the same time. He knew Randall would not be happy about Ben describing the encounter. And while not actually coaxing it out of Ben, the priest still felt guilty. He decided he must end it.

"Ben, I'd better go. But I want to say again how impressed I was with your speech. I'm sorry you didn't get more time with your uncle. Please know he is in my prayers."

#

On the drive home, Father Frank's mind swarmed over the information the boy had provided. What did Lance's statement about being fair to family mean? Was that simply the same issue as Randall had, but Lance cast it as being unfair to the family? The only thing the priest could link it to was inheritance. How else did it affect the family?

Mayfield's comment resurfaced in Father Frank's mind: *Lance Kitchen is expecting to inherit, well, expecting his wife to inherit, a good portion of Syd's estate.* If Lance knew Syd was rich, as Georgia had described him, could that possibly lead to murder? And Mayfield had also heard Lance arguing with Syd about wasting money on lawyers. Was that really about wasting Lance's inheritance?

Father Frank didn't want to think about the possibility of Syd's own brother killing him. Of course, Genesis 4 provided a precedent: Cain and Abel.

Father Frank parked the car and headed for the rectory, his mind still on the murder.

Murder. Just the thought of it sent a chill down his backbone. He heard confessions every week. People did many things that offended God and hurt neighbors, or themselves. But most of those acts were not as unforgiving as murder. It was so final. No way to change it, to see the wrong and chose another path.

Father Frank's feet dragged and his shoulders slumped as he walked to his office. Premeditated murder seemed unthinkable to him. Was suicide any better? He wanted to discount suicide, even though the medical examiner said suicide. Right now, it was Father Frank's feeling versus the medical examiner's findings. Feelings versus facts.

He turned on his computer to work on tomorrow's sermon. The gospel passage centered on charity, and so would his sermon. But he needed a few more points. Thank God for the Internet. Years ago, if he'd needed a pertinent passage, he had to flip through his Bible, relying on memory and luck. Now he just logged onto Bible.com, and typed "charity."

And then it hit him. He had a resource that might add some facts to his feelings. It might convince him that Syd really did commit suicide. Or …

Chapter 6

"Hey, Pumpkin."

Georgia grasped the phone tighter and stiffened. Normally, when Mike called her Pumpkin she went soft in the head. And tingly in the tummy. When he first called her that, he said her hair reminded him of spun gold, but he didn't think she'd like it if he called her Goldie. A golden pumpkin was close.

Today, it just reminded her she was angry with him.

She responded with a chilly, "Hi."

"Well, that didn't start off too good. So, I won't invite myself over. Instead, why don't I pick you up around 7:00 and we go out and have some good catfish?"

"I've already eaten, Mike."

"Eaten? I'm not talking about lunch. It's only 4."

"I'm not in the mood for eating."

Mike cleared his throat and proceeded in a low and soft voice. "Georgia, you're not still stuck on that suicide bit, are you?"

"Wasn't suicide. And yes, I'm still stuck on it."

"So, you're letting my work decide whether we go out or not?"

Georgia frowned into the phone, as if Mike could see her. "No. Not your work. Your bull-headedness."

"Georgia, the M.E. reported …" He stopped and there was a moment of silence before he continued. "Okay. Let's go out for a nice, quiet dinner. We won't discuss the Cranzler case at all. We'll talk about your work, or music, art, the Academy Awards, anything, except my work. How's that?"

For several seconds Georgia did not reply. He was thoughtful and funny, kind and interesting, and made her feel good about herself. And except for this situation, they generally thought along the same lines.

Her harsh treatment of Mike wasn't fair to him. "All right. Come on by around seven."

Besides, she thought as she hung up the phone, *I'll have a better chance of changing his mind under soft lights and music.*

#

Mike had opted for Catfish Heaven, the site of their first date. And as on that date, Georgia had lamb chops, not catfish.

They discussed the East Texas Symphony Orchestra, how much they had enjoyed the last concert. Ultimately, they made plans to attend the concert scheduled for the middle of next month. From that, the conversation moved to Georgia's job at the Pine Tree high school. She had opted to substitute-teach this semester, rather than continue her full-time position. This led to a lengthy discussion on teaching that carried through to the end of the meal. Georgia declined dessert and Mike asked for the check.

The waiter brought the credit card slip and left it on the table.

"Are you going to sign the slip," asked Georgia.

Mike's forehead wrinkled. "Of course I am." He focused on the check, added in a tip and signed the slip.

"Why do you suppose Syd didn't sign the suicide note?" A sweet smile adorned Georgia's face. She had promised herself she would not antagonize Mike—if she could help it, and still get him to see her point.

"Oh, it's too beautiful an evening to get into that, don't you think?"

"It's too nice to get into an argument. But we can have a nice, friendly discussion." She patted his hand. "What do you think? About the no signature?"

"Didn't take the time. Didn't see the need," Mike said cautiously.

"Let's back up a step. Why did Syd write the note?" When Mike didn't respond, Georgia tried again. "Okay. We can't know that. But, why do *you think* he would write such a note?"

"Could be any of a dozen reasons. To tell his relatives what he was doing. To make a statement about Lockey. To clear his mind, define what he was doing and why." He paused only a second before saying slowly and deliberately, "To let the police know it wasn't a murder."

"All possible reasons. But, if he were telling his relatives, he would have signed it. You wouldn't send a letter to your brother without signing it, would you? And if you wanted to make a statement about Lockey, surely you would sign it. The people who wrote the Declaration of Independence certainly signed it, even though it put their lives at risk." She took Mike's hand in hers. "And if he were trying to tell the police it wasn't murder, he would certainly sign it—otherwise the police might think it was the murderer who wrote it." She smiled innocently.

After a moment, she continued. "Of course, maybe it was an accident. He took the wrong pills, or took too many." Suddenly, she looked shocked. "Oh, but then, he wouldn't have written a note at all, would he?"

She wrinkled her forehead. "Hmmmm. If we've eliminated suicide and an accident, what could it be?" She opened her eyes wide and sat up a little straighter. "Oh, I know. Murder! That's it. Isn't there a word for that? Oh, I remember—homicide!"

For a long minute, Mike just looked at her, his eyes intense, his teeth clamped together. Georgia couldn't tell if he was irritated or considering her logic, but she maintained her wide-eyed, excited look. Finally, he said, "Let's go walk by the lake and not think about suicide or murder. Just about the beautiful evening."

"But, I think I just –"

"Georgia. I'm off the case. It's closed. You can tell all of that to the M.E., or my boss, if you'd like. You and I are going to enjoy the moon shinning across the lake. And you can tell me how much fun I am."

Georgia slid out of the booth to stand beside the detective. "Yes, you are fun. And bullheaded." But now her smile was warm and genuine.

Mike took her hand and they started for the door. "We're similar in that respect. But I like you anyway."

Chapter 7

Father Frank sat with his hands poised over the keyboard. Where to start? He typed in "eminent domain." In less than a minute, the screen filled with the top choices, the first ten out of four million. Way too many.

He added "Pine Tree, Texas" to the request. This time, only eighty-seven references were found. The top one referred to a ruling by Judge McFatage granting eminent domain to The Lockey Corporation for a shopping center. Father Frank clicked on the link.

An article in the Longview News covered the judge's ruling. The priest scanned the article. The judge had said the arguments indicated that it was in the best interests of Pine Tree that the eminent domain petition be granted. The city would gain much needed jobs and tax revenue. McFatage quoted another judge, "I'm not going to substitute my business judgment for that of these commissioners. The City knows best."

Farther down in the article, Duke Heinz was quoted as saying this was a victory, not for The Lockey Corporation, but for the city of Pine Tree.

Father Frank entered Judge McFatage as the search criteria, and Google brought up thirty-four references. The priest found two that indicated an appellate court had overturned rulings by McFatage. *So maybe he wasn't always as careful as he should be.*

Next, Father Frank searched Duke Heinz. Google found over two million references. Most were about the university, low-level royalty or ketchup. He tried it again with quotes around Duke Heinz, and added a plus sign and the word "land." That cut the number of references to a manageable size. The Duke Heinz Father Frank was interested in accounted for only six references. What caught his eye was an article covering Duke Heinz as a land man for a large oil company. In fact, the only reference that linked Duke with Lockey was the one on the eminent domain ruling.

One link was to a blog where someone was complaining that Duke Heinz had used unethical tactics in obtaining a lease. Another indicated Duke Heinz had been arrested for assault.

Chapter 8

Father Frank promised himself he would not think about the circumstances of Syd's death on Sunday. And for the most part he managed it. At one point, his mind rebelled. This time, it reminded him that all his points thus far were simply circumstances. To be fair, he had nothing that should cause Mike to reopen the case. The fact that Syd had money was a circumstance, not a motive. The fact that Randall and Lance had argued with Syd about money was a circumstance. It did not suggest murder. Lockey Corporation already had the eminent domain ruling. They had won. No need to murder anyone. What did Duke's job as a land man for oil companies have to do with anything? And the fact that Syd did not sign the suicide note merely meant he didn't sign it, nothing more.

The medical examiner had ruled it suicide. Father Frank didn't have to like it, or agree with it. At this point, he could not really dispute it. He and Georgia had been too hard on Mike. *Tomorrow, I should go apologize to Mike.*

#

Monday after breakfast, Father Frank headed over to Glass Pharmacy. He desperately needed a new toothbrush, and he was out of mouthwash and vitamin C. He was studying the array of battery-powered toothbrushes when Rich Glass spoke to him.

"Father, I'm really sorry to hear about your parishioner. I was planning to come to the funeral, but my assistant called in sick, and there's no one else who can fill prescriptions. So, I had to be here."

"I understand. People need their medications. That's your first priority."

"I was flabbergasted. I mean, Syd was in here that very day. Said he was out of digitoxin. I guess I shouldn't tell what drug he took, but he's dead, so I'm not going to worry about it."

Father Frank almost dropped the toothbrush he was holding. "The day he died?"

Rich nodded.

"He got a refill on his digitoxin?" The priest's voice was ragged. "The day he died?" He remembered Mike saying the prescription bottle was completely empty. *And I was so certain it was not suicide. I've questioned people, stirred things up. I admitted I had no proof, no evidence even. But I thought I knew better than the police. God forgive me for my self conceit.*

The pharmacist pressed his lips together and shook his head. "No. I said I could have it for him in fifteen minutes. But Syd said he was in a hurry and couldn't wait. Besides, he'd already taken his pill for the day. He'd pick it up tomorrow. Of course, he was dead the next day."

For a moment, Father Frank just stared at Rich. He replayed what Rich had just said, a frown encompassing his face. His mind raced through the ramifications of what he had heard. Syd didn't have *any* digitoxin. He'd ordered it, but didn't pick it up before he died. *It couldn't have been suicide.* He paused. *Or could it?*

Tentatively he asked, "Is it possible Syd had a bottle at home, and was just getting a spare to have on hand?"

Rich shook his head. "No. I mean, I could check my records. But I can almost guarantee you he didn't. Why?"

Father Frank didn't want to say too much. But this certainly put a different light on things. This was more than a circumstance.

"Are you going to be here this afternoon?"

"Sure. I'll get out for lunch sometime. Otherwise, I'll be here until 6. What's this about?"

"I'm not sure, myself." Actually, in his mind, he *was* sure. But Mike might not be. "But, if you could look up Syd's records, I'd like to talk with you about them this afternoon." *And more to the point, let Mike hear it first-hand from you.*

\#

Father Frank practically dragged Mike into the pharmacy. "If this is about the Cranzler suicide, I'm going to be mad as hell."

"It's not about the Cranzler suicide," Father Frank said.

"Then what?"

"Oh, hi, Father," called Rick Glass from behind the counter.

"Hi. You know Mike Oakley, don't you?" the priest asked. "He's with the Pine Tree Police Department."

"Not really. But I've seen him in the store a few times. Hi, Mike."
The two men shook hands.

"Did you get those records I asked about?" All of a sudden, Father Frank felt weak. What if the records showed Syd *did* have a spare bottle? Why hadn't he waited until he had looked at the records before he dragged Mike down here?

"Got 'em right here." Rich came around the end of the counter, carrying a sheaf of papers in his hand. "Let's go in my office."

They entered a small office barely able to hold the three chairs crowded in there. "First, will you tell Mike exactly what you told me earlier?"

"Sure." He turned to look at the detective. "Syd came in here on the afternoon he died and asked to have his prescription for digitoxin refilled. But he was in a hurry and couldn't wait. Said he'd pick it up the next day."

Mike looked at the priest, his muscles suddenly tensed and anger slipping out of his eyes. "You said—"

"Let him finish," answered the priest.

The pharmacist looked from Mike to Father Frank, and back to Mike. When neither said anything more, Rich continued. "He said he had taken his last pill, but wouldn't need any until the next day. Of course, he never came back. I still have the prescription here."

"And what did you find in the records?" asked Father Frank quickly, before Mike had a chance to object.

"I've checked back to the time he first started taking these." The pharmacist held up a thick sheaf of papers. "Normally, I wouldn't give out any information on a customer's health. I guess it doesn't make any difference now, with Syd dead. Syd had atrial fibrillation, an irregular heartbeat. That's oversimplifying it, but—"

"That's good enough," said Mike, his jaw still tense and his anger just held at bay.

"Dr. Rankin prescribed digitoxin to regulate it. Syd needed to take one 1250 mcg, ah, microgram, pill each day to keep the heart pumping at a nice regular rate. If he took them as directed, he didn't have any problems functioning as normally as you and me."

"He had to take one every day?" asked Mike.

"Oh yeah. Every day."

"What if he forgot?" Mike pressed.

"His heart would remind him before very many hours passed and he would take it later in the day. But, he *would* take one. It is a rather unpleasant feeling. And once it starts, it doesn't go away—without medication. But the digitoxin straightens it out pretty quickly. And based on what he gets, ah, has gotten over the past year and five months, since he started on them, he had no extra pills." He crossed his arms across his stomach and stared at the detective. "What's this about?"

Father Frank answered. "The police think, no, the police *know* that Syd died of an overdose of digitoxin. And they think it was suicide. But what you're telling us is, he didn't have any digitoxin pills to take, much less enough for an overdose."

Both men looked at the detective. Mike rubbed his nose and stared at the floor. He pulled a small leather notebook out of his pocket and opened it, made a short note and looked up. "He could have gotten some from another pharmacist."

Rich shrugged. "I guess that's possible. But he would have needed a prescription. I keep the ones that Dr. Rankin prescribes. He would have needed another one."

"Couldn't he have saved some up?" Mike asked. "A pill here, a pill there?"

"Anything's possible." Rich shrugged. "But he said he didn't have any. And if he had saved some up, then why come in and order some more?" The pharmacist tilted his head to the side and waited for an answer.

Mike wrote a few words in his leather notebook. "How many would he need for a lethal dose?"

Rich looked down for a moment. "I would say, based on Syd's age and build, it would take about 10 miligrams to be lethal. So, he would have needed eight of the 1250 mcg pills."

Father Frank jumped in. "And if he was going to commit suicide and already had the pills he needed, why come in and order more?"

"Forgot he had the extra pills. Hadn't decided to commit suicide yet." Mike shook his head. "I don't know. I only know the M.E. said it was suicide."

The priest leaned closer to the detective. "But at the very least, this casts doubt on the suicide argument. You have to consider that someone else poisoned Syd."

For a time, no one spoke. Finally, Mike took a deep breath. "I'll explain all this to Chief Flag. It's up to him if he wants to re-open the case."

A glimmer of hope shone in Father Frank's eyes. "But will you present it to him as a real problem with the suicide theory, or just as nonsense you're obliged to pass along to him."

"Neither. Just plain facts. No prejudice one way or the other."

"And you'll let me know what he says?"

"Oh, you'll be the first to know." The detective got up. "Thanks, Mr. Glass. I appreciate the information. I'll probably come back with more questions." Mike turned and walked out.

Chapter 9

By mid-afternoon, Father Frank had still not heard from Mike. He almost called Georgia to tell her of the news Rich had provided. He decided to wait, see what Mike had to say.

The priest found plenty of work to keep him in his office, near the phone. When the clock showed 4:00, he grabbed the phone and dialed the PTPD and asked to speak to Mike.

"No information. No decision," Mike said. "The chief hasn't called me and I'm not calling him again. The case is closed and now, maybe we've got to say we goofed and reopen it. That does not tend to bring a smile to the chief's face. Said Cranzler could have another doctor, any number of explanations." Mike let out a long breath. "But, he said he'd think about it and get back to me."

"Another doctor?"

"Happens all the time. People get several doctors to write prescriptions for the same drug to get more of it than one doctor can, or will, prescribe."

Father Frank felt his neck getting hot. "Syd was not a drug user. He had a heart problem. And a doctor."

"Did you know him well enough to say he didn't abuse drugs?"

"I did. He wasn't." The priest had a second's doubt. How well did he really know Syd? Not well at all. But surely he would have noticed if Syd had used drugs. Then, maybe not. He saw Syd mostly on Sundays. What was he like on Tuesday, Wednesday, Thursday? Still, the police needed to take another look. They'd made a decision. To be fair, it was based on the M.E.'s report. Now, they didn't want to look stupid.

"Well, Flag said there could certainly be other explanations."

"Sure. He could have found a bottle of digitoxin by the side of the road. Maybe he started a year ago, saving one pill a month just in case he wanted to commit suicide. Come on, Mike. At least take a look."

He dropped the phone in its cradle.

Instantly, he felt remorse. He was being unfair to Mike. And, the priest was letting his frustration cause him to lose his temper. He picked up the phone and dialed.

"Sorry, Mike. That was rude and un-called for. I apologize to you and the Pine Tree Police Department. You do a great job."

"Just not this time?" the detective asked with a quiet chuckle.

"Let's just say we are not in agreement today. Maybe tomorrow."

Father Frank hung up again, leaned back and closed his eyes. What to do? Wait. Exercise patience. Give the police a chance.

The telephone rang, and the priest almost jumped.

"Prince of Peace Parish. How can we help you?"

"Tell me the police have re-opened Syd's case," said Georgia. "I couldn't get Bullheaded Mike to budge an inch."

"Now, Georgia. Don't be too hard on Mike. Besides, he has talked to the chief."

"How'd you do that? What did you say to him?"

The priest laughed. "It isn't what I said to him; it's what Rich Glass said to him."

"Which was what?"

Father Frank related Rich's story about the prescription and all the records he checked.

"So, what did Chief Flag say?"

"He's looking into it. Said there could have been a different prescription, different doctor, any number of explanations."

Georgia snorted. "Like murder. Who was Syd's doctor?"

"A Dr. Rankin. Know him?"

"Indeed I do. Quite well. Nice man. Good doctor."

"How do you know everybody?"

"It's a small town. I've lived here all of my thirty-four years. Went to school here. Teach here. I'm going to give him a call."

"Now, Georgia," the priest began. "The doctor can't—"

"Call you later." And she hung up.

#

An hour later, Georgia was back on the phone.

"Well, I tracked the good doctor down. No easy task nowadays." Georgia sounded like she had been running. "Let me catch my breath."

Father Frank waited.

"Okay. I talked with Dr. Rankin. He said that actually, he didn't give Syd any prescriptions. He gave those directly to Rich's pharmacy. And only Rich's pharmacy."

"What about—"

"He doubted Syd ever saw another doctor. Couldn't say for certain, of course. But Syd had told him more than once that he hated going to the doctor, and refused to see anyone else. One time, Dr. Rankin tried to get Syd to see a specialist. Syd said no way. One doctor was one too many." She paused only a second. "How's that grab you?"

"Not conclusive. But it does add weight to our feeling that Syd did not commit suicide."

#

Father Frank put up the dinner dishes. He thought about starting on his sermon for Sunday, then decided it was only Monday. He could postpone it for a day. He'd started *The Grass Kingdom* by Jory Sherman over a week ago, but the hectic events surrounding Syd's death had kept him from reading any fiction for days. He picked up the volume and settled in his easy chair, adjusted the light, and started to read.

He had finished two pages when the telephone rang.

"Hi, Father. Norm Winters. Won't take but a minute of your time. I called everybody else earlier in the day, but seemed to keep missing you or getting a busy signal. I didn't want to leave a message on your answering machine. We're going to read Syd Cranzler's will on Friday. Ten o'clock in my office. Can you make it?"

Creases formed on the priest's brow. *Why is he telling me this?* "I'm free then. But, there's really no point in my being there, Norm."

There was a slight pause. "Actually, Father, you need to be there. You have an interest in the estate."

Chapter 10

Georgia answered the door. "Better have good news."

Mike smiled his brightest and said, "I thought maybe we'd not talk about police work tonight. Maybe just some soft music and, ah, quiet conversation."

Georgia giggled. "Quiet conversation, huh. I'll bet that's what you have in mind." She opened the door wider. "Come on in. Actually, I'm glad you're here. I made some egg custard, just fresh out of the oven. If you hadn't shown up, knowing myself as well as I do, I would have eaten the entire thing. It's more than I need. But I would have risen to the task. Now, *you* can help me eat it."

They took the custard and coffee out to the patio and settled into comfortable chairs. The sun was just above the horizon, hidden behind the trees, but casting a warm glow on the yard. The light made the colors of the flowers vivid. Hummingbirds were racing to get in their final meal of the day. It was Georgia's favorite time.

"Great custard," Mike said after taking his first bite. "I can see why you might have eaten it all."

"It's one of my many favorite desserts." It was not the time to talk about murder or suicide, but the next words out of her mouth were, "So, what has Chief Flag decided?"

"I don't know. He hasn't favored me with his decision – or his thought process. But, the information from the pharmacy didn't jolt him into re-opening the case."

"You and the chief both know I'm right. But it's easier to stick with the M.E. report and do nothing. Saves a lot of time and energy. No rummaging around for clues, then suspects, motives, means, opportunities. No work at all. Easy choice. It's like looking at the left-over pizza in the fridge and trying to decide between that and peeling potatoes, fixing a salad, and frying pork chops. Easy choice. Pop the pizza in the microwave." She spooned some custard into her mouth and savored it before continuing. "But, since I knew Syd, I'm going to skip the microwave approach, turn on the oven and stove, and start chopping vegetables."

Mike just looked at her and shook his head. "Georgia, just for a moment, step back and look at this dispassionately. You're saying it was murder, and you're going to go look for the murderer. If you're right—and I'm not agreeing it was murder—but if it was, then you should stay away from it. The man has already killed one person. Not nearly as difficult to kill the next one. Most people have a predisposition not to cross the line. He's already crossed it. He put that tendency aside."

"So, you're conceding it might be murder." A small, smug smile played on Georgia's mouth.

"No, I'm not. What I'm saying is this. There are two possibilities. One, it was suicide. That's my choice. And if that's the case, there's nothing for you to look into. You're wasting your time. The other possibility—not likely in my opinion—is murder. And if that's the case, you need to stay out of it because it would be too dangerous. In either case, stay out of it." The last sentence had the weight of authority barely concealed in it.

Georgia sucked on her spoon before speaking. "Well, I'm not going to stay out of it. So, I guess you'd better keep an eye on me, so I don't get into any trouble."

For several moments, Mike looked at Georgia, like he might look at a suspect. "I certainly intend to keep an eye on you." Then his face opened into a big grin. "But since I don't believe there is a murderer, it will be a more romantic look."

"I can deal with that." She leaned over and gave Mike a light kiss on the cheek.

She sat back and surveyed him for a moment. "I talked with Dr. Rankin today."

"Cranzler's doctor?"

"Right." She repeated what she had told Father Frank about her conversation with the doctor. "It's making it harder and harder for you to ignore the murder scenario."

Mike let out a long, slow breath. "I'm not ignoring it. But right now, the case is officially closed. I'll keep an open mind. But Chief

Flag has to okay any reopening. I can't go off on my own. He wouldn't take kindly to that."

Georgia smiled and scraped the last of the custard from her bowl. "Fortunately, I am not restricted by the blind chief. I'll do the work. You won't have to do anything but pick up the mur-derer, as soon as I identify him."

Chapter 11

"Thank you for seeing me," said Father Frank as he sat down in Dr. Rankin's office.

Dr. Rankin had the serious, no-nonsense look of a doctor, a few pounds overweight, light brown hair with just enough grey at the temples to look distinguished. *He could play the part of a doctor on TV*, the priest thought. *I sure hope he has a lot more in-depth knowledge.*

"What brings you here, Father? The nurse said it was not a medical problem."

How to begin? "I believe Georgia Peitz talked to you about Syd Cranzler's death."

Dr. Rankin nodded, but said nothing.

"As I'm sure she said, we're not convinced it was suicide. And we're, basically, just asking a lot of questions, hoping some of the answers will prompt the police to re-open the case."

The doctor tilted his head to the side and said, "I didn't see Syd as the type of personality that would take his own life. And in fact, when I witnessed his new will just a little before his death, he was in good spirits, talking about taking his case to the Texas Supreme Court. Admitted he wouldn't win, but he'd have a lot of fun, and maybe make some people see how eminent domain can be abused."

"Yes, he had Norm Winters drawing up papers to file an appeal."

The doctor laughed. "Yes. They talked about it, Norm as serious as cancer, and Syd acting like he'd taken some nitrous oxide or ecstasy." Suddenly, the doctor's expression turned serious and he leaned forward. "Not that I ever knew Syd to use any drugs. No, he was very much against them. Wasn't even happy about taking digitoxin." Rankin laughed again. "Said the only stimulant he approved of was the kind he put in an oil well."

"We don't think it was suicide either."

The doctor leaned back in his high-backed leather chair. "But I understand the medical examiner has declared Syd's death a suicide. An overdose of digitoxin. And Syd always had digitoxin in the house." He steepled his fingers. "So, what do you want to ask me—that I can tell you?"

"First, I'd like to know about digitoxin. How much is enough to kill you, or rather Syd, with his heart condition? How can it be delivered? What is its shelf life? How long would it have to be in his system before it …was fatal? Anything you can tell me that might help me understand how this happened."

The doctor nodded several times. "First, the easy part. Digitoxin is a cardiac glycoside used in the treatment of cardiac failure, due to its anti-arrhythmic effect. Actually, it's making a comeback. An old drug we're now deciding is better than the newer ones. In Syd's case, it had been an effective cardiac regulator because it did the job without the side effects of nausea or vomiting that sometimes accompanies digitalis based drugs."

"Whoa. Too technical," Father Frank said with a laugh.

"What I'm trying to say is that it was a very appropriate drug for the atrial fibrillation—irregular heartbeat—that Syd had. I can tell you that because it was common knowledge. He made no secret of it. But, like most medicines, too much can be bad. In the case of digitoxin, it can sneak up on you. Toxic levels produce a progressively slower heart rate. This could happen over a period of time until the heart slowly stops. However, in Syd's case, as I understand it, he took a very large dose and his heart stopped quickly."

"I have no problem with the cause of death. What I'm questioning is, who administered that large dose? The M.E. says Syd administered it. But couldn't someone else have given it to him?"

The doctor rubbed his nose and stared at the desk top for several seconds. "Certainly that is possible. But digitoxin is a little bitter. If this was not administered over a period of days, he would know if someone put it in his drink."

"But the taste could be masked in a strong drink?"

Rankin nodded. "It's possible. Remember, this is a prescription drug. You can't get it unless a doctor prescribes it. And any ethical doctor would only do that for a heart patient." When the priest didn't say anything for a moment, Rankin continued. "Keep in mind, Syd's condition was demanding. If he didn't take his digitoxin each day, his heart would let him know in a very uncomfortable way. I doubt Syd ever missed taking a pill each day."

"How many pills would be needed to … cause his heart to stop?"

The doctor stared at the ceiling for a moment, then looked back at the priest. "He was taking the twelve-fifty pills. That's 1250 micrograms. Given the condition of his heart, probably ten pills would do it."

"How big are those pills?"

"Not very big. About the size of an adult low dose aspirin.'

"And you could crush them up and mix them in a drink?"

"Yes. But remember, they've got a bitter taste. Ten would be hard to disguise in a drink."

"How long would it take to kill him?"

Rankin stretched his neck and rubbed the back of it with his hand. "Depends on the dose, of course. It could be pretty quick with a large dose. To make a decent guess, I'd need to know how many pills he ingested."

Father Frank nodded several times. "What if he ingested ten pills?"

The doctor pursed his lips and looked down for a moment. "About an hour, I would think."

"One last question. Are there generics? What names do I have to look for?"

"You're in luck," said Dr. Rankin. "It's most likely going to say Digitoxin or Lanoxin. And so far, the generics have not guaranteed therapeutic equivalence, so most doctors won't allow them."

"Digitoxin or Lanoxin."

Father Frank got up. "Thanks, Doctor. I appreciate your time and help."

The doctor stood and came around his desk. "I liked Syd. And I don't see him committing suicide. And if he didn't, I hope you—the police, that is—catch the guy." They shook hands. "Any suspects? Motive?"

"No suspects I'd be willing to name just yet. But, Syd had quite a bit of money, which often makes for a motive. And, he was trying to delay or stop the new shopping center. Once the police reopen the case, they'll find suspects and motives. The M.E. believed it was suicide and the police followed his lead."

"If I can be of any help, don't hesitate to ask," said Rankin.

#

Debussy played in the background, very softly. The lights were out. First, Father Frank had prayed, asking the Lord to help him look at things impartially, see only the true facts, not let his previous feelings influence his analysis tonight. He leaned back in his chair, eyes closed, completely relaxed, no preconceived notions, impartial. And then an image of the glowering Randall popped into his mind. With an effort, he pushed it away and replaced it with a picture of a bottle of pills.

Syd would have needed at least ten pills, and according to Rich's records and Rankin's take on Syd's opinion of doctors and drugs, he most likely didn't have any extra pills. The pills were small enough to be crushed and put in a drink. But Rankin thought ten pills would be too bitter to go unnoticed.

Mike didn't mention finding any glass sitting on the counter or table. So, did Syd take pills to commit suicide and then wash the dishes while he waited for the pills to do their job? He could have gone out for dinner, or a drink, and taken the pills there. Would he crush the pills in the restaurant? Or did he crush them before leaving home? Someone might have seen him, might have wondered why he was taking so many pills. And he would have no guarantee of getting back home before they took effect. Of course, maybe he didn't care where he was when it happened.

Rich said he shouldn't have any extra pills, quoted Syd as saying he had no pills. So, where did the pills come from? And if someone else spiked his drink with digitoxin, why hadn't Syd tasted it?

The M.E. hadn't found much food in Syd's stomach, just the digitoxin and some chocolate.

Father Frank's head jerked up. Chocolate. A strong chocolate, or a dark chocolate, might be able to obscure the bitter taste. A hot chocolate would do it. But it was too warm for hot chocolate. He remembered Ben saying that Syd would take him for ice cream. And frozen chocolate would mask the bitterness as well as hot chocolate.

The priest opened his eyes. He had the what and the how. What he didn't have was the who.

But it wasn't Syd.

Chapter 12

Wednesday, Father Frank had planned to get a much-needed haircut. Instead, he drove to Tyler to see Monsignor Decker. Not by choice. The monsignor had summoned him, ordered an immediate meeting. His tone indicated he was not happy. But Father Frank didn't have a clue what had caused the anger he sensed in the phone call.

Decker had always been an ad hoc mentor and Father Frank had always enjoyed their visits.

Maybe not today.

#

The monsignor opened the door and said, "Come in, Father Frank."

In those four words, the priest knew this was serious. First, no pleasantries. No "Top of the morning." No "Are ya keepin' well, Frank?" Second, Decker always addressed him as "Frank," not Father Frank. His mind traced back. Monsignor Decker had called him Father Frank the day he was ordained, a congratulation on having achieved his goal of becoming a priest. Since that day, it had always been "Frank."

With no other words, the monsignor led the way into his office. Another bad sign. Previous visits had taken place in the living room.

"I don't know what's going on up there," Decker began. "But I don't like what I hear. Have you forgotten the vows you took? Have you forgotten your training, what your position is?"

Father Frank's head tilted to the side and worry lines creased his face. He had no idea what the monsignor was talking about. He hadn't violated—or even come close to violating—any vows. He had been fulfilling his priestly duties to the best of his ability, happily. He wasn't even aware that anybody in the parish was unhappy with him. He shook his head.

"I have no idea what you're talking about."

"I'm talking about money. You took a vow of poverty. You receive a stipend from the parish. You don't amass a fortune from outside. Your real compensation is knowing you are helping bring people closer to God. It is not in acquiring earthly treasures. Have you forgotten that?" His tone bordered on harsh.

The priest's eyebrows crowded down over his eyes. He looked down, confused, his teeth grinding together. Finally, he looked up and again shook his head.

"I don't know what you're referring to. I've taken no money from anyone. In fact, I haven't even taken my last month's stipend. What money are you talking about?"

"Right. You haven't gotten it yet. But I understand you are to receive a sizable inheritance from one of your parishioners."

"Inheritance?" Deep furrows formed across Father Frank's forehead.

"Not from a member of your family. From a member of your parish." The monsignor shook his head. "It couldn't be worse unless it was from a female parishioner. And I understand it came from a parishioner who committed suicide and you took it upon yourself to give him a Catholic burial."

Father Frank's eyes opened wide, and his neck began to get hot. He sat up straighter. "I am of the opinion that Syd Cranzler did *not* commit suicide. In fact, I don't know anyone convinced he did, except the medical examiner."

Decker rolled his eyes up to look at the ceiling, then back at Father Frank. "And you know better than the authorities."

"I knew Syd better. He was not the kind of person who would commit suicide. In my opinion, he did not commit suicide and therefore I gave him a Catholic burial. And I make no apologies for that."

The monsignor stared at Father Frank for several seconds. "Okay." For the first time, his voice lost its hard edge. "The Church has become more open in that area. We don't know what a person's state of mind was in the time before they expire."

"No, we don't," Father Frank said aggressively. "In this case, I am convinced Syd did not even set anything in motion. But, that's not an issue—in my mind. What is this about an inheritance? Who told you I was inheriting anything?" His eyes bore into Decker.

"Who told me isn't important." Once again, his words were biting. "But, they had it on good authority that you were the principal beneficiary in Mr. Cranzler's will."

"That's nonsense." A part of Father Frank's mind shuddered to hear himself talking to the Monsignor that way and in that tone. "And it is important to know who told you such a thing. Who was it?" The last was a demand.

"I am not obliged to tell you anything. But, since you have resorted to an aggressive mode, I will tell you that I received a phone call, but the man did not identify himself."

"And you've called me on the carpet on the basis of an anonymous phone call? What exactly did he say?"

"Exactly what I told you—that you were the principal beneficiary in Mr. Cranzler's will, and it was a sizable amount. Are you telling me that is not true?"

"I certainly am. Besides which, the will hasn't been read yet. Unless it was the lawyer, who would know what was in the will?"

Father Frank stopped abruptly. He lowered his head, resting his forehead in his right hand as his mind raced through his last conversation with Norm Winters. *Actually, Father, you need to be there. You have an interest in the estate.* He raised his head and brought his hand up to cover his chin. After a moment he let out a long breath and looked back at the monsignor.

This time his voice was soft and his tone subdued. "I got a call from the lawyer who handled Syd's legal matters. He asked me to come to the reading of the will on Friday. He said I had an interest in the estate." Father Frank inhaled deeply. "I took that to mean I was interested, since I felt Syd had been murdered. Maybe the will would shed some light on that angle. I certainly did not—*do not*—think I would be mentioned as a beneficiary. Certainly not for any money. Maybe a small keepsake or something."

For more than a minute, neither man said anything. Finally, Monsignor Decker spoke, as strong and accusing as before. "Find out. Set it to rest. Even the suggestion is bad for the Church, bad for you. Being mentioned in the will of parishioners can only be bad for the Church. I do not like it. And clearly, the rumor—as you put it—is circulating."

Without another word, the older man stood up, walked to the front door and opened it. The meeting was over. "Keep me informed. Regularly."

#

Father Frank slammed his car door and laid down rubber driving away. He gripped the steering wheel until his knuckles were white. *He simply assumed I've done something wrong. I've never given him any cause for that. Yet, I'm called on the carpet. Dear God, give this man some sense of charity."*

He slammed on the brakes, skidding to a halt across the crosswalk. He had almost run a red light. An old woman started across the street, then stopped at his car and scowled at him. He checked behind, saw it was clear, and backed up a few feet so the woman could walk straight across between the two white painted lines.

He took several deep breaths. *Okay. Calm down. You're angry and irrational. But, you don't want to injure someone because you're mad.*

When the light changed, Father Frank eased forward. His mind switched gears. Who would call Decker? And why? Who would even know what was in the will? Norm, of course. The priest shook his head. It was highly unlikely that Norm would have called the monsignor. But who else could it have been?

And was there any truth to the inheritance bit?

Chapter 13

Father Frank arrived back at the rectory to find Mike Oakley's car sitting in the driveway.

"Come on in. I need something to drink and you can tell me the good news," the priest called as he got out of his car.

In the kitchen, Father Frank opened two Dr Peppers. He handed one to Mike and took a long drink from the other.

The detective set his drink on the table, and inhaled. "First, you have to realize Chief Flag puts a lot of stock in the M.E., and rightly so. The man handles cases over the entire county. He nails the cause and time of death with amazing accuracy."

Father Frank did not like what he heard. "Okay, that's first. What's second?"

"The chief has decided to re-open the case." A big grin spread over the priest's face as Mike continued. "He's still not convinced it wasn't suicide, but he's given me a week to settle it one way or the other. If I've not found something clearly pointing to murder by the end of one week, it's closed again, labeled suicide and that's that."

"A week's not very long, but I'll take it. Where are you starting?"

The detective picked up his drink and drained half the can before setting it back down. "I'm starting with a list of suspects. People who might or could have a reason to want Cranzler dead."

"Duke Heinz is a good start. Or somebody else at the Lockey Corporation," offered Father Frank.

"He's on my list. Anybody else you want to suggest?"

The priest thought for a moment. "I guess anybody who might benefit financially, but you probably started there. I suppose you have to include his brother and sister, though I can't imagine either of them killing their brother. Of course, I still find it hard to believe anybody can deliberately kill another human being."

Mike finished his drink and carefully placed the empty can on the table, and for several seconds he held Father Frank with a steady gaze. "And then there is Father Frank DeLuca."

Father Frank's mouth fell open. "Is that a joke?"

Mike cocked his head to one side. "Do you see me laughing? Have you ever seen me joke about a murder case? Or even a suicide case? Less than a minute ago, you said anybody who would benefit financially. I got a call today saying you were the main beneficiary in Cranzler's will. So, by your criteria, you're on the list."

"You got a call?"

"Well, the chief got the call."

The priest just shook his head. "That's the second time in the last few hours that someone has said that. I'd ask who told you, but I'm sure he didn't give a name."

"No. You don't know anything about that?"

"No. Syd and I weren't close. I mean, we talked after mass sometimes, but never more than a few minutes. Never anything of substance. Mostly, he was complaining about yet another way the government was trampling on people's rights. Of late, it's been eminent domain."

"Did you sympathize with him? Tell him he was right, that you agreed with him?"

The priest smiled at the detective. "I try to offer sympathy to anyone troubled about almost anything."

"Never mentioned anything about his estate? Leaving you anything at all?"

Father Frank shook his head. "Never." He put down the drink and held his hands out. "Remember, I'm the one who's been pushing you to re-open the case."

"You and Georgia."

"Right. Would I have kept that up if I'd been the one who killed him?"

"Probably not. Unless you were being very smart and trying to throw the police off. You'd be amazed how often the guilty party offers to help us."

"But, you weren't going to look for anybody, if Georgia and I hadn't pushed. The case was closed. This doesn't make any sense."

"True. But your name stays on the list. For now, at least. Same for Syd's brother."

"Randall?"

"He found the deceased. Often, the person who calls in a crime is the person who committed it." Mike put his lips together in an almost smile. "For the record—no, *off* the record, I don't think you did it."

"So, I'm off the suspect list?"

"Oh, no. You're on there until we find who actually did it, or prove it was suicide. The chief will want to know who benefitted financially. Your name better be on the list, or I'm in trouble."

"Maybe it's all a joke. Maybe I'm not a beneficiary at all."

"We'll find out Friday morning."

Chapter 14

Father Frank answered the door. The man standing there with the big smile was not a member of the parish. Or the community. But he was acquiring land here. Heinz stood about two inches over the priest's six foot one, and probably weighed fifty pounds more, but there was no apparent fat on the big body. He looked like he could have been a linebacker in the NFL. His dirty blond hair was almost light enough to hide a little grey at the temples.

Father Frank recognized the smile. It was not one of friendship.

"Yes?"

"My name is Duke Heinz. We met at Syd Cranzler's funeral. You may remember I represent the Lockey Corporation. We're bringing a new shopping center to Pine Tree."

And everyone should hold on to their wallets, thought the priest. "I remember. And you've come to Prince of Peace because …"

"Can I come in? I just need a few minutes of your time."

I'd like to say goodbye and shut the door in your face. But that wouldn't be very Christian, would it? I guess it won't kill me to hear what you have to say. The priest led Duke into the living room and they sat down.

"Nice room. Did the church decorate it, or did you select these furnishings yourself?"

"Mr. Heinz, you don't care anything about this room or this house. And I am working on the Sunday homily, so let's get to the real reason you're here."

A tiny smile crept up Duke's face. "Okay. I appreciate a man who gets right down to business. You know that Lockey has been granted eminent domain over Syd Cranzler's property. Lockey would like to compensate Mr. Cranzler's estate fairly for the property. But at the same time, we'd like to expedite this as quickly as possible. It *will* happen. It would benefit all parties if it is handled quickly, and out of court. We're willing to –"

Father Frank interrupted. "That's all very interesting, Mr. Heinz. But I have nothing to do with Mr. Cranzler's estate. You're talking to the wrong person."

Again, the tiny smile. Father Frank likened it to the wolf's smile when he approached Little Red Riding Hood.

"We have reason to believe that is not true. We believe you will have a great deal to say regarding the Cranzler estate. But, since you don't think so, let me ask you a *hypothetical* question. What would be your inclination on settling with Lockey, *if* you had to make decisions on the Cranzler property?"

"I don't waste time on speculation. So tell me why you have reason to believe that. Why do you think you know what's in Syd's will?"

"We've heard from a reliable source—"

"Who? What reliable source?"

"I can't say at this point."

Father Frank's back stiffened and his voice rose. "At what point can you say?"

"That's not my decision."

Father Frank stood up. "Then, I think we have nothing more to talk about."

Duke remained seated. "Let me ask you one question. Do you have any positive or negative feelings about the Lockey Corporation?"

"I don't know anything about it."

"So, Mr. Cranzler never discussed Lockey with you?"

"We never discussed Lockey."

"How do you feel about the new shopping center? Did Mr. Cranzler ever discuss it with you?"

"I have no feeling about it at all. And no, Syd and I never discussed it. But I am well aware of Syd's feeling about eminent domain being used to benefit private corporations in business to make money."

"But this project will benefit all of Pine Tree." Duke held his hands wide apart, smiled broadly and sounded like he was running for a political office. "Taxes, jobs, increased services."

"Mr. Heinz, as I said, I have to prepare a homily. And I don't waste time on speculation. So, we have nothing to talk about." Father Frank started toward the front door.

Duke eased up out of the chair and followed the priest. As Duke stepped onto the porch, he said, "Thank you for your time. I'm sure our paths will cross again."

#

Friday morning, Father Frank said Mass, had his usual breakfast of coffee and toast, and just enough time to check his e-mail and scan the Pine Tree Post before leaving for Norm Winters's office and the reading of Syd's will.

When Father Frank arrived at the small conference room of Winters & Associates, LLC, he saw that the reading of Syd Cranzler's will was playing to a full house. The room, used mostly for real estate closings, was windowless but had good lighting. A kidney shaped table filled most of the space, with ten chairs spaced around it.

He was surprised to see Ben Cranzler there, sitting by himself, head down, eyes focused on a book in his lap. Was he simply accompanying his parents? Some of Ben's words spoken at the funeral replayed in Father Frank's mind. Even now, they made him tear up. Syd probably was closer to Ben than anyone else in this room. And maybe Ben was closer to Syd than anyone in this room.

Randall Cranzler, dressed in a black suit, white shirt and blue tie, stood a few feet away, talking with his wife, Abby. As usual, Randall looked sharp. He carried the right amount of weight for a six foot man. His brown hair was neatly trimmed. His blue eyes observing, not giving away how their owner felt. Abby probably carried an extra thirty pounds, and on her short stature, it looked like more. She wore a flared, black skirt, a white blouse, and a bolero jacket. Her light brown hair was pulled back in a chignon. To Father Frank they seemed solemn more than sad.

Judith and Lance Kitchen huddled in the far corner of the room and appeared to be arguing. Judith wore a simple navy blue dress which hung loosely on her thin body. She looked as if she had applied her makeup in a hurry, her small, cupid's bow mouth only partly covered with lipstick. Her hands clung to one another and she was biting her lower lip. Lance leaned in toward his wife, a steady stream of words flying at her. Only a low hiss carried across to Father Frank, no clear words or sentences, but the tone and the body language suggested a serious disagreement. Lance was of average height and build. In fact, the main distinguishing characteristic was the angry look on his face. Father Frank couldn't decide if Lance was actively cultivating the Miami Vice look, or just hadn't shaved in a couple of days. The priest had met Lance only once before, perhaps a year ago.

At the table across from Ben sat W.C. Mayfield. At first, Father Frank was surprised. But, then he remembered W.C. saying he and Syd had been friends for many years.

Father Frank spotted Mike and went over to him.

"I have a question for you, Detective. Do you always tell suspects they're suspects?"

"Not always."

"Well, I'm glad you clued me in. I think." He grinned. "I can watch my step."

He laughed. "Just remember, *I'm* watching your step."

"I was surprised when you said you'd be here."

Mike's tone turned serious. "Normally, I wouldn't be. But now that we're investigating whether this could have been a murder, I need to see all the players."

"I guess what we have here—."

Norm Winters entered the room, followed by his son, Sammy, who closed the door and took a seat at the end of the table. The young boy looked ill-at-ease. When he saw Ben, a grin crept onto his face. Then he looked away, folded his hands on the table, and focused on them.

Norm put a folder on the table and addressed the group. "Good morning everybody. If you'll take a seat, we can begin." Norm had the look of a lawyer—tall, a tad too much weight, rich grey hair, a serious demeanor, and expensive looking clothes.

Father Frank took the closest chair. Why was Sammy Winters, a high school student, here at the reading of the will? It wasn't likely he was here as part of a "Take your child to work day." The priest observed one last, emphatic comment by Lance to Judith, complete with a jabbing finger. Then the couple took the last two remaining chairs at the table.

Norm opened the folder and took out several papers, glanced through them, then laid them on top of the folder. Slowly, he looked at each person at the table, smiled, nodded, and addressed each one by name. "Mike, Father Frank, Ben, Randall, Abby, W.C., Judith, Lance. I'm glad all of you could make it today. I think it wise, always, to have everyone who has any participation in a will to be present at the reading. That way, everybody hears the same thing, hears the questions that arise, hears the same answers. It tends to eliminate misunderstandings."

Once more, he made a point of looking at each individual seated around the table. "What I intend to do is read the will in its entirety, explain anything that does not seem crystal clear, and then answer any questions that anyone might have. Having said that, it is certainly possible that questions might come up that I cannot answer satisfactorily during this meeting. If that happens, I will research the problem, find the appropriate answer, and then mail that answer to everyone. I want everybody to have complete access to what anyone else in the group knows—regarding this will. Okay?" He scanned the group. "Are there any questions before we start, or on what I've just said?"

Lance Kitchen spoke up. "When I talked with you, you said only those directly involved in the will would be at this meeting."

"That's right," said Norm.

"Then, who are the two people to your right, and why are they here?"

Norm looked to his right and said, "This is my son, Sammy Winters, and he is mentioned in the will. And that is Detective Mike Oakley of the Pine Tree Police Department. I'll let him tell you why he is here."

Mike nodded. "Syd Cranzler's death has been tentatively classified as a suicide."

"Tentatively? What's that mean?" Lance's tone was argumentative.

"If you'll let me finish. Tentatively classified as suicide. However, there are some unanswered questions. It is possible that it may be reclassified as a homicide."

Judith Kitchen let out a small gasp. Father Frank tried to study the face of each person as soon as Mike announced that they were now looking at Syd's death as a possible homicide. Both women looked shocked, but Judith's look was also tinged with fear. Fear of what, the priest wondered. Randall's expression never changed. Lance was angry before and that didn't change. The word that came to Father Frank as he watched W.C. was "detached."

Mike continued. "Therefore, I feel it necessary to be aware of everything connected to Mr. Cranzler's death, and that includes the will."

Judith jerked her head around to look at her husband, Randall, W.C., and then the detective. "Who? How? What are you …"

Mike said, "We are rechecking many facts since Mr. Cranzler's death. Yesterday afternoon, it was determined there was enough evidence to warrant a closer look, one grounded as a possible homicide. At this point, I'd rather not say anything more. It is an ongoing investigation, but in its early stages. I will be talking with each of you today or tomorrow. And at that time, you can ask me questions—which I may or may not answer."

Norm leaned over and whispered something to Sammy, who immediately got up and left the room.

Judith looked on the verge of tears, but said nothing more. Abby reached over and took Randall's hand. Ben's face was white, and he turned to look at Father Frank. The priest could not tell what emotions were playing in Ben before the boy turned his head away and stared at the table top.

Sammy returned with a lacquered tray on which sat a large pitcher of water, a half dozen glasses, and napkins. He placed the tray on the center of the table. Judith filled one of the glasses and quickly took a drink. Abby also helped herself to a glass of water.

Norm cleared his throat. "Okay, then if there are no more questions, I will read the will."

Chapter 15

"I, Sydney Benjamin Cranzler, being of sound mind and body, do ... "

Norm read through all the usual legalese that starts most wills drawn by lawyers. For the next two minutes, Father Frank tuned out of the reading and studied those sitting around the table. Lance seemed to hang on every word and found each one distasteful, while Judith sipped water and stared at the table. To her left, W.C. sat relaxed, almost bored, perhaps wondering why he had come. At the end of the table, Abby looked on the verge of tears, even as the impersonal legal phrases were read. Randall appeared to be doing the same thing that Father Frank was: studying the people at the table.

Ben was watching the lawyer, his fragile features on the verge of collapse, his eyes ready to spill pent-up tears. Mike's focus swept from Lance to W.C. to Randall and back. Sammy was sitting perfectly straight, looking at his father, perhaps thinking about school or basketball, his face giving nothing away.

"Be it known to all parties," Norm continued reading, "that if any person or persons try to render this will invalid, or in any other way try to invalidate any portion of this will, then any bequest to that person or those persons will be voided, and if any bequest has already been passed to that person or those persons, such bequest shall be returned to the estate to be distributed in accordance with the provisions of the will as if that person or those persons had not been mentioned in the original will at all."

Norm paused and looked around the table. When no one spoke, Norm continued reading the will.

"To W.C. Mayfield, I bequeath the sum of $10,000 in cash. W.C., I'm sorry our joint oil venture didn't pan out. And I'm sorry you weren't in the one that did. But, at the time, I knew you couldn't sustain another loss, and the oil patch is full of dusters. Here's the money you invested in our dry hole."

Father Frank watched W.C. from the moment Norm mentioned his name. W.C. listened with interest, a small smile materializing as the will spoke of dry holes. But the priest couldn't quite make it out. Cynical? Covering disappointment? Acceptance? W.C.'s facial muscles moved ever so slightly, revealing no motivation. But it didn't come across as happy.

"Next, to Ben Cranzler, my favorite among the bunch. Ben, my choice would be to spend time with you, watch you grow, develop into the exceptional adult I know you will become. But, I'm guessing that won't happen, and if you're hearing this, I guess it didn't. As you know, I believe people need to make their own way, so I don't aim to destroy you by giving you a lot of money that might turn a great person into a bum. But, I want you to have the diamond-bit chance to recover all your proven reserves, to reach your potential (that's Norm's word). So, I'm setting up a $50,000 scholarship fund, a trust fund, which will grow and should be enough to take you to the college of your druthers. And to lend a hand, I'm throwing into that college fund a one-third chunk of the oil revenue I get. Once you graduate from a four-year college program, with a legitimate degree, you can get your hands on any money left in the trust, and the continued one-third interest in the oil revenue. Norm Winters, attorney in Pine Tree, at least he was on the date I'm signing this thing, will be the trustee of this fund, because I know he plows a straight line."

Father Frank thought a hint of color might have crossed Norm's face as he read the compliment.

Unlike W.C., Ben's face reflected his emotions. Tears ran down his cheeks, and he brushed at them with the back of his hand. But, beneath the tears of sadness for his lost uncle, a warm glow revealed the memories he had for the man he said had taught him important things and was "there for him."

Father Frank couldn't help but be moved by the feelings this twelve year-old had for a seventy-two year-old uncle whom most people would say never smiled.

Across the table, Lance appeared impatient to get on to what he considered the important part of the will.

Norm continued to read. "Now, I don't want anybody complaining." Norm stopped reading and looked up from the paper.

"I'm just reading what Syd insisted on putting in the will. I'm embarrassed that my family is mentioned, but it's what Syd wanted. You may all come and read it for yourselves when we finish today."

Again, he looked around the table, then looked back at the paper in his hand and began to read again. "Now, I don't want anybody complaining. I told Norm to put this in, had to insist. But, it's my will and you all know I like to get my way. I'm leaving my car, whatever I have at the time, to Sammy Winters. Sammy got on the wrong track when he was about sixteen. But he straightened himself out. Now, he's as fine as West Texas crude. Always has a big smile and a kind word for me. I'd be happy to have him on my rig. Don't worry, Sammy. The car is paid for, 'cause I don't like to pay interest. Insurance is up to you. If you're lucky, I bought a new car just before I lit a shuck for the pearly gates."

Sammy's eyes opened as wide as dessert plates and his smile was just as big. He looked at his father, then down at the table, grinning.

"Next, my little sis Judith. She tried to make a husband out of a jackass and it ain't worked. But I love her. So, I'm setting up a hundred and fifty thousand dollar trust for you, Judy. I've asked Randall to be the trustee, so you don't get sweet-talked out of it. Randall's got a good head on his shoulders and he loves you, so it will work out just fine. And for you and Lance together, you get one-third of the oil revenue each and every month. It'll help. And I hope things go well for you two."

Father Frank watched the couple opposite him while Norm read this part of the will. Judith watched Norm with sad eyes, tears trying to push out and Judith desperate to hold them in. Her expression didn't change. Only when Norm had finished did she look at her husband. To the priest, it was the look of a child hoping she would not get punished. Not good, Fr. Frank thought.

Even before Norm had started reading, Lance's expression was one of antagonism. His eyes narrowed and took on the hard edge of a hunting knife when Syd referred to him as a jackass. His mood swung to anger. At the end, Father Frank might have expected disappointment on Lance's face. Instead, he saw hot rage. White knuckles topped his tight fists. Every tendon in his arms and neck were stretched bow-string tight. His breathing was shallow and rapid. He didn't look at Judith, his fierce look directed at the messenger.

Under other circumstances, Father Frank would have thought to call

911 for EMS. In this case, he thought he should recommend an anger management specialist to Lance. Or to Judith. She would have to deal with Lance, live with him, find a way to calm him before his wrath caused real harm to someone.

Father Frank recalled Ben's statement that his Uncle Lance was angry about Syd's handling of his money. If Syd were here in the room, it would be easy to believe Lance might attack him. Had Lance seen Syd recently? Perhaps Monday before last. Could Syd have told Lance about the will?

Chapter 16

Norm poured a glass of water and took a healthy drink before continuing.

"Next, my brother Randall and his wife Abby. Randall and I are as different as an oil well and a water well. But Randall's as straight as a drill stem. And they've raised Ben, who means more to me than a gusher. So, I'm instructing Norm to fork over one hundred and fifty thousand green backs (Norm says I gotta say 150,000 US Dollars) to Randall and Abby, plus one-third of the oil revenue each month. I know you two don't need it, but I don't think it'll hurt you either."

Randall's expression remained in neutral. He nodded once, as if to say thanks, I appreciate it. Abby smiled, a "thank you" smile, not a greedy grin.

Although the bequests to Syd's siblings were essentially the same, it apparently did nothing to improve Lance's mood. His scowl deepened and a muscle in his jaw twitched. Judith placed her hand on his arm. Lance jerked his arm away, as if it had come in contact with a hot poker.

"And lastly, the balance of my estate, after Norm takes his cut, pays taxes and bills and stuff, will go into a trust for the Prince of Peace Church."

Lance slammed his fist on the table. Norm stopped and looked at the angry man.

Father Frank's gaze never left Norm, but his mouth gaped. What had Norm said? What did it mean? The priest couldn't get his mind around the concept. Prince of Peace was inheriting some part of Syd's estate. And how would the rest of the Cranzlers feel about that? He was still trying to grasp the meaning when Norm began reading again.

"I'm asking Father Frank DeLuca and Norm Winters to serve as trustees of that trust. And whatever they do with the money from the trust has got to have both votes. We've got a trust document which spells out everything. They can pay off the church's debt. They can start new church programs, or charity programs, or community programs, whatever. What I'm saying is, they both gotta agree on where and when the money will be spent. Randall, I could have put you on there, but it's work and Norm's getting paid to handle this stuff. And Father Frank's as honest as a good horse. He doesn't pray for easier tasks, but to find better solutions. Whenever he has to choose between what's right and what will give him an advantage, he always picks right. I like that.

"When you hear this, I'll be gone, so I can just throw out a little advice. Here goes. Randall, loosen up. Enjoy life a little bit more. You're as good and honest as can be. I just want to see you laugh a bit more. Lance, I know you're mad as hell with me right now. But you need to learn that trying to make things easy usually ends up causing problems. The world may owe you a living, but you have to work to collect it. Try listening to Judith. Try *really* listening to Judith. She's a good person and she loves you."

Father Frank heard a little cry and looked over at Judith. She held a tissue to her eyes and sobbed softly. Lance did not seem to appreciate the advice Syd had given. Nor did he offer any comfort to his wife.

The lawyer continued reading. "That's it. I'm off to better places. No eminent domain. No dry holes. Ben, remember to look at the stars and dream big. Then make it happen for Uncle Syd."

Norm shuffled the papers and surveyed the group. "That's it. Of course, it has been signed with adequate witnesses. It is all very legal. The trusts that the will talks about have all been drawn, signed, witnessed, filed with the proper authorities, and funded."

"Everything?" asked Lance.

"Everything," answered Norm. "Oh, except the car. The title has not been transferred yet."

Under his breath, but still audible to everyone, Lance said, "Who gives a damn about the car."

Father Frank looked around the room. The two teenagers smiled at one another, but Ben's smile contained the shadow of regret. The priest suspected Ben would rather have his uncle alive than the college fund.

Except for Sammy, no one at the table looked happy. Maybe the reading of a will was not a time of happiness. Even if you receive something, you've lost someone. Randall's expression had not changed; it remained perfectly neutral. Abby looked … not happy, maybe at peace, accepting Syd's death, perhaps pleased with the confidence he had placed in her husband.

The tiny smile on W.C.'s face was more amusement than pleasure. It was as if he were saying, "I wondered how you were going to handle this, old friend." Of course, it might also indicate how he felt about the reaction to the will from the others around the table.

Distressed best fit Judith; not from the size of the bequest, Father Frank guessed, but from the attitude of her husband. Or perhaps unhappy with the terms of the bequest *because* it upset her husband to such a degree.

Lance looked like a dog that had just seen a possum take the last of the food, and he could do nothing about it. Angry. Frustrated. And clearly, Syd's publicly professed opinion of Lance did nothing to improve his mood. Two people had told Father Frank that Lance was expecting his wife to get a sizable inheritance. He probably wasn't expecting there to be any strings attached.

How did I look to others? Did they view me as a money-grabber? Maybe I convinced Syd to leave all that money to me and the church. Not only did Prince of Peace get the money, I'm one of the trustees. I wouldn't be surprised if someone thinks I was glad Syd died.

Father Frank thought back to the announcement. How *did* he feel? Surprised. Amazed. Humbled. Perhaps grateful. And underneath all that, worried that the good fortune of Prince of Peace might cause others anxiety. But it seemed no one was really left out. Syd had not forgotten anyone.

Prince of Peace thanks you, Syd. And I pray that the true Prince of Peace has welcomed you into his house. Dear Lord, help me and Norm use this resource to honor you and to do good for those of your children most in need.

"Are there any questions that I can answer at this time?" the lawyer asked.

Lance was the first to speak. "Yeah. Who witnessed Syd signing the will?"

Norm smiled for an instant, then returned to lawyer mode. "It was witnessed by my secretary, Tina Antigua, and Dr. Rankin. Syd insisted on Dr. Tom Rankin being one of the witnesses, to assure anyone who might ask if Syd was of sound mind."

"Did Syd read all of it before he signed it? Make sure nothing was changed."

Father Frank saw the smallest shake of the lawyer's head as if he thought   , *Is this man for real?* "Yes, he did. In fact, Syd initialed each page, to indicate that he authorized each page."

Everybody was focused on Lance. No one else made a sound.

Lance looked down at the table for a second, then raised his head and stared at Norm. "Just how big is Syd's estate? You've mentioned about $360,000. Does that include the house and land?"

Norm closed his eyes for a minute, and Father Frank wondered if the lawyer was calculating or deciding how he wanted to answer. He opened his eyes and looked straight at Lance. "Not counting the house and land, and the oil revenues, there was approximately $587,000. Plus the car."

Lance stood up. "Are you telling me he gave over $200,000 to this priest and his church?"

"That is correct. Plus the house and the land."

Lance slammed down in the chair. "For the love of God," he yelled.

Norm's voice remained calm. "That's exactly what Syd had in mind."

"Very funny," said Lance. "And you and the priest get to decide what to do? Nice. Take an expensive vacation to South America? What happens if one of you dies? The other one can spend it however he wants?"

"No. Each of us will have to name a successor trustee who will fill the trustee post in the event of death, or any other reason he is unable to continue as trustee." Norm's voice remained calm and even.

Abby spoke up. "Norm, you said the trusts were already funded. Is there anything we have to do regarding those?"

"You can spend it tomorrow," said Lance under his breath. "Judith and I have to get permission from Sir Randall."

Norm ignored Lance. "Not really. I will be giving a copy of the appropriate trust to each person involved with a trust. After you've read it, you can come to my office and ask any questions you wish. They're all pretty straight forward. Nothing tricky."

Lance jerked up out of his chair. "Are there any other surprises you're going to dump on us, or can we leave now?"

"I'm through," said Norm. "That is the complete Last Will and Testament of Sydney Benjamin Cranzler."

Lance stomped to the door, then stopped. "How much is that oil royalty that we get a third of?"

Norm looked at the ceiling for a moment, then back toward Lance. "Of course, the amount varies from month to month, depending on the price of crude at the well-head, and the amount of oil being pumped. But, over the last couple of years, it has averaged about $6,000 per month. That's the total, not a one-third share."

Father Frank had not turned to watch Lance's departure. So, he saw W.C. Mayfield's head jerk up when Norm said $6,000. W.C. slowly shook his head but said nothing.

Lance threw the door open, banging it against the wall, and left.

Abby moved to the chair beside Judith and put her arms around her sister-in-law. Judith's eyes were closed, her head bowed, and her hands clenched on the table. Abby whispered something to her.

W.C. Mayfield rose and started out the door.

"Mr. Mayfield," said Norm. "I will put a check in the mail to you this next week."

W.C. nodded and left. He had not spoken one word inside the room.

Father Frank felt glued to his chair. He still could not grasp the full meaning of this. If he understood Norm correctly, the Prince of Peace Trust could amount to $400,000. That much money could provide the resources to do many charitable works.

Or it could provide a motive for murder.

Mike had said Chief Flag put Father Frank at the top of the suspect list.

And I don't have an alibi for the night of the murder.

Chapter 17

Everyone had left, except Father Frank. He sat in Norm's office, still bewildered by the unexpected bequest.

"Currently, the trust is funded with $200,000, plus the deeds to the house and land. I've held out about $27,000 for expenses yet to come in, and my fees. Various bills will dribble in over the next month or so. I've already gotten the bill for the funeral. But my guess is, all those won't come close to that figure. Once all expenses are taken care of, whatever remains, and I'm guessing that will be about $10,000, will be added to the trust."

Father Frank shook his head. "I'm just flabbergasted by all this. Syd never mentioned anything at all. And I had no idea he had that much money. Frankly, when he offered to pay for the air conditioning last year, I asked him if that would put him in a hole. He just smiled and said he'd manage; not to worry."

"Syd didn't spend much money. After the oil well he had invested in started paying off, most of it went into CD's. He paid cash for everything. He didn't owe anything on the house or land."

"And what do we do about those?"

Norm grinned. "About a week before he died, he asked me to try for a court order to stop execution of the eminent domain order with regard to his land. Of course, that didn't happen, since he was dead. Now, we can follow his request and try for an injunction while we file an appeal. Or, we can drop that line of action. He didn't expect to win. But, he wanted to make a statement about people's rights and private property."

"What do you think we should do?"

"I don't know. Haven't thought about it. But, we need to decide in the next couple of days, because if we want to file an appeal, we need to do it next week."

Father Frank lowered his head, and tapped his fingers on the edge of the desk. After a minute he looked up. "I want to respect Syd's wishes. On the other hand, I don't relish getting into a court battle."

"I don't mind a good battle, if I think I have a chance to win. I don't think we do on this."

"Let's talk about it Monday. Give me a little time to pray on this."

#

Father Frank drove home in a daze. He still found it difficult to grasp the idea that Prince of Peace had been given a fortune. More than enough to pay off the mortgage on the church hall. *Or we could set up a first class community program, something special for the young kids. Or establish a scholarship fund. The town could use a food pantry. A summer camp ...*

He parked the car, walked over and entered the church. He knelt in the last pew, bowed his head and prayed. *Father, give me your guidance so that I may use this money wisely for the good of Prince of Peace and the community. I know money cannot solve all problems, but it might make it possible to do certain good acts that had been impossible in the past. The glitter of gold can be blinding. Please help me not to lose sight of what is important to You.*

#

As he made his way back to the rectory, he saw the large, square silhouette of Duke Heinz standing on the porch waiting for him.

"Hello." Duke's booming voice embodied the cheer and good wishes of a long-time friend. "Congratulations on your windfall. That should make balancing the books a lot easier."

Father Frank invited Heinz in, not because he had any desire to talk with the man, but because he didn't see how he could avoid it. He took him into the kitchen and prepared a pitcher of iced tea, then poured a glass for each of them.

"Ah, that hits the spot," said Duke after taking a long drink.

The priest sat down and indicated a chair, but Duke remained standing. *Perhaps he wants to look down on me, or perhaps he believes towering over me makes him more intimidating.*

"Now that Cranzler is out of the way, perhaps—"

"Mr. Heinz," Father Frank interrupted. "Syd was a friend of mine, a member of this church, a brother to one of my parishioners, and an uncle to a young boy who misses him a lot. If you want to talk to me, you will have to change your attitude toward Syd. For that matter, your attitude toward any deceased person. Otherwise, this conversation is over."

Duke's expression turned contrite. "I am so sorry. That was extremely rude of me. I apologize. I didn't mean any disrespect. Sometimes, I don't express myself very well." Duke's face now broke into a large smile. "Guess I should have worked harder in my English classes." He sat down. "What I really meant was, Mr. Cranzler cannot participate in the discussions regarding his property. And as I understand it, you'll be handling that."

How had Duke come by that information so quickly? The priest's mind flicked back to his meeting with Duke yesterday. Even then, he seemed to know the church would get the land. But how? The will hadn't been read, and Father Frank was certain that Norm would not leak that information.

"Norm Winters and I will jointly make a decision on those things Syd left to Prince of Peace," Father Frank said carefully.

Again, the big smile. "Of course. But I'm sure Mr. Winters will go along with whatever you think best for the church. Now, I had offered Cranzler $200,000 for his house and land. Keep in mind, the court has ordered the land to be sold to Lockey. In light of that court order, I thought that was a very fair price."

Duke paused, waiting for a response. When Father Frank said nothing, Duke continued. "Because the money will be going to the church, and probably some very worthy community projects – and remember, Lockey is interested in the community – I'm authorized to raise that to $220,000, *if* we can get the papers signed quickly."

Father Frank did not respond, and this time, Duke just sipped his tea and remained silent.

Finally, the priest set his glass down. "Mr. Heinz, this bequest by Syd to the church was completely unexpected. I haven't even grasped what's involved yet. I know that Syd had asked Norm to file an appeal to delay the execution of the eminent domain ruling. That was his wish. I will have to decide how the church will respond. Should we respect Syd's wish? Should we continue the appeal? That's the real question."

"That was a stupid act of an old man. I think his suicide says he chose not to pursue any such court action."

Father Frank stood, his teeth clinched so tightly a muscle in his jaw twitched. His hands balled into fists. He pinned Duke with a laser-sharp gaze.

"I'm sorry, Father. I didn't mean to speak poorly of the dead. But even your church doesn't think kindly about those who commit suicide."

"The police no longer consider it suicide. Syd was murdered." Maybe a slight exaggeration, but they were looking into the possibility of homicide.

Duke glanced down for a moment, then looked back at the priest. "I hadn't heard. Do they have a suspect?"

Father Frank's jaw muscles relaxed and he almost smirked. *He knows all about the will before it's read, but he doesn't know the police are now considering that Syd's death might be a homicide? I don't think so.* "Mr. Heinz, I'm not prepared to discuss Syd's land this soon. It may be a week before I feel at all competent to make an intelligent decision. I'll call you when I'm ready."

He turned and started walking to the door. "Right now, I have other work I must attend to."

At the front door, Duke reached in the inside pocket of his jacket and pulled out some papers. "Here's the contract – with the new offer. Read it over. You'll see it's pretty simple and straightforward. And fair. I'll be back in touch in a few days." Father Frank took the papers. His tone somber, Duke said, "I'd like to get it right this time."

Chapter 18

After Duke left, Father Frank made an effort to get various pieces of parish business done, but no matter what he tried to do, his mind jumped to the inheritance. If he looked at parish finances, he speculated on what it would mean to pay off the note on the parish hall and eliminate those horrendous monthly payments. When he looked at the youth program, he began to consider other programs that the parish could do with the additional money. Even as he began to work on the Sunday sermon, Syd's generosity popped up. The first reading was from First Corinthians, touching on charity, which naturally led him to the inheritance and what it meant to the church.

After an hour and a half, he had made little progress on the finances or the sermon, but had a list of possible places Syd's money could be spent. He tossed his pencil onto the desk and rolled his chair back. He walked into the kitchen, got a Dr Pepper out of the refrigerator, and had just popped it open when the phone rang.

"Prince of Peace. How can we help you?"

"How about a loan?" Georgia let out a mischievous laugh.

"Right now, I might just give it all to you. Somehow, at least at this point, that money is keeping me from getting anything done."

"Now you can better understand the problems of some of your parishioners. Only, with them, usually it's not having *enough* money. Unfortunately, money dictates a lot of what we do."

"I'm learning that lesson. Other than a loan, why are you calling?"

"Could be I need some spiritual counseling." She giggled. "Or maybe some financial advice."

"Can't help you there."

"Well, really I just wanted to know if you got any insight into the murder when Norm read the will."

"Surely Mike filled you in."

"Actually, no. He did tell me that Syd left a sizable chunk to the church, including his house and land. But, he didn't give me any info on the reactions of the various recipients. I don't know why he's so closed mouthed."

"On-going invest—"

"Don't give me that," she interrupted.

The priest took a sip of the soft drink and thought about her question. "Certainly nothing jumped out at me. Lance Kitchen—that's Judith's husband, Syd's brother-in-law—."

"I've met Lance."

"He came in unhappy and left angry. He appeared, to me at least, to feel he was cheated. Judith was just sad from start to finish. She tried to calm Lance once or twice, but had no effect whatsoever. Randall, Syd's brother, was pretty stoic throughout. Sammy seemed to be the only happy person there."

"Sammy? Sammy Winters?"

"That's the one. Syd left his car to Sammy. He was so excited he could hardly contain himself." The priest thought for a moment. "Ben was pleased with the college fund Syd set up for him. But it was bitter-sweet for Ben. He was truly fond of his uncle."

He paused for another drink, then continued. "W.C. Mayfield was there. Syd left him $10,000 which he said was what W.C. had invested in a dry hole. I couldn't read anything from W.C.. He was just there."

"So, no suspects from the reading of the will? Darn. In the mysteries I read, the murderer is always there and gives himself away."

"He didn't this time. Or she didn't." Father Frank chuckled. "Or I wasn't clever enough to see it, if they did."

"Guess we'll have to cast a wider net, as they say. Of course, Duke Heinz wasn't there."

"No. But he was here at the rectory, waiting for me when I got back."

"Trying to find out what was in the will?" Georgia asked.

"That's the funny thing. He seemed to *already know* what was in the will. He certainly knew about Prince of Peace getting Syd's house and land."

"Wow." Georgia was silent for a moment. "How could he know that?"

"Beats me. I suppose Syd could have told him. But that doesn't seem likely."

"Have you asked Norm if he knows? Or has any idea where Duke might have found out?"

"No, but you can be sure I will."

"Oh, I was talking with one of my girl friends and she told me Carl Douglas and Syd had fought bitterly over the last months. She didn't know what it was about. But Carl was apparently very angry. Yelling. Cussing. Shaking his finger in Syd's face." She laughed. "And you know Syd. I'm sure he gave as much as he got."

"I don't know Mr. Douglas."

"I don't either. But one of us ought to talk to him. I nominate you."

Father Frank sighed. "You know where he lives?"

"Near Syd."

"Okay. I don't know what I'll say, but I'll see what I can find out."

#

The Pine Tree telephone directory listed only one Carl Douglas and his property was adjacent to Syd's. Father Frank knocked on the door of a small house desperately in need of paint as well as a complete new front porch. He surveyed the sky as he waited. The day had turned grey, but there didn't seem to be any threat of rain. Or promise of rain, more accurately. Pine Tree needed rain. After a minute, the priest knocked again, louder.

"Hold your horses," a voice yelled and after a few more moments, a tall, thin man, with hollow cheeks and rheumy eyes sunk deep in his face opened the door. "What do ya want?"

"Sorry to bother you. I just thought you might have been at Syd Cranzler's funeral," said Father Frank, suggesting, but not really saying, he had seen Douglas there.

"No. Wouldn't of gone to his funeral."

"Oh? He was your neighbor." The priest's face posed a question.

"We lived close, but we weren't neighbors. Old fool only thought of himself."

"How's that? I didn't know him that well."

"Consider yourself lucky. He had money. Didn't care about us what live on Social Security, and could use a break."

Father Frank looked puzzled. "I don't understand."

"Lockey ain't gonna pay me nothing 'til Syd signs the papers. He's the only holdout. Well, he was. I don't know who's got his land now. I tried to tell him months ago what a blasted fool he was. And if you weren't a minister, I'd tell you exactly what I called him."

"But you'll get the money eventually. Right?"

"Eventually I won't be here. I needed it back then. Still do. But things would've been better if I got it back when they first come. Damn, selfish fool. Sorry Reverend, but that's what he was and I'm not sorry to see him gone."

Father Frank started to say something, but Douglas went on, getting angrier by the sentence. "Air conditioner broke at the start of summer. I ain't got the money to fix it, but if that s.o.b. had signed, I could'a bought a new one. I suffered the whole blazing summer cause of Syd. Good riddance."

"I'm sorry you feel that way, Mr. Douglas."

"You don't even know how strong I feel." The dark eyes blazed. "I'm glad he's out of the way. Maybe now we can get it moving. Sorry he didn't commit suicide sooner."

Father Frank's eyes opened wide and he stared at the man, hardly able to believe what he'd heard. "The police aren't sure he committed suicide. They believe Syd could have been murdered."

Douglas waved his hand as if to dismiss it. "Whatever."

"That doesn't surprise you?"

"It don't matter to me one way or the other. Either way, didn't happen soon enough."

Carl Douglas turned and walked away.

Chapter 19

Father Frank sat in his office puzzled. He had thought Syd Cranzler to be a simple man who probably had no enemies. Obviously he didn't know Syd very well. He did have strong opinions. Sometimes those produced adversaries.

For awhile, Father Frank sat with his eyes closed, thinking about Lance's reaction to the will. Syd had left a very nice amount of money to Judith, but it didn't seem to please Lance at all. He certainly didn't like Randall having anything to say about it. Of course, the priest could see that. You didn't want outsiders having any say over your finances. But it was more than that. Father Frank had the feeling that even if Randall were not involved, Lance would still be unhappy with the amount left to Judith. Plus, Lance left no question how he felt about the money left to the church.

The priest could see how Douglas would be unhappy. He blamed Syd for the miserable summer he'd had to suffer through. What surprised Father Frank was the man's reaction, or lack of one, when Father Frank had told him Syd was murdered. No surprise. No questions. No feeling, except that it should have happened sooner. One would expect a little interest if there was a murder right next door.

Father Frank had no way of knowing if Douglas might need the money for something else. Certainly there were plenty of reasons that might provoke such strong feelings against someone who was keeping you from a windfall. Still, why no semblance of surprise? Why no interest?

Then there was Duke Heinz. How did he know what was in the will before it was read?

With a jolt, the priest remembered his meeting with Monsignor Decker on Wednesday, questioning why he was receiving a bequest from Syd Cranzler. Who was Decker's anonymous caller? Even if he did get it a little wrong, he—whoever he was—had to have some inside information of what was in the will. How?

And Mike had said the Chief of Police had gotten a call saying Father Frank was a beneficiary. *Clearly, somebody was trying to make trouble for me.*

Father Frank believed in Norm Winter's integrity. Obviously, Syd did too. The priest couldn't believe Norm would have revealed the contents, or any part, of the will. Not without Syd's permission. Could Syd have told people? Not likely he'd talk to Monsignor Decker. And if Syd *had* told him, then the monsignor would have known it wasn't Father Frank who was getting the bequest, but the parish. The same thing would be true if Norm had talked to Decker about the will.

Father Frank got up and paced around the room. This business of the will and Syd's murder was making him antsy. He needed some physical activity. He needed to shoot some hoops. Ever since his college days, playing basketball at UT/Arlington, whenever problems plagued him, he would shoot some baskets to relax his mind. He could go down to the public court in City Park. But there would be other people there; kids from the summer league he'd run; people who would want to talk. He needed private time.

He had talked about putting up a basketball goal at the church, encourage the young kids to run off some of their boundless energy. But the money was never quite available. Why not do it now? It was a trivial amount if one considered what Prince of Peace was about to get.

He picked up the phone, called the Pine Tree Sporting Center and without even asking the price, ordered a basketball goal to be installed, and four basketballs. It wouldn't be there for him today, but it would be there in the future.

Next, he called Georgia and gave her a report on his meeting with Carl Douglas.

"You're not exaggerating, are you, Father?" she asked.

"I'm not prone to exaggeration, Georgia."

"Then, I think we have another suspect."

"Maybe. I'd have to say he's got more than enough anger to commit murder. The thing that impressed itself on my mind was his total lack of reaction when I said it was not suicide, but murder. It just seemed like old news to him."

"What do you make of that? Maybe he heard it from somebody else before you showed up? It hasn't been on the news, has it?"

"I don't think so. The Chief of Police still considers it suicide. He's just given Mike a little time to investigate more thoroughly."

"Mostly to shut us up," Georgia said with a laugh.

"That, too. Why don't you ask Mike tonight?"

"What do you mean by that?"

"Surely you two are going out tonight, aren't you? It *is* Saturday."

"No, we are not. I told you I'm mad at the lunk."

"Because it took him awhile to realize Syd did not commit suicide?"

"He didn't believe it until we stuck his nose in it. I'm not sure he believes it yet. This is probably just an act to keep us happy."

Father Frank laughed. "Georgia, he's the detective, not us. Of course he has to find it on his own."

"Oh, I don't know. Okay, fine. I'll calm down. Actually, he hasn't asked me out for tonight."

"Am I surprised? You were pretty rough on him Thursday. Why don't you call him and invite him over for dinner?"

"Not likely."

"And after dinner, ask him how Chief Flag got the idea I was in the will."

#

Father Frank stared into the refrigerator. He had salad materials, but he wasn't in the mood for salad. He shut the door, deciding to pop a frozen pizza in the oven. He was opening the freezer when he saw the menu held to the door by a magnet which declared: A balanced diet is a cookie in each hand. The menu was from a Chinese takeout, and at that moment, Chinese sounded good to him.

He took the menu down at the same instant that the telephone began to ring. *Probably Georgia telling me she relented and called Mike and they're going out after all.*

He answered the phone with a cheery "Prince of Peace. How can we help you?"

"Give back the money you stole."

Father Frank's first impression was that Lance had been drinking, but then decided it was anger, not alcohol affecting his speech.

"I'm sorry you—. "

"No you're not. I know exactly what you did. You got him to church each week and brainwashed him. Made him believe the only way to save his soul was to give you all his money." He snickered.

"'Couse, he didn't have no soul."

"We all have a soul, Lance. And our goal in life is to return that soul to the House of the Lord."

"Yeah, yeah. I'm sure you spouted that stuff to Sick Syd. And damn if he didn't buy it. I knew he was a fool; I just didn't know how big a fool. But I'm not, and I don't buy any of your drivel. And I intend to get that money back. One way or another. The money belongs to this family, not your stupid church."

His voice was ragged with rage. "You believe in the sanctity of the family, don't you, Frank?" He didn't wait for an answer. "So do I. And that money belongs to our family, not to a Bible thumping, conniving, con-man."

Anger began to spread in Father Frank's stomach. "Lance, you heard the will, the same as I did. And at the same time. I had no idea Syd was doing that."

"Yeah, yeah. You just stooped down and picked up the winning lottery ticket. Didn't even have to buy one. Well, don't start spending it yet. We're getting it back. You can count on that. One way or the other, that money is coming back to its rightful owners. And the police might be interested in how you, no relation at all, an outsider, managed to get the biggest share. They might even wonder if you helped dear old brother-in-law Syd go meet his maker."

The receiver slammed down.

Father Frank knew the ranting probably meant little. Nonetheless, he sat down and tried to look at the other side. Was Prince of Peace receiving an undue amount? How did the rest of the family feel about it? Had Syd been unfair? Prince of Peace was benefiting at the expense of the family, but it was, after all, Syd's money and his choice. Lance's implication that Syd was not in complete control of his faculties was ridiculous. The will, while a little unusual, did not sound like it came from someone with dementia.

He picked up the telephone, hesitated a few seconds, then put it down. He didn't want to deal with it tonight, but the problem wasn't going to fade into the background. He might as well get this settled sooner rather than later. He picked up the phone again and called Norm Winters and then Randall Cranzler and asked if they could come over for a short meeting in a couple of hours. It looked like rain, but this shouldn't take very long. He didn't realize getting money could be such a big problem.

He walked back into the kitchen, replaced the Chinese menu, and pulled out the frozen pizza.

Chapter 20

Norm Winters pulled his Lincoln into the driveway just as Father Frank was opening the door for Randall Cranzler. The promise of rain had fizzled. It turned out to be what people in Pine Tree called a six inch rain—the rain drops were six inches apart. The priest ushered them in, and as coffee brewed, he started.

"Syd made a very generous gift to Prince of Peace, and let me start by saying how grateful I, and I'm sure the entire parish, will be over such a generous gift."

"Have you told the parish council?" asked Randall.

Father Frank shook his head, then looked at Norm. "I'm not sure if this is relevant, but right now, I'm not sure of much. What was Syd's disposition when he made up this will?"

The lawyer looked puzzled. "Disposition?" He took only a second to reply. "Perfectly normal. What are you looking for?"

The priest looked down, trying to think how best to explain. "I don't want Prince of Peace to take money from the family unfairly. I want to be clear in my mind that this is what Syd *really* wanted. I mean, long term. That it wasn't just some spur of the moment thing. He wasn't mad at some family member and took away some of their money."

Norm started to speak, but Randall put up his hand to claim the floor. "Father, this is what Syd wanted. He wasn't mad at anybody, well, anybody in the family. Despite what he said about Lance, he wasn't actively angry at Lance. He'd just been frustrated with him for a long, long time. He didn't think he was good for Judith, and I'm afraid much of the family agreed with him on that count. But, Judith loved Lance. Still does, as much as Abby and I can tell."

"Father, you can relax," Norm said. "He talked about this with me over a period of several weeks. Of course, he wanted to be fair to the family, but he also wanted to—as he put it—allow Prince of Peace to expand the good works it was doing. He was very impressed with what you have accomplished, Father, not only in the parish, but in the whole community. It wasn't some whim, I can assure you."

"Thank you," said Father Frank.

"There's one other point you should keep in mind," said Norm. "If there are no minor children or a spouse, then there is really no criteria for 'fair.' Lance was way off base when talking about 'fair.' There's no moral, legal, or for that matter, social obligation to anybody."

"And he was very generous to the family," said Randall. "He didn't owe us anything. I really should leave something to my *children*. But, if I leave something to Judy, my sister, that's just being nice to her. I don't *owe* her that. And she wouldn't think I did. Syd didn't owe me or Judy anything. It was nice that he left us a very generous gift. But it wasn't owed to us."

Norm shifted in his chair. "Syd was completely clear-headed on this. We talked about it a lot. He considered making some suggestions on how the church might use the money. But in the end, he said your judgment on such matters was better than his." He put his hands on his knees and leaned forward. "This was what he wanted. Nothing in the will was casual. Even the amounts. He calculated carefully on each one. He looked at what Ben's trust would earn, how much the oil revenue would add. He even had me get figures on what college expenses would be by the time Ben is ready for college. Syd was very careful with his money." He turned to Randall. "He asked you about your mortgage, didn't he? A couple of months ago?"

Randall looked surprised. "Yes, he did. Of course, I didn't want to discuss that with him, but he kept pushing until I told him."

"He was calculating how much to leave you and Judy. Nothing was quick or casual. Nothing was done in anger. He thought Lance was a jackass--."

Father Frank laughed. "Yes. He said that in the will."

Norm smiled. "He did indeed. I suggested he leave that out, but you know Syd. He wasn't bashful about saying what he thought. He didn't want to slight Judy because of her husband. But he didn't trust Lance. He said he could see Lance blowing the money. Or taking it and leaving Judy."

The coffee pot signaled it was ready. Father Frank filled three cups, retrieved half-and-half from the refrigerator then set that and a sugar bowl on the table.

"I appreciate your comments," he said, "and it makes me feel much more comfortable. I must say, receiving this money has cost me some sleep."

"Lance has a problem. He wouldn't have been happy if Syd had left him everything." Randall shrugged. "I don't know what Judy sees in him, but she loves him."

Father Frank sampled his coffee then set the cup down. "He called me yesterday. Said I had stolen the family money and he intended to get it back. He shouted and cursed and, frankly, unnerved me a bit."

"Does he ever get violent, Randall?" asked Norm.

Randall thought about that for a moment. "Not recently. He used to have a problem, but he went to some anger management class. I think, though he would never admit it, that Judy gave him an ultimatum. He was better for awhile."

"I think he needs a refresher course," said the priest.

They all laughed.

"Norm, did anybody know what was in the will before Friday?"

Norm pressed his lips together and shook his head. "No. I mean other than Syd and myself. He didn't even want my secretary to see it, so I typed it up. I should have charged him extra for that," he said with a chuckle. "Why do you ask?"

"Two days before the reading, Monsignor Decker told me I was a beneficiary. I wasn't personally, of course, but Prince of Peace was. I didn't know anything about it, said it wasn't true. Then Duke Heinz came by and indicated that I would have something to do with the disposition of Syd's property."

Norm frowned. Randall's mouth opened but no words came out.

"Is there someone who could have seen it? Maybe it was on your desk when another client came in?"

Norm looked down at the table and shook his head again. "I can almost swear that no one else saw it. Once Syd signed it, the will went into a locked file cabinet in my office. I'm the only one who knows the combination. There's a copy in my safe deposit box, but again, no one can get into that except me—unless I'm dead."

For several minutes, the three drank coffee and tried to understand how the information had gotten out. Finally, Norm said, "Father, if you want me to, I'll call and ask the monsignor how he found out."

"Would you? I didn't leave in the most congenial way. I think you'd do better with the monsignor than I would right now."

"I'll call him on Monday. Have you given any more thought about the appeal, whether we should file it or not?" asked Norm.

"Not really. Randall, what's your opinion? Syd asked Norm to file an appeal on the eminent domain ruling to try and stop the project—or at least delay it. Should we continue his case or let it go?"

Randall smiled. "Syd and I discussed that. I told him it was a waste of time and money, but you know Syd. He said he had the time and the money. Frankly, I see it as a waste of the court's time. Nothing is going to come of it. But Syd really believed that eminent domain was being abused—not just in this case, but all over the country. He wanted his day in court. He wanted to make an issue out of it so the media could pick it up and give it some exposure. He didn't expect to win. Just get press coverage."

"Judge McFatage came to my office this week, a day or two after Syd died," Norm said. "He wanted to know if the appeal would be dropped and if the court should remove it from the docket. I told him I wasn't ready to do that just yet. Of course, he wanted to know why not. Syd had committed suicide and obviously wasn't going to continue it. I said, the beneficiaries might."

Deep grooves carved themselves into Father Frank's forehead. "You didn't—."

"No, no. I didn't tell him who that was. Just said I'd have to consult with them and get back to him."

"Why would he come to you with a request like that?" asked Randall.

"I don't really know. I mean, he has an interest in the case. He was the one who signed the eminent domain order. Of course he doesn't want it challenged."

"Interesting," said Randall.

"What's even more interesting, I saw him again this morning when I was getting gas at the Valero station," Norm continued. "He pulled up to the pump next to mine. While he was filling his car, he started visiting with me and after a minute, asked if he could mark Syd's case off the calendar. I said no, it was mostly up to Father Frank and you were still considering honoring Syd's intent to appeal." Norm put his cup down and rubbed his chin. "I had the funniest feeling the meeting was *not* accidental. If I were a betting man, I'd bet his car was sitting down the block from my house, and he followed me to the gas station."

Norm got up, ready to leave. "The pump shut off automatically in less than a minute. I'd say his new Lexus needed about one gallon to fill it."

Chapter 21

Georgia relented, called Mike and said she was cooking if he wanted to stop by. She refused to be too ingratiating. He accepted. Dinner at 7:30.

At first, Georgia thought she would just pick a pizza out of the freezer. That would do for the lunk-headed detective. Then she decided she *could* add a salad. The pizza morphed into homemade lasagna. And what was a meal without dessert?

Dinner went very well, as they discussed the state of the union, what the president should and should not be doing, the new library building, and how the high school football team was doing. Nothing they could change. Georgia suggested that the October night was too beautiful to waste, so they carried the still-warm crème brûlée outside and settled into comfortable chairs on the patio. A slight breeze carried the sweet fragrance of her night-blooming jasmine.

"How did Chief Flag find out that Prince of Peace was mentioned in the will?" Georgia smiled at Mike as she took a bite of the rich custard into her mouth.

Mike's back tensed slightly. "I thought we weren't going to talk about the case tonight."

"And we haven't." Georgia licked a bit of crème brûlée off the spoon. "It's just one simple question. I wouldn't introduce any controversy into such a lovely setting."

"An anonymous call." His manner had turned guarded.

"Surely the police department has caller ID."

"We do. But if you call from a pay phone, caller ID doesn't help."

"What did the caller say? Exactly."

Mike took a deep breath. "He said a good suspect is someone who's going to inherit a lot of money—like Father Frank."

"That was all?"

Mike nodded.

"The chief didn't keep him on the phone long enough to trace the call?"

"He hung up too fast."

"Didn't the switchboard start tracing it as soon as they saw it had no caller ID?"

"No." The detective sighed. "We can't run a trace on every call made from a pay phone, or a phone with caller ID blocked."

"Why not?"

"Georgia." A slight hint of impatience crept into his voice.

"Was the call made from within Pine Tree?"

"We have no way of knowing." The impatience progressed beyond slight.

"Did the caller have an accent, or any distinguishable mannerism?"

Mike didn't answer.

She resumed nibbling small bites of the crème brûlée.

After a few moments, with her spoon poised just outside her mouth, she asked, "Have any suspects?"

"Georgia, this is an on-going case. You know I can't discuss it with you."

"You don't have any, do you?"

"Yes we do."

"Who?" When he didn't say anything, she added, "I'm not one, am I?"

"No."

"Then who is?" She knew she was pushing him, but maybe she could wheedle some information out of him. Thus far, he'd told her nothing new. "You know I'm a trustworthy person. I won't go to the Pine Tree Press. Or KLTV. Or even Bonnie, who can disseminate news better than radio."

"I'm not telling you, Georgia. So, you can quit trying."

"You don't trust me?"

"That's not the issue."

"Then what is?"

"Department regulations." With each answer, Mike's voice became a little tighter.

She raised her shoulders and fluttered her eyelashes. "Okay. Don't tell me." Mike relaxed a bit. "Are you looking at Carl Douglas?"

Now, the detective was puzzled. "Who is Carl Douglas?"

"Come on Detective. Douglas is the guy who has been seen in heated arguments with Syd—the deceased. And who has said Syd just didn't die soon enough."

He scowled. "Where did you hear that?"

"A little bird told me."

"Father Frank, I'll bet." His scowl deepened and his voice became sharper. "It would help if Father Frank would stick to preaching. I'm the detective. I don't preach; you and the father don't investigate." He looked away. "Frankly, you and that priest spend too much time together. Is there anything going on between you two?"

Georgia's mouth fell open. "I can't believe you said that. *He's a priest.*" She leaned away from Mike and her shoulders sagged. "I'm offended by that, Mike. It tells me you know nothing about Father Frank, and you *think* nothing about me." She turned away from him, heat rising up her neck and enveloping her face.

Mike put his hand on her arm, but she pulled away. Her eyes became moist. "Good night, detective."

"Okay, Georgia. I'm sorry I said that. It was stupid. I apologize."

She turned to face him. "Yes. It was stupid. I thought … I thought we had a better understanding of each other. I thought I knew you better. And I thought you knew me better than that." Again, she turned her back to him.

Mike set his plate down. "Georgia, the more I move to your position, that this was murder, the more I want you to stay out of it. We don't know who or why. But, a murderer will protect himself. And if you're getting close, he'll find it much easier to kill the second time. I don't want you in his line of fire." He paused and again touched her arm. "You mean too much to me."

Georgia did not turn to face him, but she did not move her arm.

"Can you just forget that I said that? I didn't mean it. I'm just worried about you, and frustrated that I can't keep you away from … out of harm's way."

"I'm sure I'll forget. Sometime." She sat up a little straighter and her voice became stronger. "But, you can't control me, Mike. If I want to look into things, even dangerous things, I will. And if that's too much for you, then this isn't going to work. If you want to open doors for me, act like a gentleman, terrific. I'm happy with that. But I won't be treated like a delicate violet that has to be protected from everything."

"I'm just worried."

"Worrying is okay. But you crossed a line tonight. And I'm hurt. Now, go away."

"When can I call you?"

"I don't know." She turned to face him. "Do you know why I called you tonight? Invited you for dinner? I wasn't happy with you for refusing to even consider our ideas on Syd's death. I was mad at you. But Father Frank said I was being too hard on you. I should invite you for dinner." She turned her head away. "I'm sorry I listened to him."

"Georgia, --."

"Just go, Mike. You've hurt me. I need to lick my wounds in private."

Chapter 22

Father Frank stood at the back of the church, shaking hands and speaking with the parishioners as they left after Sunday's mass. The breeze whipped in, ruffling the priest's chestnut hair. The tall southern pines that lined two sides of the church property swayed in a wind heavy with moisture. Rain was not far away, but he thought everyone should be able to get home before getting wet.

Norm stopped and leaned in. "Still feeling okay with our discussions last night?"

"Yes. And I really appreciate the advice and insight you and Randall provided," Father Frank said as he touched the hand of another departing parishioner and smiled acknowledgement to her greeting. He looked back at Norm. "I forgot to tell you last night. Duke was on my doorstep when I got home from the reading of the will Friday. He was pushing for me to sign the papers on the spot. I guess he doesn't know I can't do anything without your okay."

Norm laughed. "What did you tell him?"

"I said I needed some time to think about it. I told him, although I'm sure he already knew it, about the appeal Syd had asked you to file." He stopped, waved to an elderly man who maintained his balance with the aid of a walker. "Glad to see you're doing better, Myron."

The man gave a small wave and continued to ease slowly out the door.

The priest turned back to Norm Winters. "He raised the offer." Father Frank's bushy eyebrows arched up.

"They're anxious. If the court agrees to hear the appeal, it will stall the project. And even if we lose, and we will, the delay could be substantial."

Georgia walked up. "You two look like you're planning some covert action. Heads together. Whispering. What's going on?"

"Just talking about the trust," said Norm.

Georgia looked at the priest. "And you, always being so open about things. Now that there's a big stash of money, you're getting secretive." She turned her attention to Norm. "With lawyers, I expect them to be secretive. The more mysterious it is, the more money they can charge."

"There's nothing secretive, Georgia. If you want to listen, feel free," Norm said.

"If it's not secretive, why would I want to? Probably boring. But, I'll listen for a few minutes."

Norm looked at Fr. Frank. "Aren't we lucky."

"What's the topic?" asked Georgia.

"We were discussing whether we should file Syd's appeal," the priest said. "And I told Norm that Duke had upped the offer for the land."

"Oh." Georgia gave an exaggerated nod. "You don't jump at the first offer and they try a bigger one. Very clever, Father."

"I wasn't trying to be clever, or get more money. I just haven't had time to consider what course of action is best."

"Now that you're working with Norm, you're beginning to sound like him. 'Course of action.' Did it ever occur to you that you may be dealing with a murderer?"

"Duke's not dangerous to me. I'm not standing in … his …" Father Frank's voice trailed off, and his face lost some of its color.

Norm and Georgia were shaking their heads. Norm spoke first. "You're standing in his way now just as much as Syd was. So am I, for that matter." The lawyer looked at the priest, his expression deadly serious. "If you think he had a motive to kill Syd, that same motive applies to you. And to me."

#

Father Frank fixed himself a hamburger, opened a bag of chips, popped open a Dr Pepper and sat down in front of the TV to watch the evening news.

He had taken one bite of his hamburger when someone pounded on the door. The priest put the sandwich down and went to the door. Carl Douglas stood there, his face red, his mouth set, the muscles in his neck stretched as tight as a bow string. Without waiting for Father Frank to say anything, he jerked open the door and stepped inside.

Chapter 23

Douglas pushed past Father Frank and focused an angry look on him. "You didn't tell me you was the one holding things up now," he snarled.

"You walked off; didn't give me a chance to tell you anything."

"Yeah. Like you were about to admit you was the cork in the bottle."

Father Frank didn't know whether to ask the man to leave, offer him something to drink or a chair, or just listen. But a small voice in the back of his head asked, *Why didn't you tell him? Were you ashamed to say the church had received such a big bequest?* In fact, the priest *did* feel a little guilty receiving the largest part of Syd's estate. Of course, *he* hadn't received it, the church had. Still... .

"Well, what's the holdup?" Douglas asked. "We finally get Syd out of the way, and now you got your hands on his property. What you waiting for?"

"Actually, Syd had asked his lawyer to file an appeal of the eminent domain ruling."

"That was to show what a big man he was. He's dead. Don't need no appeal now. Let's get on with it."

Once again, the priest was shocked to hear how Douglas talked about Syd. "Actually, he was trying to make a point about how eminent domain was being misused to the advantage of a private corporation."

"Court said it was okay. What's Syd know about it?"

"Eminent domain was set up to—"

"I don't give a hoot 'bout any of that. I just want to get my money and get out. And you're holding me up. What the hell I gotta do to get you to sign the papers?"

Father Frank found it difficult to tolerate the man. *Be calm. He is a child of God. Treat him as such.* "I plan to sit down with Syd's lawyer this week and decide what the church should do about the appeal. Whether we should continue with Syd's appeal, or drop it. As soon—"

"Ain't nothing to decide. A state judge has approved it. Leave it be." The old man stopped and leveled a sinister frown at the priest. "Do I gotta wait for *you* to die 'fore things can get done?" He turned and started for the door, then stopped and turned back. "Just sign it. Next time I come back I won't be so nice."

With that, Carl Douglas banged out the door, hitting the screen so hard one of the hinges pulled loose and the door hung at an angle. Father Frank had to lift it back into place.

He went back to his supper. The hamburger was cold. He considered putting it in the microwave, but decided to just eat it. *Is that penance for Prince of Peace inheriting Syd's house and land?* He grinned. *No. Just lazy.* But the evening news had ended and his Dr Pepper was flat. Maybe that was penance.

#

An hour later, the doorbell rang. He answered it, somewhat hesitantly. Douglas had banged on the door, so it probably wasn't him. *I hope.*

Bill and Sue Granger, members of Prince of Peace parish, stood there, neither smiling.

Good grief. I completely forgot I had an appointment with them this evening.

"Come in, come in," said Father Frank. He opened the screen door, only to have it break off the remaining hinge. He set it aside. Tomorrow.

He led them into the living room, Bill practically dragging his feet. The priest asked if they wanted anything to drink, and when they declined, he motioned them to take a seat and he sat in his usual chair. Sue sat on the couch. Father Frank noted that Bill chose not to sit beside her. *Not a good start*, the priest thought.

#

It was nearly ten o'clock when the couple departed. It had taken over an hour to get to the heart of the matter: money. When Sue first broached the subject, Bill noticeably stiffened. He tried to switch to a different topic, and when she came right back to money he said he did not want to talk about it, particularly in front of the parish priest. It took the priest several minutes to get Bill to agree to discuss it. Even then, he remained rigid, his hands clenched and his jaw twitching at each item his wife mentioned.

Sue saw herself struggling to keep bills paid, food on the table, and clothes on their two children. Bill, on the other hand, spent too much on beer. "And why does he just *have* to have a new rod and reel when I can't even afford new shoes?"

"I thought you wore those 'cause they were comfortable," said Bill.

Sue snorted. "See what I have to deal with, Father?"

Father Frank held up his hands. "Whoa. Let's cool off a minute." He looked from one to another. "You both need to be aware of what you spend money on. Perhaps a common ledger would help, where each item is entered along with the reason for the expense. Categorize each, say like food, clothing, entertainment, etc.. Go over it together each month. Find out exactly where your money is going."

For several minutes, Father Frank laid out a simple plan to help the Grangers deal with their money problems. Nothing too involved that could easily get skipped. When he finished, they both agreed to give it a try.

While they were not holding hands when they left, Father Frank thought now that the problem was on the table, and both had expressed their views, perhaps they could come to an amicable resolution and improve their relationship. And they both had agreed that if things weren't better in a month, they would come back.

Father Frank sat down and closed his eyes. *How difficult married couples have it. There are so many rocks on the path; it must be hard not to stumble. And lack of communication over irritants, large or small, is all too common.*

He walked over to the church, knelt and prayed. *Help me, Lord, to counsel in such a way that it brings your people closer to You, and also to help them overcome, or to accept, their earthly problems.*

He locked the church and started across the parking lot toward the rectory. The tiny sliver of moon offered little distraction from the stars. The big dipper stood out so clearly Father Frank felt he could reach out and touch it. As he turned his head slightly to locate the North Star, he saw movement. Something much closer than the stars flew toward his head.

Chapter 24

With the instincts and quickness honed on a college basketball court, Fr. Frank dodged as a piece of lumber came slamming down toward his head. It caught him on the arm and knocked him to the ground. He landed hard on the elbow, creating an electric jolt of pain. His eyes scanned above him as he rolled, moving his weight off the injured arm. The long board was swinging toward him again.

He jerked to the left, his mind trying to decipher what was happening. *Someone is trying to kill me.* This time, the board missed him completely, hitting the ground just inches from his head, a small piece of the wood splintering off and grazing his ear.

He rolled away from his attacker, and yelled. "I don't have any money!" But already, the man was preparing to swing again. *Is this a mugging? What does he want?*

The priest twisted to his right, trying to get his feet under him. He almost avoided being hit, but the club came at him from the diagonal and caught his leg, driving Father Frank down to the asphalt. Pain blasted through his leg and he thought for an instant he might black out. He blinked his eyes and shook his head. *You can't black out. He'll kill you if you do.*

"What do you want?" he yelled.

He rolled again, ending up on his back. From Father Frank's position on the ground, the attacker looked very tall, and appeared to have a mask covering his face. But the small amount of light available revealed little else. Father Frank could see the man raising the lethal weapon over his head, preparing for another assault. The priest positioned his hands and feet, ready to dodge once more. He jerked to the side at the last instant. The wood smashed into the pavement, creating a hole in the blacktop. As the attacker started to lift the board again, the ragged edge of the asphalt snagged it. It slowed the movement only an instant.

But it was enough.

Father Frank's hand shot out and grabbed the wood. The assailant tried to pull the board away. *Hold on. Hold on,* the priest encouraged himself. *This might be your last chance—ever.* He got his other hand on the two-by-four. The thug was pulling hard, so instead of pulling, Father Frank shoved, knocking the man off balance. The priest then pulled it back and twisted it sharply. Quickly, he gave it another sharp twist wrenching it free from his attacker. The priest swung the plank around forcing the man to jump back.

Father Frank leaped to his feet, the six-foot long two-by-four firmly in his hands, ready for any attack that might come. His breath came in gasps and adrenalin coursed through him. He adjusted to a more solid stance, the board raised over one shoulder like a long baseball bat.

The assailant looked at the weapon and the priest's strong position, turned and ran across the parking lot. The priest took two steps and stopped. He was fast. He was certain he could catch the man. But his leg didn't feel up to running. And what was he going to do if he caught the man? *Hit him with the board?* He massaged his leg and watched his assailant disappear in the darkness.

It took several minutes before his breathing and heart rate returned to normal. He walked over and dropped the wood beside the rectory porch. He ran his hands over the injured areas as he entered the house. He locked the door, stripped off his shirt and studied the damaged arm. Already, it was swelling and beginning to discolor. But, it wasn't broken. It would be sore for a few days, but no real damage done. His leg supported him well enough, even though it hurt to put weight on it.

He went into the kitchen, got some ice, wrapped it in a dish towel and held it against the darkening bruise on his arm. He stepped across the hall to the laundry room and found a face towel. Retrieving more ice, he wrapped it in the towel and placed it on his leg. With luck, he could stop the swelling.

For the first time since locking the church, he had a moment to think without fear clouding the process. *What had happened? A mugging?* Father Frank played back the encounter in his mind, trying to determine exactly what had occurred and who the man could be. He had said nothing during the entire attack.

The priest had not been able to see any features of his ... mugger. Dark clothes, black sneakers, over six feet tall. *He had on a ski mask, so basically I have nothing.* Father Frank looked at the telephone and debated calling the police, while holding his makeshift icepacks against his bruised arm and leg. *Waste of their time. The guy's long gone and I have no idea what he looked like. A waste of the guy's time, too,* he thought. *I might have all of four dollars in my pocket.*

He got a fresh Dr Pepper. As he walked back to his office, his stomach began to cramp and he felt nauseous. Someone had tried to … to injure him. Now, in the bright light and quiet of the rectory, he couldn't bring himself to say "kill him." Yet, a blow to the head with the six-foot long two-by-four would most likely have done just that. He thought of the hole the board made in the asphalt and shuddered. *I should have chased him down and pounded him into the ground. An eye for an eye.* In his mind, he saw a picture of himself hitting the man. Slowly, he shook his head. No, he chastised himself. He shouldn't resort to violence. But he could have held the mugger and called the police.

He picked up his Bible, and settled in his chair to read. He shifted to adjust the ice pack on his arm and the book fell off his lap onto the floor. He reached down to pick it up. The leather bound book had landed on its spine and fallen open to Matthew 18. The priest began to read at the top of the page, verse 21.

Then came Peter unto him and said: Lord, how often shall my brother offend against me, and I forgive him? Till seven times? Jesus said to him: I say not to you, till seven times; but
till seventy times seven times.

Chapter 25

Monday morning, Father Frank was going over plans for a youth retreat. Maybe they could have it out at the lake and the kids could stay overnight. They could afford it now. He was thinking about how they would feed forty teenagers when the doorbell rang. He let Mike in and they settled in the living room.

Mike seemed agitated, didn't even respond when Father Frank offered him something to drink. "What brings you to Prince of Peace today?" he asked.

"Is there any way I can get you and Georgia to stop meddling in the Cranzler case? It's ruining my relationship with Georgia. She invited me over for dinner Saturday, and before the evening was over, we wound up having a big fight over the case."

Father Frank started to smile, but when he saw the anxiety on Mike's face, he turned serious. "What happened?"

"You haven't talked with Georgia? Since Saturday night?"

"Just briefly after Mass yesterday. Norm and I were talking about Syd's land and she joined in for a little bit. That's all."

"Well, she kept pushing me on the case and I said some stupid things." Mike stared at the floor. He ran his hand over his face. "I said she was, ah, spending too much time at the church." He looked up. "I know that was dumb, and I apologized."

"Spending time at church is a good thing, Mike. And she's not neglecting any duties."

"She doesn't even want me to call her."

"Women are more sensitive than men. If we say the wrong thing to them, they pick up on it. Often more than we intended. With men, half the time, we don't even recognize when we're being insulted. But I know Georgia. She'll get over it. Have patience. And remember how to say, 'I'm sorry.' Let her know how much you regret hurting her."

"If you and she would just stay out of this investigation, that would help a lot."

Father Frank grinned. "I think you and Georgia are a good pair, and I hate to see anything cause a rift between you. But, we believe Syd's death was murder. We've yet to convince the Pine Tree Police Department of that. So, we're still working on it. I can't say I'll stop doing that, and I don't think I could in conscience ask Georgia to. But it will help if the police really believe it was murder."

"I'm coming around to your position. But Chief Flag hasn't. He got a call this morning telling him that Syd changed his will recently, which is when you were added. Prince of Peace, I mean. And then, Syd is killed. The implication being, you got him to change his will and then killed him. So, if the chief fully endorses the murder scenario, he puts you at the top of the suspect list. He made that very clear."

"And of course, he has no idea who called him?"

"No."

The priest closed his eyes and put his head in his hands. After a few seconds, he opened his eyes and straightened up. "Be that as it may, it was not suicide and if the chief has to check me out to get on with the murder investigation, then let him do it."

"I know you didn't do it, Father. I'm just telling you how things are. I doubt the chief really thinks you did it either. He's just mad because you're making him reopen a case he thought was closed."

"But he does want to see justice, doesn't he?"

"Yes, he does. But he thinks we've got that and now we're going to waste a lot of time. And if we think it's a homicide, you had motive and no alibi."

"And I had a ready supply of digitoxin."

"I know. I know. And I think down deep he does too." Mike smiled. "So, I won't be hauling you down for interrogation."

"I appreciate that. By the way, have you checked out Duke Heinz yet?"

Mike looked down at his shoes for a moment, then looked up and stretched his lips into a thin, straight line. "It's an on-going investigation. I can't really discuss it."

"So you are investigating it as a murder."

"We're checking into it to determine if it was a suicide or a homicide."

"Did you know Duke Heinz made threatening remarks to Syd the afternoon before he was killed."

"Or committed suicide."

Father Frank ignored that. "Duke had a lot to lose if Syd held up the project. So did Lockey Corporation. And Rich and Dr. Rankin have given you enough evidence to rule out suicide."

"They gave me information, not evidence. They have cast a doubt on it, but I wouldn't say that rules out suicide. I'm looking at other avenues. But I'm not dismissing suicide altogether, either."

"If you haven't already, you need to check out Duke. And Lockey." Father Frank held up both hands. "Let me put that a different way. If you check them out, then I won't have to."

Mike just shook his head.

"You know Duke has been to see me twice already. Once, before the will was read, he came and indicated that I would have some say over the disposition of Syd's land. How did he know that before the will was read? And then on Friday, an hour after the will was read, he's on my doorstep wanting me to sign papers on Syd's place." He leaned closer to the detective. "He had the papers typed up, all prepared, before I even got back here from Norm's office. Doesn't that sound strange to you?"

The detective sighed. "I'm sure we'll be checking on Mr. Heinz." He got up and started out of the room, then stopped. "I see you're getting a new basketball hoop in the parking lot. Result of your new found wealth?"

Heat and color advanced up Father Frank's neck. Mike's illusion to wealth, particularly with reference to the basketball goal, showered guilt over the priest. "Been meaning to put one up for some time. I guess Syd's gift made it easier." He almost said something about how good it would be for the kids, but recognized that as a cop-out.

Mike laughed. "I was just kidding. Glad to see it go up. Hope you find time to shoot a few baskets. I still remember that incredible display when you single-handedly beat S.M.U. when you were playing for UT/Arlington."

"Now, don't go spreading that story around. You make it sound better than it was."

"Ha. Seven points in the last twelve seconds. Tell me that's not incredible. If I hadn't seen it, I wouldn't believe it."

"Well," Father Frank said. "Nobody else in Pine Tree saw it, so they won't believe it. Let's just forget it."

"And that beautiful black-haired coed. With those long, great legs. You know, the one who said she was going with you."

The priest put up both hands, palms facing the detective. "And for certain, let's not bring her up. She was—is—a great person. But, that was before I entered the seminary and a part of my history best forgotten. Please."

Chapter 26

Mike backed out of the driveway as a red pickup pulled in. Father Frank watched Junior Unger get out and amble up to the rectory.

"Hi, Father. Got a few minutes?"

"Sure, Mr. Unger. Come on in."

The two men settled into chairs in the priest's office. "What's on your mind?"

Unger took a minute to fiddle with his hearing aid, then looked at the priest. "I just heard that Prince of Peace got Cranzler's land. That true?"

Father Frank nodded. He felt a slight twinge of worry that there might be another person unhappy with the bequest. "Yes. Syd left his house and land to the parish."

"Well, perhaps you know what's what. A guy named Duke—funny name, don't you think—came to me with a bunch of papers, wanting to buy my land. Says the courts have said he could. Know anything about that?"

The priest rubbed his chin and looked down for a moment. "I know a little about it."

Unger pulled out his left hearing aid and adjusted a dial. "Just a minute. These damn—sorry, Father—darn things won't hold a setting." He put it back in his ear. "Okay, what was that last thing you said?"

Father Frank repeated his comment.

"This Duke guy shows me the court order and says I don't have any choice."

The priest cocked his head to one side. "Sounds like they're after a lot of land."

"He said something about not knowing how many other stores might want to come in when this thing takes off. He's thinking it might become a regional shopping ... destination. I think that's what he called it. Might need a lot of parking, or something."

Father Frank nodded a couple of times.

"Anyway," Unger continued, "I just wondered if you knew anything about it, and how much I should get."

"How much land do you have?"

"Forty acres. Used to grow yams on it. Back when I was younger. Not doing much with it now. Jack, that's my son, wanted to use it, grow yams and make some extra money. But it turned out to be too much work for him. He sits in an office. Doesn't know what real work is. Anyway, his yam growing lasted all of one year. Since then, I've just leased it to Bill Hazlet. Pays the taxes."

"No house?"

"Nothing on it. It's fenced."

"I don't really know too much along those lines yet, Mr. Unger. But I'll ask around, and let you know what I find out."

#

After the man left, Father Frank sat down and closed his eyes. What was going on? Why would Lockey need or want that much land?

He picked up the telephone and called Norm Winters. "What do you make of that?" he asked once he'd related the gist of Junior's visit.

There was a slight pause before Norm said, "I don't know what to think about it. I've talked with Judge McFatage. I've seen the order. It states one hundred sixty acres, which seems too much already. I mean, this is Pine Tree, not Dallas, or even Tyler. One of the points Syd wanted to make is that the plans they've published require less than one hundred acres. So why did the Judge approve eminent domain for one hundred sixty? It seems Lockey is grabbing more land than they need for this project. I have no idea why, but then again, I'm not a shopping center developer."

They were silent for a moment, then Norm asked, "How much land does Junior have?"

"Forty acres. What's a fair price for that?"

"Twelve to fifteen hundred an acre. On forty, that's between forty-eight and sixty thousand." Norm laughed. "Of course, I'm just guessing."

"I'll relay the information to Junior. Thanks."

"A real estate agent would be more attuned to the market for land around here.' He cleared his throat. "I *did* have a worthwhile conversation with my secretary."

The priest waited, having no idea what to expect.

"I told you the Judge came by my office a few days after Syd died. Asked if we were going to withdraw the appeal."

"I remember."

"And I told you the will was locked away at all times. But I wanted to confirm it. So, I asked my secretary if she remembered the judge coming to see me. She said she did, thought it was strange that he came to my office. I agreed. So, I asked her if he asked anything about the will while he was waiting. She said no, he didn't mention it at all. I asked her if by any chance I was working on Syd's will that day. She said no, it was locked in the file cabinet. I asked her if she was sure? She said yes." Norm paused just a second. "She said I was working on the Prince of Peace Trust that afternoon. It was sitting on my desk when the Judge came in."

Father Frank sat up a little straighter. "Could he have read it?"

"I seriously doubt it. I would have stacked up all the pages. But, he could have seen 'Prince of Peace' on it, easily. And the legal description of the property is on the first page."

"That would have been difficult to read upside down," said the priest.

"Yes. But he could easily have read 'Prince of Peace' upside down. He could have seen that the trust included land. Not what land, but *some* land. And he knew I handled Syd's legal affairs. He knew that Syd had just passed away. And he certainly could have read Syd's name upside down." He took a deep breath and let it out. "The Judge is a smart man. He could put all that together and make a very educated guess that Syd's land was going to Prince of Peace."

Father Frank shifted the phone to his other ear. "And he has been dealing with Duke Heinz and the Lockey Corporation. Easy to imagine his mentioning it to Duke. So, that could have been the leak on the will."

"Add that to the fact that he came to my office to see if I would drop that injunction. I've been a lawyer for twenty five years. I've never had that happen before. Oh, I've had judges call me into *their* office. But never had one come to see me."

Both men were silent for a minute. Father Frank broke the silence. "Why would he leak that information? What does it gain him?"

"Hard to say. But you said Monsignor Decker called you on the carpet. Maybe they wanted you to dump the whole thing. Get rid of it as quickly as possible. And you said Duke was on your doorstep before you got back from the reading of the will."

"And he wanted me to sign papers on the land right then."

"They couldn't know that I was also a trustee," said Norm. "If the monsignor made you nervous, you might have signed on the spot."

Father Frank thought about the call to the police. "So, maybe McFatage told Duke, and Duke called Monsignor Decker and Chief Flag. Both for the same reason. Put pressure on me, get me to sign quickly and get those two off my back." He paused a moment. "I know this is all just speculation. But do you suppose McFatage knew what he was doing, or just passed along some gossip?"

Norm said nothing for a moment. Father Frank could hear him tapping his fingers on the desk. Finally, the lawyer said, "I think the Judge always knows what he's doing."

Chapter 27

Father Frank called Junior Unger and relayed the information Norm had supplied on a possible price-range. He hung-up, then dialed the Pine Tree Police Department.

"Mike. A quick question."

"Shoot."

"Since the official position of the Pine Tree Police Department is still that Syd committed suicide, does that mean his house is not a crime scene?"

"Ah, where are you going with this, Father?"

"If it's not a crime scene, then I'm free to enter the house and look around."

"It's not a crime scene. Officially. But since you're trying to get it to be one, I'd think you wouldn't want it contaminated," said the detective. "Just in case we reclassify this a homicide, in which case, it would become a crime scene."

"I wasn't planning on contaminating it," the priest said with a chuckle.

Father Frank could hear Mike breathing, apparently thinking through the consequences of what he might say.

"You know I'm doing some investigating on the case. If I find something, I don't want anyone to question the veracity of anything I might pick up at the…Syd's house."

"I'll be very careful. You won't even find my fingerprints there."

"But, I will have to say in court that an unauthorized person was in the building before such and such evidence was found."

#

Father Frank opened a Dr Pepper and fixed a sandwich for lunch while he mulled over Mike's last statement. Would he, Father Frank, cause some important piece of evidence to be thrown out of court? He picked up the telephone.

"Norm, would you accompany me to Syd's house? I'd like to look around."

"Of course you can go take a look around. What are you looking for? And why do you want me to go with you?"

Father Frank hesitated. How best to put this? Straightforward. "Mike said, while it isn't a crime scene, it could become one. Right now, the official position is that there was no crime. But if they find evidence of homicide, then it could be one."

"And you want me there because?"

"You're a member of the court. You could state that no evidence was tampered with, contaminated."

Norm took in air. "I'm not sure that would work in any event. But in this case, I'm not a disinterested party. I am one of the trustees for that property. I don't think my testimony would be worth much."

The priest thought about that for a moment. "Would you come with me anyway?"

"Sure. When?"

"How about now?"

#

They pulled up to the mailbox on the edge of County Road 493. Norm reached in and pulled out a few pieces of mail.

"I'd have thought there'd be more," said Father Frank.

"It's being forwarded to my office. There are bills to pay, things to cancel. Syd's gone, but a lot of loose ends remain. You'd be amazed how much business remains after someone dies. These just got delivered before I put the order in."

As they were getting out of the car, a blue and white Ford pulled in behind them and Mike got out. "Norm called and said you two were coming over. I decided I better protect the integrity of the scene, in case it becomes a crime scene."

The three men entered the house. Father Frank wrinkled his nose, and said, "Let's open the window and get some fresh air." He started across the room.

"Don't touch it. Just opening the window changes things," said Mike. "You can suffer through the smell. Forensics couldn't get any evidence that someone broke in by that window if you touch it."

"Oh, I think Syd knew his murderer. Let him in the front door," said the priest.

"What are you looking for?" asked Mike.

"Haven't a clue. Actually, *that's* what I'm looking for—a clue. And I hope I recognize it when I see it."

"We've been over the place."

"But you—sorry, the M.E.—quickly classified it a suicide, so you weren't looking for clues to a homicide."

Mike reached in his pocket and pulled out three pairs of latex gloves. "Here, put these on. Just in case you find a clue."

Father Frank walked into the kitchen where Syd's body was found. The counter was clear—not a glass, not a spoon; nothing.

"I guess the police took the empty pill bottle," said Father Frank.

"Yes," said Mike.

The refrigerator held eight cans of beer, five cans of soda, some jelly, part of a Subway sandwich, a half gallon jug with very little milk left in it, some individually wrapped slices of cheese, mustard, pickles, and three apples. The freezer had two cartons of ice cream, one nearly empty—chocolate, the priest noted— two frozen TV dinners and one frozen pizza.

"Looks like he kept a neat kitchen."

"In my dealings with him, he was always neat," said Norm. "He always had the papers he needed, neatly filed in a folder. He looked like a dusty version of Mr. Dithers, remember, Dagwood's boss?"

The priest laughed.

"But Syd was organized," Norm continued. "His mind was, too. To look at him, you'd think he would ramble around from one topic to another and back. But his thoughts were as organized as his papers. Like I said the other day, he calculated carefully what he would leave each person. He wasn't casual or careless about anything that I know of."

"Did he have an office here in the house?" asked Father Frank.

"Yes," said Norm. "Follow me."

Norm led the way down a short hall and turned into a room crowded with a desk, a table, a filing cabinet and a single secretary's chair. The wastebasket occupied a spot outside the door.

"The murderer might have been looking for some papers," said Father Frank.

"Try not to disturb anything. You can look, but don't move papers. Don't change their position," Mike advised.

The room was too small for all three of them, so Mike stayed in the hall, leaning on the door jam and watching the two men inside.

Father Frank began looking through the papers neatly arranged in a stack of trays. Each tray appeared to be devoted to a single topic. The Lockey Corporation occupied the top spot. The priest took a pen from his pocket and used it to lift a sheaf of papers. Underneath was a contract much like Duke Heinz had given Father Frank last week. The third tray down held a sheet with a hand written reminder to check on any seismic work nearby within the last few years. Again, Father Frank used his pen to lift the paper. Nothing below it, and nothing written on the back.

"Norm, did you know about any seismic work Syd might have had an interest in?"

"He never mentioned any to me," Norm answered without looking around.

Norm had opened the file drawer and also used a pen to separate the hanging folders enough to read the labels and get a glimpse of the contents.

"Find anything interesting?" the priest asked.

"Not that I can tell. Mostly bills and receipts for utilities, credit cards. That kind of stuff. Here's a copy of last year's income tax return. Medical insurance policies, social security, investments. I've got copies of a lot of this stuff."

Norm closed the drawer and opened another. "Well, I'll be. Who would have guessed?"

"What?" Mike straightened up and craned his neck to see.

"He's got a whole drawer on genealogy."

Father Frank leaned over to look.

"I can see copies of court records, baptismal certificates," said Norm. "This looks like rubbings off grave stones. I never pictured Syd as one to create family trees. And I thought I knew the man."

The last drawer contained maps, pictures of oil derricks, family photos. "There's a separate folder for pictures of Ben. Poor kid." Norm pushed the last drawer closed.

#

Thirty minutes later, the three left Syd's house.

"Well," said Mike, "anything helpful?"

The priest hunched his shoulders. "Nothing grabbed me. In fact, the only interesting thing—other than the genealogy stuff—was that scrawled note reminding him to look into some seismic work. I have no idea what it means, if anything. But, it surprised me."

"See you guys later," Mike said and he headed for his car.

"Want to come over for dinner tonight?" Norm asked. "I don't know what Irene is fixing, but you're welcome to join us."

Father Frank sucked air through his teeth. "Boy that sounds good. But, I'd better not. I've spent no time on Prince of Peace today. I better get home and do a little work on my real job."

Chapter 28

Georgia parked in front of Judy and Lance Kitchen's modest brick home. For a brief moment, she considered driving off. She had seen Lance lash out at a woman who disagreed with something he had said. Still, it pained Georgia to see the rift between Lance and his in-laws. And she had witnessed the pain it caused Judy, one of the sweetest persons Georgia knew.

She put her keys in her purse, took a quick look in the mirror, and finger-combed her hair. No turning back. This needed to be done.

Even as she waited after ringing the doorbell, the thought of escape resurfaced. But then, Judy opened the door.

"Well, hello Georgia. I, ah, well, ah, come in, come in. What brings you to our neighborhood?" Judy's faded brown hair, pulled back in a messy ponytail, hadn't even gotten a finger-combing.

Georgia walked into the living room, which was neatly furnished in washed oak furniture, a beige carpet, and lots of small photographs of children. "Actually, I came over to talk with Lance. I know this business with Syd's will has made him quite upset with Father Frank and your brother. And Norm Winters, for that matter. I hate to stick my nose in where it doesn't belong." *And I hope I don't get it flattened.* "But I sense Randall is disappointed, and I know Father Frank is disturbed that you, as a family, are unhappy with one another."

Judy arched her brows and tilted her head. "Well, Lance was a bit disappointed."

"Disappointed about what?" Lance asked as he entered the room. "Oh, hello, Georgia."

"Hello, Lance." *I'm in the lion's cage with the lion. I guess I'd better get my lion-taming act together.* "I was in the area, and thought I'd stop by and see how you and Judy were doing?"

Lance looked puzzled. "We're both fine. Why wouldn't we be?"

"I was saying I hated to see family members at odds. And also that I think your feelings toward Father Frank are unwarranted." *There, I've thrown down the gauntlet.* She sat down in a floral covered chair, hoping Lance wouldn't tell her to get out.

For a moment, Lance just stared at her, as if trying to process what she had said. His expression turned hard. "Is that any of your business?"

"Now, Lance," Judy began.

He stopped her with a look.

"I'll get something to drink," Judy stammered. "Would you like a glass of tea, Georgia?"

"That would be nice," Georgia answered, barely able to keep her voice steady.

Judy turned and slunk out of the room.

"It is my business when it affects people I care about." Lance started to speak, but Georgia continued on. "Let me finish. Randall had nothing to do with writing the will or what was in it. You're mad at him because of what Syd wrote. That's unfair."

"It's hard to be warm to a person who can *never* do anything wrong, when you're considered the person who can never do anything right." His voice was hostile and sarcastic.

"That's not Randall's fault." She leaned forward, hoping she could make Lance believe her. "Has he ever put you down? Has he ever told you how great he is?"

Lance said nothing, which Georgia considered a victory, even if a small one. She continued. "And the same thing is true of Father Frank. He knew nothing about the will until Friday morning. He had never talked to Syd about it. The bequest took him completely by surprise."

"Yeah. So he says."

"So *I* say." She said it more forcefully, even as Lance's attitude intimidated her. But he saw any weakness as an invitation to dominate. She couldn't give him that edge. "Again, Lance, you're mad at Father Frank because of something Syd did. And it was, after all, Syd's money to do with what he wanted."

"And just how do you know Frankie-boy didn't bend Syd's ear? Particularly when Syd was vulnerable. Huh?"

"Father Frank told me," said Georgia.

"Well, that proves it." Lance snorted and shook his head. "That might do it for you, but it doesn't cut it for me. That money should have stayed in the family."

Georgia thought the snort was appropriate. Lance was acting pigheaded. "It was Syd's money and property, not yours. If he had had some children, they might have some claim. But brothers and sisters certainly don't."

"That's your opinion."

"Okay." *Maybe just one thing at a time.* "What about Randall? What did he do to cause your displeasure?"

"For one thing, he has the say-so on what we do with the money Syd *did* leave us."

"First of all, he didn't ask for that. And he gets no money for doing it. I imagine he finds that as big a problem as you do. What do you want him to do? Say, 'Too bad, brother Syd. I'm not going to do it.' Or, 'Too bad, sister Judy. I'm not interested.' You do know that if Randall won't or can't be the trustee, it reverts to Norm Winters. Would you rather have a stranger, a lawyer, be the trustee? I'm sure Randall would be glad to be rid of that task. Particularly when you're in such a snit." She braced herself, fearing how Lance might react to that last sentence.

For several moments, Lance said nothing. He had thrust his hands deep into his pockets and just stared at the floor. When he looked up, his gaze was not as hard as it had been. "How do you know Winters would take over if Randall didn't do it?"

"Randall told me. He said he hated to be in that position, particularly when Syd was concerned that Judy might lose it." Georgia folded her hands in her lap and waited for a response.

Judy crept in and placed a tray on the coffee table. She handed Georgia a glass and placed one on the end of the table near where Lance stood glowering.

"Thank you, Judy," Georgia said. "Lance and I are discussing the uncomfortable position Randall is in."

"Humph," said Lance.

"Do you think Randall likes this role?" Georgia asked Lance.

"Gives him control. And I think Randall likes to have control."

"Lance," cried Judy. "You know Randall has always wanted the best for us. Tell me one time when he didn't."

Georgia's eyebrows shot up. In all the years she had known them, she had never heard Judy challenge Lance before.

Lance gave his wife a sharp look. "He put down my job when I worked at L&M."

Judy took in a deep breath. "He did not."

Georgia's mouth fell open. Judy had contradicted Lance.

But Judy raised her chin and continued. "He said you deserved better. You were better than that job."

"Did he offer me a job where he worked?"

"He couldn't; you know that. He didn't have the authority." She thrust her head forward a little. "And you wouldn't have taken it if he had. Tell me if I'm wrong."

Lance said nothing.

After a moment, Georgia stepped in. "Lance, just think about it. See if you can't come to better terms with Randall. You know how he feels about his sister. But if you and he are fighting, it makes it tough. He hasn't done anything to you."

"Not yet. But wait until we want to spend some of the precious money Syd left us."

Georgia smiled. "You're right. Wait. See what happens. Right now, you're mad over something that *might*, just *might* happen in the future. The mood you're in right now, you'd probably be unhappy if he fooled you and said yes to whatever you asked."

Georgia got up   . "Judy, thanks for the tea, even though I didn't get around to drinking it." She turned to Lance. "Give it a try. Randall is not the enemy. And it would make Judy so happy if you and he … at least didn't fight. Right, Judy?"

Judy smiled for the first time since Georgia arrived. "Oh yes."

#

Georgia drove home with a smile on her face. *It's a start. Lance didn't promise, or even agree, to anything. But I've sowed the seeds. They'll need some water from time to time. I can do that. Today was the hardest.* She laughed. *Lance's beef with Father Frank can wait*

.

Chapter 29

Georgia followed Father Frank over to the rectory after Tuesday morning mass.

"First thing is breakfast, Georgia. Everyone knows the first thing I do after weekday mass is have breakfast. You seem to have a thing about delaying, or eliminating, my breakfast at least once a week." He raised his hand and pointed forward. "Breakfast."

"Fine. I'll just have a cup of coffee. And I can tell you about my visit to Lance last night."

As they entered the rectory, Father Frank asked, "I saw Candice leave mass early. Is she sick or something?"

"Not that I know of. But I'll ask," said Georgia.

"If she's sick, I'll give her a call."

"I'll let you know if she is."

Father Frank fixed two eggs and toast while Georgia filled him in on her visit with Lance.

"Sounds like a start to healing the relationship," he said when she finished. "Good work. I know Randall and Abby will be happy if Lance can get over his anger. Abby told me she really missed time with Judy. And I know Randall would like to maintain contact with his sister." He poured two cups of coffee and handed one to Georgia.

"I'm not saying all is well. But it's a beginning." Georgia seemed pleased with herself.

Father Frank opened the refrigerator, grabbed a carton of half-and-half, and offered it to Georgia.

She was spooning sugar into her cup. "Go ahead."

The priest poured a healthy dose of half-and-half into his coffee, put the carton on the table and started spooning sugar into his cup. Georgia picked up the carton, raised it to her nose and smelled it.

"Georgia, it's fresh. I just bought it Saturday."

"Sorry. Just a habit of mine," she said, but her face twisted into a question mark. She held the carton out, looked at it and then gave it another short smell.

Father Frank raised his cup.

"Stop," Georgia yelled as she jabbed her hand over to push the cup away from the priest's face. Hot coffee spilled on his hand and all over the table. "Don't drink that! Don't even smell it."

He put the cup down, grabbed a dish towel and wiped the hot liquid from his hand. "The half-and-half is fresh, Georgia. And even if it were a little bit beyond prime, it wouldn't kill me." He tried a smile as he dropped the towel over the brown puddle on the table. "But my hand may never recover." He looked back at Georgia. She was shaking and her face was nearly the color of the cream.

"I think... ." She started haltingly. "I think it's poisoned." She sank down onto a chair.

He tilted his head to the side. "Poisoned? Are you serious?" He reached over and picked up the carton. "Even sour half-and-half won't poison you."

"Don't taste it," she almost yelled. "Smell it. Just a little. What does it smell like?"

The priest lifted it to his nose. "Not sour." He took another sniff. "But there is a funny little smell to it. Too faint for me to tell."

"Almonds." Her face was still pale. Her voice was grim. "I think someone laced your half-and-half with cyanide."

Chapter 30

Detective Mike Oakley's Ford skidded into the driveway six minutes later.

In the kitchen, he slipped on a pair of plastic gloves, then lifted the carton to his nose and said, "Certainly has that tell-tale smell." He looked inside. "Looks like you've used some of it. When did you buy it?"

"Ah, Saturday. I used it Sunday and Monday mornings. I only use it in my morning coffee."

"He doesn't smell it before he uses it either," said Georgia. "Good thing I do."

"Well, it might have been your last cup of coffee," said Mike. "You wouldn't have smelled it in the coffee."

She turned to Father Frank. "Can I use your computer? I want to check something on the Internet."

The priest nodded, and Georgia left the room.

Mike pulled out his cell phone, called the police department and requested a crime scene team, then disconnected. "Now, tell me exactly what happened – in detail," said Mike.

Father Frank described everything, beginning with Georgia following him in the rectory until the detective arrived.

"Okay, who has access to your kitchen?" Mike asked.

Father Frank looked puzzled.

"Who could have come in here and spiked your half-and-half? It didn't come from the store like that. You said you used it Sunday and Monday. So, who could have come in here and put cyanide in it? Between yesterday morning and this morning?"

"I never lock the rectory during the day. I usually open it when I go to say morning Mass and don't lock it again until night. There's nothing in here worth stealing." He looked at the detective and raised his shoulders. "I guess anybody could have come in."

"Who knows you have coffee every morning?" The detective pulled out a small notebook and started jotting down notes in it.

The priest laughed. "Everybody. Some joke I can't function without coffee in the morning. And I guess a lot of people have seen me drink coffee in the Pine Tree Café."

"'Course, I'd just dump creamer in my coffee," said Mike. "Who knows your routine?"

"Anybody could know my morning routine. I say mass every weekday at 8. Even if they don't go to Prince of Peace, it's stated clearly on the sign at the entrance to the parking lot."

Mike snapped his notebook closed. "Who smells the half-and-half—except Georgia. We'll get it to the lab right away and have it tested. But honestly, I'm pretty sure Georgia's right. Somebody slipped a little cyanide in—"

"Mike, Father Frank," Georgia yelled. "Come here. Right now. You've got to see this."

Father Frank and Mike hurried down the short hall to the office.

"Look what's sitting in your printer," she said, nodding toward a Canon ink jet..

Both men stepped over to look at the page. Father Frank read it out loud.

"*I know I shouldn't have killed Syd, but when I learned he was leaving me all that money I couldn't help myself. Then monsinyor Decker called me in and I knew I was finished. Goodbye to all at Prince of Piece.*"

"You even wrote a suicide note, Father," said Georgia.

"But I didn't do a good job of spelling," said the priest, but he was not laughing.

Mike studied the note for a minute without touching it. He looked at the stack of clean paper in the printer. "I guess he didn't need to touch the paper to do this."

Father Frank's head came up and his eyes opened wide. "How about fingerprints off the keyboard? He had to touch the keys."

"Great idea," said Georgia.

"What have you touched, Georgia?" Mike asked.

"Nothing. Let me think." She paused. "That's right. I looked around, saw the note in the printer. Read it, but didn't touch it. And called you guys."

"Okay. Don't touch anything. I've already called the crime scene guys. The perpetrator had to touch the computer keys, and the half-and-half carton, too."

"How was the suicide note at Syd's?" asked Father Frank. "Misspellings?"

"As a matter of fact, there were a lot. Much worse than this one," answered Mike.

Mike started out the door. "Both of you—outside. I don't want to take a chance on contaminating the crime scene any more than it has been already. Go to the parish hall. Both of you."

#

Father Frank and Georgia walked outside. The morning sun had not developed any real heat as yet, but was just a brilliant, orange ball in an incredibly blue sky. The tall pines that lined two sides of the church parking lot swayed gently while two squirrels played tag underneath. An altogether peaceful setting, in stark contrast to the kitchen and its cyanide-laced half-and-half.

"What a gorgeous morning," said the priest. "I'd say perfect, if someone hadn't tried to poison me." He laughed. "If it *is* poison."

"I told you to give a better sermon. I'd say someone *really* didn't like one of them," Georgia said with a soft chuckle.

"Maybe they haven't liked any of them. You want to preach Sunday?"

"Not on your life." Georgia giggled. "Oops. I guess that's not a good thing to say, right now."

They walked over and sat on a bench in front of the church hall.

"It's a little unnerving to have the police call your home a crime scene," said the priest.

"I think now, even the police will finally rule out suicide for Syd's death and admit it's murder," said Georgia.

"You think this and Syd's murder are related?"

"If Pine Tree has a murder and an attempted murder in a two-week span, I'd certainly give that serious consideration," Georgia said.

"Could be a coincidence."

"Could be. But, you—rather Prince of Peace, but you represent the parish—received a bequest from Syd. Not everybody was happy about that. Then, you've been asking a lot of questions about the murder."

"So have you."

"Yeah, but nobody pays any attention to me."

Father Frank thought about the attack Sunday night. Yesterday, he had gone back to thinking of it as a mugging, nothing more. Now, if this turned out to be cyanide, he'd have to face a fact he had tried to put aside. Someone was trying to kill him.

Almost as if he were thinking out loud, he said, "I guess I need to tell Mike about Sunday night."

Georgia's eyebrows crowded down over her rainforest-green eyes and her mouth fell open. "What? What are you talking about?"

The priest related what had happened in the parking lot late Sunday night.

"Let me see your arm," Georgia demanded.

He pushed up the sleeve on his left arm. An angry bruise covered an area the size of a baseball on his forearm.

"It looks terrible. Does it hurt?"

Father Frank laughed. "Not as much as it did Sunday, or yesterday. And not as much as my head would have, if he had hit where he aimed."

"You did call the police, didn't you?"

He waved a hand as if to dismiss the notion. "What could they have done? I couldn't give them a good description. I guess they could have checked around to see who was missing a two-by-four."

"If you'd called right away they might have seen someone walking around with a ski mask on. Or in dark clothes." She sighed. "But if you don't tell them, they certainly won't find the guy."

"Okay. I feel properly chastised."

"Good. You should. Did he take the two-by-four with him?"

"No."

"Maybe the police could get fingerprints off it."

"I doubt it. The surface isn't that smooth." Georgia opened her mouth to object and Father Frank held his hands up in surrender. "Okay. When Mike gets back, I'll tell him what happened. He can decide if the lumber holds the identity of ..." He narrowed his eyes and his voice became sinister. "...the night crawler."

Georgia laughed. "Who says old dogs can't learn."

"Gee, thanks." He tried to give a hangdog look, but failed. "Now, back to Syd's murder. Can we come up with any suspects?"

"You listed money, power, revenge, and love as the prime motives for murder. Who would have money as the prime motive?"

"I visited with W.C. Mayfield the day of the funeral."

"Who's that?"

"A friend of Syd's. He was at Syd's house the afternoon before Syd was killed. He came to the funeral. Anyway, he said he had heard Lance Kitchen yelling at Syd about wasting money. Why would Lance care unless he thought he might get some of it?" He shifted his position and stretched his legs out in front. "Then, Ben Cranzler told me he had heard his father and Lance arguing over money. Ben didn't hear any details, just about money. Could have been Syd's money, could have been some other money."

He laughed. "Of course, Mike said I was on the suspect list. In fact, he said Chief Flag put me high on the list."

"Is that a joke?" Georgia sounded incredulous.

"Mike said it wasn't to the chief. Since there was a lot of money involved, everyone—including me—has a money motive."

"You're kidding."

"I'm not and from what Mike said, the Pine Tree Chief of Police was not."

"I've never seen that man smile. Probably doesn't have a woman to brighten his life."

#

It was just after ten when two Pine Tree Police cars pulled into the drive. Mike walked out to meet them.

"What would you like me to do?" Father Frank asked Mike.

"Stay outside. They won't disturb anything, but it's easier if the owner isn't looking over their shoulders and asking questions. And telling them how to do their job," said Mike. "I don't think it will take them too long."

Georgia said, "If I can't tell them how to do it, then I'm going home." She turned and started to leave.

"Actually, they need to get fingerprints from both you and Father, so they can eliminate those. Won't take but a minute."

"And get ink all over my clean, delicate, pink fingers," said Georgia.

"They'll even give you a nice cloth to clean your delicate, pink fingers," Mike said with a chuckle. "Wouldn't want you walking around town looking like you just got hauled into the police station for prints and a mug shot."

#

The crime scene crew had scoured the tiny house and were now gathering up their stuff, ready to leave. Mike joined Father Frank and Georgia on the porch.

"I guess this takes me off the suspect list now," said the priest.

"Not in the chief's eyes. When I talked with him an hour ago, he remarked that since you didn't get killed, it could be a smoke screen. Makes it look like there's another killer, and he's after you too."

"Good grief," snorted Georgia. "He was about to drink the stuff. If I hadn't stopped him, he'd be dead by now."

Mike looked at the priest and grinned. "Well, the chief *did* say that if you had drunk the cyanide and died, he'd be willing to take you off the suspect list."

"What a guy," said Georgia.

"You did tell him that Syd left the house and land to the *parish*, not to me, didn't you?"

"He said since you have control over the house and land, it might as well have been given to you."

The crime scene crew came out the door, carrying their equipment, and headed toward their cars.

"What'd they find?" Georgia asked.

Mike spoke to the shortest of the men, lots of grey hair and wrinkles. "Tell Georgia what you found."

"Too early to tell. But to give you a clue, there were no fingerprints on the computer keyboard. None. And I suspect all we're going to find on the milk carton will be from you two." He nodded at Father Frank and Georgia. "Not even a stock person at the grocery store." He started off then stopped. "We got a partial shoeprint that doesn't match any of the reverend's shoes in his closet." He looked down at Father Frank's shoes. "Or the one's he's wearing now. Too small." He glanced at Georgia. "And too big for her." He waved.

"When will we—," Mike started.

"You'll know when I know."

The two police cars left and Mike turned to Georgia and Father Frank.

"Okay. I'm convinced Syd was murdered. And I'm convinced that someone tried to murder you, Father. Now, are you convinced that you two should stay out of this? Leave it to the police? We *will* solve it without your able assistance." He gave the priest a hard look. "As Georgia tells it, you'd be dead now if she didn't have this fetish about smelling things. And a quick hand."

"I might have smelled it before I drank the coffee," Father Frank said.

"You would have smelled coffee. And even if you did smell it, didn't Georgia say you didn't recognize what it was?"

"And someone tried to kill him with a two-by-four," said Georgia.

"What?" Mike exclaimed.

Georgia proceeded to tell of the attack on Father Frank.

Mike looked at the priest. "Were you planning on telling the police about this assault?"

"He wasn't," Georgia answered. "And he wasn't going to tell you he has the two-by-four. Can you get fingerprints off a piece of lumber?"

Mike let out a long breath and shook his head. "Okay, where's the two-by-four? You know, I could charge you for withholding evidence."

Georgia and Mike followed Father Frank over to the side of the rectory, where he pointed to a two-by-four. Mike put on another pair of plastic gloves and picked up the piece of wood.

He continued to grumble as he started to leave, then turned back to glare at the priest. "I'm now ordering you to stay out of this investigation. Officially. And the same goes for you, Georgia. I do not want to have another murder to solve. Especially one of yours."

Chapter 31

Father Frank was almost out the door when the phone rang. He retreated to answer it.

"We got the results back from the lab. Definitely cyanide. They believe it went into the half-and-half as hydrogen cyanide, which remains a liquid below 78 degrees. So it would remain that way in the cream. Put it in hot coffee and some of it would likely be released as a colorless, odorless gas. Breathe that and you could be dead in seconds. Of course, drink it and you could be dead in minutes. You have no idea how lucky you were."

The priest stood motionless, the facts like a slap of freezing water in his face. When he said nothing for a minute, the detective continued. "I just got that report. When I get more info from the crime scene guys, I'll let you know."

After Father Frank put the phone down, he replayed the scene in his mind. He'd been about to smell the coffee when Georgia pushed his hand away. And if she hadn't, he would have drunk the coffee, and the cyanide.

He had tried to discourage Georgia from coming over after mass this morning. He had a number of things to do today and didn't want to stop and visit. What if she hadn't been there? Or what if she hadn't smelled the half-and-half? Or he had just been a little faster on smelling the coffee, or drinking it?

Dear Lord, thank you for watching over me. Thank you for placing Georgia where she could protect me. Mike said I was lucky. I know that it was Your protection, not some random luck. As always, I am indebted to You for keeping me from harm. I know I am not worthy of Your watchful eye, but I am grateful for Your continued protection. I pray that You watch over Georgia, and Mike, and that no one else falls prey to the soul who has lost his way, and that he returns to Your fold.

Father Frank tried to think what it was he had planned to do today. But the morning's excitement had knocked it completely out of his head. While he was trying to conjure up the tasks he needed to do, the telephone rang.

"Prince of Peace. How may we help you?"

"This is Monsignor Decker. I understand that Prince of Peace has come into a large sum of money."

The abruptness, no preamble at all, startled the priest. "One of our parishioners mentioned the parish in his will," said Father Frank while he wondered how the monsignor had heard of the bequest so soon. Given the fact that he knew about it, what was the purpose of this call?

"That was very kind of him. Now, the parish can continue that kindness, and make a donation to the diocese."

Father Frank flinched. "A donation?"

"Yes. Call it a gift to God's work. A great opportunity to show a little charity. And the diocese is having a hard time just now. From what I hear, you could donate a hundred thousand and still have quite a tidy sum to work with."

Father Frank gaped in stunned silence.

When he said nothing, Decker said, "How does that sound? We can't insist, of course, but it would certainly put you on good terms with the Bishop."

"I, ah, I don't really have the authority to do that. The bequest was put into a trust and the trustees would have to decide."

"But surely they will follow your recommendations. Who are the trustees?"

"A lawyer and myself."

"Well, there you are. Meet with the lawyer and vote to make a charitable donation. Can you think of a better place to donate a large sun of money?"

Father Frank's shock had morphed into anger. But, having had an angry outburst with the monsignor less than a week ago, he swallowed the sharp reply. "I have no influence over the lawyer. But I will bring it up at the next meeting." He paused to consider what he had planned to say, then decided to rephrase the idea, not change it. "I promise you we will consider it, along with a number of other proposals. But I do not want to imply or offer hope that such a donation will be forthcoming, Monsignor."

The last statement hung in the air, and the monsignor did not immediately reply. So, Father Frank said, "Right now, I'm late for an important activity. I'll call you when a decision is made on your suggestion."

He put the phone down, stalked into the kitchen and got a Dr Pepper. *I've heard of people winning the lottery and being besieged by requests from strangers. I didn't expect the first to be from my friend the monsignor. A hundred thousand? No point in thinking small.*

He put on his sneakers, grabbed a basketball and headed out to shoot some baskets. *I told Decker I had an important activity. It is important to my mental health, after an attempt on my life, to relax on the basketball court.*

#

Twenty minutes later, Father Frank walked off the "basketball court." He had painted a strip at the appropriate distance from the basket for the free throw line. It wasn't a complete court yet, but he still thought of it as the Prince of Peace basketball court. Maybe next week, he'd paint in the circle.

The argument with Monsignor Decker had vanished from his mind and he felt invigorated. He was smiling as he jogged toward the rectory.

Duke Heinz stood at the edge of the parking lot. "I see you've put some of Syd's money to work already." He had a smile on his face, but his tone was disparaging. "Sign these papers today and you can put a roof over it, play rain or shine."

"Oh, I think that won't happen, whether I sign or not," replied the priest. "I do have a question, though. What did you say to Syd the afternoon before he died?"

Duke's smile evaporated. He licked his lips, stuck his hand in his pocket and jingled his keys. "Ah, I don't remember exactly what I said. We were talking about the eminent domain order and how much the Lockey Corporation was willing to pay him in compensation."

"And you said it would all be asphalt within two months. To which, Syd said something like 'Over my dead body.' What was your reply to that?"

"I don't really remember. I guess I said the court would decide."

Father Frank chuckled. "Of course you remember. It was the last thing you said to a man before he was killed. Murdered, actually."

Duke licked his lips again, and swallowed.

"Fine. Okay. I said he wouldn't make much of a bump in the

pavement." He put up both hands, palms facing the priest. "We were both mad. Syd was being stubborn and yanking my chain. And I just popped off. Trying to be clever. It didn't mean anything."

"Except he's dead."

"Now listen, Father. I didn't kill Syd. Nobody at Lockey did."

"Are you sure Lockey didn't have a hand in it?"

"Of course I'm sure." He let out a long sigh. "We didn't need to. We had the eminent domain ruling. We had the law on our side. That battle was already decided. We were just quibbling over details of the surrender."

For nearly a minute, neither man said anything, Then, Duke smiled and said, "Let's get back to today's problem. And I won't get angry and say anything stupid. Have you read over those papers I left you? Are you ready to sign?"

Father Frank took a deep breath before answering. "I haven't studied them. And I haven't made a decision yet on whether to continue Syd's filing for an appeal. But I did look over some of those papers. And I have a question."

"Shoot."

"What does the term 'fee simple' mean?"

For an instant, a frown crept across Duke's face, but then it was gone. "If that's the only problem, we're in business. 'Fee simple' just makes things neater. It covers all the things there. Say there's a small out-building, or several. We don't have to list each one, give a legal description, location, all that stuff. I mean, technically, if there was just a little shed, no bigger than four by four, say to house a riding lawn mower, we'd need to have all sorts of language to include it. And sometimes, there are a number of those things on a piece of property. If we didn't get all of them down, the owner could come back on us later and demand to have, or use, that building. Or demand additional payment. 'Fee simple' means just that, simple. We're buying everything, and we don't have to specify each and every item, giving legal descriptions, locations, dimensions, materials, use, legal ownership, appraised value, age, year in use, taxable value, and on and on. 'Fee simple' saves all that. And with 'fee simple', Lockey pays the agreed upon amount, in cash, up front. None of this paying it out over years." Duke chuckled. "It's that simple."

Father Frank had the feeling he was being fed a line. Duke was trying too hard. That long string of items was beyond ridiculous. But, the priest nodded. "That would certainly seem to make it … simple."

Duke had a big smile on his face.

Father Frank said nothing, but he thought, *that's a crocodile smile: too wide, and too ready to eat somebody alive.* "Mr. Heinz, I've got to read those papers again, carefully this time. Then, as you know, I've got to sit down with Mr. Winters and make a decision. I'll let you know as soon as we do."

"That additional twenty thousand I offered last week is only good if we can get this signed quickly—like this week. And remember, Syd's house and land are covered in the eminent domain ruling. We have a right to the land. We're just trying to be good neighbors, keep everybody happy, do the right thing."

"Sounds good. That's what I'm trying to do also. Do the right thing. I just haven't figured out what that is. As soon as a decision is made on the appeal, we'll call you."

Duke Heinz shook the priest's hand, gave him another big smile and left. Father Frank thought about counting his fingers.

Chapter 32

Father Frank spent the better part of an hour reading over the papers from the Lockey Corporation. For the most part, it seemed relatively straight forward, at least as much as legal documents ever were. Except the words "fee simple" seemed to jump off the page at him. Did it really mean what Duke said it did? But, he ought to know. Fr. Frank laid the document aside.

He puttered around in the office, trying to work on the financial books, but he couldn't seem to focus on the accounts. He sat down, closed his eyes, and considered the topic for next Sunday's sermon. But his mind kept returning to his meeting with Duke.

Suddenly, an image popped into his mind. On the Lockey papers in Syd's house, Syd had drawn a red circle around the words 'fee simple'.

Father Frank grabbed the phone and dialed. When he got through to Norm he wasted no time. "What does 'fee simple' mean in a deed, or a transfer of title?"

"Fee simple is the most inclusive form of ownership. It means everything."

"That's what Duke said."

"I'm guessing he didn't explain 'everything' completely. It really does mean everything: the land, everything that's on the land, everything that's below the surface—everything."

"Okay."

He could hear Norm take a deep breath before answering. "For example, in most countries, all mineral rights belong to the government. Not so in the United States. And a few other countries. Here, mineral rights were originally granted to whomever owned the surface. So, these property owners had the 'fee simple' ownership— they owned the surface and they owned whatever was below the surface. With this ownership came the right to sell, lease, give, or bequest it. Many years ago, probably when companies began digging for coal, these 'fee simple' owners realized that they could sell the surface to one person, but keep the rights to the subsurface—what we now call mineral rights. Or, sell the mineral rights to someone else."

Norm paused a minute and Father Frank could imagine him taking a drink of water. "Now, when you buy a piece of property, you may or may not get the mineral rights. In fact, the chances are that today you will *not* get the mineral rights. The previous owner, or someone else, still owns the subsurface rights."

"Are you saying that I might own a house and property around it, and someone else could come in and start mining coal?"

"Exactly. You can't stop them. And you wouldn't get any royalties on that coal, either."

"What if they damaged my house?"

"There are rules on that. If they damage the surface or anything on the surface, they must compensate you for that damage."

"But now I have a coal mine on my property. Or an oil rig."

"Yes, although nowadays, states put a limit on how close the rig can be to your house. Could be two hundred feet, could be five hundred. But, outside the limit, they can put it there whether you like it or not."

"Wow. Who would have known?"

"Lockey would. I'm guessing you're talking about those papers."

"Yes."

"Fee simple means they are taking complete ownership: surface, subsurface, and air space. All mineral rights. I don't know if there are any commercially viable minerals below Syd's property—and Syd did own the mineral rights—but if there are, or might be in the future, then they belong to Lockey—*if* we sign a 'fee simple' deed."

"But, the contract does not mention mineral rights at all," the priest said .

"No need to. Fee simple covers the mineral rights. If they have fee simple in there, you won't find a mention of mineral rights."

"Hmmm," was all the priest said.

"Many years ago, a huge parcel of land was acquired through eminent domain for what is now the Dallas/Fort Worth Airport. The deeds the people signed all had 'fee simple' clauses. Just a few years ago, the DFW Airport Authority sold the mineral rights for $185 million. Plus, it will collect royalties on all the gas and oil extracted from under the airport land. The original owners get none of that. They signed a 'fee simple' contract. I'm guessing most of them had no idea they were signing away all mineral rights."

"$185 million?"

"Plus royalties."

The priest sat there, phone to his ear, trying to grasp what he had just learned. When he said nothing for a minute, Norm spoke again. "By the way, you asked me to talk to monsignor Decker and ask how he knew about the bequest to Prince of Peace before the will was read. I did, and he said a man called and said you were inheriting Syd Cranzler's house and land. The man didn't identify himself, and when the monsignor asked the man's name, he hung up."

"Sounds pretty much the same as with Chief Flag. Thanks for calling the monsignor."

"Glad to do it."

"By the way, the monsignor called me and wanted Prince of Peace to donate one hundred thousand dollars to the diocese."

"What'd you tell him?"

"I was shocked," said Father Frank. "I said I didn't make that decision. He said I could convince you. Frankly, I thought it was presumptuous."

Norm was silent for a moment. "Not entirely. You weren't here in the early days of Prince of Peace. Back then, we were a small parish and couldn't really pay our own way. The diocese helped support us for several years. Bailed us out on a couple of occasions. They still do that for other struggling parishes. Of course, we need to look at all our financials, and make a decision. But frankly, I could see us donating some of the proceeds from Syd's estate to the diocese. Maybe not a hundred thousand. But a nice gift. Sort of a repayment for the help they gave us years ago."

After Father Frank hung up, he felt guilty. Money could make one do strange things. So could the lack of it. He must remember that money problems were not easy, not black and white. He had a lot to learn about how it could affect a person's thinking.

His mind jumped back to the Lockey contract and the "fee-simple" clause. *I wonder how many other people have signed, not realizing they were also signing away all mineral rights.*

He picked up the parish directory, looked up a number and dialed.

"Mr. Unger. This is Father Frank. I've got a question on your property. Have you signed the Lockey contract yet?"

"Yeah. They offered me an amount your lawyer said was fair. So, I took it. Signed this morning."

Father Frank felt a slight wave of foreboding. "Do you own the mineral rights to your land?"

"Yes, sir. Sure do."

"You didn't sign them over to Lockey Corporation?"

"Not on your life. They want to put in a parking lot here. They don't need the mineral rights to do that. And who knows, someone might find oil here one day."

"They might. I was looking over the papers Lockey gave me to sign. They have a term in there, 'Fee simple'."

"Yeah. Had one in mine, too. I asked that Duke guy what it meant and he said it meant I was selling everything. You know, fences, out-buildings, all the stuff on the land."

"That's all he mentioned?"

"That's it. Said I could keep my old tractor if I wanted to haul it off."

Father Frank let out a long breath. He hated to be the bearer of ill-tidings."Ah, Mr. Unger, I spoke with Norm Winters, the lawyer who handled Syd's estate."

"Yeah. I know who he is."

"He told me that 'fee simple' was a legal term that meant complete ownership. Everything on the land, above the land, and below the land." When Unger didn't say anything, Father Frank continued. "He said it included mineral rights."

Unger remained silent for a few moments. "What are you telling me? There was no mention of mineral rights in the contract. I didn't sell the mineral rights."

"I'm afraid you did. 'Fee simple' includes mineral rights."

This time, it sounded as if Unger was speaking through clenched teeth. "Duke didn't say anything about mineral rights." He paused and the priest could hear Unger's breathing get quicker. "He said 'fee simple' meant everything, like fences, out-buildings, stuff like that. He never said mineral rights."

"He gave you some examples. But when he said 'everything,' he meant everything, including mineral rights. You said he didn't mention mineral rights. Did you ask him about mineral rights?"

"Well, no." Unger's voice was strained. "I mean, why should I? I wasn't selling the mineral rights."

Father Frank didn't know what to say. If it was not intentional, Lockey would probably straighten it out. But he had a gut feeling this was not an accident. Thinking back on his conversation with Duke, the man answered too easily. Maybe too easily. Almost practiced. But it sounded reasonable. *I accepted it at face value. So did Unger. I wonder how many others have done the same thing.*

"I suggest you call a lawyer and ask about it. Show him the contract and get his opinion. I can suggest Norman Winters. However, if you've used another lawyer, or know one, contact him. I hate to tell you this, but I think, at least I'm worried, that you *have* signed over your mineral rights."

"Not what I intended. That Duke guy never mentioned mineral rights." He paused for a second and it sounded to Father Frank like Unger was grinding his teeth. "Does eminent domain give them any right to my minerals?"

"That's a good question. I wouldn't think so, but I don't really know. But the contract includes them." He thought for several moments. "I'm not a lawyer and don't know much about it, so you really need to get an expert opinion on this. But I'm afraid it's more like this. If the eminent domain gave them a right to 100 acres, you could choose to sign a contract selling them 150 acres. And that would be a legal contract. In this case, eminent domain gave them a right to the surface, and you've signed over the surface *and* the mineral rights."

Unger's voice was growing husky. "I wasn't selling my minerals."

"Please go see a lawyer. The sooner the better."

Chapter 33

Father Frank sat in his office, staring at the bank statements and bills and checks spread out on his desk. But his mind kept straying to digitoxin and cyanide and two-by-fours and "fee simple" contracts. When he looked up, the bright yellow circle on the calendar above his desk seemed to be pulsating. "Yes, yes. I know the parish council meeting is in ten days," he murmured. "I've got to get all the financials up-to-date." How did Syd's bequest work into that? The cash portion could be incorporated now. Maybe. It was in a trust. He needed to talk with Norm about that. Just how did that show up on the books? And what about the property? Floy Muldoon was an accountant. That's why he had insisted she join the parish council. He'd get her advice on how to handle that.

The thought of the bequest brought Syd's death to the front of his brain. *And why had someone tried to bash my brains out and then poison me? Surely it had something to do with Syd's will.*

The bequest was actually left to the parish, not to Father Frank personally. Still, what other reason could there possibly be? An unnerving thought popped up. What if there were two different criminals, one with a two-by-four and one with poison? If there were two criminals, did they have two different reasons? Were they working together? Could these have been two uncoordinated attempts on his life? He didn't like to think of "attempts on his life." But, there it was.

The priest made a pact with himself. If he'd work on the church financials—without letting his mind stray—then he could think about Syd's murder, the cyanide attack, or whatever. But first, an uninterrupted hour of parish work. It was only Tuesday; he could wait until tomorrow to think about next Sunday's sermon.

\#

An hour and a half later, he closed the ledger, satisfied that the church books were current and that except for the bequest, he was ready for the parish council meeting. He walked into the kitchen and got a Dr Pepper. He looked at the brown spot on the table. In all the confusion this morning, he hadn't wiped up the spilled coffee. He picked up a dish cloth, then stopped. Coffee *and* cyanide. Maybe a paper towel he could throw away would be a better choice. Just in case.

How close he had come. If Georgia hadn't been there, and quick, he might be lying in the morgue at this moment. He wiped the stain, got another sheet and washed it and another paper towel to dry it.

His eyes opened wide. What if the guy put the cyanide in something else? He left a suicide note. He wiped off all fingerprints. He was careful. Why not put the poison in more than one place? Father Frank looked in the refrigerator. The Dr Pepper cans were sealed. He could wash them. Reluctantly, he began to drop all unsealed food in the trash.

After he finished cleaning out the refrigerator, he picked up the telephone and dialed. "Hi, Georgia. I just realized that I never said 'Thanks' for saving my life this morning."

"Wow. That sounds dramatic. I'm impressed. I'm going to picture it as racing into a burning building and dragging you out as the flames singed my hair. Burning timbers falling on either side of us. The floor giving way as I stepped on it and having to pull myself back up out of the flames that filled the basement. Even as the flames crowded around us, the door was stuck. I picked up the holy water font and used it to smash open the charred door, then carried you out on my shoulder to the applause of the awed crowd."

Father Frank laughed. "Well, you can think of it however you wish. The result was the same."

"Maybe I dove into a raging river and managed to get your head above the water. But the strong current was carrying both of us toward the thousand foot high waterfall. No, toward the power turbine, whose steel blades would slice through our bodies as easily as it did through the water. To hold your head above water, I had only one arm to try to bring both of us to the rocky shoreline. I was tiring. A log smashed into my hand, and now, precious blood was pulsing into the water."

"Georgia," the priest interrupted. "Have you ever thought about being a writer?"

"Me? Heavens no. I have no imagination for such things." A demure giggle came over the line.

"By the way, I talked to Norm today. He had a possible source of the leak on the will information. He couldn't be sure, but it's possible that Judge McFatage could have seen the trust document with the Prince of Peace name on it, and a legal description—indicating a land transfer."

"How could he have possibly seen it?" Now, Georgia was all seriousness.

Father Frank repeated what Norm had said about the judge's visit to his office.

"Sounds strange to me. Did he say why the judge came to his office?"

"To see if the appeal was going to be dropped."

"I didn't think judges did that. I mean, go to a lawyer's office about a case."

"I don't think they usually do. At least, Norm was surprised."

"But surely the judge wouldn't have called Monsignor Decker. Or Chief Flag, for that matter."

Father Frank said nothing as fragments tried to form into a thought. At last, the pieces fit together. "Judge McFatage issued the eminent domain order. I would guess he worked with a Lockey lawyer on it. And maybe Heinz was involved."

"So, what are you suggesting?"

"I don't know if I'm really suggesting anything. But, I can more easily imagine Duke calling the monsignor and the chief than I can imagine the judge doing it."

"I can't," Georgia said. "Of course, I haven't had any dealing with Heinz. That could change my mind. But it is my humble opinion, which I would only express to you, that McFatage is a slug. I don't even want to know how he ever became a judge. It would only depress me."

Neither said anything for several seconds. Then Georgia asked, "What motive would the judge have for calling and spreading the news?"

The priest put his drink down on the newly cleaned table. "I've asked myself that same question. A couple of ideas have been percolating in my brain. One is that you and I were pushing to have Syd's death declared a homicide, not a suicide. If the monsignor got on my case and instructed me to keep my nose out of it, then perhaps the police would stick with the suicide and the murderer would be home free."

"Gotcha."

"And that almost worked."

"Wouldn't have kept me out of it," Georgia said.

"True. But cutting the agitators down to one, instead of two, would help."

"Okay. What else has been percolating away?"

"If the chief begins to consider me as a suspect, again, I might be less interested in pushing for a murder investigation. While I would know I was completely innocent, there are certainly cases of innocent people being convicted of crimes on pretty skimpy evidence, sometimes crimes they didn't commit."

"Particularly, if the judge hearing the case had an axe to grind."

Chapter 34

Father Frank finished Mass and, without taking off his vestments, walked toward the back of the church. He had seen W.C. Mayfield standing there, arms crossed, feet apart, apparently waiting for someone.

"Hello, Mr. Mayfield. Glad to see you at Mass today." They shook hands.

"Well, I'm not a Catholic, but I enjoyed the service you had for Syd, so I thought I'd come see one without a funeral."

"I'm certainly glad you did. What'd you think?"

"Nice. Before the funeral, I'd never been in a Catholic church. Just curious; that's all."

"You're welcome anytime." Father Frank had the distinct feeling there was more to this visit than "just curious." W.C. was either looking for information, or ready to supply some. "Have you had breakfast?"

"As a matter of fact, I haven't."

"Give me three minutes to change, and let's go have something at the Pine Tree Café."

#

Fifteen minutes later, the two men sat in a back booth of the café, stirring sugar and half-and-half into coffee. The Pine Tree Café was Father Frank's favorite café, partly because it was bright, clean and the staff was always pleasant. But the main reason was that it was seldom crowded and he could most always get a booth away from other patrons, one that would allow some privacy for conversations. Usually he came here for a private talk, not for the food or coffee.

This morning, there were a few tables occupied at the front of the café, and two men sat at the counter, each reading a newspaper. The waitresses moved with quiet efficiency, only noticed when they took or delivered an order. Coffee was the overriding aroma, although occasionally the smell of fried eggs tickled the nose.

"How did you like today's service?" the priest asked. "I mean, a funeral is not the best service to attend." He chuckled just a little. "Of course, today you didn't get to hear me give a sermon. You should come on Sunday so you can hear me expound on some holy topic."

"As I said, I'm not a Catholic. But I may come hear you talk one day."

"Thank you." Father Frank took a sip of his coffee. "Now, what did you want to talk about today? Syd's murder?"

"Well, I didn't..." He trailed off awkwardly.

"I hope you enjoyed the service. But I'm sure you had something else on your mind."

W.C. pushed the eggs around the plate with his fork. "Well, actually, I got the check from the lawyer yesterday and I had to come this way to deposit it anyway. So, I thought I'd just stop in."

"The check? Oh, the money Syd left you."

"Yeah. Ten thousand. Very nice of Syd to remember his old friend." He looked down at his coffee cup. "'Though I'd much rather have him alive than the money."

Father Frank couldn't quite tell if W.C. was sincere. "In the will, Syd said something about an oil venture that went bad, or something like that."

Mayfield nodded a couple of times. "Yeah. We sunk a lot of money into a dry hole. At least, it seemed like a lot of money to us at the time. Didn't get one red cent out of it."

Lines formed on the priest's forehead. "I thought Syd made his money in oil."

"He did. But not with me. He did another well later. Turned out to be a really good one. I wasn't in on it."

"Pardon me for being nosy. And tell me it's none of my business, if you wish. But why weren't you in the next well? As you said, you were friends for many years."

W.C. stirred his coffee and then took a long drink. "Syd didn't invite me to join him. Money was tight for me at the time, and he figured I couldn't—or shouldn't—pony up the bucks. That's just the way life goes sometimes. Two wells. The one I put money in was a duster. The next one was a big winner. Still is."

"That must have been disappointing."

Mayfield raised his shoulders. "The rub of the green. The breaks of the game."

The priest nodded. "A bad break for you. Of course, money doesn't always solve problems. Sometimes it creates more problems, bigger problems."

"You know what they say. Money can't buy happiness." Mayfield gave a sheepish grin. "But then, neither can poverty."

"But you two stayed friends?"

"Oh, yeah. I was really sorry to see him go."

Father Frank shoved the last of the toast into his mouth and washed it down with some coffee. "Was there something else you wanted to tell me?"

"Oh, not really." W.C. waited a beat, then raised his head slightly and said, "However, I did hear something interesting. I don't know if it means anything or not. And I can't tell you how I know this. But, a little while after Judge McFatage handed down the eminent domain ruling on the Lockey case, he bought a new car."

Father Frank waited. When Mayfield offered nothing more, the priest said, "As lots of people do around here. Good times or bad."

"A Lexus."

"Out of my range, I'm afraid. But, I'm not a state district judge."

"I've been around here for a long time. I've never seen the Judge drive anything even close to that. Usually a mid-sized Chevy."

"Maybe he came into some money, like an inheritance," said the priest.

"No family that I'm aware of. Anyway, just something I thought you might find interesting."

#

Father Frank hadn't been back at the rectory more than ten minutes when the phone rang. Almost before the priest said hello, words were tumbling out of Georgia's mouth. "I saw somebody at Mass this morning. Was that Mayfield?"

"Yes, Georgia. W.C. Mayfield was there."

"What did he want?"

"Perhaps to get closer to God. Did you ever think of that when someone comes to church?"

"Oh, stop it. He doesn't belong to Prince of Peace. The only time I've seen him there was at the funeral. I'm invoking the freedom of information act. Why was he there?"

Father Frank laughed. "The freedom of information act does not apply here. Anyway, he said he just wanted to see what a service was like without being a funeral."

"Then why not come on a Sunday, when there's a sermon and all?"

"Maybe he didn't want a sermon." This time, Georgia didn't say anything, just waited. "Okay, he said he'd gotten the check from Norm. The ten thousand Syd left him."

"He didn't come to tell you that." It was a statement, not a question.

"He did mention that Judge McFatage bought a Lexus." He paused a second. "Just after he issued the eminent domain ruling. Mayfield said he thought I'd find that interesting."

Georgia let out a low whistle. "I don't know about you, but I certainly do. The Judge has driven cheap cars all his life."

"And how do you know that?"

"Okay, I don't—exactly. But I do know that's true for the last..." Father Frank could almost hear her counting. "The last fourteen years. At age twenty I started paying attention to local politics." She giggled. "So he bought it right after he issued the eminent domain ruling. Very interesting."

Father Frank felt a little prickling sensation on his neck. "Georgia, don't make me sorry I told you that."

A bubbly laugh came over the phone. "Oh, no. No. I won't make you sorry."

The prickling sensation progressed down the priest's back.

Chapter 35

He was downtown anyway. Why not?

"Hi, Mike. How's it going?" Father Frank didn't wait for an invitation. He picked up a stack of papers on the visitor's chair, plopped them on Mike's desk, and sat down.

The detective looked up and frowned. "What brings you to the Pine Tree Police Department?"

"Just passing by and thought I'd see how things are progressing. Or if there *was* any progress." Father Frank checked out the marker board behind Mike's desk. Four cases merited a spot on the white board. *I wonder how many cases he has at one time.* Two had been on the board last week, or was it the week before? The priest couldn't remember when he'd last studied the board. Today, there were two new cases. One appeared to be a breaking and entering case in a private home. The one on the far right was attempted murder. He read the word "cyanide" two lines down. Suddenly, his stomach felt queasy. There it was in black and white. Father Frank had been only seconds from being a statistic, a victim, a body. Dead. Under the word "suspects" nothing was written.

Mike dropped the pencil he'd been holding and leaned back in his chair. He picked up a Styrofoam cup and took a sip. He wrinkled his nose and frowned at the cup as he swallowed, then put the cup aside. "Yuck."

"Is that a comment on the coffee or Syd's case?" the priest asked.

"Both. The case is as stale as the coffee."

"Find anything on Duke Heinz?"

"This is part of an on-going investigation, Father. I'm not at liberty to discuss it with you." He leaned forward and lowered his voice. "Certainly not here in the police station." He raised his eyebrows and tilted his head toward the door for an instant.

Father Frank stared at Mike. Was that an invitation? "Since the coffee is so bad, why don't I buy you a cup at the Pine Tree Café? Have you got time?"

Mike looked at his watch. "Yeah. Why not. Maybe a decent coffee will get my juices going again."

Five minutes later they sat in the back booth, Father Frank spooning sugar into a brown mug, Mike testing his hot coffee. Father Frank repeated the question he had asked in the police station. "Have you found anything on Duke?"

"Oh yeah. Plenty. Seems to have a history of bad behavior. Assault, battery, intimidation, heavy handed tactics all over the place. Plenty of complaints, a few arrests, and one indictment. No jail time ... that I've found." He took a bite of the glazed donut he had ordered with his coffee. "He roughed up one man who kept holding out, refusing to sign. The guy signed but then later, filed a complaint. Heinz got a slap on the wrist."

"And Lockey?"

"Not much better. Maybe that's not fair. Let's just say they have not won any good neighbor awards."

"For instance?"

"Oh, mostly minor things like having no regard for adjacent neighbors during construction, improper placement of lights so that they shined into people's homes, and a refusal to even listen to neighbors' complaints."

"Any of the complaints concern mineral rights?"

Mike frowned. "That seems like a strange thing to ask."

"The contracts, at least the one they gave me and another I've seen, are 'fee simple' contracts. Which means they're getting mineral rights along with surface rights. If they're simply getting land to build a shopping center on, then why are they acquiring the mineral rights? And two people I've talked to didn't know they were giving up all mineral rights." He scratched his cheek and looked at the detective. "Eminent domain, certainly one for a shopping center, doesn't give Lockey the right to the minerals."

He waited a moment to see if the detective would make any comment. When he didn't, the priest continued. "I asked Duke about the 'fee simple' clause. He gave me a practiced speech about just covering their bases, so there'd be no later complaints about not paying for fences, or any outbuildings. He never mentioned mineral rights."

"So, you're saying he was deceptive. At least, deceptive by omission."

"I am. Somehow, I think mineral rights could be more important than fences. This isn't ranching country."

Mike closed his eyes and leaned back, stretching his neck, working it around a little as if maybe it was sore. When he straightened back up, he looked straight into the priest's eyes. "Lockey built a shopping center in El Molino which now has four producing oil wells, one sitting on each corner of the property." The priest started to speak but the detective held up his hand. "Yes, Lockey had acquired the mineral rights, perhaps in the same fashion, with a 'fee simple' clause. I don't know that. There were some challenges by former owners, but the contract stood up in court."

"So, they may have given away the mineral rights without knowing it," said the priest.

Mike did not comment. The large round clock behind the counter ticked off the seconds as the two men stared at each other.

Father Frank finished his coffee, laid some money on the table, and got up. "Okay if I go back into Syd's house and look around?"

"No. It is not."

"But –."

"It's a crime scene now. I'll let you know when the crime scene guys release it." The detective got up, tossed a couple of dollars on the table, and looked at the priest. "You might be a little careful in your dealings with Heinz. He's big and we're finding out he's tough."

#

Father Frank dreaded doing it. But it needed to be done. He drove slowly up to Carl Douglas's house. It looked as dusty and run-down as before. Today, however, there was a light on inside, and shinning through the window shade. Somehow, it looked like a giant, angry yellow eye.

Come on. You're making more of this than necessary. He's probably calmed down by now.

The priest parked and walked up to the door and tapped lightly. When no one came, he knocked a little harder.

"Keep your britches on. I'm coming," Carl Douglas yelled from somewhere inside. In a minute he arrived at the door. "It's you. What do you want now?"

Father Frank smiled and tried to look as friendly as possible. "I just wanted to check if you had signed the Lockey Corporation contract."

"Yeah. I signed it, months ago, but I ain't got no money yet. You're holding that up. Have you signed it?"

"No. But—"

"Then we ain't got nothing to talk about." His face sullen, Douglas turned and started off.

"Did you retain your mineral rights?"

"What's it to you?" He turned to face the priest, but did not come back to the door.

"The contract they presented to Syd, and also to another land owner, contained a 'fee simple' clause. When you sign a contract with 'fee simple' in it, you also transfer all mineral rights, unless you have words in the contract specifically saying you are retaining those rights."

Carl Douglas didn't say anything. Nor did he move.

"I just wanted to warn you. I didn't know what 'fee simple' meant. And when I asked the Lockey Corporation representative, he didn't tell me that. I had to find out from a lawyer."

"Well, I've already signed, whatever it said."

"If you have not gotten any money yet, it may not be too late to have that changed. If they haven't paid you, the contract has not been completed."

Again, Douglas said nothing.

"That's all I wanted to tell you. Watch out for the 'fee simple' clause."

When Douglas made no response, Father Frank turned and left. He was at his car when he was assailed by a loud, reverberating noise. He looked back at the house. The front door was now closed, and the screen door was still shaking.

Chapter 36

Father Frank stood at his neatly painted free-throw line and launched the basketball toward the rim. The ball swished through the net. He retrieved it and returned to the line. It was a perfect autumn day to be outside shooting baskets. The temperature hovered around 78 degrees; the breeze was gentle enough not to disturb any but the longest shots. A half dozen puffball clouds only enhanced the sapphire sky. He had dropped seven clean shots in a row. Not bad for a has-been, he thought. He squared up to try for eight in a row, and as his arm went up to release the ball, a horn blared across the parking lot. The shot hit the rim and bounced off.

He turned to see Georgia getting out of her car. He retrieved the ball. Georgia came striding across the asphalt.

"You made me break my string of successful free throws."

"Enough of playing. Come on inside and I'll give you something better than another meaningless basketball shot."

#

Inside the kitchen, Father Frank retrieved a Dr Pepper for each of them and they sat at the small wooden table.

"Okay. What is so important that I should miss a shot?"

Georgia was beaming. She wore a green shirtdress that complimented her eyes, which were sparkling with anticipation.

"The judge paid cash for the Lexus. Well, after his trade-in."

"Doesn't happen too often, but people do, sometimes, pay cash for things." Father Frank laughed.

"I don't mean a check. I mean real cash. Greenbacks. He handed over $49,000 in hundred dollar bills."

Father Frank's eyes opened wider and he whistled softly. "That *is* unusual." He took a drink of his soda. "With stacks of fifty bills, that's about ten bundles. You'd need a briefcase."

"He had one." Georgia couldn't contain herself and burst out laughing. "It was just like in the movies. Only, he got a luxury car, not a few bags of dope. She said he came in, put the briefcase on her desk, opened it and turned it toward her. She said her jaw dropped down to her knees. The whole briefcase was filled with bundles of money."

"Who is she?"

"Ruthie. She's the mother of one of the prize students I had last year." Georgia glowed with the excitement of this new information. "The Judge said there was fifty thousand there."

The priest shook his head in dismay. Then he stopped and fixed Georgia with a steady look. "And how did you find this out?"

"Ruthie handles the paperwork on new car sales at the Toyota/Lexus dealership. I talked to her. She was *very* secretive about it. They don't like to give out that kind of information. You know, how a person finances a car."

She paused to take a quick sip, and Father Frank said, "I don't think you should have asked."

"I didn't. Well, not exactly. I just mentioned the Judge's name. You know, 'I hear Judge McFatage bought a new Lexus.' She grabbed me and pulled me into her office and closed the door. She was so excited. And this is weeks after it happened. Said she *never* had a person actually pull out dollar bills and pay for a new car, let alone a Lexus. Not even a used car."

"And he used hundred dollar bills?"

"That's what she said. Counted out 490 bills. She said they didn't give him much for his old Chevy he traded in. He got back about twenty-seven dollars, that's twenty-seven *one* dollar bills." Georgia giggled. "Ruthie said she counted those hundreds at least five times, afraid she'd make a mistake."

Father Frank just shook his head, unable to get his brain around such a transaction.

"She said they got the police department to escort her to the bank to make the deposit. Said they take in a lot of money at the dealership, but mostly it's credit card slips or checks. Said people rarely pay cash, even for repairs. The bank teller wanted to know where all that cash came from. Of course, she didn't tell him anything." Georgia's complexion still maintained the radiance of discovery.

\#

Father Frank leaned back in the big, Lazy-Z-Boy chair in the living room, a Dr Pepper in his hand, his eyes closed. He wondered if this Ruthie could be pulling Georgia's leg. And Ruthie, after a good laugh, would tell her what really happened. But why? And surely Georgia would know.

If true, and for the moment Father Frank would work on the assumption that it was, it didn't necessarily have a direct bearing on Syd's murder. *"But, I'd bet one of my new basketballs it had something to do with the eminent domain ruling."*

There was another explanation, of course. The Judge could have been saving up hundred dollar bills for some time, a growing pile tucked under frozen pizzas in a deep freeze. And finally decided to treat himself to a little more than pepperoni on his pizza. Didn't pay high interest rates. Didn't deplete his bank savings account. Just emptied out part of the freezer. Father Frank didn't know the judge, but would an officer of the court manage his affairs that way?

Or, maybe the freezer quit. Began to thaw and had to be emptied. What to do with all those hundred dollar bills? Why not buy that impressive car he'd always wanted? Many of the judges had luxury cars. Why was he still driving a four-year-old Chevy? Even the police had newer and bigger cars.

The priest had read about huge sums of money being found in freezers, sometimes after a person died, sometimes not. More often than not, these cases involved something illegal. And if this horde of cash was a result of the judge issuing a favorable ruling for some corporation... Bribes definitely fell into the illegal transaction category.

But, it wasn't likely it had anything to do with Syd's death. Bribery but not murder.

Father Frank got up and started into the office. An idea flipped up in his mind. What if Syd had found out about the bribery and threatened to expose the judge? That could be a powerful motive. Even as he sat down at his desk, he shook his head. No. If Syd had known about it, he would have told Norm. He was preparing the appeal. Knowledge of a bribe to get the ruling would be a strong reason to overturn the Judge's ruling.

The priest grinned. With just a little change in Pigmeat Markam's famous "Here Come da Judge" line, he had "There go da judge."

Scratch McFatage off the suspect list.

Chapter 37

Father Frank arrived at Norm's office precisely on time for their 4:30 meeting to find the outer office empty and the door to Norm's office open.

"Hello," he called.

Within seconds, Norm appeared. "Tina had to run a quick errand. She'll be back any minute. In fact, here she is now." He spoke to his secretary. "We'll be in the conference room. Unless it's really important, I don't want to take any calls."

Norm ushered Father Frank into the conference room and closed the door behind them. They took seats on opposite sides of the table.

Father Frank looked a little uneasy. "This is my first ever trustee meeting. Do you think we need to keep minutes?" the priest asked.

Norm laughed easily. "I think it would be a good idea. If we keep good records and there is ever any question—which I strongly doubt there ever will be—then we have the documentation to back everything up. I can keep notes, or I can have my secretary come do it. Which would you prefer?"

Father Frank looked down at the table and squeezed his lips together, then looked up at Norm. "Why don't you keep them for this first meeting? Since I have no idea what I'm doing, I'd rather be a bumbler in front of as few people as possible."

Norm laughed. "We're just going to discuss some points. There's nothing to bungle. But, I'll keep the notes today. Where do you want to start?"

"First, I've thought about what you said, regarding the diocese and all. And you're right. We can certainly make a donation to them. I guess when people who have never had money get some, they either blow it or squeeze it to death. I was squeezing. What's a reasonable amount? I still have a problem with a hundred thousand."

"There's nothing magic about the hundred thousand. It was a nice round number—a nice *big* round number—that the monsignor threw out. Who knows, maybe you'd do it. Nothing ventured, nothing gained. I'd say, twenty-five to fifty. Remember, Syd gave his money to be used for this parish and this community. So, the large majority of it should be used here."

"What if we start with twenty-five? Then, after we've decided on how to use some of the money, we can give some more, or not."

Norm began writing. "I move that the Prince of Peace Trust authorize a donation to the Diocese of Tyler in the amount of twenty-five thousand dollars."

The priest said, "I second that motion."

"The motion carries with both trustees agreeing. It's not clear that we have to be that formal, but it certainly does not hurt." He finished writing and looked up at the priest, who had a puzzled look on his face. "What?"

"I'm just wondering. Do I need to get the approval of the parish council to do this? Normally, on any expenditure out of the ordinary, or of any sizeable amount, I would take it to the council and get their approval."

Norm shook his head. "Technically, this is not the money of the parish. It's money in the Prince of Peace Trust. That money can be dealt with only by the trustees. We are legally and ethically correct in authorizing this expenditure. And, in fact, the parish council *cannot* authorize any spending out of the trust." When the priest nodded, Norm said, "Is there anything else you want to discuss regarding the trust?"

"Actually, there is. I've been wrestling with this question of the appeal. Do we want to continue that process as Syd would have done? Or do we say, that was Syd's battle, not ours? Frankly, I don't relish a big court battle. On the other hand, I do want to carry out Syd's wishes."

"I agree with you that we want to carry out Syd's wishes—but the wishes he had at the time he set up this trust. That is, he wanted the trust to expand the good works and influence of Prince of Peace church. He wanted to help with projects that benefit the parishioners and the people in need in this community."

"But he was going to fight this ruling. He was going to spend some of this money to follow the appeal process. Maybe even to the Texas Supreme Court. Should we also use some of this money to finish what

Syd had wanted?"

Norm shook his head. "That's what *he* wanted to do. That's not necessarily what he wanted the Prince of Peace Trust to do. His orders, or rather comments, on this trust were pretty simple. The money can be used to pay off the church debt, develop church programs, charity initiatives, or community programs. He did not mention anything about finishing what he had started."

"Still—"

"We could continue his appeal. Under his guidelines, I guess we could call it a community project. But I don't think that's what he meant by community projects." The lawyer leaned back in his chair. "If we continue the appeal, I'll bill a lot of hours. Financially, it will be good for me." He moved forward and rested his elbows on the table. "Father, I honestly don't think he wanted us to continue it after his death. Syd was very pragmatic. The abuses of eminent domain were his fight, not a fight for Prince of Peace."

Father Frank slowly nodded. "Okay. That had been on my mind. What to do about the appeal. Whether we should continue it. Frankly, I didn't want to get involved with it. Now I think I can feel good about dropping the appeal. So, is there any reason we shouldn't go ahead and sign the contract with Lockey Corporation?"

Norm raised a finger. "I'd like to redo it; take out the 'fee simple' clause. Make a specific mention that it does not cover mineral rights. Otherwise, I think we can sign it. I'll leave you to negotiate the price."

"Do you think the $220,000 is a fair price?" asked Father Frank.

"I do. You could get an opinion from someone in real estate, if you'd feel better about it.

Remember, Lockey has eminent domain on their side. The law requires them to pay fair market price, but they're not obligated to pay any more. Frankly, I think the two twenty is more than we could get on the open market."

#

Father Frank called Duke Heinz, but only got voice mail. He left a message asking Duke to call him. The priest was relieved that the decision on Syd's property had been made. He had been conflicted about whether to continue the appeal process or not. Norm had eased his mind on that.

The doorbell rang. Duke was standing on the porch. "Are you ready to sign?"

"Almost. Norm Winters, the lawyer for Syd's estate, wants to redraft the contract slightly. Once that's done, we're ready."

The smile on Duke's face sagged into a puzzled frown. "Redraft? What does that mean? I'm not authorized to accept a different contract." He moved closer to the priest, stretching up, trying to tower over him.

Father Frank turned and walked into the living room and sat down in a chair. Duke came in behind him. "Have a seat, Mr. Heinz," said the priest, and he indicated a chair. Duke hesitated a minute, apparently preferring to stand over someone rather than get at his eye level. After a moment, he sat.

"When you were describing 'fee simple' to me, you failed to mention it would also include all mineral rights."

Duke flinched, caught himself, and slid a sickly smile onto his face. "Never even thought about that. Doubt there's any viable minerals under that land anyway. The 'fee simple' just makes things easier."

"Easier for Lockey, maybe. But in Texas, I would certainly expect minerals to be mentioned. You ignored that, or purposely left it out. If you were worried about fences, as you said—"

"And out-buildings."

"And out-buildings, you could have simply added a sentence saying the seller retained all mineral rights." The priest just looked at Duke for several seconds. "We're not willing to give up the minerals, if there are any. The Lockey Corporation needs the surface rights to build a shopping center. They do not need the mineral rights. So, we will take out the 'fee simple' and specify that we are not selling the mineral rights."

Heinz started to get up, but Father Frank motioned him to remain sitting. He dropped back down. "I don't know if Lockey will accept that," Duke said. "The eminent domain order does not say it is limited to surface rights."

"Nor does it say it includes mineral rights."

Duke glared at the priest. "That may change the amount Lockey is willing to pay for the land."

"Does Lockey want to build a shopping center, or drill for oil?"

"Lockey wants to build a shopping center. And they don't want someone coming along and drilling an oil well in the middle of our parking lot."

"Like Lockey itself did in El Molino?"

Heinz aimed a scorching look at the priest. His lips curled and his neck turned red.

"We might be willing to drop the appeal of the eminent domain ruling and sign the contract, slightly revised," said Father Frank. "But don't try to start re-negotiating it. The appeal is still in the clerk's office. And even if we lose the appeal, you lose a lot of time." He tried to look as pleasant and non-threatening as possible. "I'd say, if Lockey doesn't drill, no one will."

Duke looked like a volcano on the verge of erupting. His face developed splotches of red and purple. The veins in his neck stood out like red ridges. He gripped the arms of the chair tightly enough that the priest could see each tendon in Duke's wrists.

Father Frank maintained a neutral expression and said nothing. As the seconds crept by, the priest could tell the big man's breathing was slowing down, could see the muscles in his jaw slowly loosen. But his fingers still dug into the chair.

"Would you like a glass of water?" the priest asked.

"No." Duke's lips barely moved. "When will your lawyer have this revised contract?"

"He could probably have it by tomorrow. The changes are minimal, just what I said."

The big man stood. "I'll pick it up tomorrow and present it to Lockey's lawyers. I'll be back in touch."

"We're in no hurry, Mr. Heinz."

"Winters? Is that the lawyer?"

"Yes."

"You'll be hearing from me." It didn't sound like a friendly farewell. And Duke Heinz stalked out the door.

Chapter 38

Georgia knew it was a risk, but she felt it was one worth taking. She had invited Randall and Abby, and Lance and Judy over to dinner. She had told each couple that the other would also be there. Abby immediately accepted. Judy said she would have to pass it by Lance. When she called back to accept, Georgia could tell Judy was stressed. Probably hadn't been an easy sell to Lance. Nonetheless, they were coming. Perhaps the healing could begin.

Within minutes of Judy's acceptance, the Pine Tree high school called asking Georgia to substitute tomorrow. It would put a squeeze on her preparations, but the school was in a bind. Besides, Georgia could use the money since she wasn't teaching full time this semester. She said yes.

#

Now the question was whom would she invite to be her partner. It might seem strange if she had two couples and just herself. Father Frank would be an excellent choice. He was diplomatic, cheerful, and likely would have some words of wisdom to help bridge the chasm that existed between the brothers-in-law. And with no parish meetings that night he should be available.

"I don't think that's a good idea, Georgia," the priest said when she invited him.

"And why not?" Georgia was surprised. She had assumed he would be glad to come. "You don't like my cooking?"

He laughed. "No, no. That's a good reason for me *to* come, and I'll take a rain check if one is offered. But Lance is not happy with me, to put it mildly. He feels that I, as the representative of the parish, and a trustee for the Prince of Peace Trust, have stolen money that rightly belonged to the family, or more specifically, to Judith and him. He has made it very clear that he intends to fight this and prevent me from benefiting from, in his opinion, my brain-washing of Syd. He was so angry that I was worried he might have a heart attack. I don't think the evening would go well if I were there."

"Oh." A hint of disappointment colored her voice. "When I talked with Lance, I thought there was a reasonable chance of getting those two families back on speaking terms."

"And I think if anybody can, you can. But my being there would sabotage any chance of getting Lance in a friendly mood. Why don't you invite Mike? He would make more sense anyway."

She felt herself bristle at the suggestion. *Like, "Okay, a simple apology makes up for your Neanderthal behavior."* She grumbled, "I'm still mad at that clod."

"Look, I know Mike did something that made you mad. Whatever it was, the Christian thing to do is to forgive and forget—and invite him to dinner."

She couldn't answer his implied question about what had caused the riff. It would be unfair to repeat Mike's remark about her and Father Frank. Mike had retracted it. But it still irritated her that such a thought could even materialize in Mike's mind, even if she knew it was anger, and not logic, that made him say it.

When she didn't answer, Father Frank said, "Give the guy a break. Invite him. It will make me feel better if you do."

#

Against her better judgment, she had invited Mike. If it made *her* feel better, it was short lived.

The evening started out tentatively. Randall and Lance exchanged a few words, Randall nearly cordial, Lance almost civil. Judy and Abby helped Georgia put the finishing touches on the meal, happy to be removed from the two men who were like boxers in the first round of a fifteen-round bout, feeling one another out, trying to decide what would work and what would fail. If Mike were here, maybe he could act as referee.

Mike was the last to arrive. Georgia ushered him into the living room where the other two men were, then she returned to the kitchen. Abby and Judy were laughing as they filled salad bowls.

"What did I miss?" Georgia asked.

"Just remembering a camping trip we took together twenty years ago," said Judy. "The guys took off for about an hour. They came back with two fish about the size of goldfish, and said, 'Here's dinner.'"

"Good thing we weren't very hungry," said Abby.

From the living room, Lance's voice boomed, "That's none of your business."

That was followed by Mike's, "Wrong. It's part of a murder investigation."

All conversation in the kitchen stopped.

"So, investigate away. Just leave me out. I don't have to answer your idiotic questions," bellowed Lance.

"You're not going to be left out. And if you won't answer my questions, we'll bring you down to headquarters and get some answers there."

Georgia threw down a dish towel and raced into the room.

Had it not been so serious, she would have laughed. The two men stood about three feet apart, but were leaning in so that their faces were barely a foot apart. Even at that, their voices were raised so that shoppers in the grocery store two miles away might have heard.

"And just why am I being singled out? I don't see you asking almighty Randall anything. And how about the man who got the most out of Syd's death?"

"Because I saw you angry enough to kill someone. Because—"

Georgia thrust her hands between the two men and shoved Mike back. "Stop it. Right now. Both of you. Stop this nonsense." She looked daggers at Mike, her own anger flashing from her eyes.

Mike moved back and said nothing. Lance also stepped back a foot but said, "Did you invite me over so he could grill me?"

Georgia could hear the anger erupting from Lance. She turned toward Lance. "I did not. I expected both of you to act like adults. Reasonable adults. Silly me." She turned back to Mike. "Would you come into the dining room so I can talk to you?"

Mike gave Lance one last look, more of disdain than anger. Georgia put her hand on his shoulder and guided him toward the dining room.

"Mike, I can't believe you started questioning one of my guests, at a dinner where you are also a guest." Her fury rode just below the surface.

"I just asked him a simple question and he blew up. I think the man has something to hide." His tone was quiet, but not apologetic.

"I don't care if he does or doesn't. You don't investigate my guests at my party." She blew out a short breath. "I don't know why I invited you. I knew it was a bad idea before I called."

Mike started to speak, but Georgia held up her hand. "Let me think a moment." She closed her eyes briefly, her breathing deep. She opened her eyes and looked straight at the detective. "Mike, I'm going to have to ask you to leave. I'm sorry, but I'm trying to get Lance and Randall back on friendly terms and with you here, Lance won't be friendly to anybody. If you don't leave, I expect Lance will grab Judy and storm out the door."

"I'm truly sorry. I won't ask Lance anything. I promise." Now, he sounded apologetic.

She shook her head. "It's too late for that. Please, Mike. Just say goodbye to everybody and go. Call me tomorrow." She laid her hand on his shoulder and guided him toward the living room.

#

Dinner began in a rather subdued fashion. Lance kept his head down, neither looking at nor talking to anyone. Randall joined in the conversation with the three women. The conversation was light and guarded. Georgia felt as if they each considered how Lance would react before uttering a sentence. But dinner finished with no controversy.

Georgia and Abby had cleared plates and were retrieving the dessert from the refrigerator. Even in the kitchen, Georgia could hear Lance.

"Just explain to me why you should have any say over how I spend my money?"

Georgia strained to hear the conversation. Randall apparently said nothing.

This time, Lance was even louder. "I asked you a question."

Randall exhaled loudly, then said, "Syd named me trustee of the account he left in Judith's name. You would have to ask Syd why he did that. I am only following the rules given me."

"Yeah. And enjoying it." Lance's voice was thick with accusation. "Well, I don't like anybody poking their nose into my finances."

"Lance, this is money left to Judith. That doesn't mean you won't benefit from it. But quit telling me it's your money. At least admit Judy has an interest here."

Georgia picked up the dessert and headed back into the dining room. Randall was looking at Judy but she had her eyes closed, her hands folded in her lap. He looked back at Lance. "Certainly if you and Judy want to spend some money for ... " He shrugged. "Whatever, I'm not going to stand in the way."

"Yeah, yeah. I'll just— "

Georgia cut him off. "Lance, this is a social dinner. I want no unpleasantness here. I sent Mike away to avoid any more unpleasantness. Don't start with Randall." She paused a second. "We're to enjoy good food and good fellowship. So, enough of this. If you want to discuss the trust, do it elsewhere." She glared at him.

Lance was grinding his teeth, but made no response. Finally, Judy reached over and patted his hand. "Lance, honey, relax. We're out for a pleasant night visiting. No business here. Georgia has gone to a lot of trouble to cook for us. She's prepared your favorite dessert. Not mine. Not Randall's. Yours. So act civil, and start by apologizing to Georgia."

Georgia could hardly believe her ears. In the twelve years Judy and Lance had been married, Georgia had never heard Judy speak up to Lance before this week. This made twice in four days. She waited for the outburst, knowing that if Lance started in on his wife, she— Georgia—would smash the key lime pie in his face.

For a moment, Lance aimed a scorching look at Judy. Then, it began to fade. Finally, the veins in his neck still throbbing, he turned to Georgia. "I'm sorry I got carried away. I won't talk about the trust again tonight."

"Good," Georgia said. *I doubt you're sorry but at least you didn't bite Judy's head off.* She looked around the table. "Is everybody ready for some fresh key-lime pie?"

#

Georgia started the dishwasher, relieved to be by herself at last. She poured a small glass of white wine, walked out to the patio and sat down.

What an evening. After her last visit with Lance, she'd had high hopes that tonight would result in some real healing between him and Randall.

Then Mike sabotaged the evening. She took a small sip of the wine. *That's not quite fair. He didn't mean to cause a problem. But he should have realized how Lance would react.*

She leaned back and stared off into space. Why did Lance have such a temper? It didn't take much to set it off. He was very angry with Father Frank, as if it was his fault that Syd left a lot to the church. Her eyes came back into focus. Could Lance's anger and temper cause him to …?

She shook her head. She would not go there. Yelling was one thing. Acting violently, particularly attempting to kill someone, was another creature altogether. She fought to keep the thought out of her mind. She refused to allow images of an angry Lance, and Father Frank with the tainted half-and-half to enter her mind at the same time.

What to do about Mike? This whole thing had messed up... What? She was going to say romance. *Is it? Or is it just the excitement over having a special male friend, one who thinks you're special too? It's been four years since Jimmy was killed in Iraq. I've been single for four years. I think I'm ready for ... romance. Is Mike the one? Or is it just nice to be held and feel like you're desirable? I must admit he does make my toes tingle when he kisses me.*

She took another sip of wine. Tomorrow, she would call Mike and apologize. No, not apologize. What she did was the right thing under the circumstances. She would say she was sorry the evening turned out badly. Perhaps they could try again, without Lance in the picture.

And what to do about Lance and Randall? She wasn't likely to get them back at her house for a dinner. Nor did she really want to. The stress had almost done her in. Only now was her stomach untying itself and her blood pressure dropping back in the direction of her normal range. But, she would think of something to try to rebuild the bridge between the two families. *Get serious. The only real task is to improve Lance's attitude.*

Crickets chirped. An owl somewhere in the distance called for his mate. The moon shown as brightly as a half-moon could. The sweet fragrance of her night-blooming jasmine called her to look at the lovely plant, its pale green flowers delicate in the moon light. The wine tasted fruity on her tongue.

But none of it could surmount the overriding fact that to-night had disaster stenciled all over it.

Chapter 39

After mass the next morning, Father Frank called to Georgia as she walked out of the church. Georgia never left without stopping to talk to him, but this morning it looked as if she were trying to sneak out. As he approached her, he noted she did not have her usual bright smile and dancing eyes.

"How did the dinner go last night?"

"Don't ask."

The priest arched his eyebrows and cocked his head to one side. "Oh. Maybe you'd better come over and tell me while I fix breakfast. I'll even offer you a cup of non-poisoned coffee."

#

In the kitchen, Father Frank plugged in the coffee maker and started his breakfast of eggs and toast. "You're sure you won't have anything? This is really good twelve-grain bread. Makes good toast."

"No. And don't even bother trying to cheer me up. Last night was a disaster." She opened the refrigerator and retrieved the half and half. She raised the carton to her nose and sniffed. "At least no one is trying to poison you today." But even with that flippant remark, no soft smile made an appearance.

"Okay. Tell me about last night."

Georgia gave the priest a blow-by-blow description of the disastrous dinner. By the time she finished, Father Frank had consumed his breakfast and was sitting with coffee cup in hand.

"Well, have you called Mike yet and tried to make-up?"

She lifted her nose a bit higher. "I. Have. Not."

Father Frank decided her will was not as definite as the words. "You did invite him, and then kicked him out."

"And he sabotaged the evening."

"Or Lance did."

"I didn't hear the very first of the argument, but I believe Mike asked him a question, like, 'Where were you when Syd was killed?' or something like that. Well, you know that sent Lance into fighting mode. So, I think Mike set it up. Of course, Lance grabbed on and escalated it."

"How did it go after Mike left?"

"Better. But Lance held tightly to his anger." She grinned. "You won't believe this, but Judy actually spoke up to him and settled him down. I almost went into cardiac arrest. And we all held our breath, awaiting a scathing remark." She shook her head. "I was almost blown away when he actually apologized. *Apologized.* At least as close as Lance has ever gotten to an apology. I was so proud of Judy." She took a drink of the coffee and then said, "How did your day go yesterday? Find out anything on Syd's murder?"

Father Frank described his day, including what Mike had told him about Lockey.

"Wow," said Georgia. "Lockey gets an eminent domain ruling for the surface rights, finagles the mineral rights with the 'fee simple' clause, then drills wells."

"So I understand. So they could be planning a similar arrangement here. The best I can figure, it's not actually illegal, but certainly under-handed. Deceitful."

Georgia looked thoughtful. "Do you suppose that's the pattern they follow on all their shopping centers?"

"Don't know about all, but they've certainly done it before. Looks like that's their plan for Pine Tree's shopping mall."

#

After Georgia left, Father Frank drove down to Norm's office to deliver the Lockey Corporation's contract.

"Duke said he'd come by today to pick it up," said Father Frank.

"He'll have to wait a day. I can't get to it today."

"He won't be happy. Just stay out of arm's reach," said the priest. He started to leave, then stopped, hesitated a moment.

"Something else?" asked Norm.

Father Frank turned back to the lawyer. "I have a hypothetical question for you."

"Hypothetical. Gotcha."

"Suppose one hears about an action that is illegal. No, the action is legal. But it may, or may not, be an indication of something illegal going on. Should that person take that information to the police?"

Norm raised both hands to his face, ran his fingers over his eye lids and then down across his cheek. "That's tough. With all the concern over terrorism these days, many things should be reported to the police that wouldn't have been in the past."

"I don't think this has anything to do with terrorism."

"No. I didn't think so. But my point is, people are more inclined to take such information to the police and let them decide what to do with it. Sort of passing the buck, but with good intentions. Legally, you're under no obligation to do so. And even if something bad comes of it, you're not legally responsible. On the other hand, you might feel guilty if someone got killed and you might have prevented it. That would be a heavy load to carry."

"I think the action …" The priest stopped and stared at the floor.

When he didn't continue, Norm said, "Maybe the point here is, there is no real downside to telling the police. That's not like starting a rumor, or some gossip. The police will consider it, perhaps look into it, and if there's nothing to it, they'll drop it and not publish it in the newspaper. But if they find there is a problem, they'll be a step ahead for having the information—if they don't know about it already. And if they do already know it, you've certainly done no harm." He pursed his lips and twisted his head to the side and back. "I see little problem with telling them. Unless you think they might harass some innocent and fragile citizen. And frankly, if you're talking about here, Pine Tree, I can't imagine that scenario."

#

Father Frank walked the two blocks to the police station. The skies had turned grey and he could smell the coming rain. The area needed it. The weather man claimed the Pine Tree area was fully ten inches below average for this time of year. Of course, it had looked and smelled like rain several times in the last month, and only once had it actually rained. Maybe today.

Mostly, he was thinking how he should present his suspicion to Mike. Certainly it was hearsay. Second or third hand. He wasn't sure how one counted these. And did he want to name Georgia as the one who had supplied the information? Or Ruthie? He could honestly say he didn't know her last name.

Even as he entered the detective's office, he still hadn't decided how to offer this information to Mike. Mike was not in his office. Off the hook, the priest thought.

He turned and started down the hall.

"Father Frank. Did you want to see me?" Mike called. "Come on back. I was just getting some coffee."

They settled in the detective's office. Mike took in some caffeine and looked over the rim of the cup at the man in front of him. "What's on your mind?"

The priest squirmed, looking for the most comfortable spot on an uncomfortable chair. He knew part of the discomfort resulted from his uncertainty. Was he was doing the right thing or not? He looked past the detective's shoulder. The far right of the white board still read "attempted murder - cyanide." What he had to say wouldn't help on that case. Would it help on any case?

Mike cleared his throat, a signal that he was waiting.

Father Frank's mind flashed back to his talk with Georgia. Maybe he could just ask about last night. How did the evening go? What was his take on Lance? That would sidestep the cash for Lexus topic. Of course, that could be just as dangerous an area. He focused his eyes on the detective, took a deep breath, and started. "Mike, are you aware of any large cash transactions recently in town?"

"No." Now Mike sat up a little straighter and placed his coffee cup on the left edge of the desk, out of his way. "Should I be?"

"Are you aware of the police being asked to accompany a car dealer employee to the bank?"

Mike shook his head. "No."

"Probably three weeks ago."

The detective looked down at his desk for a moment, perhaps replaying events of the last three weeks. He raised his head. "Yeah. I remember one of the patrolmen saying something about it in the lunch room. From the Toyota dealer, I think. They don't usually get much cash, so they don't have an armored car come by. But that one day, they had a lot of cash, for some reason. Willie, the patrolman who accompanied the woman, said she was nervous, almost giddy."

"But she didn't say why they had a large cash deposit, or how much it was?"

"No."

Father Frank shifted again, still uncomfortable. But there was no backing out now. "Mike, I don't know if this is the right thing for me to be doing or not. And you need to tell me if it isn't. But, it could have a bearing on …" He raised both hands then dropped them back in his lap. "Something."

"Just tell me. I'll decide. And if it isn't something you should pass on to the police, I'll tell you. And no one else."

"The story is that Judge McFatage bought a new Lexus and paid close to $49,000 for it. In hundred dollar bills."

For a moment, Mike said nothing, just slowly nodding. Then, "And how do you know this story?"

"I'd rather not say, unless it's absolutely necessary. I don't want to get anyone in trouble. But can't you check it out? See if it's true? And if it is, what does it mean? Was he just saving up hundred dollar bills?"

"I can ask around. And probably find out. But there's nothing wrong with paying cash for things. I mean, it does seem almost un-American to pay cash. But not illegal."

For a minute, silence filled the room. Finally, Father Frank said, "I wouldn't have mentioned it if the Judge weren't connected, perhaps loosely and distantly, but connected to Syd's murder. I'm not pointing a finger, or suggesting he's guilty of anything."

"That's what you want *me* to do."

Father Frank laughed softly. "Only if he is. There's probably a reasonable explanation for it. But the timing." He sucked air through his teeth. "I'm told he's always driven a much less expensive car. This is a big step up, not a small incremental move up the scale."

"I'll look into it. Probably has nothing to do with Syd's murder. But it could have something to do with the eminent domain ruling."

#

The car in his driveway looked familiar, but Father Frank couldn't place where he'd seen it. One of his parishioners most likely. He pulled his car up beside it, shut off the engine and got out. No one was in the car. The priest looked around. The church parking lot was empty. This seemed like a poor place to park if someone were going to the church or the parish hall.

With a shake of his head, he went into the rectory.

Sitting in the middle of the entryway was a suitcase.

Chapter 40

Father Frank glanced around the living room. No one there. He started down the hall toward his office. As he passed the door to the kitchen, out of the corner of his eye, he saw a pair of legs. Female legs.

He jerked to a stop and took a step back.

"Well, you decided to come home," said the woman sitting at the table with a glass of milk and two cookies in front of her. She wore a hot pink polo shirt and a beige wrap skirt which revealed legs any model would be proud of. Raven eyes sparkled as if sprinkled with diamond dust. She dropped the book she was reading and jumped up. In three quick, almost seductive, steps she was across the room and wrapping her arms around the priest.

"Don't just stand here like a statue, Frank. Give me a hug. I really need a hug."

Father Frank pulled her in close and kissed her cheek. For a minute, the woman kept her arms tight around him, her head nuzzled against his neck and shoulder. He grinned. *She still smells like vanilla.*

Finally, he pulled back a little and said, "What on earth are you doing here? I mean, I'm glad, but I certainly wasn't expecting you."

"I thought I'd come spend a little time here. You're up for a visitor for a few days, aren't you?" Her sensuous mouth curved into a mischievous grin. "Or maybe weeks."

Father Frank stammered, "Well, ah, of course I'd love to have you here." His brow furrowed. He did love Maggie, but this wasn't the best time for her to come. "But why now?"

She gave him a playful punch on the arm. "Can't a girl come visit her brother if she wants to? We haven't seen each other in months." A bit of disappointment colored her voice.

Father Frank led her back into the kitchen and fetched a Dr Pepper for himself. "You're right. It has been too long. And I'm happy to see you. Except."

"What do you mean except?" She sank into a chair.

"Except, this is the first time you've been to Pine Tree and I've been here for three years. So, why now? What's up?"

"Well, certainly not me." She put her head down, her hair, black and shiny as obsidian, spilling on the table. She took several deep breaths, then looked up at her brother. "It's … I … Jeff." Tears formed in the corners of her eyes. "Jeff and I are having troubles."

Father Frank studied his sister for a few moments before speaking. "I take it, since you're here, it's serious. Not a squabble that can be cleared up by someone saying 'I'm sorry'."

"Not likely."

"You want to tell me about it?"

She pressed her lips together and waggled her head. "Yeah. But not today." She wiped her eyes with the back of her hand. "Let me pull my thoughts into some sort of order. I mean, well, I don't know what I mean. But give me a little time." She shook her head. "I haven't told Mom yet. Or Dad."

"Did you tell Jeff?"

"Oh, yes. I told him in spades. He just looked bewildered. He was clueless. But, then, you know Jeff. I had to ask him to marry me. He wanted to, but couldn't make the move."

Father Frank nodded. He did know Jeff, and was surprised when Maggie married him. A nice guy, really nice, with not much initiative. He would never be a leader. But all chiefs and no Indians was a scenario for chaos. The world needed some Jeffs. Maggie did, too. Once. Did she still?

"Okay. We don't have to talk about it tonight. But I do have just one question I'd like to ask. Do you still love him?"

She gave a demure smile. "Not today."

"As they say in press conferences, a follow-up question. Does he still love you?"

She looked away. "I think so. But …" For a moment, the priest thought she might cry. But, quickly she straightened up and said, "Another day. We'll talk about it another day. For now, show me where I can bunk and I'll get my suitcase out of the living room."

"You're planning on staying here?"

"I am. If that's okay with you. I don't really have anywhere else to go. I'm not too flush with cash right now." She looked at him and frowned. "Is that a problem?"

"No. No. Ah, I'll put you up in my room and I can move to the office. The couch in there pulls out into a bed."

"Why don't I take the office? I don't want to displace you. I just thought you might have two bedrooms. I mean, most rectories have two bedrooms. Might have a visiting priest come in to give a retreat or something."

"True. True. But not Prince of Peace. Small parish. Small rectory. No visiting priests. No second bedroom." He laughed. "But, you take the bedroom. I sometimes have people come into the office. Best if we don't have women's things in there."

"But it's okay to have women's things in your bedroom. Hmmm. I'll have to think about that."

"I can see I'd better introduce you to the whole congregation as soon as possible. I'm in enough trouble with the monsignor as it is."

"You want to tell me about it?"

"To quote my older, and wiser, sister, 'Yeah, but not today.'"

#

An hour later, Father Frank said to his sister, "I cook all the time. My fettucine alfredo is pretty good."

Maggie wrinkled her nose. "With parmesan out of a jar. I don't think so. You're putting me up. The least I can do is cook. My chicken casserole is better. Count on it." She tugged him over to a chair. "Sit here and talk to me while I cook."

#

After an excellent meal, they settled in the living room and continued to cover all that had happened to family and mutual friends since they'd last seen each other.

"And what ever happened to Hector?" asked Father Frank. "The last time I heard anything he had gotten a dog the size of an elephant."

Maggie laughed. "It's true. Let me get a drink and I'll give you all the unbelievable details."

She started for the kitchen as the doorbell rang. Father Frank answered it to find W.C. Mayfield standing on the porch.

"Hi. Got a minute?" W.C. asked.

"Sure. Come on in."

W.C. entered the living room just as Maggie came out of the kitchen, gave a little wave, then disappeared down the hall. His eyes opened wide, and his face split into a grin that would have done the Cheshire cat proud. "That's some looker you got there."

The priest held up both hands. "That's my sister. She's visiting for a day or two. We haven't had a chance to visit since I moved to Pine Tree."

"Sister? O-kay. Sure looks luscious to me."

"Don't get any ideas, Mr. Mayfield. She's married."

"Oh, no. No ideas." W.C. laughed. "Well, maybe a few. But, I'm on heart medicine as it is. She'd give me a heart attack faster'n a well blowout."

Father Frank sat in his favorite chair and motioned W.C. to sit down. "What did you want to talk about?"

"Just wanted to know if you did any checking on the Judge and his new car."

Father Frank coughed and cleared his throat, trying to buy some time and figure out where W.C. was going. Technically, the priest had not done any checking. Georgia had. So he could truthfully say, "I have not. Why do you ask?"

"Just wondered. Maybe there was more to the story. I mean, what with all the stuff going on in Pine Tree. That did seem out of the ordinary. Don't you think?"

The priest hunched his shoulders and angled his head. "I haven't been here as long as you have. It's hard for me to know what ordinary is for Pine Tree. I've never met Judge McFatage." He laughed , trying to sound casual. "Myself, I've never bought a car—here or anywhere. The parish Ford was here when I arrived. All I've done is put new tires on it."

Now it was W.C.'s turn to sit in silence. Finally, he said, "Does seem a bit strange, though, don't you think?"

Father Frank waggled his head as he worked on a non-answer. "What one person thinks is strange, someone else thinks is ordinary." *There, that said nothing.*

Another minute passed before W.C. stood up. "Well, I was just passing by and thought I'd see if you found anything. Won't keep you—from your sister."

Father Frank ushered Mayfield to the door, trying to decide if he should reiterate that Maggie *was* his sister. In the end, he decided to ignore W.C.'s insinuation. He said goodbye and closed the door, wondering if he had sounded as phony as W.C. did.

But what was Mayfield's agenda? Somehow, the priest had the feeling that W.C. knew about the $49,000 cash transaction for the Lexus. Had Father Frank played into W.C.'s hands, carried out what the man had in mind from the beginning? On the other hand, W.C. could have made an anonymous call to the police, alerting them or intriguing them to check into the transaction. Maybe he was just interested to see if I could add anything to the story.

Or, he might be more devious.

Chapter 41

Georgia answered the door to find Mike standing on the porch. His mouth drooped, matching the solemn look on his face. For a moment, he reminded her of one of her students, about to say he had not done his homework.

"Georgia, I'm sorry about last night. I know I shouldn't have said anything to Lance at your party. But at the reading of the will, he was so angry and apparently unhappy with how Syd had dispersed his money, and I hadn't had a chance to talk with him."

"And you shouldn't have at my party."

"He doesn't live in Pine Tree and here he was and I just grabbed the chance. But I know I shouldn't have and I apologize."

"I accept your apology. I'm not sure I'm ready to forgive you yet." *Okay, I am. But I don't have to let him off the hook too easily.* She opened the door, and tried to sound a little gruff, "Come on in."

\#

Georgia fixed coffee and they sat on opposite sides of the kitchen table.

"How did the party go after I left?" Mike asked.

"Not well. I mean, the mood was shattered. And Lance's anger cooled some, but never really went away."

Mike managed a hangdog look, then asked, "Is he always that angry? The only two times I've seen him he was mad enough to boil."

"No doubt he could use some anger management classes. My personal opinion is, he feels … what, around Randall. Insignificant; unsuccessful; a failure. I don't know. Somehow, he feels put down by Randall's achievements. That's my assessment. Nobody else has suggested that. Whatever, he's never happy around Randall. And yet, I think on some level he likes Randall." She inclined her head to one side. "Does that make any sense?"

Mike considered that for a moment. "I guess you could like someone, but wish they weren't better than you."

"So when Syd made Randall trustee of Judy's trust, that really tore it."

"Enough to kill someone?"

Georgia flinched. "Lance? Kill somebody? I don't think so." She paused. "I mean, I do think sometimes he loses all control when he's angry. I can see him lashing out, even hitting someone, or breaking something. It's a big step from that to murder."

"Not as big as you think. And it doesn't have to be murder. It could be manslaughter."

She was shaking her head. "Syd's death wasn't manslaughter. It was pre-meditated. And the attempts on Father Frank were planned well in advance."

For several minutes, they sipped their coffee, now getting cold.

Georgia looked up, "The purpose of my party was to try and get Randall and Lance on friendly terms. Judy is Randall's only sibling. Those two families should be close. Right now, I'd settle for friendly. That didn't happen."

"No," Mike agreed. "right now, I'd settle for friendly, too. Any chance I could I take you out to dinner?"

"Not just yet," Georgia said, but her eyes gave away that she had forgiven him. "What did the police find out about the cash the judge used to purchase his Lexus?"

"That's not really my case. I can tell you that it has been verified. McFatage did count out 490 hundred dollar bills to buy a car."

"That's a lot of counting."

Mike laughed. "Indeed it is."

"What are you—okay, not you—what are the police going to do about it?"

The detective drew his lips into a thin, straight line. "I don't know. They don't know. It's not illegal to have a lot of cash. The problem is—"

"Where did it come from?"

"Right."

"But isn't there a problem in any case? If it was a bribe, that's a big problem. If he inherited it, did he pay taxes on it? If it was in cash, I'll bet he didn't." Her eyes grew wide. "Maybe he's been moonlighting. Ushering at the movie. No, a greeter at Walmart. I've got it! I've got it!" She held her hands up and spoke as if using a bullhorn. "Big. Gigantic. Yard sale. One day only. Come early before all the good stuff goes." She looked puzzled. "Why didn't I see the signs for it?"

"He could have saved it up."

Georgia snorted. "Yeah. Right. Little old ladies save coins in a tea pot. The Judge saved hundred dollar bills in his underwear drawer. I don't think so."

"The chief is chewing on it. He doesn't want to make a mistake with a judge, particularly this judge."

"I'm willing to bet 490 pennies it came from the Lockey Corporation."

"How about dinner tomorrow night?"

"You want me to bet dinner? Will you know by then."

"No, I didn't mean a bet. Why don't I take you out to dinner tomorrow night? Forget about McFatage."

"I'm still mad at you." She smiled her innocent smile. "But if you find out where that money came from, I'd probably get over my mad."

Chapter 42

A quick call confirmed that Judge McFatage was in his office. With no plan, Georgia hopped in her car and headed for the Judge's residence.

The single-story, brick house was nestled in against a small hill. *Undistinguished*, Georgia thought. But the property deserved much more praise. Sculpted flower beds blazed with color. A variety of bushes, many of which Georgia was unfamiliar with, were trimmed precisely. Pine trees, and a thick bed of pine needles, graced the hill side. At a quick glance, Georgia could not see a single weed in the manicured lawn.

A gardener meticulously pruned a beauty berry bush, rich with bright purple berries. His muscular arms, strong hands and sun-dried skin attested to many hours of outside work.

"Hi there," she called. "Can I talk to you a minute?"

The man carefully trimmed one more branch, turned to look at Georgia, then laid down his shears and ambled over. He stopped a few feet from her car, but said nothing.

"Are you responsible for this entire beautiful yard?"

"Yes, ma'am. I am."

Georgia got out of her car. "Beautiful. Do you have time to work on my yard?"

He appeared to think about that before answering. "If you need me full-time, I come look at your yard."

Georgia laughed. "Oh, no. I mean, I couldn't afford that. Does that mean you work here full-time?"

"Yes, ma'am. It takes me full-time to keep it looking the way the judge wants it."

She extended her hand. "My name is Georgia."

The man removed a glove and shook her hand. "My name is Abiel.

Abiel Jar."

"Abiel. What an unusual name. I've never heard it before."

The man beamed. "It mean 'My father is the Lord.'"

"What a lovely thought."

"Yes ma'am. I think so." His smile turned to a self-conscious grin. "I also think it mean my mother not know who my father was."

Georgia didn't know what to say. "Well, I think it's a lovely name for a man who makes beauty."

"Thank you."

"You said if I could use you full-time you'd leave here. Why would you leave such a beautiful place?"

Abiel looked down at the ground. He wiggled his jaw. Without looking up, he said, "Judge not always nice."

"Doesn't always treat you nicely?"

The man nodded.

"Does he have many visitors?"

Abiel worked his mouth from side to side for a moment then looked at Georgia. "Only man he call Duke."

That grabbed Georgia's attention. She took a step closer to Abiel, and spoke softly, implying this was something special just between the two of them. "Did you ever hear what the judge and Duke talked about?"

He shook his head. "No. If I am close, Judge yell at me to move. And I move."

Georgia was about to ask another question when Abiel spoke again. "Maybe he not want me to see what the Duke man give him."

A car turned onto the street and headed in their direction. Georgia checked, but couldn't tell if it was a Lexus or not. She took a step back, closer to her car, and half turned as if she were leaving. The car continued on past the judge's house.

She stepped back to Abiel. "You said Duke brought him things. What kind of things?"

"I no see what Judge get. Once is little suitcase, like you take to work."

Little suitcase? Georgia brightened. *A briefcase. Like you could carry $50,000 in.*

"Did you see anything else Duke brought?"

Abiel twisted his mouth, as if that might help him remember. "'One time I see sack." He held his hands close together. "Little sack."

"Did you ever hear anything they said? Anything at all?"

The gardener studied the grass. He reached down and plucked a tiny weed that had the effrontery to enter the golf-green-smooth grass. He stuck it in his pocket. "No. Just one word: 'rats.'"

Georgia flinched. "Rats? You mean, like little grey—."

"Yes. Rats. Like run in house. I never see other people laugh when talk about rats."

"The Judge was laughing?"

"And man. Duke guy give judge little sack. They laugh more. That all I hear. Just one word."

Georgia laughed. "I can't imagine the judge having rats in his house. Did you ever see any rats or mice in his house?"

Abiel's eyes opened wide, and he shook his head. "Oh, never go in house. Judge no like that."

"See any in the garage, or outside?"

Again, he looked down at the grass, studying it in ever-widening circles. Finally, he looked up at Georgia. "No."

Georgia's mind raced, trying to think of anything she might ask this man that might add a little to her slim knowledge of Judge McFatage.

"Did this guy called Duke come by very often?"

"I see him few times. Maybe four, six. I do not know."

Abiel was beginning to look uncomfortable. Perhaps she had kept him from his work too long. Or maybe he was afraid the judge would come home and find him talking to some woman. That would probably worry Abiel, but not as much as it would Georgia.

"Abiel, I really like what you've done with this yard. If I ever win the Lotto and can hire you, I certainly will."

For the first time, the gardener smiled. "I like that."

She said goodbye and headed for her car. She had just started her car when another vehicle turned onto the street. It wasn't a Lexus.

As Georgia pulled out, the other car turned into Judge McFatage's drive. She was at the corner when a large man got out of the car, looked in her direction, then walked over to Abiel. The man wasn't the judge. But he could have been the man Abiel called the Duke.

#

As soon as Georgia got home, she fired up her computer. She didn't check her e-mail. She immediately went on a search engine and looked up "rats." When that didn't help, she tried "how to kill rats." There were tens of thousands of items. She scanned down the page, looking at the brief description opposite each entry.

Near the bottom of the page, her eyes jerked to a stop. There is was. Cyanide.

Chapter 43

When Georgia returned home after Saturday morning mass, there was a car parked in front of her house. She drove into the garage, clicked the door closed, and went in the house. By the time she put her purse down, the front doorbell was ringing.

She opened it to find a large man standing on the porch. A chill ran down her back as she recognized him as the man who had driven into Judge McFatage's drive. How had he discovered who she was?

"Ms. Peitz?"

"Yes."

"I wonder if I might have a word with you."

"I have plans. But if it's quick, okay."

"May I come in?"

"No. Since this will be short, just have your word from there." Georgia sounded confident and in control. Inside, she was quivering.

"You stopped at Judge McFatage's yesterday. Did you have a question for the judge?"

She looked at the man for a moment before answering. "That's Judge McFatage's house?"

"Yes, it is."

"A lovely place. But if I have a question for the Judge, I'll ask him directly."

The man put on an embarrassed smile and tilted his head down a little. "I'm sorry. I guess I didn't put that too well, did I? You were questioning the judge's gardener. What was that about?"

The quivering had settled down a bit, and a quick glance told her the screen door was locked. Not that that would stop anybody, particularly a man his size. But it might give her enough time to slam the heavy wooden door. "Again, I don't know what that has to do with you. Are you here on behalf of the judge?"

"Sort of."

"What does that mean?"

"Well, the Judge, being a state judge, has to be careful. What exactly were you asking the gardener?"

"Frankly, that's none of your business, nor the Judge's either, for that matter. Even a judge can't restrict whom his gardener talks to. Or what about. But to end this waste of time, I was just asking if he had any spare time to do yard work for other people. His work there is beautiful."

The big man nodded slowly and his easy expression morphed into an intimidating, sharp glower. "And why did you ask him about me?"

He didn't frown, but his cold eyes cut like lasers through Georgia's confidence, what was left of it. A chill ran down her back, even as she could feel beads of sweat forming under her arms. She willed herself to maintain a steady gaze at this man. "You're a little self-centered, I'm afraid. I didn't ask him about you. I don't know who you are, what your name is, nor what connection you have with the Judge. So, if you'll excuse me, I've got other things to attend to."

"Before you go, you did ask if I visited the judge often." It was a statement, not a question, and the tone was icy, hard, menacing.

"I did not. As I said, I do not know you. I did ask if the judge has visitors often. The yard, the entire property, is so meticulously kept, I wondered if the judge entertained a lot. What is your name? And what is your connection with the judge?"

"My name is Duke Heinz and I am a friend of the judge. It wouldn't do for a State District Judge to come running around this neighborhood looking for you to ask what you were doing. As I said, a state judge has to be careful of … people who inquire about him." The last few words sounded threatening. If they were meant to frighten, they succeeded.

"So, as a friend, you thought you'd come and ask."

"And find out what your interest in the judge was. And in me."

Fear stabbed her heart like an ice shard. *If he asks about rats, I don't know if I can keep from losing my composure. I need to end this before I fall apart.* "Well, you asked. You, and the Judge, need not fear. The gardener said he had only time for that yard. I will not be stealing him. Good day, Mr. Heinz."

As quickly as possible without looking as panicky as she felt, she closed the door and secured the deadbolt.

She watched out the peep hole until he had driven away. Then, she opened the door and her eyes tracked his car until it had turned the corner and was completely out of sight. She relocked the door and raced into the bathroom. He had unnerved her. He had terrified her.

A few minutes later, she made a cup of coffee, and sat sipping the warm liquid, calming her nerves. As soon as her insides quit shaking, she grabbed her purse and headed to her car.

#

"Georgia," Father Frank said as he opened the door to find her standing on his porch. "You don't look well. Are you all right?"

He opened the door and Georgia walked in and immediately went to the kitchen. "I could use a cup of coffee, or a Coke. Something."

Father Frank turned on the coffee maker. "Tell me what has you so … flustered."

Georgia slumped into one of the wooden kitchen chairs, legs outstretched. Suddenly, her eyes popped into focus.

"What on earth?" She sat up straight, staring out the kitchen door into the laundry room across the hall.

"What?" Father Frank asked.

"Well, it's possible you wear flowery underwear. But I'm pretty sure you don't wear a bra."

Father Frank followed her gaze. "I told Maggie not to leave the laundry room door open."

"I should think not. Some people might begin to wonder—as I am. Who is Maggie?"

"She's my sister, and she's staying here for a few days. You'll have to meet her. Right now, she's at the store, bringing in supplies. She likes to cook."

Georgia sighed. "Good. The way things have been going … Well, glad she's here visiting."

"Yeah. I haven't seen her in a while. This is her first visit to Pine Tree." The priest poured two cups of coffee and sat down. "Okay. What was bothering you when you arrived?"

Georgia tasted her coffee, then set her cup down. "I stopped by Judge McFatage's house yesterday."

Father Frank made a noise opening his mouth. "Why on earth?"

"I don't know. Just wanted to see …" She grinned and wiggled her head. "Whatever I could. The gardener was there. Have you ever seen his house?"

"The gardener's?"

"No, silly. The judge's. The yard is incredible. He has a full-time gardener who keeps the place looking fantastic. Certainly the best looking yard in Pine Tree."

"And?"

A tiny smile played on her lips. "And I talked with him. The gardener. Seems the only person to visit the judge lately is Duke. And Duke brings the judge things, like a brief case." She looked at the priest, with just a hint of a smile.

"Could have been anything."

"Yes, it could. But you thought the same thing I did. It just might match the one full of money that McFatage used to pay for a Lexus." She sipped her coffee and waited. When the priest said nothing, she continued. "He also brought the judge a small package. And the only word Abiel—that's the gardener—the only word he heard was 'rats.'"

Father Frank looked at her with a blank expression on his face. "As in, Oh, rats. I forgot my mother's birthday."

"I came up with a better scenario. As in 'to kill rats.'"

Again, the priest just looked at her, frown lines creasing his forehead.

"You don't know one of the ways they kill rats?" She paused only a beat. "With cyanide."

His stomach tightened and an image of himself about to drink the cyanide-laced coffee filled his brain. After a moment, he said calmly, "Maybe the judge has rats."

"Abiel didn't think so."

"He didn't know anything about cyanide either, did he?"

"He didn't. But what else comes to mind?"

For several moments, neither said anything. "Come on, Georgia. The word 'rats' does not mean he put cyanide in my half-and-half."

"Which one? The judge or the Duke?"

"I can't imagine either one trying to poison someone."

"Poison whom?" Maggie staggered into the room, arms filled with grocery bags. "Here, put this in the freezer while I get some of this stuff in the 'fridge." When her brother took the ice cream, Maggie opened the refrigerator door and started unloading one of the sacks. "Who was trying to poison whom?" She turned to Georgia. "I'm Maggie Deleon, Frank's sister."

"I'm Georgia Peitz. And someone tried to poison your brother. Almost succeeded."

Maggie dropped the groceries on the table, leaving the refrigerator door standing wide open. "Poison Frank?" She looked at her brother. "Are you all right?"

"I'm fine." He pointed to Georgia. "She saved me."

Maggie turned to Georgia. "What … how did it happen?"

Georgia related the events of the poisoned creamer, ending with, "I've just given him two good suspects, but he'd rather think it was Beelzebub."

"Aren't you the one going out with a detective?" Georgia nodded. "Then, give him a call and let him decide. He's more qualified than Frank." She laughed. "My brother couldn't figure out who did it before the Hardy boys did." She picked up the phone and pointed it at Georgia.

"I'm mad at the guy. I can't call him."

"'Course you can. Good way to get over it. This is business, but he comes to see you. You hold all the cards." She grinned. "Here, go ahead."

#

Thirty minutes later, Mike sat in the living room listening to Georgia explain why she was at Judge McFatage's house and what she found out.

"Brief case. Bags. That's not evidence. I can't do anything with that," said Mike. "And why would the judge want to kill Father?"

"Same reason he killed Syd. He took a bribe to make the eminent domain ruling. If Syd, and now Father Frank, takes this appeal to the courts, it might come out that he accepted the bribe."

"If there was a bribe," said the detective.

"Oh, there was a bribe. I can feel it." Georgia gave three quick nods.

Father Frank raised both his hands and spread them apart. "Based on the way the contracts are presented, with the 'fee simple' aspects obscured, I have no reason to believe the Lockey Corporation would be above a bribe." He folded his hands back in his lap. "As much as I'd like not to believe it, I have to agree with Georgia. I think there was a bribe."

Mike started to object, but Georgia waved him off. "Remember, you're the one we had to drag in, kicking and screaming, to get you to accept that Syd was murdered."

"Okay, okay. Suppose I accept your theory. What can I do about it?

I can't haul a Texas District Judge in because someone handed him a briefcase. Maybe it was his, and Heinz was returning it. And the chief would laugh me out of his office if I said Heinz gave him a sack and said 'rats.' That's just too thin. There's nothing I can do."

"Will you promise me," Georgia started in a very sweet tone, "that you will *vigorously* investigate Father Frank's death when one of them kills him?"

"Georgia." Mike's exasperation came through loud and clear.

Maggie stepped in. "If there has already been an attempt on Frank's life, can't you pursue *that* more vigorously and maybe you won't have to investigate his actual death?"

"I am. Believe me, I am."

"I mean, how many places can one go to buy cyanide?" Maggie asked.

Mike stretched his arms above his head and shook his hands, as if to loosen the muscles. "In Pine Tree, maybe no place. But in a larger city, lots of places. It's used for many purposes: various metal processes, even in medicine; rarely for murder."

Maggie scooted out on the edge of her chair and leaned on the table, closer to Mike. "Let's suppose this was not planned too far in advance. Could you check the judge's travel during the last few weeks?"

Georgia's face brightened. "In fact, the will was read only eight days ago."

"Of course, some people seemed to know the church was getting the land before the will was read," offered the priest.

"Okay. Go back ten days," Georgia said.

Mike let out a long breath. "I'll see what I can find. Of course, if Heinz brought him the cyanide, as you suggest, tracking the judge's movements won't do any good."

Georgia's face sagged a bit in disappointment. But Maggie wasn't bothered. "So, check where Duke's been. Is his name really Duke?"

"Short for Durrell, I think," said Mike. "But he is constantly in large cities."

"In the last ten days?"

"Probably Tyler, Longview. Maybe even Dallas."

Maggie remained upbeat. "So, how many places sell cyanide in those cities?"

"I'd bet Duke would know all of them," Georgia said and she

shuddered.

Father Frank looked at her. "Georgia, have you met Duke Heinz?"

She looked down at her hands, tightly clasping one another. "He came by my house today. Just before I came over here."

Mike's head jerked up. "He did *what*?"

"He came by. Asked me about my visit to the judge's house and what the gardener and I talked about."

Mike slammed his hand down on the arm of his chair. "What did he say? Did he threaten you?"

"Not in *what* he said. But in the *way* he said it." She looked over at Maggie. "He gave me the creeps."

"If he comes near you again, you call me. Immediately. If you're at home, don't open the door. Call me. I'll have his a—" He paused only an instant. "I'll haul him down to jail." Mike's face was flushed, his muscles tensed. He sat forward, his back no longer touching the chair. "I mean it. He cannot come in here and harass our citizens."

Father Frank reached a hand over and laid it lightly on Mike's arm. "I think we may have touched a nerve." He laughed. "Both with the judge and with Mike."

"And Heinz," said Mike.

"Okay. So, what can we do about it?" asked Maggie. Her brother started to speak, but Maggie held her hand up. "Somebody tries to poison my favorite brother, I'm in it."

"You've never told me I'm your favorite?"

"You just got that designation today." She gave him a big smile. "So, Mike, what can we do?"

Mike looked down for a moment. "I don't know. We haven't anything to get a warrant to search his house. We just don't have any hard evidence."

For a full minute, nobody said anything. Then, Maggie stood up. "Mike, I'll give you until Monday morning. If you don't have a plan by then, I will." She frowned at him for a few seconds, then turned and marched down the hall.

Quiet settled over the room. Finally, Mike asked, "What does Maggie do when she's not visiting Pine Tree?"

Father Frank chuckled. "She writes murder mysteries."

Chapter 44

Monday morning, Maggie called Detective Mike Oakley.

"Well, have you come up with a plan?"

Mike hemmed and hawed, but finally had to admit that he had not. "We're going to keep a close watch on Heinz and the judge and see if they tip their hand."

"That's a great plan. Let's do nothing and see if the perp will come in and confess. You sound just like the Dallas police."

"We just don't have enough evidence to do much."

"Then you have to be creative. Here's my plan."

She talked for about five minutes, and ended by saying, "Are you in on this or not? Can I count on you, or shall I just pull up in front of the police station and hope there's a cop around?"

Her fingernail tapped on the phone as she waited.

"Okay. I'll be available. But I don't like it."

"It's not entrapment, if that's what you're worried about."

"It isn't. But I have this thing about involving civilians in police work. What if something goes wrong? What if my car stops running? What if I have an emergency call?"

"What if we have a tornado? Then I'm on my own. And it's not like I'll be in a dark cave or anything. My only worry about you not being there is, I can't arrest him."

Maggie hung up the phone and looked out the window.

"Damn." She turned to see her brother enter the room. "Oops. Sorry Frank."

"What's the problem?"

"It's started raining."

"Rain is good."

"Not when you want to be outside."

#

Maggie sat in her car, waiting. The rain had stopped several hours ago, the sun was shining, and most important of all, Abiel was working in Judge McFatage's yard. She checked her watch for the tenth time in the last ten minutes. According to her information, the Judge should be home soon. She got out of the car and approached the gardener.

The earlier rain had made the grass a vivid, exaggerated green, like a beginning artist might paint. And the humid air heightened the sweet smell of the many fragrant flowers in the Judge's yard. *They have such brilliant colors*, Maggie thought. *Now it's time for some people to show their true colors.*

She had no trouble engaging Abiel in conversation. Maggie was good at keeping a conversation going. She talked about the flowers, the grass, the bushes, the trees. She asked if they had any trouble with varmints or rats. Abiel said they had some moles earlier, but he had put out mole poison and now they had no moles. Rats? No, he hadn't seen any. No, he didn't know if the Judge had any in the house.

She checked her watch again. Where was he?

Maggie wanted to know how he kept everything so clean and neat under the tall southern Pines. She had just started on foundation plantings when the champagne-colored Lexus turned into the drive. The Judge parked in the garage and came to the curb where Maggie was talking with Abiel.

"Can I help you?" he asked Maggie. The judge was round, soft, and probably fifty pounds overweight.

"Oh, hello. I was just admiring what a lovely yard you have and asking your gardener how he kept it so nice."

The judge looked skeptical and started to speak, but Maggie continued. "Your gardener didn't know, but maybe you can tell me. How do you kill rats? I mean I've tried traps and they don't work. Is there some poison you can use?" She opened her dark, sparkling eyes wide, fluttered her eyelashes, and just stared at the Judge.

When she said the word "poison" the Judge's mouth gaped and he quickly snapped it shut. For a moment, he simply stared at her, then slowly said, "I don't have rats and I have no knowledge of poisons. I would appreciate it if you would leave my property."

Eyes still wide with innocence, and assuming the role of an empty headed beauty, she said, "Oh, but I'm in the street. I wouldn't think of standing on such beautiful grass."

"Then leave my gardener alone. He has work to do."

Abiel shook his head. "No, Mr. Judge. I finish for today. I go now."

"Then go." He turned to the woman. "And if you don't leave, I'll call the police."

She raised her chin and looked totally puzzled. "Now why would you do that?"

"Because I'm a judge and I can get one out here in five minutes. So, leave."

Still playing clueless, Maggie looked at the gardener and said, "Abiel, step out here in the street so we can talk and not bother the Judge."

"Abiel, if you want to keep your job, and stay out of jail, you'd better quit talking to this woman and leave. Right now." With that, the Judge turned and stalked into his house.

Maggie took her time leaving, saying goodbye to Abiel, walking in the street to look at the yards on either side. After the Judge's beautifully manicured yard, the others looked faded, almost sad. But she inspected them. Finally, she got in her car, started it, but had to find the right radio station, get the seat belt just right.

Had she miscalculated? Or was she just impatient? She grinned. *Certainly I'm impatient.* She checked her makeup, rummaged through her purse and found some sunglasses. Getting them set just right took a few minutes and numerous checks in the mirror. Reluctantly she pulled her Chevy away from the curb, turned around in the Judge's driveway, and slowly moved out.

When she saw the midnight blue Buick round the corner, she speeded up slightly and began her odyssey.

Two blocks down, she turned left onto Madison Street. The Buick turned left also. Four blocks farther, she turned right onto Wilson Road. Fifteen seconds later, a midnight blue Buick made the same turn. After she passed the vacant lot on Jefferson, she made four successive right turns until she was back by the vacant lot on Jefferson, then drove around the block once more.

She slowed, pulled to the curb and got out. She began to walk into the vacant lot. Out of the corner of her eyes, she saw the midnight blue Buick pull to the curb behind her car. Duke Heinz got out and approached her as she studied a sign saying the lot was for sale.

"What are you doing here?" he asked with implied authority.

Maggie turned and looked at the man. She removed her sunglasses and stared at him, but made no reply.

"What are you doing here?" His tone was demanding.

"Why, I'm reading this 'For Sale' sign. Wasn't that pretty obvious?"

"And just why are you reading the sign?"

Maggie looked at the man, then laughed. "Now that's a silly question. Why on earth would a person be reading a 'For Sale' sign?"

"Don't get smart with me. Why were you at the Judge's house today?" His voice grew louder with each question, or perhaps with each non-answer, he got.

"My mommy always told me to be smart." She gave a tinkling laugh. "Course, I never managed to do that very well." She tilted her head and deep furrows creased her forehead. "What judge is that?"

"You know damn well what judge I'm talking about." He took a step closer and leaned in so his face was just inches from Maggie's. "I suggest you answer my questions before I get rough." His face was flushed, and his voice had taken on a threatening timbre.

Now, her smile vanished and fear took over. She cowered and her eyes became saucers. She started backing away. "Officer, officer. Help!" she called. "Please." Her voice trembled and tears formed in her eyes.

Duke did not turn until a calm, cold, voice spoke behind him. "Sir, please step away from the woman, and put your hands up where I can see them." Mike stood about ten feet behind Duke, his hand resting on the butt of his gun.

Heinz swiveled slightly.

"Put your hands up, sir." Mike sounded deadly serious.

Duke raised his hands and a big smile materialized on his face. "There's no problem here, officer. I was just asking the lady a few questions." He ducked his head some and slumped a little, and Maggie wondered if he was trying to minimize his size.

"Please step away from the woman."

When Duke stepped back, Mike continued, "Now, please turn around and put your hands behind your back."

The smile instantly turned into a frown. "What? What's this about? I was just asking the lady a few questions. I've done nothing wrong."

"Just put your hands behind your back." Mike lifted his gun slightly, not clearing the holster, but showing clearly that it was ready to come out.

Duke turned around. "This is some sort of a mistake. You don't want this on your record."

Mike snapped handcuffs on Duke's wrists. "Ma'am, do you know this man?"

"No, sir. I've never seen him before."

"Did you feel threatened by him?"

Maggie's lower lip began to quiver. "Yes, sir. He was scary."

"You'll need to come down to the police headquarters and fill out a complaint."

She nodded.

Mike put his hands on Duke's shoulder and guided him toward the police car. "Your problem is, I watched you follow her. She made two complete circles around this block, and you stayed right with her. It looks like stalking to me. And from what I could hear as I approached, you were threatening her."

Duke shook his head. "I wasn't stalking her. I don't even know her."

Mike opened the back door to the police cruiser and put his hand on Duke's head to insure the tall man did not hit his head on the door frame. "Not knowing her is not a defense for stalking and harassing. You have the right to remain silent ..."

#

Based on complaints from Georgia and Maggie that Duke Heinz had harassed them, Mike booked Duke into the Pine Tree jail. No doubt Duke's lawyer would have him out quickly. Duke demanded that the police go back and lock the Buick. He said he had been taken into custody—unlawfully, he added—so fast, he was not given time to lock his car. Mike said no request to lock the car had been made at the time of the arrest, but he would take care of that immediately.

Mike returned to the vacant lot and parked behind the blue Buick. Maggie was standing on the sidewalk, a huge grin on her face.

Mike got out and held up his hand. "Don't tell me what you did."

"I won't. But I have the names of several businesses we can start with."

"You know that anything you found cannot be used in a court of law."

"That I do. You'd be amazed how much I know about such things. Have to do lots of research when writing a book. But, what I'm looking for—and maybe found—is just a place to start searching for the evidence. If we're lucky, one of these places will provide us with what we need. And in a very legal way."

"But, it'll still be tainted."

"No. The evidence we hope to find will not be tainted. This just shortens our work. Instead of calling a hundred stores, we may need to call only a few. If we find the right one after five calls instead of seventy-five calls, we're just lucky. You can say in all truthfulness in court, that you started looking for the source of the cyanide and after so many calls, you found it."

Mike shook his head as he locked the Buick, got back in his patrol car and left.

A plan was already forming in Maggie's mind on how to proceed.

Chapter 45

"Okay," said Maggie. "We need to hit on both fronts as quickly as possible. The judge has to have a housekeeper. Anybody know who that might be?"

Georgia looked at Father Frank, who shook his head.

Maggie had prepared tarragon chicken breasts and invited Georgia over for dinner with her and Father Frank. Now, they sat in the living room of the rectory, each with a bowl of Blue Bell Moolennium ice cream, and tried to decide on a plan to find the person who attempted to poison the priest. Their two prime suspects were Judge McFatage, a Texas State District Judge, and Duke Heinz, a land man for the Lockey Corporation.

Georgia said, "I might be able to find out, but it will probably take some time."

"We need to move fast, so let's put that on the back burner. When do they pick up garbage at the Judge's house?"

"I don't know, but I can find out," said Father Frank.

When he didn't move, Maggie said, "How about now?"

The priest got up and went into his office. In three minutes he was back.

"Tomorrow morning. They should probably be at the Judge's house between 9 and 9:30." He plopped back down in his chair and reached for his ice cream. "When my sister asks, I deliver."

"Good. How'd you do it?" asked Maggie.

"Got a parishioner who lives only a few houses away," he said with a smug grin on his face.

"Next, we need to have somebody from the Pine Tree Police Department ready to go through the trash," said Maggie.

"I'll take care of that," said Georgia.

"I don't know," said Father Frank, still grinning. "You've been so tough on Mike lately, he may just tell you to go fly a kite."

"He might," Georgia said. "And that will make it take a bit more time. But, he'll be there."

"Great. I'll be on the phone, tracking down some place that sells cyanide," Maggie said as she spooned ice cream into her mouth.

"And what am I to do?" asked the priest.

In unison, the two women said, "Pray."

"About anything in particular?"

Georgia spoke up, "Pray that our comments about poison and rats have gotten back to the Judge."

"And that he hasn't already disposed of the evidence," said Maggie.

"If he ever had any," said Father Frank.

"If Duke brought the cyanide to Judge Fat," Georgia said, "then Duke didn't put it in your half-and-half. There would have been no reason to bring it to the Judge."

Maggie put her bowl down. "Come on, Frank. If the Judge isn't guilty, why is he so nervous about Georgia or me talking to his gardener? Why would he send henchman Duke to intimidate us?"

"Could be just the bribe," said the priest.

Maggie threw up a hand. Her voice was submissive. "Okay. I'm willing to give up on both the Judge and the Duke."

Georgia looked puzzled.

Father Frank looked amused. "You gave up too easily, sister dear. What are you going to drop on us now?"

"I'll give up on those two, *if*..." Maggie raised her eyebrows, and gave her brother a sweet smile. "You have another candidate."

"What other possibilities can you come up with?" Georgia asked Father Frank.

"Lance."

"Can't believe that. And no motive on you, Father," Georgia said. "How about Carl Douglas?"

Father Frank clicked his teeth. "Certainly has enough anger. But I don't think he has the wherewithal. There's W.C. Mayfield."

Georgia thought for a moment. "Can't see any motive for poisoning you. And he did say he was a friend of Syd's and they played golf together. How about the Lockey Corporation. Not Duke, but someone else?"

Father Frank took a deep breath. "I guess the same motive would apply there as to Duke. But we're really at a loss there. We don't know a single name connected with them except Duke Heinz."

"And they've got Duke here. Why not use him?" said Georgia.

"Same thing Frank just pointed out," said Maggie. "You know Duke and you don't know some Mr. X. They send Mr. X, you're not going to suspect him because you don't know him, not even a name, and don't know he's connected with Lockey."

Georgia laughed. "I don't guess Bud Wilcox would have the gumption to do anything."

"No, I don't think so," said the priest.

"Then, unless we can think of a plan to get into the Lockey inner circles, it sounds to me like it's back to Duke and the Judge," said Maggie.

#

Mike and Detective Harry Sacs sat in a pickup just down from the driveway of Judge McFatage.

"We're really going to go through his garbage?" asked Harry, for the third time.

Mike ignored the question and looked up at the gathering clouds. "Be glad it isn't raining. And hope it doesn't start before we finish sorting through the trash."

Mike had stopped the garbage truck a couple of blocks away and handed the men on it several large, heavy-duty contractor bags. He showed them his shield and told them exactly what he wanted and how he wanted it handled. They'd looked at him like maybe he had been dropped on his head at an early age, but agreed to follow his instructions.

Mike had positioned the pickup where both he and Harry could see the garbage in front of the Judge's house. They could watch the garbage men pick up the bags and see the bags until they were deposited in the back of Mike's pickup. Both Mike and Harry needed to be able to say without a doubt that the garbage they inspected had come from the Judge's house. No missing time when a bag might have been exchanged for someone else's trash.

#

"I got rats in my barn. Have you got any poison that will kill them?"

Georgia and Maggie had been on the phone for half an hour, running down all the stores and phone numbers Maggie had found in Duke's car.

Maggie listened for a few moments. "Naw. I've tried that stuff. Got any cyanide?"

She listened again.

"And you think this other stuff will work? Okay, maybe I'll give it a try again. But it didn't work last time." She paused only a second. "You know of anybody who still carries cyanide?"

She hung up and scratched another name off their list. Next, she consulted her paper, and then the Internet to find a phone number. She dialed again.

"Want me to take the next call?" asked Georgia.

"Naw. But I sure would like some coffee. If you—Hello, I've got a rat problem in one of my barns." Maggie waved Georgia toward the kitchen and then continued her call.

#

The two detectives stood at the back of the pickup, now parked next to a large dumpster behind the police department. The garbage truck had stopped, and two of the men had quickly loaded three bags into the bed of Mike's pickup. As soon as the garbage truck drove on, the pickup moved out, slowly, hoping to draw little attention.

Now, the two detectives from the police department sorted through a pile of garbage.

"How are we ever going to recognize a bitter almond smell with all this other smelly stuff?" Harry grumbled.

"That's why you've got to get your nose up close to each sample. You can't hold it out at arm's length and expect to tell. It will be a faint smell," said Mike.

"I'm not getting my nose too close to this stuff. It's bad enough to pick it up."

"What a pansy. Look at it this way. If we get to the end and haven't found it, we'll just have to go through it again."

"No way. What if there isn't any in here at all? Huh? We're just gonna keep going through it 'till it gets time for our pension?"

Mike laughed. "Could be. So, let's get it right the first time. If we check every little piece carefully, maybe we won't have to go through it but once."

Harry, a detective for less than two months, was smelling a mildewed head of lettuce. "Pay attention," said Mike. "We're looking for a container. You don't have to smell all the rotten food. Just containers."

"Gotcha."

"Hey, this isn't as bad as last month when I had to help you scrape a dead dog out of the mud and gravel because its owner thought it had been poisoned *before* it was run over by a cattle truck. Talk about a bad smell."

Harry laughed. "Yeah. That was bad."

Mike reached for the third bag. It was much smaller than the others. He was beginning to believe they wouldn't find anything.

Of course, if—and it was a big if—the Judge did put the cyanide in Father Frank's half-and-half, that was nearly a week ago. Surely he would have disposed of the container, and any cyanide left over, by now. What would he do with it? Flush it down the toilet? Maybe. And the container? In the garbage. And this was the first pickup since then. It sounded good back in the office.

Mike glanced over at the young detective. He seemed to be hesitating over a small container. He smelled it and started to throw it away. Then he smelled it again. Now, he was taking a third sniff of it.

"What've you got?" Mike asked.

"Judge live alone?"

"Yeah. Why?"

"Take a whiff. This is a women's perfume. No musky, leathery man's stuff." He handed the bottle to Mike.

He sniffed. "You're right about that. But my understanding is the Judge does live alone. Could have had a female visitor." He tossed the bottle into the sack. "And how do you know about men's fragrances? Don't tell me you put that stuff on after you leave work."

"No. No." The young man was definitely on the defensive. "I don't use that stuff. But I know some guys who do. They claim the girls like it. But I ain't into that."

Mike laughed. "Me neither."

Harry handed Mike another container. "Check this out."

Mike took it. "What's this? Women's powder."

"I don't think so."

Mike lifted the container and smelled. He moved the box closer.

It was faint. But amidst all the different odors arising from the back of the truck, up close the container gave off just a hint of bitter almond.

"Great work. We've done it. You've done it." Mike gave his partner a high-five. Then, he carefully put the container in a clear plastic evidence bag, pulled out a marker pen, labeled the bag and signed it.

"Here, put your John Henry on this. We don't want any mistakes on this."

Harry signed the bag. "You forgot the time and date."

"Good point. Put it on. And I owe you a drink for catching that—and for finding the container."

"If this becomes the critical piece of evidence, you owe me a whole dinner."

Mike put the evidence bag in the front of the truck and then helped gather the rest of the garbage and put it in the dumpster.

#

Maggie hung up the phone and crossed off the last name on the page. "Okay. That's the end of our list. We've got three places Mike can survey. Of course, he needs to check several others. Don't want the defense lawyer to wonder why he drove straight to the right store."

"I hope he's got a good picture of Duke," Georgia said. "And maybe one of the Judge, too."

"At the least, they've got a mug shot of Duke. And I can't imagine the Judge would do that himself."

"Doesn't make sense. But crooks do stupid things all the time."

Georgia laughed. "Yeah. Like paying for a Lexus with hundred dollar bills."

Georgia jumped as the phone rang. "Prince of Peace. How may we help you?"

"By being nice to your local policemen."

"That may be beyond our capabilities," Georgia said, grinning. "It's Mike," she whispered to Maggie. She returned to the phone. "However, we do have some good locations for you to check out in Longview." She was feeling pretty smug.

"That's good. Really good. Now, about dinner."

Georgia let out a little cry. "You traced the money."

"No. But maybe better. I found a container in the Judge's garbage. It had a slight smell of bitter almonds."

"Wow. Fantastic."

"It's already gone to the police lab for testing."

"Double wow." She relayed the information to Maggie.

"Dinner?"

"I'll be ready at seven."

Chapter 46

"Tell me again, where did we get the list?"

Mike drove down highway 300, heading for Longview. Tall pine trees flanked the wide, four-lane highway and for most of the trip between Gilmer and Longview, no houses could be seen from the road. It was a beautiful drive. However, the sun had yet to make an appearance today, and didn't look like it would. The clouds were beginning to give up their moisture and he turned his wipers to intermittent.

Father Frank held a list of businesses and their addresses on a clipboard in his lap. "These are the stores in Longview that sell cyanide as a rat poison. Actually, they say 'rodent control.' Maggie and Georgia compiled it this morning, while you were playing in the garbage."

Mike turned his head and gave the priest a disgusted look. "You can't imagine what nasty trash the Judge has. He sits up there on the bench in his robes and everybody thinks he's so neat and clean. If they only knew about his garbage."

"You brought the pictures of the Judge and Duke?"

The detective patted his left breast pocket. "Right here."

They rode in silence for a few minutes.

"You look like you're solving a difficult math problem," said Father Frank.

"Not math. I'm just thinking how the DA is going to see all this. 'Circumstantial,' that's what he will say."

"But, if you found a package that had contained cyanide in his garbage, and we get lucky and find a supplier, that ought to be pretty clear. A direct trail."

"A direct trail to his house. But not to *your* house," said the detective.

"But why would he have cyanide? He told Georgia he did not have rats." The priest looked puzzled.

"That's what he told Georgia. He might tell the court he did have rats. He just didn't want to share that with some nosy woman. Or he has other rodents. We can't place him at your house. And we haven't got a rock-solid motive."

"There's fear that if I kept the appeal going, his acceptance of a bribe would come out. Same motive as for killing Syd."

"*If* there was a bribe. We haven't proven that either. Yet."

"So, where did the money come from?"

"Maybe he got lucky at a casino." Mike hunched his shoulders. "Maybe out of his bank account and he just wanted to play the big man, spread cash on the car dealer's desk"

"Maybe."

"Or he had a nice, old aunt who saved for forty years. Then, on her deathbed, she handed the Judge the key to her safe deposit box. Actually, Harry's checking on dead relatives and big Shreveport payouts today." Mike signaled to turn off the highway. "You see, lots of evidence, but no irrefutable piece of evidence." Mike looked at the priest. "What was the number?"

"4975."

The detective scanned the buildings, looking for the correct number. "And the DA will not take a Texas District Judge into court, or even make an arrest, without something a lot stronger than what we have. Even if some sales clerk says, 'Oh, yes. I remember Judge McFatage coming in and buying some cyanide.'"

Father Frank let out a long breath and squirmed in his seat. *We aren't going to get a smoking gun and we don't have a bloody fingerprint.*

#

At the fourth store, Mike once again asked his questions. This time the clerk, a man probably in his early sixties, said he had sold some to a man with a rat problem last week. Early last week.

"To a man named Duke Heinz?" Mike asked.

"Don't know. Let me look."

The man disappeared for several minutes. When he returned he said, "Thought so. Last Monday. Bought half a pound. Said his name was Don Smith." He pushed his glasses up on his nose and checked the paper in his hand. "Said he lived out on County Road 9218. Thought that was strange. Ain't no houses on 9218. But maybe that's where his mailbox is. Anyway, here it is, half pound, last Tuesday, $8.75."

Mike pulled out a picture of Duke and showed it to the man.

Father Frank glanced at the photo. Duke looked sharp in his pinstriped suit. He didn't look like a killer. But the picture didn't capture the hardness in Duke's eyes.

"No. I don't think that's him."

The detective showed the clerk a picture of Judge McFatage. The clerk shook his head again.

Mike thanked the man and they started out the door.

"Hold it," said Father Frank. He picked up a sales flier that had a picture of blue coveralls for sale. The priest tore out one of the pictures. "Let me have Duke's picture."

Mike handed over the picture without a word. Father Frank maneuvered the two pictures until he had Duke's head atop the coveralls. He clamped them together with his thumb and forefinger and walked back to the counter. "Would you take a close look at *this* man? Was he the one who bought the cyanide?"

The clerk studied the picture. "I think so." He adjusted his glasses and moved his head closer to the pictures. "Yeah, that's the man."

"Are you sure?" asked Mike, who had followed Father Frank back to the counter.

The clerk took another look. "Yeah, that's the man."

"Can I have that slip?" asked Mike.

The clerk nodded. "Let me make a copy for our records," he said, and disappeared into the office.

#

In the car, as they headed back to Pine Tree, Mike shook his head and chuckled. "Just goes to show you. People put you in categories by your clothes. Duke with a coat and tie on just didn't look like the type that would buy cyanide to kill rats in his barn. Put coveralls on him and, 'Yep. That's the man.'"

"So, we're filling in the trail," said the priest with a grin on his face.

"But it still stops at the Judge's house, not your house."

Chapter 47

Maggie had fixed one of her favorite dishes for dinner and had invited Georgia and Mike to join her and Frank.

"Fabulous soup, Maggie. What is it?" asked Georgia.

"It's a curried zucchini. The nice thing about it is, you can prepare it the day before, or in the morning. Get that part of the dinner out of the way before you even begin to think about cooking the rest of it."

"Well, it's delicious," said Mike. "Probably helps that I can't find any zucchini. Can't find anything to identify. But it's great. And I don't usually like cold soup."

"Since the telephone always rings in the middle of my meal," said Father Frank with a chuckle, "I usually end up with cold soup."

The aroma of the main dish preceded Maggie into the room. A sweet, tangy smell tickled the noses of those waiting in the dining room. The large platter Maggie carried contained a work of art. A dark red glaze covered a golden brown pork roast and trickled down to mingle with large pecan halves. It looked like a dark lake with a mountain jutting up in the middle. Four lines of asparagus spears curved gracefully around the outside. White peaks of mashed potatoes, with pools of melted butter, filled a side dish.

"And what is this beautiful concoction called?" Georgia asked.

"It's called Earlene's Special Pork Roast," answered Maggie.

"And who's Earlene?" asked Mike.

"A friend. And a very good cook."

Accolades for the dinner dominated the meal and Maggie beamed at her guests.

When they had finished the main course, Georgia said, "That entrée was so good, I don't think I need any dessert."

Me neither," agreed Father Frank.

"I bet I can change your mind," said Maggie.

Maggie disappeared into the kitchen and a minute later returned with a tray containing four small bowls filled with strawberries, covered in a honey-colored sauce.

"Heavenly," said Father Frank after his first bite.

"What is this?" asked Mike.

"Fantastic, that's what it is," Georgia said.

"Thank you. And Charlton Heston thanks you also," said Maggie.

"Charlton Heston?" said Mike.

"Another close friend of yours?" asked Georgia, a grin on her face.

"I'm told this was his favorite dessert when dining at the Beverly Hills Hilton," said Maggie, with just a touch of satisfaction.

#

They had just adjourned to the living room when the phone rang.

"Just let it go to the answering machine," said Maggie. "It's probably Duke wanting to know if you've signed away your mineral rights yet."

Father Frank chuckled, but hopped up and answered the phone. "Prince of Peace. How may we help you?"

"You can start by explaining to me why you have a woman staying at the rectory. A very attractive, young woman."

Father Frank's mind bounced between anger and amusement.

"Well?"

"Would it be better if she were homely?" asked the priest with some annoyance.

"Why is she there?"

"Let me guess. You got another anonymous phone call."

"Answer my question?" The monsignor's indignation came through as clearly as if he had been standing, red-faced, in front of Father Frank.

"Monsignor Decker, you need to either start ignoring anonymous phone calls, or give them some serious thought before you start accusing people."

"I did not accuse you. I asked you for an explanation."

"So you did—in as angry a tone as I've ever heard addressed to me." By now, Father Frank's temperature had risen. He breathed deeply, trying to calm his anger. *Probably Carl's tone was worse. Or Duke's.* "The caller was right. I do have a very attractive young woman staying at the rectory right now. However, he failed to mention that this very attractive young woman is my sister. And before you say anything else, I have every right to have members of my family stay with me, whether they are female or male."

From the living room, Father Frank heard a cell phone ring, then heard Mike's voice answering it. The priest turned his attention back to his own telephone conversation. All he could hear was a slight cough from the monsignor.

When the monsignor didn't say anything, Father Frank said, "And, Monsignor Decker, you'll be happy to know that I introduced my attractive, and young, sister to the entire congregation at Sunday services."

The older man recovered somewhat. "But, to those outside your flock, it looks bad."

"I don't know how many outside my flock keep tabs on who is in the rectory. But if you would like, I'll put an ad in the local newspaper explaining to the entire town that the very attractive young woman is my sister, visiting for a few days."

"Well," the monsignor started hesitantly. "Well, that won't be necessary. But remember, appearances are very important. How long will she be there?"

"As long as she needs to, or wants to. Now, I have guests. If you have any other questions, please call tomorrow."

Father Frank hung up and returned to the living room just as the detective snapped his cell phone closed.

"Good news from the techs. They recovered a partial print on the two-by-four,"—he nodded toward the priest— "that you deigned to provide to the police. What is even more incredible, they've matched it—as well as you can with a partial, but a likely match nonetheless—to a person who lives in the area and is 'known to the police,' as we would say."

"Duke's?" asked Georgia.

"Lance's?" said Father Frank, the irritating call from the monsignor forgotten.

"The Judge's?" asked Maggie.

"Wrong, wrong and wrong," said Mike, grinning at the three.

"Okay," Georgia said. "Who is it?"

"Actually, nobody you'd know. We call him Shakey. And I'm pretty sure he has no connection with Father Frank. So, I can only imagine someone hired him. Unless it was simply a mugging that didn't work."

"Yeah, like mugging is a big problem in Pine Tree," Georgia said.

"And coming just two days before the cyanide attack, that would be quite a coincidence," said the priest.

"My thoughts exactly." Mike said. He turned to Maggie. "That was a great meal. If you stay here very long, Father Frank's going to put on so much weight I'll be able to outrun him. Something I've yet to do. I really do hate to leave, but this is the best time to find Shakey. I'm going to meet Harry at headquarters and go check out the seedier side of Pine Tree."

Chapter 48

Mike sat in a chair across the table from Shakey. Harry leaned against the wall behind the vagrant. "So, why did you attack Father Frank Sunday before last, a little after ten-thirty?"

Shakey, no novice to interrogation, shook his head. "Don't know what you're talking over. Don't know no Father Frank."

Mike just smiled at the man. "Trying to play dumb. And you're good at it. But, the problem is, we've got you this time. You didn't know we could take fingerprints off a piece of lumber, did you? Well, they can and did. Now, you want to start over. Why did you attack the priest?"

"Ain't talking to you. Don't know nothing 'bout no priest." Shakey's words were firm, but he began to fidget, moving his hands to his lap, then back on the table.

"We can play this game as long as you like. We can start each morning with it. Who knows, maybe for weeks."

"You can't keep me here that long. Ain't done nothing."

"I can and will. You'll love the jail food. And the nice guys there to keep you company."

"You ain't scaring me."

Harry moved off the wall and put his hands on Shakey's shoulders and began to squeeze, his thumb just behind the collar bone, his fingers on Shakey's back. "Mike might not mind, but I do. And I'm going to make sure that each day gets harder and harder for you." One of Harry's hands slipped off Shakey's shoulder and on to his neck. "And this will give me a chance to exercise my hands, strengthen them, you know?"

Shakey wiggled and tried to get out of Harry's grip. "Hey, cut it out. I know my rights. You ain't allowed to hurt me."

"You're right. You're right. So, tell me when this begins to hurt."

"Already does. Cut it out."

"Just let me know."

"I'm telling you now."

"I'll sure stop before I hurt you," said Harry.

"At least before we take you to the hospital," offered Mike.

"I wanna call my lawyer," yelled Shakey.

"Okay. Who is your lawyer?"

"I don't gotta tell you. Just take me to the phone."

"Since I don't think you have a lawyer," said Harry, still squeezing Shakey's shoulder and neck, "I'm thinking you're going to call and try to get someone to break you out of jail. Frankly, I'm a little scared."

"I ain't gonna do that. I'm calling a lawyer."

"Oh," said Mike. "You're going to call Judge McFatage."

"Bingo," said Shakey. "And he'll have your badge for treating me bad."

"Okay. You get to make a call. And you can call the Judge, if that's what you want."

They led Shakey to a public telephone and managed to see what number he punched. Sure enough, it was the residence of Judge Edward McFatage. The conversation was short and apparently did not go as Shakey expected. At one point, the prisoner raised his voice saying, "How long?" And another time, "I want more?"

Back in the interrogation room, Mike again sat opposite Shakey. "So, that didn't go too well. You're going to sit in jail awhile."

"Fingerprint probably ain't any good, what coming off a two-by-four," said Shakey.

"Two-by-four? Who said anything about a two-by-four?" said Mike.

Shakey gritted his teeth and looked down. "Yeah, well you said something like that."

Mike spread his hands wide and sucked air through his teeth. "Look, we've got an eyewitness. We've got your fingerprints which back up the eyewitness. We don't need anything else."

"So, why you jawing at me?" He gave a defiant jerk of his head.

"I'd like to know why you did it."

"And why should I tell you anything?"

"Maybe so you won't spend the next few years in jail."

"Ain't gonna happen"

"Shakey, let me tell you the real problem you've got." Mike put his elbows on the table and rested his chin in his hands. "You're not going to Judge McFatage's court. I know you think, probably he told you, that he'd be the judge and he'd see you get off with a few weeks."

At the mention of the Judge's name, Shakey winced. "You don't get to decide what judge I see."

"Actually, in this case, I do." Mike didn't know that, but he would certainly push the DA to make sure McFatage didn't hear this case. "So, you're looking at long jail time."

"Long time? Simple assault, Won't get me more'n a week, with good behavior."

Harry stepped up and laid his hands on Shakey. The prisoner jerked, even though Harry had applied no pressure. "Shakey, you got bad advice. You're going down for assault *with intent to kill.* You're looking at long time. And not here. You're going to Huntsville. As the Judge probably said, 'so long sucker.'"

"Intent to kill? I wasn't trying to kill nobody. Nobody said nothing about killin' the preacher."

"Six-foot two-by-four. Aimed at the head. Then a second time when he was on the ground. There's a gouge in the asphalt. We've got a picture of it for the court. That's intent to kill. That's long years in Huntsville." Harry snickered. "'Course, you won't live that long down there."

Shakey's head drooped forward and perspiration began to form on his forehead. He put his hands in his lap, clasped tightly together to stop the shaking.

Harry wrinkled his nose and took a step away from the prisoner. He shook his head and grinned at Mike.

The clock on the wall made a distinct click as the second hand jumped forward at each interval. Mike had insisted on one that made a noise. Tick. Tick. Annoying, but more disturbing to many criminals when they sat there wondering what was going to happen to them.

"There weren't no intent to kill," Shakey mewled. "What do you want from me?"

"Start with why you did it," said Mike.

"Just to ... to ... to rob him. Get some money."

Harry let out a loud guffaw. "Shakey, you're so stupid. He's a priest, for God's sake. He don't have any money. You don't rob the homeless; you don't rob a priest. Not if you want money. You got to come up with a better reason than that."

Shakey held his head up and set his jaw. "I ain't stupid. I was gonna get paid for putting him in the hospital." He looked smug for a minute, then quickly changed. "Wasn't trying to kill him."

"We can end all this," said Mike, "when you tell us who was going to pay you."

"And how much," added Harry, laying his hands on Shakey's shoulders again.

Once more, Shakey's head drooped and he said nothing.

After a few minutes, Mike leaned forward and spoke softly to his prisoner. "Shakey, it's late and I'm tired. So, I'm going to say this once. And I'm going to wait just one minute for your answer. Either tell me who paid you to attack Father Frank, or I'm leaving and writing this up as assault with intent to kill. So decide if you want to take a chance on that. And to help you decide, keep in mind, you won't be in McFatage's court."

Tick. Shakey's breathing came faster now. Tick. Tick. He twisted his hands together and a slight tremor took hold of his body and didn't let go. Tick. Tick. Tick. Mike kept his eyes on Shakey's face, so whenever Shakey looked up, Mike's eyes were focused on him, unblinking lasers, boring into the man.

Tick. Tick. Tick. Tick.

Chapter 49

"**I** want a baby, Frank. Is that asking too much?"

Father Frank and Maggie sat at the kitchen table, the remnants of breakfast cold and unappetizing.

He blinked, mouth forming an "O". He recovered quickly and a grin covered his face. "That's fantastic, Maggie. I'd love to be an uncle." His grin faded and he turned serious. "But, are you saying you're having trouble getting pregnant?"

Maggie stretched her lips wide, her eyes moist. "I guess you can say that. Jeff isn't interested. He says we have each other. Why mess up a good thing?"

Father Frank nodded several times. "You had a fight about it, and that's why you're here?"

"Not exactly." She waggled her head. "I mean, yes, we had a fight about it. And that's why I'm here."

The priest placed his elbows on the table and leaned on them, moving a bit closer to his sister. "So, what's the 'not exactly' bit?"

"I'm not here because of the fight. I'm here trying to sort things out. What to do about this?" She looked at her brother, eyes ready to overflow with tears, pain all over her face. "This is important to me. Really important. Jeff knows what it means to me. And indecisive Jeff has picked this time to make a decision. The wrong one."

Her eyes could no longer hold the tears and they overflowed down her cheeks. Father Frank reached over, took her right hand and pressed it between his. After a few minutes, she looked up at him. "I don't always cry over this. Sometimes I'm so mad I just scream at whomever is around, or at the walls." She brushed the tears away with the back of her hand and looked up at her big brother. "Am I being selfish? Am I saying my wishes are more important than his? Or is he just being a stubborn, mule-headed jackass?"

"It's not that simple. Neither of you is right or wrong. But, as your brother, I don't want to get between you and your husband."

She jerked her hand out of his hold. "Well, tough. Your job, part of your job, is to counsel married couples. To help them stay married. And I'm telling you right here, the thought of divorce has crossed my mind. In fact, it's taken up residence there." She sat up straighter. "You can think of it as your duty as a big brother, or your duty as a priest. Whatever. I need some help." She slumped back down a little. "Do you have any idea how hard it is for me to tell you this? I'm desperate. I don't know what to do. I cry some. But mostly I'm lost. Which way to turn? Which way to go? What to do?"

For several minutes, neither said anything. Father Frank leaned back and closed his eyes for a minute. *Please, God. Help me to say the right things to your troubled daughter.*

"Maggie, this is a decision only you can make. But let me just pose some questions. You asked if you were being selfish. On the one hand, it is in the nature of the female to want to reproduce." He paused. "That sounds too clinical. Most women want to have children. It's part of your genetic makeup. But, to put your wants above your husband's is a little bit selfish."

Maggie started to speak, but her brother held his hand up. "Let me finish. The other side is that Jeff is putting his wants above his wife's. And that's not good either. So, what I'm saying is, at this point, both of you are being a little selfish.

"Now, I've said that woman's natural inclination is to be a mother. Though perhaps less strong, as a rule, a man's inclination is to have children also. Maybe for different reasons, but nonetheless, it's still there. So, your question should be: Why is Jeff adamant about not having kids. Has he said why?"

"Things are great now. Why change it?"

"So, perhaps he fears, maybe subconsciously, that a child will come between you and him. A child will change his life."

Maggie's head bounced a little bit. "Maybe."

"And of course, it will. A child changes a lot of things. A baby will get a tremendous amount of your attention, attention that might be going to Jeff right now. And as the child grows, it will take a lot of attention from both of you. You'll get less of Jeff's attention."

"Yeah, I guess."

"If that is the reason, you have to convince Jeff that his gains will exceed his losses. Whatever loss of attention he gets from you will be more than made up for by the love and attention a child will provide."

Father Frank got up and refilled their coffee cups. He remained standing. "I think you have to find out *why* he doesn't want to have a child. You've said it's because he doesn't want to change." He laughed a little. "I'll bet marrying you changed his life a lot."

Maggie had to grin. "You can say that. Big time."

"Was that change bad? Was his life better, happier after the change?"

"I think he'd agree it was better after he got me down the aisle and in the sack."

He chuckled. "Well, you don't need to tell me all the details. My point is, find out what the real objection is. It might be a legitimate one, one you'd agree with. Or it might just be the uncertainty of change. He knows how he is today. He doesn't know how he'll be after the change."

She picked up her coffee and started into the living room. Father Frank followed.

"Sit down with him and try to get a deeper reason than, 'I don't like change.' Then you can figure out what to do. And you have to be open to listen, to really hear what he's *thinking*—not just saying."

Maggie sprawled on the couch and Father Frank sat in his favorite chair. "One last point. You need to look deep into yourself and ask why *you* want a child. Remember, a child will not make a happy marriage out of an unhappy one. Do not expect a tiny baby to hold two people together who are drifting apart. It can happen. But that's not a good reason to make a baby."

For a long time, they sat in silence.

Finally, Father Frank broke the quiet. "If you think my talking with Jeff would help, of course I'll do it. But, you two need to have some serious, non-accusatory, probing talks."

Maggie got up and started toward her room.

"Maggie. You and Jeff need to find out what each of you wants, and perhaps more important, what each of you fears."

Chapter 50

There just isn't enough, Mike thought. Mike shuffled through the evidence again. *Not enough for a search warrant.* He turned and looked at the white board behind him, the list of clues all too meager. *Especially for a judge's house. Maybe it's time to bring Heinz in.* His stomach growled. He glanced at his watch. It was only 8:45, but he had skipped breakfast. Now he needed something to counteract the department's acid coffee. He threw his pencil down on the desk and got up

"Where you headed?" yelled Harry.

"Out for donuts. Maybe they'll give me some great insight."

Heavy clouds hovered low in the sky, threatening to water the grass in town at any moment. *Good thing I didn't turn on the sprinklers this morning.*

He had just come out of the donut shop, a bag of twelve assorted sweets to take back to the office, when he saw Duke Heinz get out of his car and start for the Professional Building.

"Hey, Mr. Heinz. Got a minute?" he called.

Duke turned and frowned. "You hauled me in on Monday. Now what? Is this some sort of harassment?"

By now, Mike had closed the distance to Duke and stopped in front of him. "Just a couple of questions. You can answer them right here if you'd rather not go into headquarters. Your choice." Mike smiled, trying to look friendly and non-threatening. He knew he couldn't force the man to answer, at least not at this point.

"What do you want?"

"Why did you buy cyanide?" asked Mike.

"Cyanide? I didn't buy any cyanide." He made a definite statement, but his lip twitched.

"You didn't?" Mike turned his mouth down in surprise.

"No. Is that all?"

"Not quite. You see, I've talked to a man in the Longview Farm and Ranch Supply who identified your picture as a man he sold cyanide to a week ago."

Mike could see Duke's jaw tighten. "Guy probably made a mistake."

Mike smiled. "Could be. I can get him up here and we can do a line-up."

Duke looked down at the sidewalk for a moment. "Last week? In Longview?" He frowned, still studying the walk. "Yeah." He looked up at Mike. "Maybe I did. I just told the guy I needed some stuff to kill rats. Could have been cyanide. You're probably right. Sorry. Had a lot going on this week and it slipped my mind."

"Okay." Mike tucked the donut bag under his arm, then took a little notebook out of his pocket, and clicked open a pen ready to write. "Where is that barn? Is that where the cyanide is now?"

Duke hesitated only a moment. "I used it all. Threw away the package."

"That's okay. My guys can find residue. What's the address of the barn?"

"Look, Oakley. You've already yanked me off the street and kept me in jail overnight. I consider this harassment and I'm going to call my lawyer if you keep it up." Duke's face was becoming redder by the minute.

"You've already lied to me about buying the cyanide. Why should I believe you about the barn? You call your lawyer. But in the meantime, what's the address of your barn?"

Duke started to speak, then stopped. He took a deep breath. "I'm not giving it to you until after I talk with my lawyer." He turned and started to enter the building.

"Did you give the cyanide to Judge McFatage? Was that what my witness saw you hand to the Judge?"

Duke jolted to a stop, and the flinch was noticeable. His breathing accelerated. With angry eyes, he said, "I'm not saying anything until I talk with my lawyer."

"If you didn't give it to the Judge, did *you* put it in Father Frank's half-and-half in an attempt to kill him?"

"No. I did not. Why would I want to kill him? He's ready to sign the contract. In fact, I'm just going into Mr. Winters's office to get the papers."

"Right. But Father Frank had not agreed to stop the appeal at the time of the cyanide attack." He paused for several moments. "Maybe you should come into the police station. You can call your lawyer from there."

Duke's shoulders sagged and his eyes glazed over. The two men stood on the sidewalk, neither speaking. Someone called Mike's name, but he ignored it. A few drops of rain began to land on his head.

Duke's eyes regained focus. "Okay. I was trying to keep the Judge's name out of this. Yes, I bought the cyanide. The Judge said he had a rat problem and needed some cyanide to get rid of the problem. So, I got some for him. Just doing a favor. That's all. I don't know what he did with it."

#

Back in his office, Mike slumped into his chair, bit into a glazed donut and studied the notes in front of him. A break loomed in the path of the cyanide. For all the pieces of evidence he was collecting, he could not connect the Judge to Father Frank, could not put the Judge at the scene of the attack.

The phone interrupted his thoughts. "Detective Oakley."

"What are you doing?" asked Father Frank.

"Eating a donut and spinning my wheels."

"Bring me one and meet me at the back door of the court house in five minutes."

"It's raining," said Mike.

"Right. That's why we're going there. Hurry." And Father Frank hung up.

#

Mike found the priest just inside the back door of the red brick courthouse built in 1921 and, some would say, not renovated since. He had on a pair of faded jeans and a knit shirt that said, "Smile. God Loves You." The priest laid a piece of newsprint on the floor and pulled the detective into a small closet.

"What on earth are you doing now?" asked Mike as he brushed a few rain drops off his jacket and handed the priest a chocolate-covered, lemon-filled donut.

"Great. My favorite." The priest started to take a bite, stopped, and whispered, "Shhh."

The outside door opened and a man walked in, a little water

dripping off his hat and jacket. As soon as he had passed, Father Frank jerked open the closet door, reached down and yanked up a piece of newsprint off the floor, then replaced it with a clean piece. He moved back into the closet and pulled the door nearly closed.

"What on earth are you doing?" asked Mike.

"I'm looking for a possible piece of evidence we don't have. When—." He put his finger across his lips.

Again, the outside door opened. This time a man and a woman walked in. The man continued on into the building. The woman removed her rain hat and shook the water off and proceeded into the courthouse. As soon as she stepped into the restroom, Father Frank again replaced the wet newsprint with a dry piece. Back in the closet, he took another bite of the donut.

Father Frank repeated the process three more times as dampened people arrived.

"I can see that you're providing a public service, Father. Trying to keep people from tracking water into the courthouse. And I'm proud of you. But why am I here.?"

"You're here to observe. Something to do with the chain of evidence, I think you call it."

Again the outside door opened. Judge McFatage walked in, a scowl on his round face. He did not bother to brush any water off his clothes. He carried a black umbrella which he closed as he walked down the hall, dripping water as he went.

Father Frank jumped out of the closet just as the outside door opened. "Wait!" he said and motioned to a man to stop. "Just one second." He grabbed up the piece of newspaper McFatage had stepped on. "Okay. Thanks. Sorry I slowed you down, but I wanted to get this paper out of your way."

The man looked at the priest as if he were crazy, but ventured on down the hall without saying a word.

"You didn't put down a dry piece," Mike said.

"Got what I wanted. Let's go."

"And what do you have?"

"A shoeprint from the honorable Judge McFatage."

Chapter 51

Father Frank walked in the front door to once again find a suitcase sitting in the living room. He looked around and saw Maggie lounging on the sofa, a book in her hand.

"Time to go, big brother," said Maggie.

"So soon? Seems like you just got here."

"Yeah. You have so many things going on, there's certainly no time to get bored."

"Isn't always like this. I mean, it isn't every week that someone tries to poison me, or split my head open with a two-by-four."

"Or your little parish gets four hundred big ones," she said with a little chuckle. "That's a lucky break."

"Believe it or not, I'm finding it difficult to suddenly come into all that money. I know it's the parish's. But I have to decide how to use it. It's not that easy."

"Beats the alternative." She tucked the novel in her purse and rose. "We've had times when we had to decide which bills got paid and which ones got put off. It takes a toll."

"It certainly can."

"So, Jeff and I will sit down for a long talk. Actually, many. And maybe we can decide what each of us *really* wants. And what we really fear. I've said Jeff doesn't listen to what I'm saying, what I really mean." She stretched her mouth into a long thin line and shook her head slightly. "Maybe I don't listen to *him*. I'm going back to see if we can change that."

Father Frank nodded and smiled. "I'm glad to hear that. I'll pray that the two of you figure it out. And if you do, I truly believe you'll get your marriage back to a happy and rewarding union."

"Now you sound like you're counseling a troubled couple."

"I am."

Maggie stepped over and wrapped her arms around her brother. "Yes you are, and did. You said some very important things to me. Opened my eyes. Now I hope I can open my ears." She laughed. "And get Jeff's open as well."

A tiny smile played on his face while he hugged her back. *She's still my vanilla girl.*

She unwound her arms and held him at arm's length. "And I'm impressed. You really do know about this counseling stuff, Frank. Hate to admit it, but I'm a little surprised."

"Gee, thanks."

"Now don't get the big head." She walked over to her suitcase and picked it up. "And don't get complacent. I'll be back to check up on you. And to spend some more time with Georgia and Mike. They're neat people. I really like them."

"So do I."

"Wish me luck."

"I'll do more than that. I'll pray for you."

"Jeff's a great guy and I do love him. But sometimes it's hard to know what's really going on in his mind. I think he says one thing and means something else."

"And when he says he loves you?"

A big grin spread across her face. "I believe he's telling the truth and I believe him."

She turned to leave.

"It's been raining. Be careful on the wet roads."

"Hey, Frank. I've got this new invention on my car: windshield wipers."

"Give my love to Mom and Dad. And stay in touch," Father Frank called to her.

"Count on it."

#

Father Frank went to the kitchen and grabbed a Dr Pepper out of the refrigerator. He wandered out onto the front porch. The rain had stopped and the clouds seemed to be breaking up. But the rain had played its part and the police had a chance at eliminating the Judge. Or not. But even if today's wet print from the judge's shoe *sort of* matched the partial print found in the rectory, it wouldn't be enough. They needed stronger evidence.

Tomorrow he'd scout around the area, see if anybody had seen the judge's new Lexus parked nearby. He picked up the phone and dialed.

"Hi, Georgia. You said you saw the judge's new car. Describe it to me, please."

"And hello to you. You're not wasting any time on me, are you?

"Sorry. I guess I was a little preoccupied."

"I understand. It had just a touch of gold, like champagne. Wait a minute. I think Ruthie called it satin cashmere metallic. I must say, it was outstanding. Why?"

"I thought I'd ask around and see if anybody had seen his car around here."

"You think he might drive his car up, park it in the driveway and enter your house? Even McFatage wouldn't be that stupid."

Father Frank laughed. "No, I think not. But he could have parked it a few blocks away and walked over."

"So you're going to canvass the neighbors."

Father Frank took in a deep breath. "I don't know what else to do. We need more evidence."

"Want some help?"

"No. Maybe only one of us needs to be wasting his time. I know it's futile."

"But you're going to do it anyway."

"Yeah. Besides, it might be safer walking the streets in broad daylight than sitting in my house."

Chapter 52

Mike spent Wednesday afternoon and part of the evening getting all the paperwork in order. He had the newspaper shoe print from Father Frank, which wouldn't stand up in court. There was the container from McFatage's garbage which the lab boys determined contained cyanide at some point, but might or might not be connected to the attempt on Father Frank's life. Shakey's testimony was--shakey. The large cash transaction could be innocent. And Duke's statement about delivering cyanide to the judge could be self-serving. After all, Duke had purchased the cyanide. Lots of pieces. None of it conclusive. But there was a growing body of evidence and it should merit a search warrant.

Mike scrutinized every detail in his paperwork as if he were checking the numbers on a winning lottery ticket. Getting a search warrant was seldom easy. Getting an arrest warrant from a judge was worse. And getting them both—to serve on another judge, no less—was simply asking to be booted right out Judge Alwright's window. And since the judge's office was on the second floor, that wouldn't be good.

#

Attention to detail pays off, Mike thought as he walked out of Judge Alwright's chambers Thursday morning with the warrants. It had gone so smoothly Mike promised himself he would prepare his next case with equal care.

When Mike, Harry and a patrolman arrived at the Judge's house, Abiel was working in the yard. Mike presented the search warrant to him.

"I only work in yard. But the maid is cleaning today." Without waiting for a response, Abiel went back to work.

Mike rang the front doorbell. When the maid opened the door, Mike presented her the warrant. She looked at it, not really reading much of it, and then back at Mike.

"I'm not supposed to let anyone in. Maybe I should call the judge," she said.

Mike smiled and tried to sound pleasant. "Ma'am, this is a legal search warrant and the judge does not have a choice to allow it or not. The court has ordered this action. You can call the judge, but it will not change anything."

She looked uncertain, checking the paper once more, and looking at the three policemen. She stepped aside and the policemen entered the house.

Mike said, "Okay, guys. Shoes for the right foot. Any signs of cyanide. Digitoxin. Anything regarding money that might seem out of the ordinary. In fact, *anything* that might seem out of the ordinary."

The patrolman rolled his eyes but said nothing.

"Don't complain," said Harry. "You didn't have to sort through all his garbage."

"Wrong," said Mike. "He has to go through any and all garbage we find today."

#

Someone was leaning on the doorbell and banging on the door at the same time. Father Frank hurried to see what the emergency was.

"What's going on?" Duke Heinz demanded. His face was flushed, and his breathing accelerated. The priest could see the anger radiating from Duke's eyes.

"Come in, Duke. Let me get you something to drink. You look like you're about to have a stroke."

"I don't need a drink. I need an answer. What's going on? You told me there were a few minor changes and you were ready to sign the contract."

"That's right."

"Well, I went to pick it up at that attorney's office. And he told me you weren't going to sign it."

Father Frank was as puzzled as Duke. "I'll have to talk with Mr. Winters before I can answer you."

"You gave me your word. Doesn't a Catholic priest's word mean anything?"

The priest didn't know how to respond. When he had talked with Norm, everything was on track. The few changes that Father Frank had outlined to Duke earlier were to be made and the contract would be ready to sign. Now, apparently, Norm had changed his mind.

"As you know, the house and land are in a trust." Father Frank hated to dump this problem on Norm, even though the priest didn't know what had happened. "Both trustees will have to meet and discuss the contract and then both must sign it. I *will* get back to you as soon as I have an answer for you."

Duke glared at the priest for several seconds. "Yeah. We'll see. But let me tell you something. Lockey will not take this easily. We have the right of eminent domain and we can take that land with a much smaller payment. Don't push us." For a moment, the man glowered at Father Frank. "And don't push me. I push back—harder. I know how to play dirty, if that's your game. You may regret messing with Duke Heinz."

He turned and stomped off the porch, got into his car, and laid down a streak of rubber backing out of the driveway.

#

An hour and forty minutes after they arrived at Judge McFatage's house, the three policemen left. They carried four shoes for a right foot, and a pad of paper with indentations that read "Shakey 555-7894." His warrant didn't cover telephone records, but the old-school method provided a link between the judge and Shakey. They found nothing indicating cyanide had been there, and no digitoxin.

Mike walked out with shoulders slumped and feet dragging. He had really expected to find digitoxin.

#

After a quick stop at headquarters to deliver the shoes and pad of paper to the crime scene officers, Mike and Harry entered Judge McFatage's courtroom and took seats just inside the back door. Harry had wanted to march into the courtroom, interrupt the trial McFatage was hearing, cuff him and lead him out. Mike had convinced him that patience was an easier approach. He pointed out that the Judge would get the bailiffs involved resulting in a possible standoff. Then, there might be reporters at the trial and that always made things worse. And lastly, on the outside chance that the Judge returned to the bench in the future, neither of them wanted to have embarrassed the Judge.

Just before noon, the Judge called for a recess and left for his chambers. Mike and Harry followed the Judge.

As soon as they entered his chambers, the Judge yelled, "What are you doing coming in here? Get out this minute before I call the bailiffs."

"Judge McFatage, we have a warrant for your arrest," said Mike, feeling just a tad uneasy. "If you will come with us quietly, we won't handcuff you. You can simply walk out naturally, and no one else has to know anything."

In a flash, Judge McFatage's face glowed red and his eyes became lightning bolts, slashing first at Mike and then Harry. "What do you mean a warrant? Let me see it." When Mike did not produce the document fast enough, McFatage raised his voice. "I said, give me the so-called warrant. Who issued it?"

Mike handed him the warrant and the Judge raked his eyes over it. "Judge Alwright. I might have guessed. Always been jealous of me. You know what we call him? All Wrong. He hardly knows how to wield a gavel. This is garbage." He wadded the warrant and tossed it on the floor. "You're taking the word of a dope head? I'm a Texas District Judge. I don't—"

"I didn't mention anybody. But I believe Shakey." The Judge didn't take Mike's bait. After a moment, Mike said, "Judge, it is a legal warrant. If you do not come with us peacefully, we *will* handcuff you." His voice was low but firm.

"You pull out handcuffs and I'll have the bailiffs in here in a second. Do you want to fight with them?"

"No sir, Judge. But you know better than anyone, we have no choice but to execute this warrant."

"What is your name?" He turned to Harry. "And yours?"

"I am Detective Mike Oakley and this is Detective Harry Sacs."

"I'll remember you. Both." He put his foot on the warrant and crushed it. He glared at each of the officers. "You can count on it."

Mike knew the judge was accustomed to judging people, in and out of court. He was the one who dictated what happened. Clearly, he didn't like the alternative.

"Let's go," McFatage snapped.

Harry started to read the Judge the Miranda statement. "You have the right—"

The Judge cut him off. "I know more about that than you do, sonny. Just can it."

"Yes sir," said Harry. "Would you like me to drive your car to headquarters, or to your house?"

"I do *not*. Nobody drives my car but me."

"Could we call someone?" asked Mike.

"You deaf? I said *no one* drives it but me."

"Yes sir," said Mike. *We are pleased to know that nobody drives that car but you.*

Chapter 53

"I know what you gave Judge Alwright," Chief Flag growled. He pushed aside the papers Mike had spread out on the table in the interrogation room. "What have you got that's new? You got a warrant to search his house. Please tell me you found something. He's a State Judge. You get it right or your neck will be on the chopping block."

"They're checking the partial shoe print we found at Father Frank's against the shoes we found at the Judge's house. We should know something within the hour."

"Any sign of cyanide?"

Mike shook his head. "No. Other than the container we found in his trash Tuesday."

"Which he'll claim someone else dumped there. How do you know the cyanide was put in the half-and-half that morning?"

'Father Frank had used it the day before."

"What time the day before? Don't you see, the Judge can claim it was put in the half-and-half Monday afternoon, when he was in court." The chief shook his head and slumped in the chair. He had a ruddy complexion, a mouth that had forgotten how to smile, a ping-pong ball nose, and eyes trained to reveal little. But right now, they indicated displeasure. "Come on, Mike. You gotta do better."

"Yes, Sir. We're still working on it." The room had no windows and the chief had closed the door when he came in. Mike believed the temperature in this interrogation room had risen twenty degrees in the last few minutes. Sweat rolled down his side, and glistened on his forehead.

"What about digitoxin? Cyanide—okay, we can make a case for Father Frank. But if he tried to kill the priest, he most likely killed Cranzler, too. But you gotta have some evidence. Not logic. Cold, hard evidence. If you haven't got it, then get the hell out of here and find it. I don't want to see you until you've got the smoking gun."

"Yes, Sir. But we do have the cyanide container and maybe a shoeprint." Mike felt like he was being interrogated for the crime of not having enough evidence.

The chief slammed his hand on the table. "Who bought the cyanide?"

"Duke Heinz."

"Right. So you have it in Heinz's hands, not in the Judge's." Mike started to speak but Chief Flag kept right on talking. "Don't tell me it was in his garbage. Did Heinz visit the Judge at his home? Yes. So, he could easily have dumped the container in the Judge's garbage. You tell me this Heinz has had bitter arguments with the priest. Tried to intimidate him. If I'm the Judge's defense attorney, I'm thinking that Heinz looks guiltier than the Judge, and I can probably convince a jury that he is." He took a deep breath and let it out slowly. "McFatage is probably out on bail already and working on his plan to crucify you. And the department. You know what that means?" He scowled at the detective. "It means me as well. And I won't like that. Or the person who got it started. Understand?"

"Yes, Sir." Mike was grasping for any lifeline. "We've got him on conspiracy to commit murder, or at least assault with bodily harm."

"Did the priest go to the hospital?"

"No, Sir."

"So, how you going to make that 'bodily harm' stick?"

"The guy, Shakey, tried to club Father Frank in the head with a six foot two-by-four."

"So, you can get a conviction on Shakey. Big deal."

"But, he'll testify that McFatage hired him to do it."

The chief smiled. "And right now, you believe Shakey."

"We found Shakey's name and phone number on a telephone pad in the Judge's house."

"Sure, the Judge hired him—to haul trash for him, help in the yard, paint the garage. After a good defense attorney finishes with Shakey, even *you* won't believe him." The chief put his elbows on the table and his head in his hands. Without looking up, he said, "Get out and get something that will last more than ten seconds in court. Get me some hard evidence on something. Anything." Flag shook his head again. "I don't know why I let you talk me into getting that warrant. I'm not going to sleep until this is over." He looked up at Mike. "And you better not sleep until you have solid, unimpeachable evidence on McFatage. And have you forgotten about the Cranzler murder? Do you recognize the difference between a murder and attempted murder? So far, you've told me lots about the attempted murder and absolutely nothing about the actual murder. Are we back to thinking it was suicide?"

"No, Sir."

"Then get out of here and get me some evidence, solid evidence on the murder case. I don't want to see your ugly face until you have evidence in your hand on the *murder* case."

#

Mike didn't know where to start. He grabbed a coffee from the department pot, and sat down in his office with Harry.

"I take it the chief wasn't happy," said Harry.

"Right. And how did you manage to get out of the meeting?" asked Mike. He slumped in his chair and blew on his coffee.

"Had to go deal with a domestic disturbance call. Rather have faced the chief."

"I hate those calls. Both sides hate you."

"So, what did the chief say?"

"You mean other than we should be focusing on the murder case," said Mike.

"McFatage is probably good for both."

"Yeah. But Flag wants some evidence on the murder. Bottom line, none of our evidence is worth a cow patty." He tested the coffee, then took a long drink.

"Eyewitness. He didn't like that?"

"Figures a defense attorney will destroy Shakey."

Harry nodded a few times. "Probably true. Let's go see him. Make sure he's going to testify. Make him understand the serious trouble he's in if he doesn't come through."

Mike finished the coffee and the two detectives headed over to the county jail.

#

"Hi, Jake. We're here to see Shakey," Mike said when he and Harry entered the jail.

"Well, you ain't."

Mike gave the jailer a slap on the back. "Don't give us a hard time.

The chief's already beat you to it. He chewed on me for half an hour."

"Bet you'd rather a been here." Jake, a man almost as big around as he was tall, settled down on a high stool, large portions of his body hanging off on all sides.

"You are right about that," Mike said with a grin. "He told me not to sleep until I had the case wrapped up tighter'n a new boot. Let's go."

"Ain't no place to go. Shakey's gone."

"What do you mean 'gone'?" asked Harry, worry lines fanning out across his brows.

"Gone as in like he ain't here."

Mike's was getting a sinking feeling in his stomach. "What happened?"

"He posted bail. Walked out of here 'bout twenty minutes ago." The jailer smirked. "I told you you should'a been here and not jawing with the chief."

"Bail?" Mike's face was one big question mark. "How could Shakey post bail."

"Well, I guess someone posted for him. But bail got paid and Shakey walked." The jailer laughed, his huge belly shaking up and down. "But now you're here, you guys can just visit with me."

Chapter 54

Father Frank had spent nearly two hours on Sunday's sermon. He needed a break. Maybe a few minutes with the basketball would rejuvenate his mind, provide a little inspiration. He slipped into some sneakers, grabbed the ball, and headed out to the "court."

Across the parking lot, Candice Leverett was leaving the parish hall.

"Hi, Candice. Women's choir have a good session?" the priest called.

"Yes, Father. Very good. See ya." She walked to her car.

A picture flashed into his mind. He called to her to wait and he jogged over to her car. "I just remembered that you left Mass in the middle one day last week. Were you sick?"

"Last week? No, I haven't been sick in months." She frowned and cocked her head to the side. "Oh, yeah. Last Tuesday. I suddenly remembered I had to take a friend to the airport in Tyler. I'd forgotten about it, or I wouldn't have come to church. We were almost late. But we made it."

"Good. Glad you weren't sick, and that your friend made the plane." He started to leave, then stopped. "You said Tuesday?"

She nodded.

"You didn't happen to notice anything unusual, or different, did you?"

The slim brunette closed her eyes for a moment, then quickly opened them. "Yes, as a matter of fact, I did. There was a man coming out of the rectory. Thought that was funny. Who would be in there when you were saying Mass? He had a little … like a little tool box. I decided maybe you had some problem with the plumbing or electricity."

"Did you get a good look at him?"

She shrugged. "I guess so. As I said, I thought it odd, so I looked."

"You think you would recognize him if you saw him again?" The priest's pulse rate jumped and he unconsciously held his breath.

"I think so." She looked puzzled. "Why?"

"There was a problem at the rectory last Tuesday. We have a suspect, but haven't really placed him in the house yet. Was there a car in the drive?"

"No, which seemed strange. As I drove out I did see a white van parked on the street, just a little to the right of our entrance. You know, where the trees are pretty thick. So, I couldn't see the car until I was on the street. What was the problem?"

The priest pursed his lips and cocked his head slightly. "I'd rather not say right now. But I might call on you to ask you to look at some pictures."

"Well, if I can help, I'll gladly look at pictures, or whatever. Just give me a call."

#

Father Frank went back into the house and dialed the phone.

"Mike, I have someone who saw a man leave the rectory during Mass that morning."

Mike let out a low whistle. "If we can add the Judge actually coming out of the house—"

"I didn't say it was the judge."

"Who was it then?"

"She didn't say. But she's willing to come down and look at some pictures. I haven't mentioned the judge. I didn't want to prejudice the case."

For several moments Mike said nothing, but Father Frank could hear the detective tapping on something. "See when she could be at the police department. Give me some options. And I'll set it up." He paused a second. "She got a good look at the person?"

"She said she did. She was surprised to see anyone coming out of the rectory during a weekday Mass, so she looked at him. I asked her if she'd look at a line-up. She said yes."

"Call me as soon as you find out when she can do it."

#

It took only five minutes to get the answer. And another thirty minutes for Mike to get the lineup arranged. The Judge had posted bail and was minutes away from walking out of the jail. Mike caught him and brought him over for the line-up.

At three o'clock, Candice stood outside an interrogation room.

"They won't be able to see you," Mike said. "You can ask any person to step forward, turn to the side, anything that will help you make a positive identification. If you're not certain, tell me."

She nodded.

Mike turned to Harry. "Bring them in."

Five men, all about the same size and age, shuffled into the interrogation room. Each one held a number, beginning with one on the left to number five on the right.

"Take your time. Ask me anything you want to know or see," said Mike. He watched her closely, trying to gain any insight into how her decision was being made.

Candice took a step forward and studied each man. "I think I knew as soon as they walked in. But I want to be careful."

"Careful is best. We don't want a mistake. And if this goes to trial, the defense will grill you."

"Can you ask number two to turn to the left a quarter turn? Clockwise."

"Mike spoke into a microphone. Please make a ninety-degree turn clockwise and hold that position." He thumbed the mike off and said to Candice, "Just to be perfectly fair. Let you see the profile of each one."

She studied each one, never shifting her gaze from the men behind the window. "I'm certain that number two is the same man I saw leaving the rectory."

Mike felt like jumping and yelling, but he managed to keep his voice level. She had identified Judge McFatage. "Do you remember when that was?"

"Oh yes. Last Tuesday morning."

"About what time did you see him leave the rectory?"

"Just about eight twenty."

Mike told Harry to release all the men in the lineup, and he took Candice back into his office.

"What happened last Tuesday?" she asked once they were seated in Mike's office.

"Father Frank didn't tell you?"

"No. He just said there was some trouble at the rectory, but he didn't say what."

Mike raised his eyebrows, surprised the priest hadn't told her. "Someone came into the rectory between late Monday morning and nine o'clock Tuesday morning and put cyanide in Father Frank's half-and-half carton. Enough to kill several people."

Candice recoiled in the chair, her eyes blinking rapidly, her face turning pale in a matter of seconds. "Cyanide? In Father Frank's half-and-half?"

Mike simply nodded.

For nearly a minute, she just stared at the detective, unable or unwilling to open her mouth and speak.

Harry popped a soda can open as he walked in. "Well, how did that go?"

Mike looked at Candice. "Can we get you something to drink? Water, a soda?"

She nodded almost as if asleep. "A soft drink would be nice. Anything."

Harry handed her the drink he had just opened.

She took a long drink, then set the can on the desk. "I'm sorry, Mr. Oakley. But that was quite a shock. Father never said anything about that. I can't imagine …"

After a moment, Mike said, "Can we ask you a few questions about the lineup? And is it okay if I record your answers, so that I don't forget anything?"

She nodded. Mike turned on a tape recorder and stated the date and time, the topic, and the people present. Then, he asked Candice his first question.

"First, did you know any of the men in the line-up?"

She shook her head no.

"Please say your answers so I'll get them on the recorder."

"Oh. Of course. No, I did not know any of those men."

"Did you recognize any of them—you know, not people whom you know, but anyone you have just seen around town or any place?"

"No. I don't think so. I mean, I might have seen one of them, but if I did, I don't remember him." She reached over, retrieved her soda and took another drink.

"Did you recognize one of them as the person you saw coming out of the rectory of Prince of Peace Catholic Church about eight twenty in the morning of Tuesday, October 4?"

"Yes. I believe that number two was the man."

Mike looked at Harry and frowned. He shook his head then looked back at Candice. "You said, 'I believe.' How certain are you that number two was the man you saw at the rectory?"

"Very certain."

"Is there any doubt in your mind that number two was the man?"

"I would swear he was the same man. Now, if you tell me that number two was in Alaska that day, then I'm wrong. But, then I'd have to say it was his twin. The man I saw coming out of the rectory looked exactly like number two. Of course, his clothes were different. But the face, the build, the size—the same."

"How can you be certain? Did you spend time studying the man?"

She took another sip of the Dr Pepper. "I looked because I was surprised. Who would be coming out of the rectory during a weekday Mass. I wondered if it might be another priest, visiting Father Frank. Or a worker. So, I took a careful look. And as an artist, I just naturally study people's faces."

"Was he just standing on the porch, walking up the steps? What?"

"He was coming out of the door. Not just closing the screen door like he had been knocking on the door. Of course, there's a doorbell, so he wouldn't be knocking. What I mean is, he was exiting the house. I watched him cross the porch and start down the stairs."

"And then?"

"And then, I got in my car and left. I was late to get my friend Frieda to the airport."

"So, you're sure of the date and time?"

"Quite. I was at Mass when I remembered I had to take Frieda to the airport. And that's the only time I've taken Frieda to the airport. So, the date and time are certain."

Mike looked at Harry and Harry nodded, a big smile on his face.

"Ms. Leverett, we really thank you for coming in. It has been very helpful to us. We may need to contact you regarding this again. And we may need you to testify in court. Are you willing to do that?"

"Yes. If someone tried to poison Father Frank, I'll do whatever I can to … to …"

"See justice."

"Exactly."

Chapter 55

"Okay, this better be better than last time," said Chief Flag. He sat in his office, his desk clear in the middle with stacks of folders on either side. He picked up his coffee cup and leaned back in his chair.

"It is," Mike said with less confidence than he actually felt. The chief had shot Mike down on several occasions. If there was a weakness in anything he said, the chief would spot it. "First, the techs have said that one of the shoes we retrieved from Judge McFatage's house matches the partial shoe print we found at the Prince of Peace rectory the day of the attempted poisoning. They said it was a perfect match, but of course only on the portion that we got from the crime scene."

"Okay. Not much yet. Next."

"We have a solid witness who picked the Judge out of a lineup as the man she saw coming out of the rectory on the day and at the time we believe the crime was committed."

The chief actually sat up a little straighter and put his cup down. "How solid?"

"She said she is positive of the identification, and she knows the exact time and day." Mike allowed himself a tiny smile. "We've got the means, the motive, and the opportunity."

"Did she see a car in the driveway?"

"No, sir. She said she thought that was strange. She did see a white van parked on the street nearby."

"Anything distinctive? Writing on the side?"

"She didn't notice anything. Said she didn't really look at it carefully."

"But she studied the man?"

Mike nodded. "She thought it strange that someone would be

coming out of the rectory during mass, so she really looked at him. She's an artist. Said she always studies faces. But she was rushing to the airport, so she didn't pay much attention to the van."

"And she didn't see him get in the van?"

"No, sir."

"So, that's worthless." For a moment, the chief just stared at his desk. He looked up. "Does she know the judge? Had any dealings with him? Any connection at all?"

Mike shook his head. "She said no. Said she didn't remember ever seeing him before."

"Did you tell her a State Judge was in the lineup, or that she had picked out a State Judge?"

"No, sir."

Flag took a deep breath and locked his eyes on Mike. "Are you willing to gamble your career? Because if he gets off, he'll know who put the case together. And he'll destroy your career in law enforcement."

The statement washed over Mike like an icy shower. Everything looked solid, but risking his future was a tough pill to swallow. For a minute, he weighed the evidence. *Of course, the D.A. will have to believe it's strong. He may be risking his career also.* He swallowed, and could feel his Adam's apple moving.

"Not totally certain?" asked the chief.

Mike took a deep breath and shifted his weight from one foot to the other. "Yes, Sir. I'm certain. I'm ready to present this to the D.A.."

"What about the conspiracy to assault with intent?"

"Someone bailed Shakey out while we were meeting this morning. We haven't been able to find him since. Without Shakey we have nothing." His shoulders slumped a little.

"Who bailed him out? The Judge?" Chief Flag had a smirk on his face.

"That's our guess. Of course, the Judge didn't do it personally, but I'm sure he arranged it and paid the bail."

"And Cranzler's murder?"

"So far, nothing. Except motive. Same one as for the attack on Father Frank." Mike pounded his right fist into his left palm several times in frustration. "I mean, Syd was more of a threat to take the appeal all the way to the state supreme court. He had the will and the means to hire detectives to investigate every little detail. He had said publicly he'd spend all his money to expose the abuse."

The chief snorted. "Good motive for the minister to kill Syd—save the money for his inheritance."

"The priest did not kill Syd. I believe the Judge did. But we found no digitoxin at his house. We've canvassed the drug stores in Pine Tree. Nothing there. I even talked with the Judge's doctor. Naturally, he didn't want to tell me anything regarding a patient. But I did at least get him to say the Judge's heart was sound and he did not take digitoxin." Mike rubbed his chin and ran his hand down his neck. "We could branch out on the pharmacies, but which way to go? And how far?"

"Then I think you better come up with another approach. The Cranzler case is murder. The priest is only attempted murder. If you think the Judge is the murderer, then get me some evidence."

"We're working on it, Sir. Are you ready to take the attempted murder case to the D.A.? Then we'll have McFatage while we find the evidence on Syd's murder."

The chief picked up his telephone. "Get me the D.A. on the phone. Call me when you have him." He put the phone down and his eyes bored into Mike. "You'd better hope this does not blow up in your face."

#

Once the D.A. was on the phone, Flag's tone changed. He listened, nodded, and said "Yes, Sir," several times.

"Yes, Sir. I *am* aware that he is a State Judge. But, we believe the judge is not only guilty of attempted murder, but also linked to the Cranzler murder."

Mike couldn't hear what the D.A. was saying, but the look and expression on Flag's face gave Mike a good clue.

"No, Sir. We're not ready to charge him with the murder." The chief listened. "We don't have enough evidence yet." He listened again, his face turning red. "You're right. I'll wait for your call." Flag slammed the receiver back in its cradle.

"Is he ready to charge McFatage?" asked Mike.

"He'll *study* the evidence," Flag said with disgust. "Of course, his is another career down the toilet if we don't win the case. You'll have company in the unemployment line." He looked down at his desk, almost talking to himself. "Convicting a judge of attempted murder is no easy task. To make a jury bring back a *unanimous* vote to convict, you need irrefutable evidence, and then some more." He looked up and his eyes drilled into Mike."Get out of here and turn over every rock, everything, and find more evidence."

Mike got up and started to leave.

"And find something *strong* linking him to Cranzler's murder."

#

Father Frank was watching the evening news when the doorbell rang.

"Hi, Mike. What brings you here? Why aren't you over at Georgia's?" the priest asked as he ushered Mike into the living room.

Mike sat on the edge of the couch. "First, I wanted to thank you for the witness, ah, Ms. Candice Leverett. She turned out to be excellent and supplied the missing piece. She placed the Judge in the rectory."

Father Frank grinned. "I thought my shoeprint would do that."

"That helped get us the warrant to search his house. And we did find a shoe there that made a good match with the partial found here. But, it is only a partial. It helps. But her testimony is much stronger. Put the two together and they remove all doubt. The Judge was in this house."

"Great. Can I get you something to drink?"

"No, no. I won't be here that long. We've given the evidence we have to the D.A. and he should decide by tomorrow if he's going to indict the Judge or not."

The priest looked confused. "You're saying he might not indict the Judge. Why not? Seems like pretty strong evidence."

"McFatage is a State Judge. Tough to get a conviction. He's got 'character' on his side. People—jurors—will have a hard time thinking of a judge as a murderer. Then, he knows the system inside and out. He'll know every loophole, every objection, every chance for a mistrial or an appeal."

"I didn't think of that."

"The chief has called in a forensic accountant to go over the Judge's books. See if he can find anything pointing to a bribe."

"If everything was cash, that could be tough," said Father Frank.

"Yeah. But those guys are good. They find things nobody ever realized were there." Mike got up, ready to leave. "And so far, we don't have diddly squat on Syd's murder. I'm convinced McFatage did it. But I don't have one shred of evidence."

"Maybe he didn't do it," said the priest.

"I think he did. Trouble is, right now, I don't have any proof. Anyway, since you really made this possible, I just wanted to bring you up to date. Thanks for the shoeprint, and the eyewitness. I owe you."

After Mike left, Father Frank went to the kitchen, grabbed a Dr Pepper and settled into his favorite chair in the living room. *More evidence. Where to look?*

Chapter 56

"Exactly what is it you want me to do?" Georgia asked.

Father Frank was driving and Georgia was a passenger. The sun was riding close to the horizon, sending bright slashes of red across some clouds, adding a warm glow to the western sky. They were being treated to another beautiful sunset.

"We're going over to see W.C. Mayfield. At some point, I want to go look in his medicine cabinet. And I want you to keep him busy, so I can snoop," said Father Frank.

Georgia studied the man. "You want to snoop?"

"That's right."

"What for?"

The priest didn't answer for several long seconds, then looked at Georgia. "I don't want to get you involved in my questionable actions. Let's just say I'm trying to further the cause of justice."

"I'm being the decoy; I'm involved. What are you looking for?"

Again, he didn't answer immediately, and scrunched his mouth right and left. *I guess it's only fair to tell her.* "When Maggie was at my house, W.C. stopped by. I said, joking, 'Don't mess with her, she's my sister.' Or something like that. He laughed and said he wouldn't. He said she looked pretty hot and he had a heart condition."

"Meaning?"

"Heart condition." Father Frank turned and looked at Georgia. "I'm looking for digitoxin. The bottle could say Lanoxin."

She scrunched her eyebrows down and looked at the priest. "You think he had something to do with Syd's death?"

"Georgia, stop with all the questions. I've said more than I intended to."

"That's okay. You've answered it for me. I'm with you."

#

W.C. was a little flustered when he saw Georgia. But immediately a smile emerged and he welcomed her. He ushered them into his living room, told them to be seated and disappeared. Two minutes later, he brought in soft drinks for Father Frank and Georgia and a Lone Star for himself.

"So, what did you want to tell me?" W.C. asked.

"I thought, since you had first mentioned to me that Judge McFatage had bought a new, expensive car, I ought to tell you where that led, and where things stand as of now."

"Well, I 'preciate that," W.C. said.

The priest then told W.C., in a round-about fashion—dragging the story out to stretch the time—about the Lexus, the briefcase of hundred-dollar bills, and the process of counting out 490 bills to cover the cost of the car after his trade-in. He threw in, at great length, the auto company calling the police for a guard to escort the car dealer's employee, and the money, to the bank. Father Frank surprised himself at the amount of detail and the length he had managed to stretch a two-minute story.

W.C. did have a few questions, and once again, the priest was very verbose. But, he had also managed to drink his entire soda and so it was not surprising that he asked to use the restroom.

"Sure," said W.C. and he pointed to a small, half-bath whose door opened just between the living room and the kitchen.

Trying to hide his disappointment, the priest made his way to the half-bath.

Georgia worked to maintain a neutral expression. She knew that wasn't what Father Frank had in mind. He wanted to search W.C.'s main bath. Her mind raced.

"As long as we're stopped, I'd like to visit a restroom myself. Do you have another bathroom?" she asked.

"Sure. Right through the bedroom there. It's on the left."

"Thanks. I'll be more comfortable if I make a quick stop," she said with an embarrassed grin.

Georgia hurried into the bathroom, and closed and locked the door. Immediately, she went to the medicine cabinet. A spray can of deodorant tumbled out as she opened the door. She let out a small gasp and amazed herself when she managed to catch it before it clattered into the sink. *Good work, gal. That noise would certainly have raised suspicions.*

An electric razor, which she decided he hadn't used in a few days, occupied the middle shelf, alongside the tipsy deodorant. The bottom shelf contained probably a dozen prescription bottles. Quickly, she scanned them. *Why doesn't he keep the labels facing front where you can read what's in the bottles?* She scanned down the row, having to turn two-thirds of them around to be able to read the label. *Oops. I'd better put them back in disarray.* She turned several so that the label faced the back.

She reached over and flushed the commode to make a little noise.

The top shelf had a toothbrush, toothpaste, and a few other things that were of no help to Georgia. Quietly, she closed the cabinet door. Turning on the water in the sink, she didn't bother to wash her hands, but rather opened the cabinet under the sink. A toilet brush (seldom used, she decided), plunger and cleansers of various types cluttered the space along with a dirty rag and an old magazine. She scanned the rest of the room, but could find nothing of interest.

She shut off the water, slipped out of the bathroom, and made her way over to W.C.'s bed-side table. She glanced at the door to the living room, then opened the drawer. It had a mishmash of articles and she poked around in it to see if there were any prescription bottles there.

"What'cha looking for?"

To Georgia's ears it was an accusation. She froze as a chill ran down her back. Afraid to move, she gazed in the drawer. She pulled her hand out and turned to face W.C., her eyes lowered, trying to look embarrassed rather than guilty. "I broke a nail and was looking for a fingernail file." She held up the metal file. "Is it alright if I use this for a minute?"

W.C. stared at her, and she couldn't tell if he bought her excuse or not. But after a few seconds that seemed like minutes to Georgia, he said, "Sure."

She noted he did not smile, nor did he leave her. He remained and watched as she smoothed a nail that had been perfect before she started.

The three visited in the living room for a few more minutes, Father Frank raising the possibility that Judge McFatage might have received the money as a bribe and idly speculating that if that were true, it could be a motive for killing Syd.

"You think so?" W.C. asked. His voice and manner were indifferent, but his eyes gave away a more serious interest.

Father Frank ducked his head and a sheepish grin crossed his face. "I shouldn't have said that. I apologize. Please forget I said that." He looked at W.C., imploring him. "Don't tell anybody I said that. Please."

"I sure won't," said Mayfield. "'Course, that thought's crossed my mind, too."

#

Father Frank and Georgia drove off. W.C. stood in his front door, watching.

"Well, the two baths threw us," said the priest. "Quick thinking on your part to take the second one."

"For all the good it did me. There was nothing in the bathroom. And he caught me before I finished going through the bedside table. But I don't think there was anything there. I mean, I got a pretty good look before he came in." She gave a small laugh. "Scared me so much when he came in and caught me, I thought I might have to go *back* to the bathroom, for real this time."

"I tried to keep him in the living room, but even as I was talking to him, he got up and went in. Didn't think it would work to yell a warning."

"It was a waste anyway. I didn't find anything."

Father Frank grinned. "I didn't think you had."

"But, we went there expecting—"

"I didn't think you had … because *I* found it, in the half bath."

Georgia's eyes grew wide, and her mouth made a perfect "O." No words came out, just a sound to match the shape of her mouth.

"The half-bath is next to the kitchen. Makes it easy to take the pill with breakfast, I guess. Whatever, I have the name of the pharmacy that fills digitoxin prescriptions for W.C. and the doctor who writes them."

"Which gives him—."

"Means, to go along with motive and opportunity."

Chapter 57

Father Frank knew he should have called first, but he was already out, and he didn't own a cell phone and pay phones had all but disappeared. Luck smiled on the priest and Norm was in and available.

"What's on your mind this morning, Father?" the lawyer asked as Father Frank sank into a comfortable brown leather chair.

"I had an angry visitor yesterday. Duke almost knocked my door down and when I opened it, I thought for a minute he was going to knock *me* down."

"He does have a temper."

"He said you told him I was not going to sign the contract, even after you modified it."

Norm leaned back in his chair and picked up a pen and toyed with it. Father Frank watched as Norm's mood changed from pleasant to agitated. His eyes darkened and he looked directly at the priest.

"He participated in Syd's death. I can't in good conscience or for that matter, any conscience, help him achieve what he may have killed a friend for." He paused and studied the man in front of him. "I can't imagine you would give aid to the enemy."

Father Frank nodded several times. "I can see how strongly you feel about this. And I could come to the same conclusions. Except." He steepled his fingers. "I don't think Duke had anything to do with Syd's death. And I don't think the Lockey Corporation was behind it either."

For a minute, the two men stared at each other. Then, Norm said, "I heard that he bought the cyanide. In fact, I heard that you went with the detective to check out the store where he bought it."

"That's true. I did. But, Syd wasn't killed by cyanide."

A frown took up residence on the lawyer's face. "But, didn't the same person …" He paused and tilted his head to the side. "Are you saying there were *two* people? The person who tried to kill you is not the same person who murdered Syd?"

"That is my opinion, and I'm trying to prove it." Other than Georgia, Father Frank had told no one about his growing conviction, not even Mike. "I can't say just yet. But I think I know who killed Syd, and it wasn't the same person who tried to ... who put cyanide in my half-and-half."

Norm just shook his head. "Hard to think of one killer in Pine Tree. Now, you're saying there's two. The motives?"

"Wait until I get a little more information. I *think* I know what happened. But right now, it's only a theory, one the police would think foolish."

The lawyer straightened in his chair. "So, what are you saying here? You want to go ahead and sign the contract?"

"I think so. I'm not sure whether or not Duke knew what McFatage was going to do with the cyanide. Probably, he knew at some level. But, —"

"Whoa. Hold it. Are you saying?" Norm shook his head and blinked. "You're saying Judge McFatage was behind the attempted poisoning?"

"I'm not saying he was behind it, Norm. I'm saying McFatage *did* it." The hint of a grin made its way onto his face. "I guess I'm supposed to say 'allegedly.'" Now, the priest's manner returned to deadly serious. "First, he hired some poor man the police call Shakey to club me on the head. When that didn't work, I guess the Judge said, 'If you want something done right, you have to do it yourself.' I think the evidence is going to prove that the Judge personally came into my house and put cyanide in my half-and-half."

"Why? Why on earth would he do such a thing?"

"The police believe the Judge took a bribe from Lockey Corporation. And when it looked like we were going to carry this appeal through the courts, he was afraid the bribe would come out and his career would be ruined. Plus, of course, he'd get jail time. If I were out of the way, the appeal probably would be dropped."

"But we *are* dropping the appeal."

"Yes, we are *now*. But at the time of the cyanide attack, we hadn't decided that." The priest rubbed his nose. "He must have believed we would carry it out."

For a while, Norm just stared into near space. Finally, he brought his eyes into focus. "Have they arrested him?"

Father Frank nodded. "They did. Of course, he bonded out pretty quickly. And surprise, surprise, Shakey—the witness who turned on the Judge and told police McFatage had paid him to whack me—also bonded out. Shakey didn't have two quarters to rub together, but he got the money to get out. And has disappeared."

"And how did Duke figure in all this?"

"I think he simply made it easier for McFatage. He was the gopher. I know, Duke has a terrible temper, and I wouldn't put violence beyond him. But in this case, I don't think he did it. Did he know, or suspect, what the judge would do with it? Maybe." The priest ran a hand over his head and down the back of his neck. "From what I've heard, what I suspect is going to happen is this. Judge McFatage will be indicted on attempted murder. Duke will be hauled in and threatened with an indictment for being an accessory to attempted murder. That will be used as a wedge to get information on the bribe." Father Frank pursed his lips. "Mike and the chief would like to charge the Judge with Syd's murder, but right now, they have nothing to connect him to it, except a motive."

"So, you want to go ahead and sign the contract with Lockey?"

"We don't have much choice, do we? It's only a matter of whether we do it before or after going to court. Who benefits if we fight them?"

Norm reached in his drawer and pulled out a sheaf of papers. "Here's the revised version. Want to read it?"

"If you say it's okay, I'm sure it is."

Norm Winters handed the papers over, along with a pen.

*

Georgia sat in her car, wondering if she had miscalculated. He should have driven past by now. She would not get any closer. She could still feel the fright of being grilled by Duke. *Maybe this is a mistake.*

For the hundredth time, she glanced in her rear view mirror. This time, she saw Abiel's van approaching. She let it pass, then started her car and followed him. Six minutes later, he pulled into a convenience store. Georgia parked beside his white van. When he emerged from the store carrying a gallon jug of milk, Georgia stepped out of her car.

"Hello, Abiel."

The gardener looked startled momentarily, then smiled. "Hola."

Georgia made a few remarks about how beautifully he kept the judge's yard, then took a step closer and lowered her voice. "Does the judge ever borrow your van?"

Abiel looked at Georgia, and then cut his eyes to the right and to the left. His expression did not change, but Georgia could see his hesitation and sense his caution. He said nothing.

"Let me be more specific." Georgia spoke barely above a whisper. "Did he use your car one day last week? Maybe Tuesday?"

"I work for judge. I need job."

Suddenly Georgia realized the position she was putting Abiel in. *What am I doing? He could lose his job, his livelihood.* "I'm sorry. Forget I asked that. It was nice to see you again." She turned to go.

"He use van one morning last week. Maybe thirty minutos. I not sure; maybe Tuesday."

She turned back and grabbed his hand and gave it a squeeze. "Thank you, Abiel. You are indeed a son of the Lord."

Chapter 58

Carl Douglas was sitting on his front porch in an old wooden rocking chair when Father Frank pulled his car off the road and stopped. He dreaded going to see the old man who seemed locked in a bad mood. Still, it was only fair. If it would make Carl's day even a little better, then it was worth enduring his anger for a few minutes.

The priest got out of his car and started across the grass. The day had started out beautiful, but now grey clouds were drifting in and there was a smell of rain in the air. Father Frank wondered if the gloomy weather foreshadowed his visit to Carl.

"Good morning, Mr. Douglas. How are you doing?" the priest said with a smile on his face and in his voice.

"Same as always. Terrible," Carl responded. His expression matched the sentiments of his statement.

"I'm sorry to hear that. Perhaps I can make it a tiny bit better."

"Doubt it."

Father Frank stepped forward, put one foot on the edge of the porch and leaned on it, watching to see if the old man would object. He didn't, so the priest continued. "We have signed the contract with Lockey Corporation this morning. So, at least we won't be holding up their payment to you."

"'Bout time."

"You are absolutely right. And I'm sorry it took so long. There have been a number of things that delayed it. Of course, Syd's death was a big factor."

Douglas rocked ever so slowly. After several seconds, he said, "Ever find out who killed him?"

"No, they haven't. I'm sure the police asked you if you saw anybody the night of the murder."

"They did. And I didn't."

When Douglas said nothing else, Father Frank took his foot off the porch and stood up straight. "Well, I just wanted to tell you the contract was signed."

Again, Douglas said nothing and the priest turned to go. His gaze swept the road. There was Syd's house, in plain view. Douglas had a commanding view of Syd's house and the road in front of it. Out of nowhere, a thought popped into the priest's mind. One of the clues that led to the judge was his new car. He had purchased it too soon, putting it out in front, almost like a sign.

Father Frank turned back to face the old man. "Mr. Douglas, did you see an old Camaro parked near Syd's house the day he died?"

"Yep."

The priest could feel his pulse quicken. "You did? On the day he died?"

"Twice."

"Twice? Do you remember when?"

"'Course. You think 'cause I'm old I'm senile?"

"No, sir. I can tell your mind is sharp as a new razor. I'm just excited. When did you see the Camaro?"

"Once in the afternoon, when that Duke guy and the city manager were talking to Syd. Then, later that night, it came back. Around nine. Maybe nine fifteen."

Father Frank felt a rush. "Same car both times?"

"I said it came back. That makes it the same car. Mud all over it. Man ought'a wash his car ever year or so."

"Did you tell the police about the car?"

"Nope."

Father Frank was thinking how to phrase the next question, but Carl went on. "Never asked me 'bout a car. Asked if I saw any*body* that night. I didn't. But I did see the car. Don't know exactly when it left, but it was gone by ten forty-five."

#

Father Frank drove home, tapping on the steering wheel, smiling and talking to himself. A fine mist began falling and he switched the wipers onto intermittent sweep. *I don't care if it is raining. This is a sunny day.*

He pulled into the drive at the rectory and turned off the motor. For some moments he sat there, his head leaning on the steering wheel. He jerked his head up, started the car, and backed out of the drive and headed for Syd's house.

#

The police had finally removed the crime scene tape and turned the house over to the Prince of Peace Trust. After three weeks of being closed up, it smelled musty. Father Frank's first instinct was to open windows, air it out. But he didn't take time for that. Instead, he walked into Syd's bedroom and checked the closet. A few clothes hung on a rod. The priest checked several pairs of shoes scattered on the floor, all run down at the heels, but found nothing of interest. The shelf above the rod had a variety of caps, most bearing the logo of some business. The only other item was a box of shotgun shells, no doubt to go with the double-barreled shotgun leaning in the corner.

He looked under the bed. Nothing but dust. Next he checked the office, a bathroom, and a cabinet in the living room. Finally, he headed to the garage. It took a minute, but he found a light switch and flipped it. Thank goodness Norm hadn't turned off the electricity. The one car garage contained so much stuff—Father Frank thought of it as mostly junk—it would have been impossible to put a car in it. It served as a big storage building. Dozens of cans of oil lined a shelf that ran the length of one side wall. Beneath it, hoes, rakes, an ax, picks, shovels, clippers and other tools hung on hooks. A garden hose was coiled around a piece of two by four nailed to a wall stud. Two tires that clearly came from poorly aligned front wheels were stacked in the middle of the floor. Several boxes of books shared the middle of the floor with the tires. Fence posts, barbed wire, fence stretching implements, and other building materials that looked like they could have been there since the Revolutionary war were piled along the back wall. An incredible assortment of tools, some of which the priest couldn't identify, hung from nails and hooks and filled nearly the entire length of the other side wall. Old brooms, mops, a washtub with a hole in it, and a discarded hot water heater added to the clutter. A number of empty cardboard boxes filled some of the space, ready to receive additional junk as needed.

The priest looked in each box. He checked each corner, behind any object capable of hiding anything bigger than a deck of cards. Combing through the garage consumed twice as much time as the rest of the house. But it produced no more.

Father Frank locked up the house and left. Empty-handed. No golf shoes. No golf clubs. No tees, no golf balls, nothing associated with golf. He drove off, smiling and humming *Everything's Coming Up Roses.*

Chapter 59

Joan Henson, a member of Prince of Peace, had been admitted to the Pine Tree Hospital last night. Father Frank drove to the hospital to visit her.

"Hi, Joan. How are you feeling?" he asked.

"Fine as wine," said the sixty-seven year old woman.

"I'm glad to hear that. So, what are you doing in here?"

"Getting ready to leave. Wasn't anything wrong with me. I just got a little dehydrated and started shaking. My son was worried that I was going to check out on him. Young people are so spoiled. Never expect to have a single pain or problem. 'Course, I raised him, so I guess I'm to blame."

Father Frank laughed and they visited for a few more minutes. "So, I'll see you at Sunday's mass," said Father Frank.

"Oh, I'll be there."

#

After the hospital visit, Father Frank returned to the rectory and immediately called Randall. The short conversation confirmed what the priest suspected. Syd *never* played golf. As soon as he hung up, he dialed Mike's number. It took all of his persuasive powers, but the priest convinced Mike to take a ride with him after lunch.

Father Frank was half way through a grilled cheese and Dr Pepper lunch when the telephone rang.

"Guess what?" said Georgia, her voice giving away her excitement.

"What?"

"Judith called me. Randall's sister."

"I know Judith."

"She invited me over for dinner. Said Abby and Randall had already accepted. I think she's going to invite you also."

Father Frank could almost see Georgia fidgeting, her face aglow, her feet moving back and forth. "That's great. That is, if Lance knows about it and approves."

"Are you sitting down? Here's the most amazing part: Lance suggested it."

The priest sat down. He felt it hard to even believe this turn of events. "What turned him around?"

"Judith said she and Lance had decided they would like to build a covered patio. Said they'd talked about it for several years. Lance had gotten some estimate of what it would cost. So, he called Randall. She described Lance as tense and angry and 'loaded for bear,' as she put it. In his patented belligerent tone—that's Judith's description but we've all heard it—he told Randall about it and asked Randall to release the money from the trust." Georgia paused just long enough to breathe. "Randall said, No problem. He'd take care of it Monday. Judith said Lance was speechless. Then Randall even suggested a builder."

"That's good news, Georgia. And I'm pleased Judy and Lance have invited Abby and Randall for dinner. But, if I'm not being too nosy, why you?"

"Judith said it was at my dinner party that Lance talked to Randall about the trust, and Randall said he wouldn't stand in the way of how they wanted to spend the money."

"Okay, I can see that. Why me?"

Georgia giggled. "I'm pretty sure that was Judith, not Lance."

"Well, I'm happy. I hope the family becomes closer."

"So do I. But, that's not my *real* news."

When Georgia didn't say anything, Father Frank said, "Are you going to tell me, or is that just a tease?"

"I'm going to tell you. But it needed a little drama. Or maybe a drum roll."

Father Frank taped his fingers on the telephone. "Will that do?"

"Yes, thank you. I talked with Abiel today, the judge's gardener. He loaned his car to the judge one day last week." She paused.

"And this is *real* news because…"

"Abiel drives a white van."

The priest sucked in air. "And it could have been Tuesday morning."

"He said it was early morning, and he thinks it might have been Tuesday."

"Wow. So that … Have you told Mike yet?"

"I put a call in for him, but he was on another call. I'll try him again when …"

After a few seconds of silence, the priest said, "Are you still there?"

"What? Oh, yes. Sorry. I was watching out the window. The same car's driven past twice while we've been talking."

"Somebody looking for an address, maybe."

"What kind of a car does Mayfield drive?"

"An old Camaro. Probably '91 or '92. It was parked in his drive last night." said the priest. "Why?"

"I thought I recognized it. That's the kind of car that's driven past twice since I called you." Her voice had lost its excitement. "Why would Mayfield be driving up and down my street?"

"It may not be Mayfield, Georgia. There are other old Camaros around." But Father Frank felt his gut tighten. *I didn't think W.C. posed any threat to Georgia.* Now, Father Frank wasn't sure. Why would he be driving past her house? *If it is W.C., and it probably isn't. Someone looking for an address is still the most likely explanation.* But, his gut did not relax.

"Maybe. But if he comes by again, I'm going to go out and ask him."

"Georgia. Do *not* go out if you see him."

Chapter 60

Mike drove and Father Frank sat in the passenger's seat. "Just how did you come by this information?" the detective asked. "It's a long story."

"Yeah, yeah. I've heard that. So just get on with it. I've agreed to do your bidding but I want to know what I'm getting into."

"I don't want to prejudice you."

They drove out of Pine Tree heading east. The grey morning and slight mist had given way to a bright sun, but clouds hung around the edges of the sky threatening a return visit. Father Frank was in an upbeat mood and kept up a lively chatter, trying to fill the air so that Mike would not ask too many questions. Father Frank had reminded Mike that he had been canvassing pharmacies, looking for the source of the digitoxin used to kill Syd. Father Frank said he'd found it.

"All right." Mike slowed the car. "We're in Oak Flats. Where to?"

"The Oak Flats Pharmacy. It's just about two blocks ahead."

"And what do we do when we get there?"

"You, as a duly authorized officer of the law, are going to ask the pharmacist about digitoxin."

Mike pulled the car to a stop at the pharmacy and they got out. "Anything else you want to tell me before we go in there?"

"Just ask about the prescriptions for digitoxin for W.C. Mayfield. When he last filled it, how many pills it contained, and anything unusual about his use of the drug over the past year."

"W.C. Mayfield? We talked to him. Cleared him."

Father Frank laughed. "Maybe you shouldn't have."

When the two men asked to speak with the pharmacist privately, the pharmacist came from behind the counter and the three men moved to a part of the store void of customers. Mike told him what information they needed. The young man, whose name tag read Pete

Brasher, asked to see Mike's badge and ID. After he studied them for a minute, he handed them back and without a word disappeared through swinging doors.

Father Frank sat down at a blood pressure machine and proceeded to take his blood pressure. "One twenty-five over seventy-two. Not bad for a sedentary person. Here, give it a try."

"The department insists we have frequent checks. Mine is okay."

Father Frank pushed. "How long has it been?"

"Not long."

"How long?"

At that moment, Brasher came back through the doors and out to his two visitors. "Mr. Mayfield has been taking digitoxin upon orders from his doctor for about a year. His last prescription was filled ten days ago, and it was for sixty pills. The doctor's instructions are for Mayfield to take one tablet each day." The man stopped and looked up from his notes.

"Has he gotten any extra prescriptions? Anything unusual?" Father Frank asked.

Brasher looked at his notes again. "Not that I can see. Regular as clockwork. Sixty pills every two months." He looked at his notes again and nodded. "The first day of every other month for the last ten months."

"So, he should have about fifty pills?" asked the priest.

"He might have more if he fills his prescription before he runs out. But he shouldn't have less, I would think." The man looked from Mike to Father Frank and back. "So, what is this all about?"

"Just wanted to make certain he didn't run out, had plenty for the next few weeks." Mike stuck his hand out and the pharmacist shook it. "Thanks for your cooperation. It would be best if you did not talk of our conversation to anyone."

Brasher nodded his head. "I don't discuss people's prescriptions with anyone - except the police."

Five minutes later, Mike and Father Frank were back on the highway, outside Oak Flats, headed for Pine Tree. "Okay," said Mike. "Let's hear the rest of the story."

Father Frank grinned. "Well, I happen to know that W.C.'s digitoxin bottle at home, dated exactly ten days ago, has only thirty-five pills in it. That leaves at least fifteen pills unaccounted for."

"He could have lost them down the sink," said Mike, his eyes never leaving the road.

"Possible. But he lied when he said Syd stole money from him. He said Syd beat him at golf even though W.C. was a better golfer. So he felt like Syd was stealing from him."

"He told us pretty much the same thing."

"But Syd never played golf. I searched Syd's place. No clubs. No shoes. No bills for anything related to golf." Mike started to object, but Father Frank kept on talking. "And Randall told me that Syd hated golf. He played tennis when he was younger. But never golf. Randall said Syd liked to compete against people, not against a piece of landscape. Looking for oil was his contest with geology."

"So he lied to us. That doesn't put him in an elite group," said Mike.

"But why would he lie about that?"

"Some people lie just to put something over on you. What was his motive?"

"He felt Syd stole money from him. W.C. told me that Syd backed two wells. He invited W.C. to participate in one. That one was a dry hole. They lost all they put into it. The other one hit big. But Syd didn't ask W.C. to invest in that one."

"But Syd couldn't know which one would hit and which wouldn't. If he knew that, just skip the duster."

Father Frank nodded. "That's the logical approach. But I think W.C. has had a tough time financially, and here's Syd with lots of money. And the resentment just grew and festered. Makes no logical sense, but I think W.C. felt Syd really did steal money from him."

"Syd left him ten thousand dollars in his will."

"Yes he did," said the priest. "And I could tell W.C. thought that was nothing. Syd had made hundreds of thousands of dollars on the well he *didn't* include W.C. in."

They drove in silence for awhile. Father Frank could tell Mike was worrying the information back and forth in his mind. The detective looked over. "Why does he use a pharmacist in Oak Flats? That's fifteen miles away."

"His doctor is in Oak Flats."

"Should I ask how you knew, or suspected, there would be some missing pills?"

"No." The priest grinned. "I was at W.C.'s house and used his bathroom. And there was the bottle of digitoxin."

"Just sitting on the back of the commode."

"Not exactly."

"And it's a new, high-tech bottle that flashed the number of pills left."

Father Frank chuckled. "No. I snooped. But you didn't. You simply asked the pharmacist. All perfectly legal. I hope."

"And not proof of a crime, yet. But, it certainly gives me another path to check."

After a minute, Mike asked, "Why did you snoop anyway? I'm guessing you went to W.C.'s looking for some evidence."

The priest's eyebrows shot up. "Me? Looking for evidence?"

"Yeah, you."

The priest looked down and let out a long breath. "I don't know if you'll understand or not. I've talked with W.C. several times. And each time, he's told me how sorry he was to see his friend dead." Father Frank rubbed his nose and looked over at the driver. "I hear hundreds of confessions every year. After a while, you can tell when a person is really sorry or not. I just couldn't believe W.C. when he said he was sorry."

"Isn't everybody who comes to confession sorry?"

Father Frank laughed. "Sorry about something. They all want forgiveness. And most are really sorry for their digressions. But not everybody is deeply sorry."

"And you can tell?"

"I think I can. And I think W.C. was not sorry Syd was dead."

"Still ..."

The priest looked appalled. "That didn't convince you?" He shook his head and sniffled a little, trying to look as if he were about to cry. "Okay, sir." Sniffle. "Would it help if I had a witness who saw W.C.'s car parked in front of Syd's on the fateful Monday night, between nine and ten-thirty?" He opened his eyes wide in expectation.

"Between nine and ten-thirty the night Syd died?" Mike's attention was at full throttle.

"At the time the M.E. estimates the digitoxin got into Syd's stomach," said the priest with a trace of smugness.

"Always nice to place the suspect at the scene of the crime. And better if it's about the time of the crime."

"I thought you'd like that."

"Could have some of the digitoxin pills in another bottle."

"Possible. When did W.C. tell you he last saw Syd?"

Mike took in a large breath and nodded several times. "Four in the afternoon."

They were about five miles outside Pine Tree when Mike's cell phone rang.

"Oakley."

"This is Harry. Is Father Frank with you?"

"Yes."

"Well, I just picked up a call for you from an Irene Winters, looking for Father Frank."

"Here, I'll let you give him the message." Mike passed the phone to the priest.

"Hi. This is Father Frank."

"Ms. Winters wanted to tell you that she was at the parish hall a few minutes ago. And a man drove up to the rectory. He banged on the door, then walked right in. A minute later he came out, slamming the door. Got in his car and drove out ninety to nothing. She thought it strange."

"Did she know the man, or describe him?" the priest asked.

"She said he was short, thin except for a pot belly, and grey fuzz on his head."

Father Frank closed the phone and stared ahead.

"Anything important?" asked Mike.

"Maybe. " Father Frank flipped open the phone and dialed. The phone rang and rang, and after twenty more rings, he hung up.

"A problem?"

"I don't know." He swallowed dryly, a lump in his throat. "Irene described an angry man looking for me, then drag-racing out. The man she described had to be W.C. Mayfield. Earlier today, Georgia thought W.C. might have been driving by her house. And now, Georgia doesn't answer her phone."

"Why would Mayfield be interested in Georgia?"

"I forgot to mention, Georgia was with me at W.C.'s when I found the digitoxin."

Chapter 61

W.C. rang the doorbell. When Georgia didn't answer, he banged on the door so hard Georgia thought he might break the door. She crouched in the hall, being careful to make no noise, trying to keep her breathing quiet. She had seen him park and come to the door. She was not about to open it.

The telephone rang and she let out a tiny gasp, then bit her lip for fear he might hear her. To answer the phone, she would have to leave her hiding place. She let it ring.

Finally, he quit banging. She eased out of the hall and crept into the living room to peek out through a tiny crack in the curtains. He was gone. Thank God. She let out a long breath.

She started to the kitchen to get a drink and try to settle her nerves. She jerked to a stop. Back at the curtain, she cautiously looked outside again. W.C. was nowhere to be seen.

But, his car was still there. Empty.

The sound of breaking glass jolted her into action. She ran to the telephone and started punching in Mike's number. She had six of the numbers in when a hand grabbed the phone from her hands.

"Whoever you need to call can wait until we have a talk." W.C. Mayfield replaced the phone in its cradle. Maintaining his iron grip on her hand, he led her into the kitchen. "Sorry about the glass, but when you didn't answer the door, I had to come in and see if you were all right. You could have been hurt or sick."

"I'm fine. You can leave now." Georgia made an effort to sound strong using the authoritative voice she used with her students. Inside, she was shaking.

"Sit down. And don't think about running. You could slip on the broken glass and hurt yourself. You might even get cut. Know what I mean?" His voice was low, not menacing, but his eyes blazed and the veins in his neck stood out as red ropes.

Georgia slumped into a chair, her entire body shaking now, her mind racing in several directions, desperately trying to come up with a plan to escape, or call for help. Each path wound up at a dead-end. What did he want? And what might he do?

"What do you want from me?" she said, still trying to control her voice.

W.C. sneered at her. "More to the point, what did *you* want from *me*? What were you looking for in my bedroom?"

Georgia's fright had scrambled her thinking so much that for several seconds she could not come up with an answer. "A nail file." Her voice cracked. "I told you that. I broke a nail and it was catching on my blouse, skirt, everything. I needed to smooth it out."

He said nothing. His steady gaze bore into her and she had to force herself not to cringe. The silence frightened her. If he would say something, she could react to it. The quiet forced her to continue. "I know it seems silly to you, to any man. But a broken nail catching on everything is so annoying to a woman." She tried a little laugh. It sounded fake even to her. "I should have just toughed it out. Sorry. I didn't think you'd mind."

He did not smile. "I looked at your fingernails. They looked just fine to me. What were you really looking for?"

"They looked good because I used your nail file. If I didn't say it then, let me thank you now for its use."

For a full minute he focused his total attention on Georgia, but didn't utter a word. She tried to think of something to say, anything to defuse the tense atmosphere. *Please God, get this man to leave.* She tried not to think about what she and Father Frank had discussed. But there it was: this man is probably a murderer.

Finally, without ever taking his eyes off her, or even blinking it seemed to Georgia, he said, "Okay. Suppose I just accept what you said."

"Thank you." She urged her voice to sound casual and friendly. "You could have just called. No need to drive all the way over here." Her whole body, tight as an E string, began to relax a little.

"So, if you were only looking for a nail file, then what was your minister friend looking for? And don't tell me you don't know. I think you and him probably discussed it." He smirked. "A little strange that both of you decided you had to go to the bathroom at the same time."

Georgia said nothing, but her shaking started again. She tried to mask it. She clenched her hands together. If he realized his question upset her again, he would be certain she knew something.

"I'll ask you politely *this time*. What was he looking for?"

Georgia decided the only way she was going to stop shaking was to get upset and push back. "Why don't you ask him?" It came out a little shrill, but she kept on. "How am I suppose to know what goes on in his mind?" *There. That's telling him.* "And as for the bathroom break, I go all the time. In fact, I need to go now."

She started to get up. In an instant, he grabbed her hand and yanked her back into the chair. He jammed her arm on the table and she cried out in pain. "You'll stay right here until I'm through with you." He let go of her, but his predatory expression made it clear she better not move.

She massaged her arm where he had smashed it on the table, and her wrist where his fingers had dug into her flesh.

No plan of escape came to her, but she did know that delaying was important. Not that anybody was coming. Still, stall long enough and perhaps he would grow tired of this and leave, or an angel would materialize and protect her.

"Okay. I see I should have asked permission first." She held up her hand. "Teacher, may I go to the bathroom, please."

He slapped her in the face.

Her head jerked back and a cry escaped her lips.

"Don't get smart with me. Tell me what you or the minister were looking for."

She rubbed her jaw, trying to ease the sting. But worse than the sting was the panic invading her. On each exchange, he got more brutal. She needed to escape, or at least delay things. "I really need to go." It was almost a whimper. "You can stand outside the door. And the window is too small for me to crawl out." She wasn't sure that was true. She'd check it out when she got there. "Come on. It could be unpleasant for both of us if you don't let me go."

She could see he was considering it. A good first step.

"Okay. But if I think you're playing me for a fool, I'll come in and stand over you. You got that?"

"Yes, sir." She almost saluted, but thought better. *Do nothing to rile him.*

He kept a hand on her and for a moment she thought he was indeed going to accompany her into the bathroom. But he stopped at the door. He looked in at the window. He squeezed her shoulder until she had to bite her lip not to cry out. She had always thought she was strong enough. Mayfield didn't look strong. But for a moment, she thought his fingers would actually break her shoulder.

He held her in such a grip she knew she could not break free even if there was some place to run. Finally he released her and in a cold, intense voice that left no doubt he meant it, said, "If I hear anything I don't like, or you take too long, I'll break this door down. And don't think this door will slow me five seconds. And if I have to break it down, that will make me mad. And guess who'll get hurt.

Chapter 62

Mike grabbed the phone and hit a speed dial button. "Come on. Come on. Pick up. Pick up the – Harry. Where are you?" He listened for a moment. "We may have a problem." He gave Harry Georgia's address. "Meet me there ASAP."

Father Frank huddled against the door, guilt weighing him down. *Have I put Georgia in the sights of a killer? W.C. had built up an anger, a resentment toward Syd. He truly did believe Syd stole from him. But Georgia has done nothing to him.* He felt marginally better. *Except, Georgia was helping me try to prove he was a murderer.* Father Frank put his head in his hands and prayed that the Lord would watch over Georgia.

The Ford gobbled up the miles quickly and they entered Pine Tree in four minutes. In deference to the increased town traffic, Mike slowed a little, but only a little. Father Frank said, "Uh oh," as they turned onto Georgia's street and he saw the Camaro parked in front of Georgia's house. *Please Lord, protect her.*

"How are you going to handle this?" the priest asked.

"Depends on what we find."

The detective stopped behind the Camaro and jumped out. He sprinted to the garage and stretched up to look through one of the small glass panes near the top of the door. He pulled out his cell phone and dialed.

Father Frank eased up near the detective.

Mike shook his head. "Car's here but no answer."

They turned to see another car pull to the curb. "There's Harry now."

#

Mike, Harry and Father Frank huddled on the driveway.

"We don't want to tip him off. We'll circle the house, check the windows. See if we can get a fix on where they are. Maybe they'll be sitting in the back yard drinking a glass of tea. Harry, take the left, I'll take the right. Father, you wait here by the car."

"That's not going to happen." The priest's tone was adamant.

"This is not the time to argue. Stay behind me. Meet you in the back, Harry."

They walked up the driveway and split up. Mike and Father Frank cautiously peered in the windows on either side of the front door, then a large living room window. Nothing. They turned the corner and checked the side window for the living room. The curtain for the dining room window was open, but revealed nothing.

Curtains completely covered the small window for the bathroom. Father Frank stopped. Was that a noise from the bathroom? He stopped, motionless, listening. *My imagination.* The curtains were pulled back in the kitchen window, and while they could only see from the counter tops up, no one appeared to be in that room.

At the back gate, Father Frank jumped up as high as he could and looked into the back yard. He did not see anyone there. They eased in through the gate.

Immediately, Father Frank saw the broken pane in the door. So did Mike.

When Harry joined them, Mike whispered, "See anything?" Harry shook his head. "Go back to the front door in case he runs. If you hear problems inside, break the door in. Be careful. I haven't had time to tell you, but we think Mayfield probably murdered Cranzler. I'll give you one minute, then I'm going in this back door."

"Is he armed?" asked Harry.

"Don't know."

Harry nodded once and left.

Father Frank prayed silently.

#

Inside, W.C. pounded on the bathroom door. "Come out right now or I'm breaking the door in."

"Just a minute. I'm washing my hands."

Georgia had checked the window immediately, but quickly saw it provided no escape. So she set about looking for anything that could serve as a weapon. She had picked up the plunger. It wasn't much of a weapon. The stick was too light to do much good, even if she could hit him with it.

I need your help, God. Now. She looked in the cabinet again. This time her eyes zeroed in on an aerosol can of cleaner. She grabbed it and started shaking it. She sprayed a heavy coat on the floor between her and the door. She weighed the can in her hand. Enough left.

"That's long enough."

"Give me a minute, will you? I'm in here and can't go anywhere else. Be patient."

"On three, I'm knocking the door in."

"Just hold on a minute." She said it with irritation, like she might speak to a wayward child, but her hands were trembling.

He continued as if she hadn't said a word. "And then, I'm going to be mad. Really mad. One." A brief pause.

"Just wait. I don't want you mad." *That's the truth.* "And I don't want you smashing my door in. It'll cost me a lot to have it fixed." *If I'm still alive.*

"Two." Another pause. "Three."

Georgia didn't open it. In an instant, the edge of the door and the door jamb shattered and the door flew open, banging on the wall, the sound reverberating in the tiny room.

W.C.'s eyes were fierce, his fists clenched. The sound of the door smashing into the wall still rang in Georgia's ears as he lunged forward. Then he hit the slick cleanser and slipped. He grabbed at the wall and the splintered door, struggling to keep his balance. Georgia pulled the can from behind her back and sprayed it in his face. As he jerked his hand up to try to protect his eyes, his feet shot out from under him and he went down hard.

His body blocked Georgia's escape route.

She hesitated only a second, then started to step over him. He grabbed her leg and held on, screaming curses at her. "You little—"

Georgia stopped that with another shot of cleanser in his face. Even as she sprayed him with the foam, he managed to keep his vise-like grip on her leg. He wiped some of the foam out of his eyes. He continued screaming at her and spitting cleanser out of his mouth.

"Let go," she yelled, and tried to kick his arm. He jerked the leg he held and Georgia lost her balance. She threw her arms out, trying to stay on her feet, and the aerosol can flew into the hall.With a shrill cry, she fell heavily onto Mayfield.

#

The sound of splitting wood and curses, punctuated by Georgia's shrill scream jolted Mike into action. He reached through the broken door, unlocked and opened it. "Stay here." He commanded Father Frank, and rushed into the house, not knowing what to expect, but intent on rescuing Georgia.

Cautiously, Mike turned the corner into the hall and stopped. Inside the bathroom, Georgia was on top of Mayfield, who was covered with white foam and struggling to breathe. Georgia was trying to get her legs free, but Mayfield had a firm grip on one of them.

Mike raced over. "Mayfield, if you move, I'm going to shoot you right here and now." His voice softened. "Georgia, are you all right?"

"I'm okay."

"Here, give me your hand."

He kept his gun aimed at Mayfield but his eyes were on Georgia as he reached down to help her up. Georgia raised her hand, but Mayfield grabbed Mike's extended hand and yanked him forward and down. Mike put his foot out to brace himself, hit the slick cleanser and tumbled down on top of Georgia. As he struggled to get off her, W.C. lurched up, shifting Georgia and Mike to the side. In an instant, W.C. grabbed Mike's pistol, jumped up and dashed from the room.

\#

Father Frank had moved into the kitchen but couldn't see or hear anything. He eased over near the door to the hall.

Suddenly, W.C. whipped around the corner and almost ran into Father Frank.

"Out of my way," he yelled and waved the pistol at the priest.

When Father Frank played basketball in college, he had been known for his quick hands. He stepped aside as if to let Mayfield pass. As W.C. started to move, Father Frank's hand darted out, grabbed Mayfield's hand that held the gun and twisted it up and around behind his back. Quickly, Father Frank moved behind W.C. who flailed at the priest but couldn't make any contact.

Father Frank continued to twist Mayfield's arm up until the gun fell free. The priest scooped it up and aimed it at the man.

A sneer formed on the man's face. "You won't shoot me. You're a reverend. You don't shoot people." W.C. turned and started for the door.

Father Frank stepped forward and kicked W.C. in the back of his knees. He went down in a heap just five feet short of the back door. He looked up at the priest. Confusion covered his face. He started to get up, but Father Frank put his foot on W.C.'s leg and pinned it to the floor.

"You're right, I won't shoot you. But I can and I *will* keep you here until the police can take you."

W.C. got a hand on Father Frank's leg, trying to pry it off. But the priest applied more pressure and W.C. let out an angry curse.

Mike raced into the kitchen. "I'll take good care of him. This time." Then to Mayfield, "Turn over and put your hands behind your back."

"I think we stirred him up," said Georgia.

Father Frank turned and in spite of the serious situation, he burst out laughing. Cleaning foam covered one of Georgia's ears, and half her hair was now white. A small ball of foam clung to the end of her nose. Her dress had wet spots scattered about and white bubbles ran down one of her legs.

She turned only slightly red. "It wasn't so funny for me. What took you guys so long?" And tears began to run down her cheeks.

Father Frank stepped over and put his arm around Georgia. "You look … so … "

"Wonderful," said Mike as he snapped the handcuffs shut on Mayfield.

"I was going to say funny," Father Frank said. "But maybe I'll just shut up for now."

She brushed at the tears, but more came. "Wise decision. And you both can help clean up the mess, once you dispose of … of … him."

Harry came running in the door, gun held firmly in two hands. "I could see everybody heading out the back. So, I came—"

Mike interrupted. "Everything's fine, Harry. Just read the guy his rights. I've got to comfort the victim."

Mike wrapped both arms around Georgia and held her close.

Father Frank stood over W.C. and silently prayed. *Thank you Lord that no one was injured today. And please help W.C. recognize the error of his ways and find his way back to You.*

Chapter 63

Two weeks had passed since Georgia sprayed foaming cleanser into W.C. Mayfield's face. Maggie had arrived, unannounced as before, just as Father Frank was leaving for a dinner invitation to Georgia's. A quick phone call, and Georgia extended the invitation to include Maggie.

On the drive over, Maggie explained that she and Jeff had several long talks after her visit to Pine Tree. "Good talks. I mean, in all our marriage, we've never talked in such depth. I could tell it was really painful for Jeff." She looked a little chagrined. "I guess for me, too."

She stopped and after some long seconds, Father Frank said, "Have you got things straightened out?"

She wobbled her head side to side. "We're not through. We've got more work to do. But it's been really good for both of us. I understand him so much better. And I'm sure he understands where I'm at better than before. I understand *myself* better. But it's also highlighted areas we need to work on."

"And a baby?"

"Not settled. But I'm addressing his concerns and I think in a year or so you're going to be an uncle."

#

When dessert was finished, they filled their coffee cups and moved into Georgia's comfortable living room. "Okay," said Maggie. "I've waited far too long. Fill me in on all that's happened." She sat on the edge of the sofa, eyes sparkling, her eagerness clearly visible.

Mike said, "Well, we arrested Judge McFatage, our renowned State District Judge, for conspiracy to commit murder. And the D.A. has *finally* decided to indict him. Thanks to Father Frank and his newspaper trick, we got a search warrant for the judge's house, which produced a shoe that matched a print found in the rectory. Also courtesy of Reverend Frank, we have a witness who can put the judge in the

Rectory at a time consistent with when the cyanide might have been put into the half-and-half. And we found a container that held cyanide in the judge's garbage. And Georgia found a link between the judge and the white van parked near the rectory the morning of the poisoning."

"And the physical attack on Frank?" asked Maggie.

"No. The only witness was sketchy, at best. Then, someone bonded him out of jail and he hasn't been seen since. So, we have no evidence. The D.A. has dropped that charge. As for the bribery charge on the judge, the D.A. has a forensic accountant going over McFatage's financial records right now. He believes he may get enough to pursue the bribery charge. Either way, McFatage's days as a judge are over."

"Why didn't he just deposit the money in the bank? Then, you wouldn't have been so suspicious? Maggie asked.

"Depositing that much cash would raise a flag at the bank, even if he spread it over all the banks in Pine Tree. Questions would be asked. But, he figured the car dealer wouldn't care how he paid for his Lexus. They got their money on the spot. And they could deposit cash without any trouble. Of course, the car dealer will have to file a form with the IRS next January about the cash transaction. I think Norm said an 8300 form, or something. So it would have come out then anyway."

Maggie looked puzzled. "Wouldn't the judge know that?"

Mike shrugged. "Maybe not. He's a judge, not an accountant. I'd never heard of it before."

"Okay. What about Duke?" Maggie asked.

"The D.A. has threatened to bring him up on conspiracy also, since he actually bought the cyanide. But, as that might be hard to make a case, he's settled for turning Duke into a state witness on the bribery charge against the Judge. And Duke's given the accountant a lot of good information. They'll slap Duke on the wrist, but he'll help the DA make the bribery charge."

"And the motive?" asked Maggie.

"The judge thought Father Frank was going to appeal his ruling. He knew if that happened the bribery would come out and he'd be in deep ... trouble," Mike answered.

"What about Syd? Did the Judge take him out?"

"No," said Father Frank. "That was Mayfield, Syd's long-time friend."

"Some friend," said Maggie. "Why?"

"It's a little complicated," the priest said.

"How about a condensed version?" Maggie asked.

"I'll try, but you know brevity was never my strong suit."

"Amen," said Georgia.

Father Frank laughed. "Okay. Syd invested in two oil wells. The first one was with Mayfield, but it turned out to be a dry hole."

"W.C. called it a duster," said Georgia.

Father Frank continued. "They lost everything they put into it. When Syd decided to put money in another well, he knew W.C. couldn't afford to risk any, so he didn't ask him. That well hit big and Syd made a ton of money on it. As time passed, W.C. let his anger fester to the point he believed Syd *knew* the first one would fail and the second would be a winner. He felt Syd had deliberately cut him out. Eventually, it ate at him so much, he killed Syd. Took him a chocolate shake, knowing how much Syd liked chocolate, and loaded it with digitoxin."

"I saw him at the rectory," said Maggie. "He seemed nice enough. As I recall, he was trying to help." She looked at Mike. "How'd you ever figure he did it?"

Mike answered. "Father Frank gets credit once more. If I get a raise, I may have to give most of it to him. He tells me, though I don't know if I believe it, that he could tell Mayfield was not sorry about Syd's death, even though he said he was. So, your brother and Georgia went to see Mayfield and discovered he used digitoxin."

"How did they find that out?" Maggie asked.

"Best not to ask," answered Georgia with a laugh.

"Then," Mike continued, "your brother found the pharmacist who supplied Mayfield with the digitoxin and they concluded there were a lot of pills missing."

"Don't forget the car," said Georgia.

"Oh yeah," said Mike. "Father Frank found a witness who saw Mayfield's car at Cranzler's house about the time of the murder."

"Ah, but don't leave out Georgia's part in all this," said Father Frank.

Mike nodded. "Right. Mayfield somehow figured they had found his digitoxin and went to Georgia's to find out what they knew. And that's a whole 'nother story in itself."

"So, what happens to the shopping center?" asked Maggie.

"Back on track," answered her brother. "Turns out, everybody was in favor of it except Syd. They probably shouldn't have gotten the eminent domain ruling. But, with Syd gone, no one is objecting. Most would have sold without the ruling."

"And the mineral rights?"

"No one knows whether there're any valuable minerals there," said Father Frank. "Lockey just tried to take advantage of the land owners. They've done it before, and brought in some producing wells. But with the bribery, Duke's role in it, and most likely Lockey's, we've convinced Lockey to rewrite the contracts with the 'Fee Simple' clauses removed. The mineral rights are remaining with the owners."

"And the city manager is salivating over anticipated tax revenues from the shopping center," added Georgia.

"I think everybody's happy now," said the priest.

"Except the Judge, Mayfield and Duke," Mike said.

#

Back at the rectory, Maggie said she was pooped. "I think I'll just head to bed. We can talk more about Jeff and me tomorrow."

"That works for me," said Father Frank. "The pull-out's still made up, so you can take the bedroom again. I've just got to go lock up the church. See you at Mass in the morning."

Two minutes later, he stepped into the dark church, where only a few candles highlighted the life-sized crucifix at the front. The priest knelt at the back.

Father, thank You for once again looking after me. I know that the good in my life comes from You. The problems I have are the result of bad choices I make. Please keep your strong hand on my shoulder. Thank You for keeping Georgia and Mike safe. Please help Duke and Mayfield and the judge find their way back to You. And may your divine presence guide Maggie and Jeff to a happy life together, each helping the other to a closer relationship with You.

Father Frank stood up, locked the church, and started back to the rectory. He stopped and looked at the basketball goal. He hadn't painted the circle yet. Maybe next week. Just looking at the hoop brought a smile to his face. He did love the game. The smile faded. *That was a little selfish on my part, Lord. But I will put it to good use. I promise I'll get the parish youth involved. And as Syd enriched Ben's life, I will work to see that Syd's bequest will enrich the lives—and particularly, the spiritual lives—of many of the youth in Pine Tree.*

Father Frank headed on to the rectory. Tomorrow, he'd see if his sister needed any marriage counseling. Then, he'd call Monsignor

Decker and make peace with him. *All the monsignor wanted to do was keep me—and the church—out of trouble. He's still my friend and mentor.*

Father Frank's mouth turned up and his eyes sparkled. *And maybe, Lord, You'll save me a few minutes to shoot some baskets.*

The end

Read the opening chapter of the first Father Frank Mystery.

Cleansed by Fire

A Father Frank Mystery

James R. Callan

~ ONE ~

"Bless me Father for I have sinned."

Father Frank DeLuca waited in the dark behind the screen of the Prince of Peace confessional. The voice sounded familiar, like he should know the person but he quickly wiped that thought from his mind. He did not want to know who it was.

When nothing more came, he said, "How long has it been since you last took the Sacrament of Reconciliation?"

"Ah, I don't remember. Kind of a long time."

"Is there something in particular that has brought you back today?"

Another silence.

Finally, "I knew about the fire Thursday."

Thursday. Father Frank's mind searched through the events of two days ago. "You mean the Pine Valley Baptist Church? That fire?"

"Yes, Father." Then he quickly added, "I didn't set it or nothin'."

When the boy did not continue, Father Frank said, "But ...?"

"I knew it was going to happen. And I didn't tell nobody, uh, anybody. I mean, I didn't tell the police."

Father Frank furrowed his eyebrows and ran a hand through his black, curly hair. He hadn't heard if the fire had been classified as arson or an accident.

"Do you mean you knew someone was going to set fire to the church before it happened?"

"Yes."

Father Frank's mind raced down several paths at once. As a rule, the priest tried not to recognize any penitent. Tonight, with news of the arson, his mind inadvertently associated the voice with a name—Sammie Winters. Did someone tell the boy they were going to burn a church? Did he have a vision or premonition? Sammie didn't seem the type.. Had he heard someone talking about it?

"How do you know this?"

The teenager remained quiet for a moment before answering, almost in a whisper. "I, uh, I heard someone say they were going to burn a church."

"Why didn't you tell the authorities?"

"I couldn't. Uh—you don't understand. I just couldn't."

The priest closed his eyes and rested his forehead in his hands, suddenly weary. Could the fire have been prevented? He took a deep breath. He was supposed to give guidance. He raised his head.

"You're right, I don't understand. But God will. Talk to Him. Tell him you're sorry for your sins, and say a Rosary for the people who lost their church."

"Yes, Father."

"I absolve you from all your sins." Father Frank made a sign of the cross. "In the name of the Father, the Son, and the Holy Spirit."

The priest cleared his throat. "There is one other thing. Since you know who committed the crime, you really should tell the police. Now. If you don't, this is going to weigh on you like a lead warm-up jacket. You have information that can help the police solve a crime, and an obligation to tell them."

The boy said nothing but Father Frank heard the door open and close. Sammie was gone.

The priest sat in the darkness, eyes wide open, as he hoped no one else came into the confessional tonight. Sammie Winters knew Pine Valley Baptist had been arson. He probably also knew the name of the arsonist. Why wouldn't he tell the police?

The priest sighed. Maybe Sammie was more involved than he indicated. Maybe he pushed someone into setting the fire. What *was* the extent of his participation?

Sammie didn't seem like the type to be involved in serious crime. He seemed like a good kid, and attended mass every Sunday with his parents. Yet, some connection existed between Sammie and the arson. Father Frank shook his head. Maybe he didn't know Sammie that well since he wasn't involved in any church activities. Nice looking kid, about fifteen. What had he gotten himself into?

~ * ~

Even now Father Frank could see the inferno—red and orange flames with yellow tongues flickering, roaring, stretching upward, trying to reach the tall pine trees that towered over the white frame church. He could feel the heat, pulsing on the breeze. First hot, then warm, then hot again, lest you forget it was consuming a building. He could hear the frustration of those trying to save something—firemen who were losing the battle, parishioners who were losing their church, and Reverend Fisher, wringing his hands, almost in tears. Just a month ago, he had celebrated his twentieth year as the minister of Pine Valley Baptist.

The church burned to the ground.

At least no one was killed. Allan Moore, one of the

volunteer firefighters, had sustained serious burns when he tripped and fell on live coals. Maybe all of that could have been avoided if Sammie had told the police what he had known before the fire was set. Father Frank said a quick prayer that Pine Valley Baptist would rebound, rebuild, and use this misfortune to draw closer to God. And the priest prayed that Sammie would go to the police and tell what he knew.

Father Frank guessed the crowd of gawkers to be over fifty. He'd been there too, watching the firemen struggle to put out the fire and work to see it didn't spread to adjoining properties. He had felt a deep loss, watching a house of God being destroyed, not knowing what he could do.

He felt the same way now. What could he do? He shook his head in the solitude of the confessional. Nothing. The seal of confession prevented him from telling anybody, even the police, what he had heard from Sammie. And yet, how could he do nothing? Someone had destroyed a church. Not his church but a Christian church, and that was like a cousin being attacked.

Cleansed by Fire is in paperback, e-pub and Kindle editions and in audio (narrated by Five-time Emmy Award-Winner Jonathan Mumm).

On Amazon at http://amzn.to/1fqgWee

About the Author

After a successful career in mathematics and computer science, receiving grants from the National Science Foundation and NASA, and being listed in *Who's Who in Computer Science* and *Two Thousand Notable Americans*, James R. Callan turned to his first love—writing. He wrote a monthly column for a national magazine for two years, and published several non-fiction books. He now concentrates on his favorite genre, mystery/suspense, with his sixth mystery/suspense book releasing in Spring, 2015.

Website: www.jamesrcallan.com
Blog: www.jamesrcallan.com/blog
Amazon Author page: http://amzn.to/1eeykvG